Good Rebel Soil

The Champ Ferguson Story

Troy D. Smith

Good Rebel Soil
The Champ Ferguson Story

Cane Hollow Press

(Originally published by Writer's Club Press, 2002)

Dedication

For my brother Tony, the forever Rebel

Foreword

Good Rebel Soil, although based on the historical record of Confederate guerrilla Champ Ferguson, is a *novel* - a work of fiction. It is not a biography. Some facts and events have been changed, in order to provide drama and flow. Also, as it is the author's intention to provide the reader with a glimpse inside the mind of this very volatile individual, I feel the need to point out that the thoughts the main character expresses are not always necessarily my own—especially the racist ones, which must be presented in order to give a realistic picture of a man from Ferguson's background and time period.

~ Troy D. Smith ~

Author's Note

It is never a good idea to weigh down a manuscript with slang or dialect to the extent that readability is impacted. I have tried to avoid that pitfall with this book, while still realistically portraying the flavor of the Southern Appalachian, or Southern Midland, dialect that was and is spoken in the Upper Cumberland region of Tennessee and Kentucky.

That being said- *y'uns* means "you ones," even as far north as Appalachian Pennsylvania, and is interchangeable with *y'all*. It is a one-syllable word, and the *u* is similar to that in the German word for dog, *Hund*. Another word I use freely is *ye* for *you*. If I made every word phonetically equivalent to the spoken version, the book would become incomprehensible, though.

Wikipedia has a pretty good article on Appalachian English, and you might want to give it a look: http://en.wikipedia.org/wiki/Appalachian_English

Good Old Rebel

(Originally written in the 1860s by Major James Innes Randolph)

I am a good old Rebel, that's just what I am
For this your land of freedom, I do not give a damn
I'm glad I fought against it, I only wish we'd won
I do not seek no pardon for anything I done...

I can't pick up my musket and shoot Yankees anymore
But I ain't gonna love 'em, that's for certain sure
I don't apologize for what I was, or what I am
I won't be reconstructed, I do not give a damn...

Upper Cumberland Region of Tennessee and Kentucky
(map by Tom Nolan)

Champ Ferguson ~ 1865

Chapter 1

It gets a mite lonesome in this cold cell sometimes, marking off the hours and the days 'til you get hung, so I reckon I'm glad you're here. It's true that I have killed a sight of men, just like the newspapers say. Most every one of them was fixing to kill me. Them as weren't, well, I could tell they was studying on it right hard. They say the Lord takes care of sheep. I reckon the wolf looks out for his own damn self – and that's just the way I like it.

You say you want to hear my story. Everything, just the way it happened. Well, here it is. If you don't like it, by God, you can go to hell.

I was born up in Clinton County, Kentucky, not far from Albany. I've spent pert near my whole life on the Tennessee-Kentucky border – racing horses, coon-hunting, mostly just doing whatever I was of a mind to. I had ten brothers and sisters. They was all born of wedlock, and there was only one of 'em – Jim – that was a son of a bitch. I'll be getting to that part.

I never went to school much. I was there just long enough to learn how to read and write some, cipher a right smart, and practice my fighting. What you might call elementary learning. I reckon I would've needed a sight more if'n I had chose to become a preacher, or a lawyer. But I was called to be a killer, and book-learning would've just slowed me down.

Everybody always likes to talk about where they was at, what they was doing, when the War broke out. Where was you when you heared the Rebs had fired on Fort Sumter?

Me, I was in jail.

What I was in jail for then was attempted murder – which means I wasn't that serious about it. Not like now.

The attempted murder come about when I went to a camp meeting at Lick Creek, over in Fentress County, Tennessee. The trouble was over a horse.

First off, I reckon I ought to tell you a little about the troubles me and my brothers was having with the Evans boys. Them Evanses bought a hog off'n us, you see, then welched out on paying. We felt it was our legal right to go and attach one or two of their horses as recompense. It was all legal and aboveboard – to our way of thinking – despite the fact we done it under cover of darkness, and there was some unfriendly gunfire exchanged.

Them Evans boys come on up to Clinton County and attached that horse right back, then took him back home to Fentress County in Tennessee. Then me and the boys re-attached him. This went on for a spell. Hell, we stole that damn horse back and forth so much it got to where I about forgot whose it was to begin with.

The last I knowed, near as I could keep up, the Evanses was the last ones to steal the horse. Since I was the innocent party at the moment, I figured it was safe to go on down to their neck of the woods and take in that camp meeting.

I always dearly loved to go to a camp meeting. It's my experience that when you get that many fellers together, there's only so much praying and such they can do before they start wanting to gamble and race horses. Add the fact that I like to reel a dance or two with the pretty young girls – but no more'n that, for everybody knows how took I am with my dear wife Marthy – why, a camp meeting ain't nothing but pure fun, whether you're a hymn-singer or not.

What I didn't know, of course, was that the night before my brother Jim had snuck down and stole that damn horse again. It wasn't even much of a horse, to be honest. Not worth getting all riled up over.

Some people ain't got no sense of balance.

I was standing amongst a crowd of upstanding brethren, shooting the breeze. I had a set of dice in one pocket and a flask of whiskey in the other. I was thinking about sneaking some of that firewater into the preacher's coffee, just to see how it would affect his religious outlook.

"Say Champ," says one feller – a fat, red-faced old boy name of Grainger. "You in the market for some good horseflesh?"

"Shoot, son," I said. "I'm always open to a good barter, you know that. But I don't know that I'd want to trade with a feller like you – you might try to take advantage of my good nature."

Everybody chuckled, and old Grainger turned a shade redder though he kept on smiling. "You sayin' I might try to cheat you, Champ?"

"No," I said, matching his grin. "You ain't that stupid. I'm just sayin' you wouldn't know a good horse if it reached around and bit your ass."

"That chestnut I got over yonder is a fleet one," Grainger said. "I'll race ye, if'n you're of a mind to, and prove it."

"Might just do that afterwhile," I said. "But not 'less'n I'm ridin' a different horse than I come here with. Which is what I had my mind set on. I've got a fine mare, but she's in foal – I'm a man on the move, I cain't be slowed down."

Jory Williams walked up and tugged on my sleeve. Me and him went back a ways. He leaned close and talked to me in a low voice.

"Them Evans boys is talkin' agin ye, Champ. They say you're a sorry horse thief."

I laughed. "I think I'm a pretty damn good horse thief."

"They say it's mighty funny you show up, same day as their sorrel mare turns up missin'."

"Maybe it just don't like 'em. I'm surprised their dogs don't run away too – they prob'ly don't get fed well enough to make the trip."

"I ain't jokin', Champ. This is their county, they can get a whole lot of folks on their side. Might be best if you lit out."

"I'll leave when I'm good and ready."

Jory protested, but I didn't pay no more attention to him. I was always a bit on the stubborn side.

"When we gonna run some coons, Champ?" Jay Marlin said.

"Soon as you're ready, I reckon," I said. "I got me some fine hound dogs – they can do the huntin' while we do the drinkin'."

"Champ Ferguson!"

I turned around. All three Evans brothers was there, with half a dozen or so friends. I snuck a glance at my horse, judging the distance to her – I decided I might not be good, but I was damn well ready.

Floyd Evans, the oldest brother, was scowling at me. I scanned over the faces of his friends, but only knowed three of them – Elim Huddleston, Jim Read, and William Frogg. I had never had no problems with Read nor Frogg, but me and old Elim never did see eye-to-eye on things. Not for any particular reason, I don't reckon, we just naturally irritated one another.

I started easing toward that mare of mine. Elim caught the movement and hollered at his friends.

"Kill him!"

Somebody chunked a rock at me.

I took off at a hard run and jumped into the saddle. Somewhere off in the back of my mind I was cussing at my brother Jim – he knowed good and well I was coming to this camp meeting. It was a damn fool notion to steal that horse again today of all days. I hit the trail full-gallop, with the whole gang close behind, and the race was on. By this time there was about twenty of them.

I run that mare through the brambles, and jumped her over creeks, and with every step I could feel her slowing down.

That whole Fentress County crew was close enough that I could hear them cussing me. The more they cussed at me the madder I got – I take that kind of thing personal.

My little ride met a quick end. I come to a broad gulley and my horse didn't make the jump, spilling me out of the saddle. I jumped to my feet without even bothering to brush off the leaves. I started scrambling my way up the side of the gulley, but it was too late. My pursuers had caught up with me. I wished I had a firearm on me, but the only weapon I had was a pocketknife. It was a new knife, and mighty sharp, but I didn't see it helping me much against such a crowd.

Floyd Evans reined up his horse and dismounted. He walked toward me. He had an uncertain look on his face, like he was trying to work up his nerve or talk himself into something.

The whole crowd was looking pretty grim and serious. I knowed I was in a bind, but I was too damn mad to be scared over it.

"Floyd," I said, my cheeks heating up, "what in the hell do you think you're doin'?"

"Shut up, Ferguson," one of the others said.

"I ain't gonna put up with no more of your thievin'," Floyd said. "Me, nor Will and Mike neither." His brothers nodded. Floyd was trying to sound blustery – when several of his friends grumbled their agreement he puffed up a little more. "We're done with it," Floyd added, more certain now.

I shook my head. "You're sparkin' that Mullins gal, ain't ye," I told him.

"That ain't none of your business."

"You're tryin' to impress her by makin' trouble for me," I said. "And all these fools with ye is playin' up for the neighbors – and y'uns have pushed it too far to back down." I seen in some of their faces that I was right.

Jim Read took a step toward me. "Folks around here ain't gonna put up with your ways, Champ Ferguson."

"I don't hardly even know you, Read. Since when is it any of your business what I do?"

Read grinned like a school-kid. "Since the mayor hired me as constable of Jamestown. Just the other day."

They all moved slowly, surrounding me. I was so mad by then that I was snarling like a cornered wolf.

"You're making the damnedest mistake of your lives," I said. "You better not start givin' trouble to me 'less'n you have a notion how much I can give back."

Mike Evans throwed a rock. It hit me in the side. "That does it, by God," I said, scooping up a rock of my own and launching it toward Mike – his nose busted like a ripe squash.

A few more stones came my way. They had the advantage in numbers, but none of them seemed willing to be the first one to close in on me. I was throwing rocks right back – one took Floyd in the breadbasket and doubled him over.

Jim Read came running at me, with Elim Huddleston a few steps behind. Read put a bear hug on me – he was a stout man. I had took my pocketknife out and opened it before he reached me, though. I broke the hold and swiped at him with the knife. Read's eyes about popped out when he felt the steel cut a narrow path across his belly. I spun around and jabbed that knife hard as I could into his upper thigh – I'd meant to plunge it into his chest, but I was off-balance. I drawed back to stab the son of a bitch again.

Like I say, I was mad.

Huddleston grabbed my knife-arm. I back-handed him with my fist, which made him let go. I stabbed at him but he twisted out of the way and started running. I chased him out of the gulley and plumb across a field, with the rest of the crowd – minus the honored constable, of course – chasing me.

I closed to within a couple paces of Elim. I launched myself forward hard as I could, striking him in the back and sending him rolling through the grass. I come to a stop and was about to dive onto him when I remembered, through my red fury, all them other fellows. Me stopping had allowed them to almost catch up to me.

I took off running again. On the far side of the field was a two-story farmhouse – I headed for that, planning to make a stand there. I didn't know whose house it was, and didn't much care.

I run right in the front door, and past an old man reading a newspaper, without even slowing down. I bounded up the stairs just as my pursuers came in the front door.

"Where is he?" I heared Floyd Evans demand of the old man.

"Here I am, by God," I said. "Come get me!"

They would have to come up the steps one at a time. No one rushed to take the lead.

"Go get him," I heared Floyd say.

"Go get him hell," William Frogg answered. "Why don't you go get him?"

"You're the one wanted him," Frogg added a moment later,

"You're a coward," Floyd answered him.

"No more'n you. Besides, I ain't so much worried about him killin' *me*. That's Champ Ferguson. He might not stop killin' 'til he gets my whole family."

"Come on up here, any of y'uns," I said.

Will Evans charged up the steps. I punched him in the face, then throwed him against the wall and slammed a knee into his groin. I sent him tumbling down the steps to his comrades.

"Send me up another'n," I said.

No one else came up. I heared them talking over the best way to get at me without me getting at them.

"Maybe we could set fire to the house," Elim said. "Or at least a part of it."

"You do, boy," the old man who owned the place said, "and I'll fill you full of buckshot."

"Maybe we could shoot him," Mike Evans said – his busted nose made the words come out funny.

"We'd have to go up there and get a bead on him," Frogg said.

I could hear more people down there now. The whole camp meeting had moved from the creek to this poor old man's house.

"Let me through," a gruff voice said.

I seen a shadow at the bottom of the stairs.

"Come on down, Champ," the voice said. "This here is Jack Wright."

"How ye doin', Jack," I said.

"I'm gettin' along, Champ. Yourself?"

I chuckled. "I'm better off than a lot of folks I know. That might not be true no more, though, if I came down these stairs."

"You know me, Champ. I've been sheriff of this county for a long time. You know I'm a fair man. I won't let no harm come to ye."

"Not from you, maybe, but there's a passel of fellers down yonder that's got theirselves all worked up agin me."

"I give you my word, Champ, that no harm will come to ye and you'll get a fair trial."

"Trial? For what?"

"Attempted murder, Champ – you stabbed the new constable. We hadn't even got him broke in yet."

"That was self-defense."

"All these men are willing to testify that *you* attacked *them*."

"That's crazy. Why would I attack twenty men at once?"

"I don't know why you do half the things you do, Champ, but that ain't the point. Throw down that knife and we'll take care of this."

I heaved a big sigh, then sent the pocketknife clattering down the steps. Before long I was in chains, being led to the county jail in Jamestown.

Everybody in town was talking about the fall of Fort Sumter, and wondering what the state of Tennessee was going to decide to do. As you can imagine, I had more pressing concerns on my mind.

Chapter 2

Marthy reached through the bars and caressed my hand.

"When are you fixin' to settle down, Champion Ferguson."

"I settled down with you."

"You was supposed to. When are you *goin'* to?"

I bowed my head and shrugged a little, like a young'un caught at the cookie jar. I give her the charmingest smile I could muster. She didn't smile back, right at first, but I knowed if I kept on throwing that smile at her, her mouth would crack a bit afterwhile.

"Shoot, Marthy," I said. "It wadn't my fault. It was them goddamn Evanses."

"I wish't you wouldn't take the Lord's name in vain, Champ, you know I do."

"Oh hell, I reckon He knows I don't mean any harm in it."

"You never mean no harm in nothin' yet here ye set in jail. You know you got things you're supposed to be doin'."

"I know it. I'm sorry. I told Edgar Whitley I'd help him build back his barn this week."

"Edgar Whitley?" she said, her voice rising a little, and I knowed I had done said the wrong thing again.

"Yeah," I told her. "Remember? Lightnin' touched fire to his barn, burned it clean down."

"What about our farm? Why are you always helping some stranger instead of your own family?"

"Edgar ain't no stranger, I've knowed him all my life. And you know good as I do, he cain't drive a nail worth shit. I mean, worth nothin'."

The prospects of that smile was growing dimmer by the minute. I decided to get Marthy's mind off my cussing – her mention of our farm did set me to fretting about it some.

"Is Ann sloppin' the hogs regular?"

"She is, you know she is. She's a good helper to me, always has been. But there ain't a reason in the world why a thirteen-year-old girl and her mama should have to be a-doin' all the hard chores, not when we have us a man."

"I know of a dern good reason," I told her. "That man of yorn is in jail. Did Jim send you my bond money?"

"Cain't nobody find Jim," she said. "He took off after you got nabbed – said he was goin' on a long hunt, might not be home for a spell."

I snorted. That damn brother of mine was starting to irritate me. "Well, I hope to hell he's huntin' somethin' useful, seein' he's the one got me in this mess to start with."

"Your mama give me part of the money. Rains Philpot is supposed to be comin' along directly with the rest of it."

"Good ole Rains. I can always count on him."

"I can always count on him, you mean – to get you into trouble."

"It's usually t'other way around. I got plenty enough help this time, anyways, from Jim."

I stared at her, still smiling, and she finally started to crack a little bit. Marthy always had been too serious, like keeping the world in line and the sun on its course was her personal task. It was sure enough easier than keeping me in line, which took up most of her time and energy.

I loved her for it, though, and I ignored her foolish notions about what-all was proper, and what-all wasn't. I took it as my task to work on her, see, get her to smile and dance and live. She did live, too, in the moments we was alone – alive and shining in a way most of the folks who knowed her would never have believed possible. It made me feel kind of guilty about all the times I was away from her. I just don't think, I reckon. I get caught up in some escapade or another and lose track of time – by the time I think about going home, a day or two has passed. I don't intend no meanness by it, it's just the way I am.

My first wife Ann Eliza was a wildcat, like me. She could keep up with me in anything I did. But the fever took her, and my boy too. It was then that Marthy came along and commenced taking care of me, dragging me out of the blues and back into the world of the living. She even let me name our only child after Ann Eliza, and I know what a big sacrifice that is to a woman. Sometimes I think she lets me have my head to roam, in spite of her feelings, because Ann Eliza did – and she lets up to prove she can, too.

Lucky for me. I always felt for them poor bastards whose wives kept them hitched to a rail like a dumb horse. I can't stand to be hitched or fettered. Or bored. So you can imagine how it was eating me up to set in that cell. Same as it eats me up to set in this one now, talking to you – only I'll be seeing some action when they get that scaffold finished out yonder. More action than even I care for.

At least they didn't have no scaffold waiting on me when I was in jail over in Jimtown. All I was waiting on was for somebody to show up with my bail money.

Marthy was rubbing on my hand again – real light and easy, like a goose-feather. Her bottom lip moved, just a tad. This added up to about as much soft emotion as she would ever let herself show, leastways in public. She come from a poor family, and had learned young to scrabble hard in the dirt with nary a sign of weakness. Folks like her show love – not like a dog, licking his master's hand and looking at him with moony eyes – but like a fine horse. Always up before the crack of dawn, eager to pull that plow or carry a man's weight, all day long with never a sound of complaint. It was a more solid kind of love. A quiet love that kindled itself up in your bones on a winter's day, instead of blazing up to singe your whiskers.

I've always been partial to dogs. But any man in these here Cumberland Mountains can tell you that Champ Ferguson knows horses as good as he knows his own self, and he loves horses above any other creatures.

Excepting my daughter Ann. And my Marthy – my tough-skinned, hard-headed, sweet-hearted Marthy. I love her the best of anything.

"I'm worried, Champ," she said.

"Don't fret none," I told her, my voice softer than before. "I'll get them crops in, you'll see. Rains'll help me. He's a better friend to me than my own brothers is, and he'll do anything I ask of him. Even work."

"Oh, I ain't worried about no crops. I'm worried about this. They got you on attempted murder, Champ."

"I didn't stab nobody but Read, and maybe one or two others."

"Read is a constable now."

"He won't be a very active constable, not for a spell, anyways," I said with a chuckle.

"They could send you to the pen, Champ – for years, maybe."

My skin drawed up. "Hold it right there a minute," I said. "I don't mind passin' a little time in this jail, sort of as a favor to 'em, but they better not go havin' any notions of makin' it permanent. They'd have to kill me first, by God, and I'd throw a few of 'em in hell afore me to break my fall."

"There you go, losin' your temper!" she said. "You get mad an' the whole world can just go hang – that's what keeps you in trouble! You don't think, you just *do*."

"I'm sorry, honey. When I get mad ever'thing just sorta turns red."

"You need to control yourself. Think about the future, and what might happen."

"I don't live in no future, and neither does nobody else. Don't live in the past, neither. I just live in the right now, movin' whichever way my heart tugs me. You love me on account of that too, you know you do."

"Well, *right now* you're in jail and you might be here awhile."

"You said yourself, Rains is comin' to bail me out."

"See there? Just thinkin' about right now. Even after ye make bond, Champ honey, you still gotta stand trial. They could put you back here then. All of them fellers you fought say you attacked 'em with a knife, for no reason."

"That's a damn lie, and they know it. They was aimin' to do me some serious harm."

"It's your word agin theirs. And William Frogg is a real respected man."

"Hell, William Frogg is our neighbor. He's a Clinton County man. He's knowed me for years."

"Just because somebody knows ye ain't no guarantee they'll love ye, Champ."

"No. But if they know me, an' they got good sense, they know to be scared of me. Nary a one of them boys is dumb enough to lie on me thataway, knowin' it'll put me in a bad humor."

"Maybe they're afraid to say anything that'll let ye go free, knowin' how stubborn an' mean you can be."

"Hell, folks can go to chunkin' rocks at me all day long, or rassle me – long as it's in good fun. But if'n they go to lyin' on me and puttin' me in jail – well, I just won't forget it, Marthy. You know I won't."

She nodded. "I know. I just wish't you would forget things, or let 'em go, ever' once in awhile."

"I don't know that I can. But I'll sure enough give'er a try, Marthy. For you. Long as they don't rile me up too damn much."

She stood. "I reckon that's the best I can ask for. I better go now. I got chores to do, an' Rains Philpot is worser'n you are – no tellin' when he'll show up."

She moved to go. I reached my arm through the cell door and grabbed hold of her, pulling her back close, and I kissed her lips best I could. Mostly I was kissing iron bars, though.

"See ye directly," I said. Marthy nodded sadly and walked off. I was left alone in the cell again, wanting nothing more in the world than to feel the wind in my hair.

Chapter 3

The boredom was relieved a little bit by the arrival of my dinner, courtesy of Constable Jim Read. Read limped pitifully as he walked over to my cell door and slid the plate in.

"Oh for heaven's sake, Read, quit actin' so damn wounded. You won't get no sympathy out of me."

"I ain't lookin' for no sympathy from you, nor nothin' else, neither." He sat down at Sheriff Wright's desk and commenced to eating his own dinner. "When I signed on as town constable, I didn't know the job entailed bein' carved on by roughneck rulicks such as yourself."

"The job's liable to entail a whole lot of things you hadn't counted on, especially if ye rile me up agin." I crumbled the cold cornbread up into my beans. "Hell," I continued. "This town ain't got more'n seven or eight people on a cool day, what do they need a constable for to begin with? I think they just felt sorry for ye, myself."

"You go on and talk smart, Champ Ferguson. You won't be such a smart aleck when I get up there on that stand and testify on how you tried to kill me."

"If I ever took a serious notion to kill you, son, it'd be your kinfolks testifyin'. Not you."

Read snorted and went back to stuffing his face.

"Hey," I said, kind of put out when I seen what he was eating. "That ain't fair."

Read chuckled. "Prisoners don't get beefsteak, Champ, you ought to know better than to expect it."

"Forget the beefsteak. They give you pinto beans at that restaurant, an' they sent me navy beans."

"Beans is beans."

"Like hell. Only picky part of my nature is my taste in beans. I don't care a whole lot for white navy beans, but I'd walk a fer stretch for some tasty pinto beans."

"Like I say, beans is beans."

"If ye feel that way about it, why don't ye trade with me?"

"You stabbed me the other day, you son of a bitch."

"Yeah, I reckon ye got a point there. Still, I don't know why they give you pinto beans."

"I asked fer 'em."

"I woulda asked fer 'em, had I been there."

"You wadn't there, though. You was in jail. Son of a bitch."

I ate the white beans, but I didn't like 'em none.

Read smacked his lips like a hog.

Sheriff Wright walked in – Rains was following right behind him. "Your friend here brung your bond money, Champ. You're free to go."

Wright fished out his keys and turned me loose. I went and stood over Read – he was only half-done with his dinner. It was a big plate, more of a platter. His face blanched a little with me standing so close to him, without any bars between us.

"About time you got your scrawny ass over here, Rains," I said.

Rains chuckled. He was a ugly bastard, but he had a good heart. "I come quick as I could, Champ."

"You got a chaw?"

"Shore do." Rains cut me off a plug and handed it over. I stuck it in my mouth.

"Now Champ," Sheriff Wright said. "When they set a trial date for ye, you better come on down here like you're supposed to. You don't, your friends and family won't see none of their money back."

"You know where to find me," I said. Then I spat tobacco juice into Read's dinner and walked off. Rains was close behind me, laughing like a drunk.

~ ~ * ~ ~

"We fixin' to go whup them Evanses, Champ?" Rains said.

"There'll be time for that later. First I want to find out where in the hell Jim has been at."

"Ain't nobody seen him in a day or two, as I know of. He's all worked up over this War business."

"He'll be worked up when I'm done with him."

"You reckon Tennessee's gonna secede from the Union, Champ?"

"Hell, I don't know. I got bigger concerns right now."

We was walking down the sidewalk of Jimtown's main street. A couple of young'uns seen us coming and scrambled out of the way. I reckon their folks had been telling them stories about how wild us Clinton County boys was.

As we walked past the mercantile a fellow who had been loading his wagon with dry goods turned to look at us.

"Howdy fellers," he said. He was not quite as skinny as Rains, and going bald in the front. I recognized him after a second - it was a farmer from there in Overton County, name of Tinker Dave Beaty. Nobody remembered where the "Tinker" part came from – Beaty his self might not have remembered – it had just always been tacked onto his name.

"Howdy, Tinker Dave," I said.

"Y'all boys been hearin' this war talk?"

"Ain't none of my concern, I don't reckon," I said.

"Mine neither," said Tinker Dave. "All me and my boys care about is gettin' our crops took care of. If ever'body thought like you an' me, Champ, I reckon there wouldn't be no war."

"More'n likely not," I said absently, thinking more about all the folks that had angered me in the past week than about what Tinker Dave was saying.

Neither one of us had any way of knowing which paths we would wind up taking, or of how our fates was bound up together.

~ ~ * ~ ~

Mama was hoeing up weeds in her garden. She stood stooped over in the bright sun, the blade of her tool hacking away slow and stubborn. Her whole attention was fixed on them intruding weeds. Since the scarf on Mama's head blocked her vision a bit, I had begun to think she hadn't seen me standing there.

"I see they finally turned ye loose," she said finally.

"Yep," I answered. "Thank ye for helping raise the money."

"I give all I had, which ain't much. Don't expect I'll be seeing it again, neither."

"I'll get it back for ye, one way or another. Don't you worry."

She turned her head slowly toward me, letting her hoe come to rest in the dirt. I suspect that the ground and the tool was both equally pleased to escape her notice for a little while, and was grateful to me for presenting her with a new target. Mama was the type that liked to stay on top of things, and on top of people. She had kept a short rein on my daddy when he was living – which was never easy, for he had a wild streak. She done her best to keep that streak subdued in him so as to make sure he was a good family man. He went along with her, but his heart was never in it. His heart was in the untamed places. I had no doubt Mama suspected he was in Hell now, for his bad intentions. Maybe that's why she was always chopping so vigorously at the dirt with that hoe – maybe she was still trying to keep the old boy's attention on important matters such as family and farm, instead of letting it drift off to whatever distractions Hell had to offer.

"You'd best behave yourself," Mama told me. "I don't know what I'm gonna do with you. I don't want my money back if'n it's stole from somewhere."

"Stole?" I said, sounding surprised at her words and trying to pretend that it was not what I had been thinking.

"Stole, yes," she said. "I know you wadn't planning on working for it. And much as it pains me to say, I surely hope you ain't planning to go stand trial in Jimtown. They'd throw the book at ye, sure."

"I ain't scared of them none," I said. "I never done nothin' wrong noway, 'ceptin' to carve on a constable a little bit. An' he's a stout feller, he can take it."

Mama shook her head. "The how's an' the why's don't matter none," she said. "The fact is, that Overton County prosecutor is a Secesh man – though most folks in Jimtown has more sense than that – and he knows that Fergusons is good Union people."

"Hell, Mama, I don't see where that matters none."

"It's the only thing that matters anymore." She took a step closer to me. "You'd know that, Champion Ferguson, if you ever listened to a word I said when I was bringing you up. Them damn Secesh fools is fixin' to tear this country apart, just you wait and see if they don't. There's gonna be bloodshed."

I shrugged. "Long as they don't interfere with my business, I don't much care. If'n they was to start shuttin' the saloons down, now, or try to keep me from wagering on a horse race, I reckon I'd sure enough be up to sheddin' some blood then."

"Just like you," Mama said. "Not thinkin' 'bout nothin' but yourself an' your fun. My granddaddy died from a British saber-cut in 'seventy-eight, and your daddy's daddy – who you was named for – was shootin' redcoats at King's Mountain when he was hardly more than a young'un. Our family has shed blood to make this country, and I reckon we'll shed some to hold it together, if'n it comes to that."

I nodded, but I wasn't really listening that close. I knowed there was no use arguing with Mama once she got to preaching and going on. And I knowed it would only make things worse on me if she knowed how I really felt – that I didn't give a damn who was shooting at who eighty years ago. The past is over and done with, and best forgot, and the future don't never come. The sun is shining and the wind is blowing right here and now, and that's where I prefer to do my living.

"I'm lookin' for Jim, Mama. Have you seen him?"

"Jim comes and goes. He's been out in the hills and hollers, scoutin' out the trails."

"Is he expecting to do some hunting?"

"He's figuring to hunt, and be hunted – 'cause he has enough sense to know that there's a war comin', an' he wants to be ready. Not like some."

"He stole that damn Evans horse when he knowed full well I'd be down yonder in Jimtown for 'em to take it out on."

"You've stole it yourself a good many times – as well as some other things you sold off or give away before the Evanses could steal 'em back."

"That don't matter," I said. "He shouldn't have done it with me down yonder."

"Jim needs some good horses. He's putting together a militia group for when the fightin' starts. So you leave him be, Champ. Ain't none of us got time no more for your childish games."

"Seemed kind of serious to me at the time, what with folks chunkin' rocks at me an' such."

Mama reached out and put a hand on my shirt sleeve – an unheared of show of affection, from her. Onliest time I ever remember her embracing me was when my boy died.

"You got a lot of fight and spirit in you, Champ," she said. "Just like your Grandpa Ferguson did. Don't waste it on brawls and drinkin' matches, not when the Lord and the flag needs strong men to defend what's right. When you find Jim, join up with him. He's gonna need you."

"If he wanted me to play soldier, Mama, he'd of asked me his own self."

"No he wouldn't of. An' he might not even think he wants you with him – but that don't change the fact that he needs you. You're brothers, Champ, an' that's what matters the most in times like this we're livin'."

"I don't know what to make of that boy sometimes, Mama. He acts like he thinks he's the oldest."

"No, you act like you think you're the youngest."

"I just cain't figure him."

"That's 'cause you ain't got no sense, Champ."

I shrugged. Maybe what she said was right. I could think of no other explanation.

Mama tugged on my sleeve. "Come here a minute, son, out of this heat." She led me to the shade of a willow tree, then sat herself down in a rocking chair that was waiting for her there. I sat on the cool grass beside her.

"You ain't got no sense."

"You done said that."

"You can be clever an' sly as a fox, Champ – you can read sign good as a Injun, and you can catch any critter you put your mind to. But there's some things you just cain't see. You're like a wild animal yourself – take you out of the woods, and you don't understand the world you're in."

"I understand all I need to."

"You don't understand Jim."

"Then to hell with him."

Mama smiled a tiny bit - her face was almost soft. "Jim wanted Ann Eliza, Champ. Ever'body knowed he did – but before he could work up his nerve you swooped in and took her. And she adored you, the way women always adore men like you."

"He never said nothin' to me about it."

"He wouldn't. But most folks could tell just by lookin' at him."

"I ain't most folks."

"No, Champ, you ain't. But it wouldn't have mattered none – even if you had knowed, you still would of took her and she still would of went."

"Of course. A feller sees somethin' he wants, he takes it – or somebody else does. No sense poutin' 'cause you didn't have the nerve to act. Besides, Ann Eliza is dead."

"That makes it worse, son, not better."

"Why are you tellin' me this now, after all these years?"

"'Cause I know you. You aim to make trouble for Jim, 'cause you figure he made trouble for you. You need to understand why he acts the way he does - on account of he's your brother, and you're duty-bound to protect him if the Secesh bastards start a fight. It's your duty to him, and to me, and to all your kinfolks alive and dead – and to the flag. And to the Lord."

I paused, my head cocked to one side. I was waiting to see if her list was finished, or if she could think of some other people I owed duties to – maybe she could think of a way to work Moses and Abraham in there, too.

I was starting to feel uncomfortable. I never have liked nobody telling me what I "had" to do, I don't care if their reasons are good or not. I couldn't make much sense of the notion that if my brother, who didn't care none for me, picked a fight I *had* to jump in, just because my dead grandpa had once shot some foreigners on a mountain somewhere. I was starting to think I was the only one in these hills that did have any sense, after all.

I stood up and kissed Mama's forehead. I could see her face start to get warm then. She wouldn't never kiss me, but I know she liked it when I kissed her. Jim never did.

"You be careful, Champ," she said, and I couldn't help but laugh as I walked away.

Some folks think that being careful is what keeps a feller alive. I've always been of the opinion that being careful is what keeps him from living.

My grandpa is dead, and my great-grandpa too. A flag is a piece of cloth, and the Man Upstairs has never introduced His self to me. I am alive, by God, and I direct my own damn feet.

Chapter 4

I always figured farming to be a worthwhile pursuit, if a feller approached it as a diversion - but if it's the onliest thing you ever do it can become tiresome to the soul. I don't mind some good hard labor, but I like to break it up every once in awhile with some funning. I didn't inherit my mama's taste for drudgery.

These same thoughts was running through my head that summer day as I stood in my fields, sweating like a bashful pig at a crowded barbecue. My girl Ann was working beside me, and not enjoying it any more than I did.

I took a deep breath and looked around, stretching my bones, then I caught her eye.

"It's gettin' too hot in the day for cuttin' hay, gal," I told her. "What say let's go fishin' for a spell?"

"But Mama says we gotta get this done."

"It'll get done, don't you worry. You know I wouldn't let our stock go into the winter without nary a bit of food."

Ann was the only person I ever run across who had a better way with horses than I did. I have always knowed what an animal's needs are, knowed it quicker and more accurate than most men, but Ann seemed to just naturally understand what a horse feels like on the inside, like she had the spirit of a wild horse herself. She could run her slender fingers through a race-horse's mane and whisper in his ear and that booger would pound the dirt like he was trying to spin the earth around with his hooves.

And she was able to do the same thing with me – with nary a word. I done most of the talking when we was together. Ann never spoke any more than she had to, but it was all right because no words was needed between us. We always understood each other. She had none of my first wife's blood, but it always seemed to me like she had a part of Ann Eliza's soul. She was free, in her own way, though she was never wild like me – her mama seen to that. Just like I tried to see to it Marthy didn't weigh the girl down and strangle her with a bunch of fool notions about rules and proper ways.

"Come on," I whispered, grinning. "Just for a little spell."

Ann hesitated for a moment – but only for a moment. Then her face melted into a smile. "Okay!" she said.

With that we set off. I had stashed my fishing gear nearby, just in case. Me and Annie ran through the bushes and briars, laughing and carrying on like we was both young'uns, instead of just her. Once I scooped her up in my arms and twirled around with her – not for no special reason, just because the notion struck me, but she wasn't the least bit surprised by it. I took joy in the warm feel of her in my arms, just like when she was a baby, and the softness of her laughing breath in my beard.

I don't know how long we sat on the moist soil on the bank of the Cumberland River, our lines drifting slow and lazy in the water. Fact is, I never have paid a lot of mind to time anyways - how long something is going to take, or how long I've been at it. All I pay attention to is what I am doing. I live in that task until it is finished, or until I decide to do something different.

"Say, you got a nibble," I said to my girl, smiling at her. "Way he's tuggin' at that thing, he must be a big bastard – there now, he's swallered the bait." The line had suddenly pulled taut like it was a dropped anchor chain.

"Don't jerk it in," I told her. "Pull him in slow. Then he won't know what a mess he really is in, until he flops in the dust. Then he'll know he's yorn – when it's too late to struggle."

Ann done like I told her, without answering me a word. The only sound she made was a satisfied giggle when she dropped that big old catfish onto the riverbank.

"I reckoned I'd find ye here," I heared Rains Philpot say, and he was giggling too. I turned around to see him standing at the edge of the woods.

"Marthy said you was supposed to be workin'," Rains said. "So I come straight out to the river. I reckoned I'd find ye here, all right, and I did."

"Set down, Rains, and quit scarin' the damn fish."

Rains plopped down beside me. "Havin' any luck?"

"Not yet – we ain't been here long. I don't aim to leave until I've caught me a catfish at least as big as this one.

This dern gal ain't beatin' me again. Last time she wound up with all the fish, and all I drawed was skeeters."

Ann laughed again, softer this time but with a touch of pride. "Oh Daddy. You know that ain't so."

"Outdone by a twelve-year-old gal," I said. "I won't stand for it."

"I should've brung my pole," Rains said. "I wasn't thinking about it when I left the house this mornin'."

"Go cut ye one. Ain't no shortage of trees around here."

"I ain't got no line."

"Just set on the bank and hold the pole out over the water – you ain't gonna catch nothin' anyway."

"I bet I'd catch me a mess of fish," Rains said, "if'n I had me some line."

"I reckon if I could produce gold turds," I told him, "I'd be rich as hell. I keep tryin', but all I get is the same old shit."

Ann laughed so hard she almost strangled herself. I wasn't supposed to be using such language around her. I hoped the child didn't run tell on me.

"Looks like you got some extry line there, Champ," Rains said.

"Quit poutin' and go cut your dern pole," I told him. "I'll share some of my line with ye. I might as well, I wind up givin' ye ever'thing else."

Rains picked him out a decent tree-limb, and when he got back I cut off some of my fishing line for him. I always have enjoyed arguing with Rains, same as I used to scratch and argue with my brothers growing up – but he was the truest friend a man could have. Rains Philpot was better than a brother to me.

Maybe Rains sensed that my mind was on the subject of brothers.

"I seen Jim while-ago," he said.

"Where at?"

"Over at your ma's house."

"I might have to go have a word with him directly."

"I seen somebody else too, when I was down at Jimtown yesterday."

"Who?"

"The sheriff. He said for me to bring ye word that he needs to talk to ye. Says it's real important."

"Huh. Reckon what he wants. Maybe they got that court thing set up or somethin'."

"I don't know, Champ. All he said was for you not to be scared, alls he needs is to talk to ye."

"Scared my ass," I said. "If I go back to Jamestown, Tennessee, I ain't the one needs to be scared."

Rains grinned. "I surely ain't seen them damn Evans boys up here no more, to steal back their horse."

"They'll get more'n a horse if'n they do." Just thinking about the Evanses and their friends made my pulse quicken with rage.

Rains reached into his hip pocket and brung out a pint of whiskey.

"Have a sup, Champ," he said.

I took a swig – the burning of the liquor mixed with the burning in my blood.

Rains turned the talk to horses, and to hunting. I chipped in my opinion on them matters too – Ann was focused on her line, and before long she'd made another catch.

Off in the back of my mind, though, there was an anger burning like a red coal. I just don't take to being attacked, like I was that day at the camp meeting.

If them people in Jimtown wasn't careful, that coal was liable to quit smoking and set off a blaze.

Chapter 5

"Have some coffee, Champ," Jim said.

I had just walked into Ma's kitchen. Jim stood over the stove - he set fire to a piece of newspaper and lit his pipe with it. He never turned around to look at me. Ma sat in a corner, mending one of Jim's shirts.

I poured some coffee into a tin cup. I was about to ask Ma where the milk was at – I always liked a few drops of milk in my coffee, when I can get it – but she beat me to the subject.

"Milk's in the jar at the eatin' table, son, same as it always is."

I nodded and poured some of the fresh milk into my steaming cup.

"I reckon I ought to whup your ass," I told Jim after my first sip, "for settin' me up to get mobbed by that Jimtown bunch. All over a dern horse you could've took any time you had a notion."

Jim finally turned, puffing on his black pipe. A mist of smoke curled around his head, making his deep-set eyes look mournful, and I took note for the first time that the hair at Jim's temples and in his drooping mustache was showing flecks of the same smoky gray that his tobacco produced.

Jim shrugged. "It never occurred to me that would happen, Champ. I had a lot on my mind. I wadn't swapping livestock back an' forth as a game, like a child - like we've always done. Times is changin' on us, an' we're gonna have to grow up. I been procurin' all the horseflesh I can for when we have to fight."

"That don't make ary bit of sense to me."

"It ought to. It will."

"This war business is all a bunch of nonsense. It don't concern me none."

Jim sat down at the table – he had no sooner stretched his legs out from his chair than Ma set a cup of coffee before him. Them two irritated me, sometimes – she never poured no coffee for me.

"Things is happenin' fast," Jim said. "Tennessee has done voted to secede from the Union. Most folks in East

Tennessee is good Americans, though, and don't want no truck with rebels – there's talk in Knoxville of splittin' off an' makin' a separate state, loyal to the Union, like West Virginia did. Probably won't have enough votes to carry, though. A lot of Tennesseans is mad about Mister Lincoln's talk of invading the South."

That got my attention. "What do you mean – send a bunch of damn Northerners down here? Invade, hell. I'd like to see a bunch of ignorant Yankees try to invade these hills."

"You're talkin' foolish, Champ," Ma said.

"Ain't no need for 'em to invade us," Jim said. "We're almost all pro-Union. Them few that ain't, we'll take care of 'em ourselves. Kentucky is officially neutral, but there's a big recruitin' and trainin' camp bein' set up just down the road a piece. Camp Dick Robinson, they're callin' it – it's for the Home Guards, but the Home Guards is Union."

"Your other brothers have done joined up, Champ," Ma told me. "They're in outfits with their friends of the same age."

"I reckon I'd better stick with old Jim here," I said, "and keep him out of trouble, though I still don't understand what the fightin' is all about. Sounds like it's Kentucky agin Tennessee."

"It ain't that simple," said Jim. "About two-thirds of Tennesseans is Reb, and about two-thirds of Kentuckians is Union. Most folks in Jimtown is Union – even the Evanses, which puts us on the same side. I done give 'em their horse back, and they're gonna be joinin' up at Camp Robinson soon."

"I'll be damned," I said, and Ma give me a mean look. I was too mad to care. "I'll be good an' damned. I don't reckon I'll be fightin' alongside of no Evanses, nor any of them other sons of bitches that ganged up on me neither."

"That's all in the past," Jim said. "They're willin' to forget about it. Preserving the Union our fathers fought for, that's what's foremost on all our minds."

I shook my head. "I don't understand Unions, or secedin', nor none of that. I do understand somebody tryin' to kill me, and if I lay eyes on a damned Evans I aim to carve out his liver. I don't care what his daddy done, nor mine neither."

"Champ Ferguson!" Ma said, shocked.

Jim shook his head.

"You're gonna have to learn discipline and self-control if you're gonna wear Union blue," he said. "Private grudges don't mean nothin' anymore."

I tried to get ahold of myself before I spoke any further. *What kind of a world is it,* I wondered, *when your own private grudges didn't matter anymore* – all that counted was the grudges that your daddy held, or the ones some state council voted for you to hold.

"It's time to rally around the flag," Jim said, "and everything it stands for. Law and order, and freedom."

I was slowly shaking my head, staring into my coffee – it was getting cold. Here was my own brother, and one-time fellow horse thief, using terms like *law and order* and *freedom* in the same breath, like they meant the same thing.

"I have some things to do," I said, standing up. "I'll talk to y'uns directly."

"You stay out of trouble, Champ," Ma said, and I smiled.

"Don't sound like anybody around here aims to stay out of trouble," I said. "At least we should see some lively times."

"It'll be lively all right," Jim said. "We aim to run all of them Reb sympathizers out of these mountains. I hear that when ye go south of Jimtown, down around Sparta, the Rebs is thick as flies."

I had done a lot of hunting near Sparta, Tennessee, and White County in general. It was pretty country, and I had a lot of friends there. I had nothing but enemies in Jamestown – yet that was no longer supposed to matter, according to my kin, not when there was bigger more important things like flags to consider.

I put it all out of my mind when I walked out of my mama's door. I was headed across the border to Tennessee, a border I never paid any mind to because the Cumberland Mountains was still the Cumberland Mountains, no matter which side of the state line a man is on. It was time to see what that damn sheriff wanted.

Chapter 6

I walked down the sidewalk of Jamestown's main street, still in a foul mood over my kinfolks' foolish notions. A group of young'uns was playing in the road. When they seen me they all hushed and got wide-eyed, so scared you'd think I was the Devil his self, just like they had done the last time I was here. I stopped in my tracks real quick-like – my boot heels thundered on the boardwalk when I did – and stared at them for a few seconds. Then I throwed my hands up and hollered "boo". The little fellers scampered off like rabbits. It lightened my mood, even made me grin a little. If their daddies had any sense, they'd do the same if they seen me coming.

When I walked into the sheriff's office my grin melted away. It still grated on me that I had been locked up in that place.

Jack Wright was setting at his desk, and there was another feller beside of him. The second feller was tall and skinny as a rail, with puffy white whiskers growing on the side of his face that seemed almost as big as he was. He was duded up in a fancy suit, with a necktie and the works.

"Howdy Champ," Jack said. "How ye gettin' along?"

"Tolerable well, I reckon," I said. "Bein' as I'm on this side of them bars today."

The skinny feller smiled. "I see your point, Mister Ferguson," he said. "It is too pretty a day by far to be locked up in a dark cell."

He stood up and held out his hand. "I have heard much about you," he said. I took his hand and pumped it. "My name is Benjamin Carver. I am the town prosecutor; I also own the hotel and the dry goods store. Should you go to trial, it is my job to convict you." He smiled.

"You don't say."

"Oh indeed, Mister Ferguson. However, Sheriff Wright and I have been discussing the possibilities. You see, it is within my purview to determine if the case against you is strong enough to prosecute. We don't want the court's time wasted with trivial matters, not if it can be helped."

"Attempted murder ain't no trivial matter," I said. "Leastways that's the impression I got."

"No sir, it is not. Unless the charge is deemed unsubstantiated."

Sheriff Wright shuffled papers around on his desk, not looking up.

"What are you gettin' at?" I said.

Carver sat back down. "What I am getting at, Champ – I can call you Champ?"

"Everybody calls me either Champ or son of a bitch. I'd go with Champ."

Carver cackled like a hen. "You are just as you've been described - Champ. Well. What I am getting at is that we live now in trying times. War is raging in this land, and all men of conscience are compelled to answer the call to arms. With such events looming over us, a squabble at a church social seems petty indeed."

"So - does that mean you're droppin' the charges agin me?"

Carver folded his hands and cleared his throat. "First let me state my political position to you. Most citizens here in Jamestown are decidedly pro-Union – I have heard that some members of your own family have those same sentiments, although I am unaware of your own stand." He paused, staring at me, and I realized he expected an answer.

"I ain't got no stand," I told him. "I stand foursquare in favor of me. And my wife and my little gal."

Carver sighed. "Many of us would like to say the same thing, Champ, but events will soon be out of our hands and neutrality will not be an option. As for myself - and Sheriff Wright, I am happy to say, is in agreement – I am in favor of secession. The Northern states must not be allowed to bully us and tell us how to live our lives, lives they know nothing about. You do not seem like a man who likes to be bullied either, if I may say so."

"Damn right."

"And yet that is what Unionists do, you know. They try to tell you how you should think and how you should live, as if you were a child."

I studied on it for a minute. It did seem like his words had a ring of truth to them – my own kinfolks had spent a good part of the morning trying to browbeat me into supporting their ideas, whether I agreed or not.

"So far as the charges against you are concerned," he said. "There are two things which could happen - and they depend upon the stand you choose to make. If you follow along with many folks in this area - and yes, I know it is hard to strike out on one's own and be different - if you decide to follow along in the Unionist cause, then you will be a danger to the State of Tennessee, as proven by your violent actions at that church meeting. I will then have little choice but to prosecute you to the fullest extent.

"If, on the other hand, you put your skills at the disposal of Tennessee and the Confederacy - why, you have proven what a valuable asset you could be, and it would be a shame to waste that asset in Tennessee's hour of need by locking you away."

Sheriff Wright looked up from his papers. "I'll put it to ye simple, Champ, without the patriotic speech. If you swear right here and now to support the Confederacy, we'll let you go and pretend that whole fracas never happened. If you don't, we'll go through with the trial and you'll be bustin' rocks in a prison yard for the next ten years. We think you'd be a big help to us in these hills - there's all kinds of Union Home Guards roaming around from Kentucky and guerilla groups formin' up around here, and we need some hard men like yourself to protect good Southerners from 'em. But it's up to you."

I walked real slow around the little room, studying. "All I do is promise to come down Confederate, and I walk out of here free," I said.

"That's right, Champ."

Or I could do what my mama and Jim was pushing me to do – and what I didn't really want to do in the first place – and go to jail.

"Seems like y'uns have got me over a barrel, Jack. One side's about as good as another'n, I reckon. You've got yourself a deal."

Carver leaned forward. "Swear to it, then," he said. "Before Almighty God, swear you'll be loyal to the Confederate States of America and give no support to the Unionists."

I drawed up to my full height, my back straight as a board. "Shitfire," I said, "I've done told you it's a deal. I reckon God heared me as plain as you did."

Jack nodded. "See that our arrangement don't get heard outside of this office."

Carver took a paper from Jack's stack and held it up. "So far as this complaint against you is concerned," he said - then he struck a match and set fire to the paper, smiling as it burned. "It might as well have never existed."

"I reckon I'll be goin' then."

Carver shook my hand again, and this time so did Jack. "I expect to be hearin' good things about ye, Champ," Jack said.

I walked out the door. For some reason I couldn't put my finger on, the air was lighter and I felt freer.

I reckon I was born to be a Rebel.

Chapter 7

Marthy was standing in front of the house when I rode up. I knowed then that she had been watching for me, for no telling how long. It hadn't occurred to me she would do that – I reckon I ought to of come straight on to the house, instead of stopping in at Yarrow's Saloon and drinking them beers, so as to keep her from worrying.

She was wringing her hands as I dismounted. "How'd it go, honey?" she said. "What did the sheriff say?"

"I reckon that's one less thing for us to fret about, Marthy," I said, then bent down and kissed her cheek. "Or leastways, one less thing for *you* to fret about. I never gave a shit, myself."

"What do ye mean, Champ? Did them fellers change their story?"

"Nope. But Jack an' this lawyer feller he had with him, they said there wadn't enough evidence. So they're droppin' the whole thing, they say it's a waste of time."

Marthy sighed, a sigh so deep I could see her ribs shake from it. "Praise Jesus," she said. "I was scared, Champ – I figured maybe they locked you up soon as they could lay their hands on ye."

"Not a-tall, darlin'. Fact is, we had us a nice chat."

Marthy sighed again and started straightening that spine of hers up, gathering back her control. She cleared her throat. I always loved that high little noise she made when she cleared her throat.

"Well," she said. "That's mighty good news. I don't see how they could just drop such a thing, though, not with so many men willin' to testify agin ye. Are ye sure it ain't some kind of trick?"

I hesitated a moment before I answered. A little tad of Marthy's control slipped away from her when I done that, for she could always read me like a book.

"There's a little more to it than that," I said.

"What is it."

"They said they'd drop the charges if'n I promised to come down Confederate when the fightin' starts around here."

"There might not be no fightin' around here," Marthy said, but I could tell she knowed better.

"I reckon there's liable to be," I told her.

"Why should you get mixed up in it?"

I couldn't help but laugh at that one. "Hellfire, woman, if'n there's a fight you know good an' well I'll be mixed up in it. I usually start it. An' if it comes down to a choice between bein' a Rebel or goin' to jail – hell, I was a rebel to begin with, I never needed no war to tell me that. It all made perfect sense to me."

"It won't make much sense to your kinfolks."

"I reckon that's their damn problem."

Marthy leaned up against me and put her arms around my waist, her head on my chest. The pure surprise of it near about knocked the breath out of me.

"Hold me a spell," she said. All of the stiff had gone back out of her spine.

"Why sure, honey," I said. "Sure. Ever'thing's all right."

"For now it is. I'm scared, though, about tomorrow. All this talk of fightin', and ever'body so serious about it – I don't know what to expect."

"Don't matter what happens tomorrow, honey," I said real soft into her ear. "Today is a pretty day. When tomorrow rolls around, I'll take care of it. I always do, don't I?"

She nodded her head against me, and I was surprised to feel the wetness of tears on my chest. I held her like that for a long time.

~ ~ * ~ ~

"You better keep a close eye on old Reuben," I told Rains Philpot. "He'll hoodoo ye in a minute. I'd check ever' once in awhile and make sure he hadn't changed the board around."

"I never had to cheat to beat you at checkers, you rascal," Reuben Wood said, without any feeling in his words one way or another. "I see no reason I should cheat this young scarecrow."

The checkerboard was set up on a barrel at Ivey's Mercantile in Albany, Kentucky, the seat of Clinton County, just a few miles down the road from my farm. All the old boys was gathered there like usual, setting on the shady porch and whittling and spitting and cussing. There was eight of us there, counting Old Man Ivey his self.

"When we gonna run some 'coons, Champ?" Len Carey asked.

"The first time it's dark an' you're still sober, I reckon," I said.

"Go to Hell," Carey said, and laughed.

"I'm on my way, brother."

Rains giggled and moved his checker-piece with a flourish of his arm. "There. What do ye think of that, Reuben Wood?"

Reuben grunted. "I'm glad you ain't on my side. You ain't doin' yourself too damn good."

I shook my head and chuckled. Reuben had a way about him like a straight-razor with a paper-thin edge. Even when you had the upper hand on him – whether it was an argument or a game of checkers or anything else – he could turn around and draw blood with his words. He would make you think you was winning only because he felt like being charitable. I had known Reuben since I was knee-high to a sheep – I done odd jobs for him when I was a young'un – and stubborn as I am, I knowed better than to try out-arguing him.

"Boys, what do y'uns think about all this war news?" Buddy Forrest said.

"I'm tired of hearing about it," said Old Man Ivey – which told me he was afraid it might affect his business.

"Sounds like the Rebs is givin' 'em a serious run for their money," Carey mumbled – he was talking around his pipe stem. He had been trying to light the damn thing for several seconds. I was tempted to take it away from him and light it my own self – or else do something with it he would like even less – but I was having fun watching the helpless fool. Run 'coons together, my ass.

"Damned secessionist bastards," Wash Tabor said with a snarl. Wash was even older than Reuben, and didn't mind speaking his opinion. I reckon he figured folks would excuse him because of his advanced years.

"What the hell are you so hot about?" I said. I was never no great respecter of age.

"Secession, that's what. I was borned in the United States of America, and I ain't never moved. Just because a bunch of idiots in Nashville decided to go along with this Confederacy shit don't mean a thing to me. I never voted for it."

"Amen to that, brother," John Crabtree said. "Anybody that's go along with that Confederacy nonsense is stupid."

"Stupider'n Hell," Carey chimed in. The idiot.

"Lots of folks feels different," I said.

"A lot of folks don't think things through," said Reuben. "They just follow along in the heat of the moment, all set to tear down somethin' that good men died for. On a damn lark." He leaned forward and scooted a checker. "Your move," he told Rains. Rains wasn't following the conversation, he was too caught up in the checker game.

"Near as I can figure the Yankees wants our niggers," Buddy said. "I ain't got no nigger, myself."

"My Uncle Jarvis, he's got a nigger," Carey said. He still hadn't got his damn pipe lit.

"Then the Yankees can have your Uncle Jarvis's nigger," said Buddy. "I don't give a shit."

"Uncle Jarvis's nigger is awful old," Carey said, like that mattered somehow. "He used to could play a pretty good fiddle, though."

"It ain't about niggers," Reuben said. "It's about the Union my grand-daddy fought for."

"Damned Rebel sons of bitches," Wash Tabor said. "I'd like to get my hands on one."

That pretty much done it. I didn't care much about niggers or unions either one, I just didn't like the turn this conversation was taking. I stood up, so sudden my chair turned over, and looked down at Mister Washington Tabor.

"I am a damn Rebel son of a bitch," I said. Wash's eyes opened a little wider, like the idea had just dawned on him that he might be seeing the last of this old world and he better not miss nothing.

"Put your hands on me," I said.

Wash's jaw worked a little, but he couldn't get no words to come out.

"Champ," Reuben said, concerned. "Are you took in by that Rebel foolishness?"

I give him a hard look. "Only thing foolish is a bunch of Yankees tryin' to tell us how to live," I said. "Sayin' that if we don't do things their way they're gonna come down here an' make us."

I was echoing the words that lawyer in Jamestown had told me, of course. I hadn't give them words any real thought. All of a sudden, though, under the circumstances, it seemed like they made sense to me.

"And once them Yankees gets here," I added, "anybody that's standin' around waitin' to welcome 'em with open arms, and go along with what they say, just because of some flag or some piece of paper – that's who's stupid. Nobody pushes me around, by God."

Wash and Crabtree, their faces colored up. I could tell that my words angered them. I could also tell they wanted to say something, but was afraid to.

"What about you, Rains?" Reuben said softly.

Rains had done looked up from the checkerboard. "Well Reuben," he said, "I reckon I'm a Rebel. Same as Champ."

"I reckon I am too," said Buddy, like it had just dawned on him. No one much looked at each other, they all looked down – except me and Reuben. It had got terribly quiet in the store. There was no longer even the sound of knives whittling.

"I hear your younger brothers is already wearin' Union blue," Reuben told me. "And your brother Jim is always around Camp Dick Robinson. Are you fixin' to shoot them?" He looked around the room. "Are you fixin' to shoot *us*?"

"I won't go lookin' to shoot my own brothers," I said. "Nor my friends neither. But I'll sure as hell shoot any damn Yankee that shows up pokin' his nose in my business. And if any of my brothers or my friends was to come lookin' to shoot *me* – well, I reckon they'd run out of luck damn fast."

Rains turned his attention back to the checkerboard. He jumped Reuben's last man.

"Looks like I win," Rains said. Reuben did not answer.

"Come on, Rains," I said. "Let's go."

Rains got up and followed me out the door. No one else spoke a word.

Once we was outside Rains looked at me kind of sad-like, but the expression faded away quick – like fog in the sunshine. A few seconds later Buddy stepped out too.

"Reckon I need to get on home and see that the stock is watered," Buddy said. He mumbled it. He sounded like a man talking in his sleep.

The next day I came back into town again, to buy sugar and coffee. A lot of folks out on the street looked away from me, like I had a disease or had become a ghost. A few others, though, they grinned real big – or else just give me a knowing look and nodded. A couple of old boys came up and patted me on the back.

"We're with you, Champ," they said as they walked off.

The air seemed heavy, even for late summer.

Chapter 8

"Come on out here, Champ!"

I looked out my window. It was Jim, and he had Mama with him. I blinked a time or two, trying to focus.

"Damn, they're out early," I said. I took a big swig out of the coffee cup in my hand – the hot liquid made me wince, but I figured I was going to need it.

Marthy and Ann was setting the table. "Ask 'em do they want breakfast," Marthy said, with a hint of sarcasm.

"They won't," I said, setting the cup down. "I reckon it's me they've come to chew on."

"Champ!" Jim hollered again.

I stepped through the door and stood squinting in the early sun. I rubbed my hand over my head, trying to make my hair lay down.

"I'm comin', brother," I said. "Good Lord. Have you ever heared of knockin' on the door, instead of standin' outside a man's house hollerin'?"

"I cain't hardly believe what I've been hearin', Champion," Mama said.

"I don't believe much of nothin' I hear."

"Don't you get smart with me, son. This is serious business."

"How's things at Camp Dick Robinson, Jim?"

"I ain't seen you there," he replied, and his eyes narrowed.

"I don't reckon you will," I said.

"Champ," Mama said, "you're bein' foolish. Everybody knows that Fergusons is good Union people."

"We've done already been over all that," I said. "No point in sayin' it again."

"You're throwin' in with traitors, Champ," Jim said. "It's a disgrace."

"And you're throwin' in with them Evanses and that whole Jimtown bunch that tried to railroad me. That's a disgrace in my book."

"This is war we're talkin' about," Jim said, his lips drawing back a little bit. "I done told you, it's bigger than your private squabbles."

"My private squabbles is pretty damn big." I heared the creak of the door hinges and the soft pad of Marthy's bare feet, and felt her presence behind me.

"Folks are sayin' them charges agin ye in Jimtown has been dropped," Mama said. "And ever'body knows that Carver feller and the sheriff over yonder is Reb plumb through. An' now I hear that you've been spoutin' off a bunch of Secesh nonsense – it makes me wonder, is all. I know you, Champ. You don't fool none with politics. If it ain't somethin' personal, you don't care about it."

"This is personal, Mama. I'm a growed man – a free man. Ain't nobody fixin' to tell me what to do or how to live. Not ary Yankee, not ary Abe Lincoln – not even you, Mama."

"You're a childish fool, Champ," Jim said, "and a damn traitor. You don't deserve the name you carry."

My muscles tensed and I could feel the blood in my veins heating up.

"You better mind how you talk," I said in a low voice.

"Like hell," Jim answered.

"We come down here to talk some sense into you," Mama said. "Jim told me it wadn't no use, and I knowed he was right – but I had to try. Once you get a notion in your head it cain't be blasted loose with black powder. But try, just this once, for all of us. Ride on down to Camp Dick Robinson and make a pledge to the Union."

"I'll do what I've a mind to. Come what may."

Tears was glistening in Mama's eyes. "Then you ain't my son no more, Champ. You're dead to me."

I think that one even caught Jim by surprise. It sure as hell knocked the wind out of my sails, I'll tell you that. She might as well have slapped me. I'd druther she would have. Marthy's hands slipped around my arm and squeezed.

"Hell, Mama," I said, but she shook her head and turned away. Jim looked like he was pert near going to bust into a big grin at this unexpected gift God had bestowed on him. Instead he just looked smug.

He took a step forward. "You ain't never been no account, and you never will be. You was a waste of God's breath."

Marthy let go of my arm. "Just a damn minute, Jim Ferguson," she said. "You got no call to go talkin' to my husband thataway."

Jim's head snapped around at her.

"I ain't speakin' to you," he said.

It was Marthy's turn to take a step toward him. Mama had done turned away and started walking off, and I knowed she wouldn't speak nor come back again – for nothing.

"How much of what you say is loyalty to the Union," Marthy said, "and how much is hate over Ann Eliza?"

Jim colored up. He could not speak for several seconds. His eyes blazed during that time, first at Marthy and then at me.

"That's crazy talk," he finally said.

"Oh, is it now?" said Marthy. "You've been ate up with jealousy for years, rotten and bitter in your bones like somethin' dead, all the while pretendin' it wadn't so – and now you use this war as an excuse to screw up your courage and speak agin Champ."

"If you wadn't a woman I'd hit you," Jim said, breathing hard.

"If she wadn't a woman," I told him, "she'd whup yore ass. She might anyways, if I don't beat her to it. Get off my land, Jim, and don't never come back."

"Oh, I won't," he said, then spit real hard. "Next time I see you I'm liable to kill ye."

Jim hurried down the road after Mama. I realized then that Ann was standing in the doorway, watching her kinfolks leave. I didn't know what to tell her.

That was on a Tuesday. Come Thursday they found old Buddy Forrest – who had just figured out he was leaning towards the Rebels – laying dead in his cornfield, his brains smashed out, and his house robbed. Late Wednesday night some old boys had gone over to Len Carey's house and choked him to death with his own U.S. flag. I reckon that by daylight Satan was lighting the poor bastard's pipe for him, but good. It was impossible to say for sure which murder happened first, or whether one sparked the other, but it didn't make ary difference.

It had begun.

~ ~ * ~ ~

On Saturday morning me and Rains was on the road into Albany. I heared a feller in town had a horse for sale, and I was figuring to have a look at it.

We was just turning a bend in the road when my mare nickered. It wasn't two seconds before several horsemen stepped onto the road, surrounding us.

There was eight of them. They was wearing regular clothes, not uniforms, but I picked right up on the fact that there was more blue there than anything else. They was all armed. Their guns was not pointed straight at us. They was pointed up in the air – but more in our direction than away from it.

I knowed all the men, of course. They was all Clinton County men. Old Reuben Wood was there, and so was John Crabtree. There was Alex Huff and the Thompson brothers, Luke and Jimmy. John Hurt was there – we used to hunt together quite a bit – he was holding a double-barreled shotgun. Bug Duvall and his cousin Van rounded out the crew; we used to play together as young'uns.

"Mornin' Champ." Reuben said.

"I figured you was too old for business like this," I told him.

"Howdy Reuben," Rains said in a real cool voice. "Is this," he nodded at the group, "is this all on account of I keep beatin' you at checkers?"

Reuben ignored him. "Ain't nobody too old to defend the Constitution and the flag," he said to me. "We're Home Guards, out of Camp Dick Robinson, and we're on patrol."

"Are ye?"

"Yep. It's our duty to defend the roadways here in the State of Kentucky – make sure there ain't no Rebels or other undesirables makin' trouble."

"Kentucky is supposed to be neutral," Rains said.

"Not where we're at, by God," Huff said. "Wherever we stand or ride, that's free Union soil."

"Get down off your horses, boys," Reuben told us.

"You wait just a minute!" I said – and then all the guns was no longer pointing in the air, they was leveled plumb square at me. I blowed a breath like an ornery stallion, but I dismounted real slow and Rains done likewise.

"I think you boys is gettin' too big for your britches," I said. Rains said nothing, but he never took his eyes off our captors.

"Reuben," Crabtree said. He chewed on his mustache for a moment, then he spoke again. "We really ought to shoot 'em. You know that."

"What?" Bug said. He wore a confused smile, like he wasn't for sure whether he was involved in some practical joke.

Crabtree ignored him. "We ought to," Crabtree said again. "What else can we do with 'em?"

"First," said Reuben, "we confiscate their mounts, and their weapons." My rifle was in its boot. I had left my Bowie knife at home, not figuring to do any hunting that morning.

"Champ can get other horses and other weapons," Crabtree said. He was looking at me the way a man looks at a copperhead slithering in his garden. "And when he does he'll come lookin' to kill somebody. Rains won't – but he will if we shoot Champ and let him go."

"You cain't just shoot these boys down like dogs," Bug said. "They're our dern neighbors!"

Bug might have been squeamish, but his cousin – and some of the others – was nodding real thoughtfully at Crabtree, agreeing with his solution. Reuben just looked real sad.

"You don't win wars without killin' people," said Huff.

"Cain't we just – lock 'em up, or somethin', fellers? Dern."

"What do you aim to do, Bug?" Crabtree said. "Lock up every third man in this state? Where do you propose puttin' 'em?"

"It ain't right to just kill 'em," Bug said. "Not Champ and Rains."

I had pulled myself up as straight as I could and squared my shoulders, ready to spit on the first man who pulled a trigger.

Reuben sighed. "Champ," he said, "you've been like a son to me. But Reb is Reb. I'd give my own son for the Union. This one time – just this one time – we're lettin' you two go free with your lives."

Crabtree started to speak, but Reuben stared him down. Then the older man continued.

"My advice to both of ye in this – change your politics or else clear out of this territory. Now stand away from your horses, they're federal property now. They'll go into service for Old Glory even if y'uns won't."

I knowed he had no legal right to take my property, but I didn't push our luck. Bug leaned over and took my mare's reins.

"Watch out for her, Bug," I said. "She's favorin' her left hind foot."

"I will Champ, thank ye."

The "Home Guards" rode off, taking our rehabilitated horses with them. I watched the bastards until they disappeared, then me and Rains started hiking.

"That Bug Duvall, he always was a good old boy," Rains said after awhile.

I didn't answer him. Anger was rising off my skin like steam.

~ ~ * ~ ~

The two of us rode into Jamestown, Tennessee, on Sunday afternoon just as the churches was letting out. I had two Walker Colts stuck in my belt and my own double-barreled shotgun across my knees. Rains carried an old Hawken. Folks scattered before us – some of them scared, some of them mad. A handful stood their ground and smiled.

"Howdy, Champ," said Bob Timmons. He stroked his scraggly beard. "Goin' huntin'?"

"Damn right," I answered. I cantered my bay gelding around in the town square until I was sure I had everybody's attention.

"Listen up," I said. "Any of you Tennessee boys that ain't joined up in the Confederate States Army as of yet because you don't want to leave your farms unattended – or your wives, whoever you think is more fertile – now's your chance to do a little fightin' after all."

More folks scattered. Timmons flashed a gap-toothed, tobacco-stained grin. "What kind of fightin' you talkin' about?" he said. Timmons was about half-crazy. He had more fights on a average day than I have meals. He was so wild I don't believe the regular army would have him – not on either side. I always liked old Timmons.

"What kind of fight?" I said, leaning forward in the saddle. "From now on, I aim to spend my time blowin' Yankees to hell, and still gettin' home in time for supper. Any of you boys wants to come along you're welcome. If not, then go to hell."

I jabbed the gelding in the ribs and headed out of town. I heared some low mumbling among the crowd – and I heared Timmons laughing – but I ignored them all. Let them follow if they wanted, or stay at home, I didn't care.

I did see something which made me rein in for a moment. Tinker Dave was standing in front of the Baptist Church, decked out in his good clothes, rolling a smoke.

"I reckon it's gettin' to where a man has to choose sides, Tinker," I told him.

"Lookin' thataway," he said, and nodded politely.

"Which side you choose?"

Tinker shook his head. "I got farmin' to do, that's all I know." He put the finishing touches on the cigarette, put it in his mouth, and lit up.

"Buddy Forrest up in Clinton County had farmin' to do, too," I said, "and the damned Unionists kilt him."

"My oldest boy joined up with the Union infantry last week. Feels mighty strong about it – young men always feel strong about things, seems like. I don't reckon I'd want to be fightin' agin him. That's all I know."

I nodded and kneed my horse back into a walk. I heared Rains plodding along right behind me.

"See ye directly, Tinker," he said.

"See ye."

A curtain moved in a second-story window as we passed the hotel, which gave me a start. I jerked my head around and seen it was Benjamin Carver. He was waving and grinning – like he was mighty pleased with his self.

I didn't wave back. I figured he could go to hell too.

Chapter 9

Things started heating up just a mite in that fall of 'sixty-one. There had already been plenty of skirmishing back east and in Mississippi, and that summer the Union Army had their ass handed to them at Bull Run and at Wilson's Creek, Missouri, but now both sides was moving in on Kentucky.

Old Leonidas Polk sent Gideon Pillow into the state with a big force, knowing that the Yankees was fixing to do the same thing. So much for Kentucky being neutral. Before long that son of a bitch Useless S. Grant had moved his troops into Paducah. General Felix Zollicoffer run the Yankees out of Barbourville, and the next thing you knowed there was word of little set-to's here and yonder: Rockcastle, West Liberty, Hodgenville, Morgantown. Then both sides kind of shored up for the winter, figuring that spring weather was more convenient for large-scale killing. They must have got a little impatient, though, because by February Tennessee and Kentucky both was hotter than hell with fighting.

The irregulars and the militia groups never took no rest at all. Kentucky Unionists like Rufus Dowdy and Oliver Brown – and that bastard Elijah Kogier – got their own little groups together and started spending their time annoying Zollicoffer's troops. They commenced to disrupting supply lines, stealing horses, burning bridges, and every once in awhile they'd raid some local farmer who made a public stand for the South, roughing him up and sometimes killing him. This went on all through September and October.

I figured, why should they have all the fun? Me and Rains had several good old boys lined up with us by now, all of them eager for action. Some of them fellers wound up riding with me for years. There was half-crazy Bob Timmons, and Harry Cropper, and Will Simmons. There was Edgar Whitley, whose barn I had helped rebuild after it was struck by lightning. There was Jory Williams, my old friend who had tried to warn me on the day of that camp meeting in Fentress County. There was John Homer – he was getting long in the tooth, but he was tough and hard and ready to prove it. We had Peter Lucas, a dreamy-eyed kid wanting to see how brave he really was. LeRoy Reese, he ended up being one of my best men – he was real quiet, always sort of on the edge of things, but willing to kill in an instant. His little brother had been murdered by Kogier's bunch.

Oliver Brown and his outfit had stole about twenty horses from the Reb soldiers, then scattered. One of his boys, name of Grainger, had got in the habit of slipping out on his wife with a neighbor girl. The wife got plenty mad when she found out about it, and in a fit of spite let it slip to some loyal Southern ladies where her old man and his buddies had their hide-out. Turns out, Brown and Grainger and a couple of others was standing watch over their ill-gotten gains at the farm of a Unionist named Bowers.

Me and the boys, we decided to re-appropriate ourselves some good Confederate horseflesh.

The moon was bright in the sky that night. It cast kind of a pale glow on all our faces as we rode silently onto the Bowers place. Nobody sounded ary alarm when we got there – the fools had posted no sentry, and didn't even have a dog to bark them a warning.

I motioned the boys toward the corral. I stood an easy guard while they opened the gate and started rounding up that little herd. I lit me a cigar and puffed on it real slow, then pulled my Colt out and held it against my leg, just in case I needed it.

The door to Bowers' house opened and a man padded out in his bare feet, rubbing the sleep from his eyes. The feller had a revolver stuck down the front of his britches. It was one of Brown's men – he was on his way to ease nature, and when he seen us his eyes about popped out of his head.

His jaw worked a couple of times before he could get any sound out. When he did, his voice was shrill as a hurt pig's.

"Rebs!" he hollered. "Wake up, wake up, it's Rebs!"

He tried to pull that gun out of his pants but it snagged. He tugged and jerked, frantic. I leveled my Colt at him and put two holes in his chest. The old boy fell backwards against the doorway – his body went limp at once, emptying itself of blood and piss and soul. It was the first time I had killed a man, but I didn't give it any real thought – not then and not later. I knowed full well it wouldn't be the last.

Timmons and Reese broke away from the rest and came toward me – the others had them horses running through the gate and back the way we had come.

Fat old Grainger came through the door next, a shotgun in his hand. I had told him way back at that camp meeting that he was no hand with horses, and it turns out he was no good at holding onto them once he'd got them, neither.

Timmons and Reese both put bullets in him, and he collapsed into a heap. He looked kind of pitiful – a fat little bastard who had no business venturing off his own front porch.

A front window busted out – the tinkle of glass could barely be heared over the confused neighing of the horses – and a rifle barrel pointed from it. Flame spurted from the gun, and I seen Timmons jerk in the saddle.

"Bob!" Rains hollered out. "You hit?"

"Damn!" Timmons said, gripping his left arm. Blood flowed between his fingers. His face showed disbelief, like a man whose favorite dog had just bit him.

"That damn son of a bitch shot me," he said. "He *shot* me!"

"They tell me that happens in this line of work," I said. I fired two shots through the window, and the rifle jerked back. Another'n was pointing out the window on the opposite side of the door.

Bob Timmons had his revolver out. His left sleeve was dripping red.

"Damn if any Union bastard's gonna shoot me and get away with it!"

He jabbed his horse's ribs and charged straight at the house.

The first rifleman hadn't reloaded yet, I reckon. The second one squeezed off a shot, but it went wild – he was too timid to take a good aim, with the rest of us laying down covering fire.

Timmons busted right through the front door, still on horseback. We heared his pistol ring out several times.

The second rifleman throwed his self out the window and hit the ground rolling. By the time he got to his feet I was sitting my mare square in front of him, covering him with my Colt – I had changed cylinders, and in the moonlight he might've even seen the lead bulging out of the chambers on the side.

"Reckon ye better set still, hoss," I told him.

Timmons walked out the door, leading his horse. His revolver was snug in its holster.

"That other'n in there was Oliver Brown," he said.

"Is he dead?" Rains asked.

"If he ain't," Timmons replied, "I'd say he's imitatin' it good enough to fool God."

"What about this'n?" Reese said, waving his rifle toward the surviving Unionist.

"I reckon we ought to just shoot him, too," Timmons said. "What do you think, Captain?"

The boys had took to calling me Captain. That suited me well enough. All these Union sons of bitches riding around the countryside with their boys, shooting everything up, got to be captains – I reckoned, by God, I'd just be a damn Captain too.

"Reckon we ought to," I agreed. "But we won't."

The man breathed a sigh of relief – the air seemed like it couldn't get out of his lungs fast enough – but Timmons sneered.

"You gettin' soft on the Union, Cap'n?"

My eyes snapped onto him. I could feel the cold fire coming out of them, and I seen his eyes shrink back. He was crazy, but not crazy enough to push me too far – at least not yet. But I knowed what kind of men was riding with me. If I looked weak they'd turn on me in a minute.

I didn't bother to answer Timmons. After that one, quick stare, I ignored him.

"You got a name, boy?" I said to the prisoner.

"John – John Goodrich," he stammered. He was about twenty, tow-headed, looked like he would make a good field hand.

"Well, John Goodrich, you go on back to your farm. If I catch you riding the roads, I'll shoot you on sight."

John Goodrich nodded, his head bobbing up and down slowly like a puppet with loose strings.

"When you talk to your Yankee-lovin' friends," I continued, "you tell 'em Champ Ferguson is patrollin' these hills and woods. And I won't put up with 'em."

I leaned forward in the saddle and let my eyes bore into the boy. I was close enough he could probably smell my breath.

"You're lucky tonight, John. You won't be lucky no more. Go on, now."

Old John Goodrich, he lit out. He was on foot, and he wasn't complaining about it.

"Come on, fellers," I said. "Let's take these horses on back to them soldier boys."

"Minus the good ones?" Reese said.

"There ain't no damn good ones."

I rode up next to Timmons. He was binding up his arm with a strip off a dead man's shirt.

"Reckon ye better get that dug out."

"Reckon so, Cap'n. Don't think it broke the bone, though."

"Damn lucky, then."

"Yep."

I reached over and took ahold of his horse's reins, pulling it up short.

"I ain't soft on the Union."

"I was just makin' a joke, Champ."

"I ain't soft on nothin', Bob."

"It was a joke," he repeated. "Prob'ly not the best time for it, though."

I let go of his reins. "You done good tonight, Bob."

"Thank ye."

We both broke our mounts into a trot – the others was already a good bit ahead of us.

Timmons tied the tourniquet with his teeth. "I hate these damn home-grown Yankees."

"I'm gettin' to where I do," I said.

I had no way to know what was coming. No way to know I was just beginning to hate the bastards.

Chapter 10

Since the end of the War, I have been accused of some mighty mean things, all of them being directed against Union men. Most of these accusations is true. Them that ain't true I wish I had thought of, on account of I probably would've done them.

But there is one thing I ain't never been accused of. No man who made his self my enemy was ever safe from me, not even in his own house, but I ain't never harmed any women or children, or dishonored them. Any man under my command who was to try such a thing, I would've shot him dead where he stood. They all knowed it.

I just wanted that fact stated plain.

Now this next part of my story, it's something I ain't never talked about to nobody. Folks has asked about it, sure enough, especially them damned reporters out yonder. It's just me and you talking here right now, and talking plain, and I promised you the whole story. But you understand, this part ain't to be repeated. I'll deny it. And if you say anything about it after they stretch my neck on that scaffold out yonder, I swear to God, they can't bury me deep enough for you to be safe. I'll come clawing my way out of hell to get to you, do you hear?

All right.

Me and Rains knowed something wasn't right when we got to my house. There was a whole passel of neighbor ladies there, and they was all grim-faced and shuffle-footed – like ladies visiting a house which death has visited first. Them same looks was on the faces of the women who I'd found waiting at my house that other time, all them years ago, to tell me that Ann Eliza and our son was dead of the fever. A couple of these women had even been in that first group.

I dismounted real slow. My legs was numb. I was swimmy-headed – everything was all blurry, and my limbs moved like I was floating underwater. *Maybe this is what it feels like to drown*, I thought, only it was dread pushing the air out of my lungs instead of water.

"What's goin' on," I said. "What's happened."

No one answered. No one looked at me.

"Where's Marthy? Where's Ann? Marthy!"

"They're inside," one of the women said.

I rushed to my front door. Rains was behind me, but a couple of ladies stopped him and whispered at him. I went in alone.

Marthy was sitting hunched over the eating-table. Ann sat beside her. Two more ladies sat with them, but they got up and left without a word when they seen me.

I felt like a rock the size of Alabama had been lifted off my chest when I seen my girls sitting there, breathing and whole. But something was still wrong. I felt it in the air. And I knowed it for sure when Marthy looked up at me, her eyes wet with tears, quivering with rage and shame, one side of her face bruised like she had been kicked by an ornery cow.

"Marthy. Oh, Marthy."

She didn't speak. She just whimpered a little, way back in her throat. That was when I noticed that my Ann was different. She had never spoke a word neither, nor moved a muscle - she just sat there, staring at the walls, *through* the walls, like her soul had done slipped away and her body was just waiting to follow.

I pulled out a chair and sat beside them. Marthy throwed her arms around my neck and sobbed. She sobbed a long time, wetting my shirt through – deep, long sobs that shook her body. Tears was welling up in my eyes now, too. Behind my own tears, though, I felt the fire – it was rising up from my heart, heating my blood, pumping through my body, burning like nothing I had ever known or imagined.

"What have they done to you, Marthy?" I said. "Have they – have they—" I couldn't find the right words. I knowed that even if I found them I could never get them out.

Marthy shook her head against my shoulder, then looked up at me. "No, Champ," she said. "They never done that to us. But they might as well have."

"Who, Marthy. Did you know 'em?"

"I knowed some of them."

My hands was balling up into fists. "What happened? Tell me, for God's sake, tell me."

It took some time, and she had to stop for a spell every once in awhile because the crying was choking her.

But she told me.

Chapter 11

Eleven. Eleven men had rode onto my property. A few was wearing uniforms – they was soldiers on leave. The rest had put together their own version of uniforms, showing enough blue to let folks know where their sympathies lay.

Ann had seen them coming down the road, and went in the house to tell her mother. Marthy waited for them on the porch, a shotgun in her hands. When the men reined in, she could tell some of them had been drinking.

Their leader had not been drinking, though. He was sober as a preacher. He dismounted and stepped onto the front porch step. Marthy raised the shotgun.

"You ain't welcome on this land, Jim Ferguson," she said.

My brother's face was hard. "We're here for Champ, Marthy."

"He ain't here."

"He will be."

"You won't."

Jim stared at her a few seconds. She stared right back.

"Champ killed Oliver Brown the other night. And some other boys, too – at the Bowers' place. If Willie Bowers had been home that night, I reckon he'd be dead too."

Marthy never said nothing.

"A feller cain't go around just murdering people like that."

"I don't reckon you're the law," she said.

"It ain't a law matter, it's a war matter," Jim said. "There won't be no law 'til these Rebels is stopped."

"Your husband is a traitor," one of the mounted men said. It was an older man, one of two older men in the group. When Marthy looked closer she seen it was Reuben Wood. The other codger was Wash Tabor.

"You and Champ was always friends, Reuben."

"He was like a son to me," Reuben said. "But if my son was a Rebel, I'd kill him."

While Marthy was distracted by Reuben, Jim's hand streaked out and jerked the shotgun away from her.

"You give that back," she said, angry.

"I'll give it to Champ when he gets here."

"It's one thing to talk Rebel," Reuben Wood said. "That's bad enough. But when somebody starts terrorizing good Union people in the middle of the night, it's got to be stopped."

"I hear Oliver Brown terrorized himself some good Confederate people." Marthy said. "In the middle of the night."

Ann was standing behind her – she didn't say anything.

"There ain't no good Confederate people," Wash Tabor said, and spit.

"I reckon we'll just go inside and wait for Champ," Jim said.

"He might not be back for days."

One of the men laughed. Marthy recognized him as John Crabtree. Him and Alex Huff was both there – the two fellers who had argued with Reuben the day they captured me and Rains, wanting so bad to kill us.

"That'll just give you a chance to get to know us better," Crabtree said.

They had all dismounted and was picketing their horses. In addition to Jim and Reuben, the leaders, there was the ones I already mentioned: old Wash Tabor, John Crabtree, and Alex Huff. William Frogg was with them. Nervous as always, he was also the drunkest – it had took a lot of whiskey for him to work up the gumption to ride onto my property, even with ten other men. The other men Marthy didn't know. When she described them to me, though, it didn't take a lot of work for me to figure out who they was. It was the Evans brothers from Jimtown, and their buddy Elim Huddleston. They had brung the youngest Evans with them, Fount, who weren't no more than sixteen years old.

Jim shoved his way past my girls – his own kin – and sat down, making his self to home in my kitchen. Some of the others followed, but there wasn't enough room in my house for them all. Reuben, Huddleston, Frogg, and Fount Evans sat outside on the porch.

"Make us some coffee," Jim commanded my wife.

"Make it yourself."

"Coffee hell," Alex Huff hollered. "Look what I found." He brung out two jugs of corn liquor that Rains Philpot's uncle had give us the week before – he had give us three jugs, as a matter of fact, but we'd only had time to finish the one of them.

They unstopped the jugs and passed them around. Ann was huddled up in a corner, uncomfortable with the way some of the men was starting to look at her.

"Looks to me," Alex Huff said, "like when a feller turns traitor, by rights he ought to forfeit all his property. By rights, it ought to all go to loyal Union men."

"My brother is still a Ferguson," Jim said. "He's the only one out of all us boys to turn Reb. Any property he's got stays in the family."

"Any property?" Huff said, grinning at Marthy. "I ain't talking about just land and horses and such, you know. There's other things in this house that Champ ain't gonna have no more need of, him bein' a walkin' dead man."

Wash Tabor giggled, while Crabtree and Mike Evans smiled real big, hunger showing in their eyes. Floyd and Will Evans looked embarrassed, which I reckon is a little something in their favor.

"You might as well get them notions out of your head right now," Jim told them. "None of y'uns is gonna lay a hand on these ladies." He gave Marthy a look of contempt. "Much as this'un here might deserve it."

"Hell, Jim," Mike Evans said, "where's the fun in that?" His brother Will jabbed him in the ribs.

"That's his own flesh-and-blood niece over yonder, you damn idiot," Will hissed.

"Well. I never meant no harm in it. Just thinkin' out loud. All kinds of terrible things happens in wars, you know. Regular laws don't have to apply, not when you're dealin' with the enemy."

"Just shut up," Floyd told his brother, and Wash Tabor took to giggling again. No one bothered to ask him what he thought was so funny.

Jim didn't touch any of the liquor. I reckon he wanted to keep a clear head for when I showed up.

"I'm still waitin' on that coffee, woman. I wouldn't mind havin' some dinner to eat, neither. Would you, boys?"

The others voiced their agreement. I reckon that talking abusive toward females works up a feller's appetite - I don't know, I ain't never tried it.

"I reckon you're gonna have to fix us up somethin'," Jim told Marthy.

"I reckon you're gonna have to go to hell."

Jim breathed out real hard, like a snorting bull. "You're tryin' my damn patience."

"What are ye gonna do, Jim, shoot me? You was scared to even come here without ten men to back you up, and even then you come when Champ ain't home."

"If he had been home, he'd be dead by now," Huff said.

"He might well be," she said, "but upwards of half of y'uns would be dead right along with him. Which ones would it be? Which one of y'uns would have died first?"

Wash chuckled. "I reckon if he was here, we'd take one of them cornstalks in that field out yonder and stick it up his ass. Wouldn't we, boys?" The others laughed.

"I done told you, I'm hungry," Jim said, his voice cold.

Marthy smiled at him, but her eyes was blazing. "Do you reckon you're even man enough to kill me, Jim Ferguson, or do you need these others to help ye? Or maybe you need your mama."

Jim was on his feet in a flash, sending his chair clattering backwards, and he backhanded her hard across the face. The blow was powerful enough to knock her down.

Ann screamed – Marthy sat on the floor, and wiped the blood from her mouth. She motioned her daughter to hush.

Reuben Wood stormed in. "What the hell's goin' on in here!"

"Family business," Jim said, still breathing hard.

"I thought you said we wasn't to touch these ladies," Huff said.

"You ain't family," Jim answered.

Reuben moved to help Marthy up, but she pushed him away. "Get away from me, you blackhearted bastard," she said.

"We never come here to cause you no harm," Reuben said, his voice soft.

"You come here to kill my husband! What more harm could you ever do me than that? And over politics! When Champ always thought the world of you – he'd give you the shirt off his back, and you know it. You're worse than any of them!"

Reuben straightened back up, flustered. "I'll be outside," he said stiffly, and left.

Jim was standing over Marthy. "I'm hungry."

Her eyes narrowed to slits. "You're hungry, all right," she said. "You're hungry to be the man your brother is. You're hungry to take what he has, 'cause no one will ever give it to ye. As long as Champ is alive, he'll be better than you. You know it, and I know it, and Ann Eliza knowed it."

Jim's face colored like he was the one that had been slapped. "Bitch."

Ann spoke for the first time, tears streaming down her face. "My daddy's gonna kill you, Uncle Jim," she said. "I hope I see it happen."

Jim reached into his belt and pulled out his Colt. He leveled it at Ann's face and pulled back the hammer. Marthy gasped.

"No!" Marthy screamed. "No, please!"

Jim's hand was shaking. It was clear how bad he wanted to pull the trigger, to hurt Marthy for her words. To hurt me, for their truth.

"You get on your damn feet, woman," he hissed, "and you do exactly like I say."

Marthy stood up, all the fire extinguished by her fear. "Don't hurt her, Jim."

All the men stood spellbound, almost afraid to breathe. Wash had even stopped giggling.

Jim reached over and grabbed the front of Marthy's dress. He ripped it down – the tearing fabric sounded loud as thunder in the room. His other hand still pointed the gun at Ann. Marthy bit her lip so hard to keep from crying out that it began to bleed.

"Take it off," Jim said. "Take it all off."

"Please, Jim."

"It's too late for any damn please, *bitch*. It's time you was taught a lesson. Take it off!"

"All right, Jim," she said, her voice breaking. "Just don't hurt my little girl."

Marthy undressed and stood naked in front of the men, trying vainly to cover herself with her hands. Her eyes stayed glued on her daughter.

Jim's gun waved at Ann. "Now you."

"No Jim," Marthy whimpered. "Don't make her."

"She'll do it or you'll both die."

Ann didn't move at all. Jim's anger smoldered even hotter. His men was still paralyzed. Shame burned in the faces of some of them. But not Huff – he was staring at Marthy's bosom, smiling.

"Move!" Jim shouted, but Ann didn't even flinch. Her mind had left her, I reckon, and traveled to some place where bad things like this don't happen. It left her body behind. Could be she figured that if her mind wasn't there when it happened, maybe it never really happened at all.

Marthy moved to her daughter's side and helped her undress. Ann's limbs cooperated by instinct. All the time Marthy whispered softly to her. Soon they both stood naked in their own kitchen, seven men's eyes upon them.

"Now then," Jim said. "You are going to fix our dinner."

He picked his chair up off the floor and sat back down in it. The other four men crowded into the house to see what the noise was about – even Reuben was surprised at the sight which awaited them, and seemed to be disturbed, but he never said a word.

Marthy cooked their dinner. She felt their eyes on her bare bottom as she worked over the stove. Mike Evans reached out to touch it.

"If you touch her, I'll kill you," Jim said.

"What?"

"You can look, 'cause she needs the humblin'. But no man is gonna lay hands on ary Ferguson woman and live."

He received no arguments. Maybe they was starting to think he was as crazy as his Reb brother.

After they finished eating, Jim grabbed Marthy and Ann each by the arm and marched them outside.

"What are you doing?" Marthy said. "We cain't go out there."

"You'll do what I tell you. You're going to take a little walk."

He let go of them when they were in front of the house. Jim mounted up. The others had followed him outside - he told them to hit the saddle, too.

He leaned down closer to Marthy. "Now walk."

"Where to?"

"Down the road."

"Please."

Jim had a little quirt in his saddlebag. He took it out and struck Ann across the shoulders with it, drawing blood. She flinched, but did not take a step.

"By God, I said walk!"

Marthy took her daughter's arm and together they walked down the dirt road, the eleven horsemen behind them. They were marched for three miles that way, past the homes of many neighbors. People came out and stared, but was afraid to say anything.

William Frogg was getting more nervous by the minute. "We – we sure are paradin' these ladies past a lot of witnesses," he said.

"You got no call to be afraid of Champ," Jim said. "He's dead, just as soon as we find him."

"Maybe I'm afraid of the Lord," Frogg said.

"You got a lot more call to be afraid of Champ," said Marthy, just loud enough to be heard.

"We'll see," said Jim.

They finally turned my girls loose at the Widow Haston's house, and they rode off together to try and find me. They didn't know that in another hour I would've arrived home.

Marthy wasn't able to face folks after her humiliation, and she sure as hell didn't feel safe anymore. I sold everything. All my boys camped out around my house in the meantime, just in case the Unionists returned, but I reckon Jim and his friends didn't care too much for even odds. Ann got her wits back after a couple of days, but she wasn't the same for a long time. Maybe she never was.

I knowed there was a war on. I knowed that when a man chose up sides, he was making his self a fair target for the other fellers. But I never dreamed that a man's family could become a target. I would never make that mistake again. I was moving my girls to someplace they'd be safe. I knowed a feller had some bottomland for sale down near Sparta, Tennessee, and a little house to boot. Everybody knowed now that Sparta - all of White County - was good Rebel soil, through and through. It would not just be a haven for my family, it would make a good base of operations. There was plenty of wild land down there, and I had hunted all of it. My boys made the move with me.

"I ain't never comin' back to Kentucky," Marthy mumbled as we drove off in our wagon. "Not never."

"I know, honey."

But I was coming back to Kentucky. By God, I was coming back.

Chapter 12

Sparta was our home now. It felt like home. The handful of hunting buddies I had down there had spread the word about me – my Rebel sentiments made me a welcome neighbor to most. That ain't to say that there was no Unionists in the county. There was a few. The difference was, in this area they was a small minority, so they kept a low profile.

My new farm was near the banks of the Calfkiller River, not far from England Cove. There was miles of woodlands around that cove, woodlands wild and twisted, and a feller that knowed his way around in them could avoid someone that was unfamiliar with them forever.

Folks crowded around me as soon as I arrived in town, welcoming me and offering their support. White County had provided a passel of boys to Confederate regiments, both infantry and cavalry, and in fact a local big-wheel named George Dibrell was colonel in command of the Eighth Tennessee Cavalry, in General Forrest's division. There was still quite a few men around who had been unwilling to leave their farms and families and commit to the army life, but who still supported the Southern cause. It didn't take very long for such men to begin coming to me, one or two at a time, and offer to lend me a hand should I need it against them homegrown Yankees in neighboring counties.

Two such fellers approached me in the general store just two days after my arrival. They come up to me while I was looking through the work jeans, trying to find a pair that looked like it would fit my large frame.

"You're Champ Ferguson," the first feller said. He was skinny as a rail, and had a long nose – all he needed was wings, and he'd look just like a buzzard. His partner was round-faced and short.

"Yep," I said. "That's who I am."

"Welcome to Sparta," the round-faced man said, thrusting his hand out at me. "We're awful glad to have ye."

I pumped his hand, and then the skinny one spoke up. "We heard what happened to your family. That's a terrible thing."

I dropped round-face's hand, and my own face darkened. "What do you mean, you heared what happened to my family? What happened to 'em?"

The skinny man was suddenly very uncomfortable. "Well," he stuttered, "um, you know."

I took a step closer so I stood looking down at him. "No I don't know," I said. "I don't know what the hell you're talking about."

"Never mind about that, then," said the round-faced man. "We was mistaken."

"But I heard the Yankees came to your house," the skinny one said. I was beginning to suspect the skinny one wasn't all that bright, and I could tell his friend knowed it as well as me.

"I heard they came to your house," he continued, "and, you know... Disgraced your womenfolk."

"*That* is a damn lie."

"Huh? It is? But everybody says—"

I reached out and grabbed hold of his shirt collar with both hands, and pulled him up close to me so that he was standing on his tiptoes.

"I said, that's a damn lie. Nothing like that has ever happened to my family. Anybody says different, I'll cut his heart out."

"Yes – yes sir."

"You had best not be spreadin' no tales like that around this town, son. Nobody had. If my wife finds out folks are repeatin' lies like that about her, it'll break her heart. That would put me in a mighty bad temper. Do you hear me?"

Skinny nodded. Round-face nodded too, a look of understanding on his face. "That was a mistake, Mister Ferguson, like I said before. Don't you pay it no mind. Things like that ought not to be repeated. They won't be anymore, not by us. We just wanted to offer you our help if you needed it."

"That I'm obliged for, fellers. If ye want to ride with me, then ye can ride with me – and, by God, we'll fight some

Yankees 'fore it's done. Let's not say anymore about that other."

They agreed. Then they bid me a good day and left. Neither one of them ever wound up riding with me, though. I reckon I scared them off. They sure as hell never rode against me. That round-faced boy, he joined the infantry and got killed in some battle or other. Skinny, I reckon he just went on back to the house and stayed out of everybody's way.

People still spread them rumors, but very rarely did anybody speak about it direct to me anymore. I done all I could to quash such talk. There was other rumors, too. There was even a story that I had a little five-year-old boy setting out on my front porch one day, waving a Rebel flag, and some passing Yankee soldiers shot him dead. That, according to some, was what set me down the road to vengeance. I swear, there was some people repeating that story who knowed good and well that my only son had died of natural causes years before the War broke out.

I have denied both stories to this day. I have never made any secret that the reason I became Confederate – in the beginning – was just to stay out of jail. In time I began to believe in the cause for real, and was willing to risk or even lose my life for it.

But that didn't account for my hatred, and everybody knowed it. I could never admit out loud that some of the stories was true. I struggled to make folks disbelieve, so that Marthy could walk down the street with her head held up high. Deep down inside of me the truth was there, though, and it ate at my guts like an ulcer. The eleven bastards who done it would not be enough to satisfy me. I swore I would kill a hundred Yankees before I quit.

Now that my family was settled into their new home, it was time to get to work. I had people to see.

I knowed William Frogg would be easy to find. He was never one to stray far from his home in Jamestown, Tennessee. I decided he would be first.

Chapter 13

"You better watch out, Champ Ferguson."

I reined in my horse and looked at the old woman who spoke to me. She was shuffling slowly down the side of the road.

"Do I know you, ma'am?"

She stopped moving too, and looked up at me. The lines in her face was so deep they might well have cut all the way down, into her soul – her face was so shriveled and lifeless that maybe her soul had leaked away out of them lines.

"I don't reckon," she said. "But I know you. I've seen you around town." We was just a little ways outside of Jamestown. The woman actually managed to muster up a little smile. "I'm for the South," she said. "So was my husband, before Elijah Kogier an' his bunch kilt him."

"I'm sorry to hear that, ma'am. Elijah Kogier's gonna be gettin' his one of these days, though."

"He ain't the only one around here that ain't any good," she said. "Like them Evans boys, and William Frogg. And Elim Huddleston."

"I know, ma'am."

"They're layin' for ye, y'know. You better watch out for 'em. I reckon they figure you're gonna be comin' after 'em one of these days."

"Is that so?"

"You be careful, son."

"I will." I decided to stay away from the roads from now on.

"You tell your poor wife that the Lord will take care of her," she said, and my back stiffened. I took her words to mean that the story of my family's dishonor had spread plumb out to here.

"God bless you too, Champ Ferguson," she called after me as I rode away. "I'll pray for ye. God bless you!"

It was a funny feeling, I'll tell you that right now. All my life folks had thought of me as either a no-account scoundrel, or as a good old boy with rough edges and the heart of a child. Now here I was – the same old Champ, doing pretty much what I've always done, reacting as I would have reacted whether a war was on or not – and folks was looking at me different. Union people hated me like I was the devil his own self, for no other reason than that I had spoke up for the South. And Confederate people, why, they was starting to love me like I was some kind of angel, for the same reason.

What if I had never got that offer to have my charges dropped if I supported the Southern cause? I reckon I might well have followed along after my kinfolks, fighting for the Union. Then the people that loved me now would hate me instead, and the other way around, and I'd still be the same Champ. It never made no sense to me, no sense a-tall.

I found Esther Frogg setting on her front porch, peeling apples. Esther was a Clinton County girl, and we was raised up together – she used to moon around after me at dances and church socials. I always thought she was a nice enough gal, but she didn't have the right amount of fire to suit me. Maybe that explains her later marriage to Frogg. Frogg was probably afraid of fire, even when it came in the form of a female, so they made a good match. Whenever I seen Esther afterwards, though, which wasn't often, I couldn't help but notice the boredom settled into her features.

She looked up at me, and her eyes danced for a moment – first with something like joy, then with something like fear. She took in a sharp breath. Her face colored, like she was embarrassed for some reason.

"Howdy, Champ," she said.

"Hello Esther."

"How's your wife doin'?" Again with my wife.

"She's fine."

"That's good."

"There's a chair yonder, if you want to set down."

"I ain't got time."

She held out a piece of fruit to me, fresh-peeled. "Ye care for an apple?"

"I done had one, while-ago," I said. "I'm here to see your husband, Esther."

"He's in yonder, in bed."

"This time of day?"

"He's took sick. He joined up with the Army, y'know – the infantry. He took sick right after he got to camp, and they sent him on home for awhile. My cousin Jack is settin' with him - you remember Jack, don't you?"

"I remember Jack." Me and Jack Mace had always got on well when we was young. That didn't necessarily mean much anymore, though.

"My baby's in yonder too, asleep in his crib." A tear had welled up in Esther's eye and it rolled slowly down her cheek. "You – you'll be careful not to wake him, won't ye?"

"I'll try not to."

I walked into the house. It took a second for my eyes to adjust to the dark. When they did, I seen Jack Mace setting beside the bed. Frogg was propped up on a pillow – the blood drained out of his face when he seen me. I stared at him, no emotion in my eyes at all.

"Howdy Champ," Jack Mace said. Then he stood up, real slow and careful. His expression said, *this ain't got nothing to do with me.* "I'll be outside, I reckon," he said, and he brushed lightly past me as he went out the door. I felt the tension in him when he passed.

Frogg raised one arm feebly, like he was trying to somehow draw Jack back to him. I could read what was going through Jack's mind, same as I can read trail in the woods, or predict the actions of a skittish horse. Jack Mace – just like his cousin Esther, Frogg's own wife and the mother of his child – had heared the stories about what happened at my house, and was disgusted. On top of that, they both knew William Frogg to be a coward. Neither of them wanted to risk defending such a man. Not even if he was kin.

I kept staring at him. He looked like he was going to cry. It was him stepping forward to swear lies against me to the law that had helped set all this in motion – that alone was enough to put him on my bad side.

"I got the measles," he said, his voice breaking.

"I reckon you caught 'em at Camp Dick Robinson."

"No, I didn't," he said. "I ain't never been there."

I drawed my Army Colt out of its holster and pulled the hammer back.

"Please," Frogg said. "Sweet Jesus." He pulled the blanket over his face. I could hear him whimpering. He was pretty good at begging. Marthy had done plenty of begging her own self, which never came easy for her, and it didn't do her a bit of good.

My eyes was drawn to the cradle over in the corner, and the baby laying in it. It was a little boy – but it still reminded me of my sweet Ann at that age, all innocent and pure and unspoiled by the world. I had promised Esther I would try not to disturb the child, but I reckon she would just have to get over it. Same as Marthy. Same as Ann.

I shot the bastard twice in the head.

The baby immediately took to squalling. He'd be better off making up memories of his daddy, I reckon, than he would be if he was raised up by such a piece of shit.

Esther Frogg was sunk to her knees on the front porch, sobbing quietly. Jack stood with his hand on the wall and his back to his cousin, shoulders hunched over and staring at the distant mountains.

As I untethered my horse, a neighbor lady showed up – Russell, I think her name was. Maybe you've noticed how many neighbor ladies keep popping up in this story. No matter what happens in these mountains, whether it's bullets flying or plagues spreading, I can guarantee you that before the smoke clears the premises will be thick with neighbor ladies. I've rarely been able to keep their names straight, even in my own neighborhood – there's just too blamed many of them.

"What's wrong?" Mrs. Russell said. "What is it?"

"Mister Frogg has expired," I said as I swung into the saddle. "I reckon you'd best see to his widow."

"What happened to him?"

"He had the measles."

"And it kilt him? I ain't never heared of measles killin' nobody."

"It all depends on where you are when you catch 'em."

I rode away. Esther's crying and the baby's crying blended together, faint as they was.

They say that was my first murder. I don't call it murder, myself – I call it self-defense in advance. Frogg was a coward, but not so much a coward he wouldn't have shot me in the back if he had a chance. Or from ambush –

especially if a few other fellers backed him up and lent him some nerve.

I killed him, and I'd kill him again. I'd kill his damn ghost if I knowed how. That's all I have to say on the subject.

Chapter 14

Fentress County, Tennessee. Clinton County, Kentucky. That was the territory of my sworn enemies. After the death of William Frogg, they was twice as watchful for me in them counties. That's why I decided to take a few extra hands with me when I rode up to Clinton County to cast my net and see what fish I could catch. I couldn't take my whole Bunch – the number of boys following me now was usually somewhere between twenty and thirty – that would attract too much attention. Some of the Union guerilla bands or Home Guards might lay into us. This didn't scare me – I just didn't want to warn my targets and give them a chance to run away.

Rains came along, of course. I also brung John Homer and LeRoy Reece. I figured the four of us could fight our way out of any bad luck we might run into.

Our first stop was the Evans house. We didn't find nobody at home there but their old mother. She came out onto her porch waving a broom at us, like we was mongrel dogs.

"Get off my property, you Rebel bastards!" she hollered. "When my boys find out you've been pokin' around here, they're gonna hunt y'uns down and kill ye!"

"Seems like I'm a hell of a lot easier to find than they are," I said, "and that right there says a whole lot."

"What do y'uns want here!"

"I reckon you know good and well what we're after. But your boys ain't here, so we'll just have to take them horses out yonder in the corral instead. Bring 'em out, boys."

She stomped her foot – I thought the old lady was actually going to come off the porch and take a whack at me with that broom.

"Damn thievin' Rebs," she said. "You're worser than wild niggers!"

That sounds kind of funny now, considering all them Yankees from Massachusetts and what-have-you that shot at me later, wearing actual uniforms, their goal being to end slavery. Fact is, them Kentucky boys that hounded me through the mountains in the name of preserving the blessed Union, a good third of them had a slave or two back home. It was a crazy damn war, all right.

We took five pretty good mounts off the Evans place with us. Word of our own return to Clinton County must have traveled fast, though – the Home Guards wasted no time getting together a reception for us.

Staying away from the roads didn't help. I reckon they knowed that if they lolled around in the woods near the Evans farm, eventually I'd come right to them.

I heared the ball clipping its way through the branches above my head before I heared the shot. I hunched down in the saddle, and even as I hollered at the boys to ride there was more shots from our rear.

We pounded through the brush, bullets whining in the air around us. Them horses we took from the Evans place was slowing us down – we had to let them go and allow them to run wherever they had a mind to. They kept going in the same direction, fortunately, shielding us from some of the gunfire. One of them, a chestnut mare, took a bullet and plowed into the ground, tripping up one of the others. I risked a quick look behind me – the two horses was tangled and thrashing. I heared hollering and cussing from a ways back. One of the Evanses must have recognized the horses.

There was about a dozen horsemen back there. I whirled around and emptied my Colt at them. One of the men managed to get off a shot – I felt the wind from the bullet – then he dropped his gun and clutched his shoulder. Before I took off again to catch up with my partners, I caught a clear glimpse of my brother Jim's face among the crowd. I was pretty sure I seen Reuben Wood, too.

Rains came crashing out of the trees in front of me. He unloaded his own pistol in their direction just like I had. While the Unionists veered off, scrambling for cover, we hightailed it out of there. Reese and Homer had held up, waiting for us – we all turned east, toward the creek. We splashed down the little stream for a ways. It was enough to throw off our pursuers for a bit and allow us to slip away.

~ ~ * ~ ~

We rode over to the Wood place bright and early the next morning. Reuben was out back slopping the hogs. He dropped the slop-bucket when he seen us trotting up to the pen. Reuben walked slowly out and shut the gate behind him. His eyes flickered to the back door of his house, and I knowed he was evaluating the risk of making a dash for it, and for the gun he must surely have placed just inside.

"How are you today, Reuben," I said.

"I'm gettin' on, I reckon," he said. "How are you, Champ?"

"Gettin' along."

"Howdy Reuben," Rains said, but Reuben ignored him.

From the corner of my eye I seen two more people coming from around the corner of the house. It was Reuben's wife and his youngest daughter Liz. Liz was a few years older than my Ann, about the age she ought to be married already. Both their faces was white with fear - they didn't walk no closer.

"Well Reuben," I said, "I reckon now you're fixin' to tell me you ain't never been to Camp Dick Robinson."

"I have been," he said, "and I don't give a damn who knows it. Me and my son Robert is both Home Guards and you know it, and my oldest boy is in the Twelfth Kentucky Union Infantry. I got a nephew in the Confederate infantry, and he can go to hell."

"You don't say."

"I do say. Ain't no room in my family for traitors to the Constitution."

"I've got to tell you, Reuben," I said. "I'm gettin' sick and tired of you Union sons of bitches and your damn sermons."

I drawed my revolver out and pointed it at him. Reuben's eyes widened for a moment, but then he regained control and pushed the fear away. His face was back to its usual proud, stubborn self at once.

His wife cried out, though. "No!" she hollered, and Liz grabbed hold of her while she sobbed.

"I've knowed you since you was a boy, Champ," Reuben said. "I've always been good to you, you know that. I even talked them fellers out of killin' you."

"Yes," I said, "you've treated me good. But how you've treated me ain't got nothin' to do with it."

I cocked the hammer, and the women started wailing. It crossed my mind to let Reuben go – a few months ago I wouldn't have even had to think about it, my heart would have already softened.

Reese and Homer, for their part, didn't seem to be very concerned by the proceedings. Rains was, though – he was all tore up, so upset I could feel it pouring out of him in waves. He kept looking from the women, to Reuben, to the pistol in my hand. He wanted to say something, I know, but he held back. Maybe he thought I wouldn't go through with it.

But my girls got no mercy, did they. I was never no angel, but I wasn't exactly what you'd call evil, neither – I always had the same kinds of feelings a normal man has.

But the image in my mind of my girls – naked, scared, and ashamed – pushed them feelings out of my soul and left it hard as tempered steel.

"Don't you beg," I told Reuben Wood, "and don't you dodge."

Then he was trying to run past me to reach the safety of his house, and I was shooting at him. The first bullet caught him in the chest, just below the left nipple. This caused him to jerk to the side and made the second shot miss him. Reuben never stopped – he reached the door and even managed to slam it behind him.

I was sliding to the ground. The boys sat and watched, impassive, knowing this was my business to handle. Reuben's wife was laying in the dust, screaming, and his daughter was keening to the sky like a she-wolf. Maybe she was praying for the Lord to send a lightning bolt to fry me in my tracks.

I bounded through the door, and immediately the old man was on me. He hadn't had the time to reach his rifle - it hung on a peg over the mantel – but he had picked up a hatchet. He swung it at my hand an instant before I fired again. The hatchet hit my barrel and the shot went wild.

Reuben launched his self at me, his chest soaked with blood, and we both fell to the floor. We rolled around, each holding the wrist of the other's weapon hand. Then Reuben head-butted me so hard it seemed like the whole world had exploded right in my face. The gun slipped from my fingers. Reuben lifted the hatchet high for the killing blow.

And then Rains was standing over us. The muzzle of his revolver was only inches from Reuben's face.

"If you touch Champ again," Rains said, his voice shaking with emotion, "I'll blow your damn brains out."

Reuben's breath was coming in ragged gasps. He backed away from me on hands and knees, still holding the hatchet, and pulled himself up onto a chair. I shook my head, trying to clear my vision, and felt around for the Colt. I could feel Reuben's wild eyes upon me. His breathing was even worse – there was one final, terrible rattle and I knowed he was dead.

The women rushed in a moment later and fell on his body.

"You killed him!" his wife said, her voice a pitiful sob. "You killed him!"

"He came to my house to kill me."

Liz looked up at me, her features turned ugly by grief and hate.

"My brothers will hunt you down and kill you, you heartless son of a bitch!"

"That's how it works, I reckon," I said as I holstered my weapon.

Rains stood, spellbound, his gun still leveled at the corpse.

"Come on," I said, touching his shoulder. "Come on."

Rains backed slowly away, a muscle twitching in his face. He had been under fire when we fought Oliver Brown's bunch, and held up fine – but today he had been prepared to kill one of his oldest friends. It had shaken him to his core.

I didn't feel nothing. All that ran through my mind was that there was nine more to go. After that there'd be Elijah Kogier and his guerillas – and one day there'd be a whole army of blue, marching from the north, hoping to trample us underfoot.

The blood was only beginning to flow.

Word would get out quick about Reuben, and the others would be on their guard. I would get them some other day. We left the stiffening corpse and the crying woman behind, and headed home to Sparta.

Chapter 15

"I think you've got a bite, darlin'."

Ann started, like she had been woke out of a dream, and tugged on her line.

"That's right, gal," I said. "Play 'er easy."

We was sitting on the red banks of the Calfkiller River. Our breath turned to frost in the air when we spoke.

"It's just a stick," she said. Sure enough, a big chunk of wood came swimming at us on the end of her line, looking almost like a baby 'gator.

"It's too cold, Daddy," Ann said, and her tone added *I told you so*. It was like she was the bored grown-up and I was the backward child. "The fish are too sluggish."

"Sluggish my foot," I said. "I'll warrant ye it's awfully dern nippy out here – it don't make me sluggish, it makes me want to move around. Don't see why a bunch of dern fish should feel any different about it."

"It's almost December, Daddy. It's way too cold to just be setting out here like this."

I nodded. It would actually make more sense to be out hunting deer – but I figured that something a little more calm and peaceful would be better for my daughter.

"I reckon this wadn't the best idea I ever had after all," I admitted. "I just figured you might want to get out of the house for a spell, is all."

She reached over and patted me on the leg.

"I love you, daddy."

I got choked up for a second. I cleared my throat. "Well," I said finally. "I reckon you're right, we ain't gonna catch nothin'. We might as well go."

"Let's stay," Ann said. "We might catch somethin' after all."

"A cold, maybe."

"Settin' here ain't really so bad," she said. "It's better than settin' in the house."

So we sat a spell longer. We didn't talk no more, we just sat there. We didn't catch nothing – we never even got a bite. Along about dark we got up and both stretched our muscles. My bones creaked when I climbed to my feet, and my joints popped, just loud enough to tell the whole world that I wasn't a young man no more. In two more days, on the twenty-ninth of November, I would be forty years old.

We trudged on home. Ann walked close to me, so close she bumped into me a couple of times. It was like she believed that my shadow would protect her from the cold, that my body would block the wind.

I wondered if the day would come when she would realize the truth. It was my shadow which had brung upon her all the cold and pain she had known in her young life. I had set things in motion – by not thinking, just like Marthy always said – then my family suffered, and I wasn't even there to protect them. All I could do was react afterwards.

At least this time, with this family, I had an enemy to vent my rage on, not just a faceless fever which came in the night and then was gone. My girls would not suffer again at the hands of my enemies. I would make it up to them, the best way I knowed how. The only way I knowed how.

Marthy never asked me no questions anymore about what I done when I wasn't with her. She never talked about it, or about the life and home we had left behind. Once Edgar Whitley was at the house – a rare occasion, my boys all had the respect to stay away from my family, all except Rains because he pretty much was family – but Edgar had come to deliver a message to me.

"I hear old Reuben Wood passed away the day before yesterday," Edgar said solemnly to my wife on his way out.

"Good," was all Marthy said about it, then or afterwards.

Rains never said much either, not about anything I ever did. He did mention Reuben though, just one time, a few days after it happened. He had been unnaturally quiet up to then.

"It don't seem right, Champ," he said, his voice sad.

"What don't."

"None of it. Reuben and them, what they done, that ain't right – it don't make ary bit of sense. And us just – just shootin' folks down thataway."

"You mean Reuben."

"I mean folks, Champ. I just mean folks."

"Do you want out?"

Rains jerked his head up, his eyes widened a little. "Oh no, Champ, I don't mean that. Oh no. I'm with ye – you're my partner come hell or high water. I never meant nothin' like that a-tall."

"All right," I said, and I couldn't help but smile a little.

"It's just – nothin' in the whole world don't feel right no more. Nothin' in the whole world."

"Nothin' ever will again, Rains, I don't reckon. The world ain't the same. Nothin' makes sense, and right or wrong don't count for anything. A feller just has to accept it, and go with it, or else he'll wind up dead for sure."

"I reckon," Rains said, but I could tell he didn't really understand. I could tell he had given up on trying to. I was glad, because that was what he needed to do – quit trying to understand and give all of his energy over to trying to survive, instead. Like the rest of us.

The message Edgar Whitley gave me that evening was from a feller named Scott Bledsoe. I had heared of him, of course. He was a Confederate guerilla, same as us – he had a bunch of boys several times the size of mine. He had already begun to make a name for himself in the Upper Cumberland, raising hell against the Union militia groups.

He wanted to meet with me. Edgar had a second cousin that rode with Bledsoe, and this cousin was going to lead us to their camp. I was told I could feel free to bring as many men with me as it would take to feel safe. I knowed it might be a trap, of course, and that feller might not be leading me to Bledsoe at all but rather to a bunch of Unionists.

I brung Rains with me, naturally. And Edgar Whitley, since it was his cousin that would be our guide. I brung LeRoy Reese because he was reliable – reliable to know when to fight like hell and when to set still. I didn't bring nobody else.

Edgar's cousin – I don't even remember the boy's name now, just that he had a head of hair so bright red it liked to have put my eyes out – never said much on the trip. We rode north, through Cookeville and into Jackson County. Bledsoe's camp was at a clearing set deep in the woods. There must have been two hundred men there. The whole thing was set up very organized and military, even though there was no real uniforms in sight.

Young Red led us through the camp and to a ragged tent, no different from all the others. A man pushed the flap aside and stepped out to meet us.

The man was short and slight of build, about ten years my junior. He had curly brown hair and several days' worth of beard stubbling up his cheek. What stood out most about him was his eyes – they was a bright, fierce blue, and they seemed to dance around without moving.

"Howdy," he said. "My name is Scott Bledsoe." He looked up at me. "You must be Captain Ferguson – I've heard a lot about you." He held out his hand, and I shook it.

"Was it good or bad?"

Bledsoe smiled. "Depends on which side a feller's on, I reckon. Step inside, Captain, we have a lot to discuss. You other boys, you just make yourselves to home – the best you can, in this damned mud."

I followed Bledsoe into his tent. I remember having a good feeling about him at the time, a sort of an immediate trust. I had no way of knowing then, of course, that this slender, intense man would become closer to me than a brother.

"Have a seat, Captain," he said, pointing to an overturned crate.

"Call me Champ," I said, and I sat down.

Chapter 16

Bledsoe rolled his self a smoke, then offered me the tobacco pouch and paper. While I was making my cigarette, he struck a match on his fingernail and lit up – he cupped the match with his hand and I leaned forward, drawing in the flame and feeling the smoke curl down my throat.

"We're fixin' to see some real fightin' in these mountains," Bledsoe said. When he seen the scowl on my face he added, "Not to say that what we've been doin' so far ain't been real, you understand. People have died. But so far it's just been a matter of partisans takin' potshots at each other, which ain't nothin' compared to what's comin'."

I nodded. "There's gonna be armies, and full-scale battles, ain't no gettin' around that. It's only a matter of time. But I reckon we can handle anything the Yankees send our way."

"We can," Bledsoe agreed, "but we've got to be organized. When the Confederate forces come this way we can join up with 'em. We can do all the things regular cavalry do – make sorties, scout. Thing is, though, them Unionist bastards like Kogier can do the same thing for the Yankees. So until the official fighting swings this way, we need to concentrate on wiping them sons of bitches out."

"Sure as hell suits me."

Bledsoe grinned. "If you and your boys are riding with us, I reckon we can sure enough do some damage. I've heard stories about you all."

"If they ain't true they ought to be."

"Are ye with us then?"

"I will be directly. I have some business I need to take care of first – I don't expect it'll take long."

Bledsoe folded his hands in front of him. "I understand, Champ." Then he grinned again. "Besides, I have a feelin' that takin' care of your business will take care of some of mine, too."

I nodded and stood up. "I'll holler at ye afterwhile, then, I reckon."

"You be careful."

"I don't believe in it."

Bledsoe chuckled and watched me walk out.

~ ~ * ~ ~

"What did y'uns talk about, Champ?" Rains asked. We was riding through the woods of Jackson County. It was drizzling rain – it felt good.

"Good news, fellers," I said, loud enough for all of them to hear. "We're gonna get together with them old boys back yonder, here before long, and kill Yankees."

"Sure as hell suits me," LeRoy Reese said. Me and him always did think a lot alike. Edgar Whitley and his red-headed cousin chuckled and joshed around – everybody seemed to be real pleased at the prospect of more fighting, everybody except Rains. He was swaying easy in the saddle with a solemn look on his face.

After awhile I slowed my mount down so as to draw even with my friend. "Why so gloomy?" I asked him.

Rains chewed on his mustache for a second or two. "I seen a couple of fellers back yonder at that camp," he said, "playin' checkers."

"Yeah?" I said, in a tone that invited him to get to the point. I waited, but he didn't say no more. He acted like the conversation was over and that I had surely made whatever connection it was that had clicked in his own brain, and then he slipped back into his own thoughts. He even forgot to duck when we rode under a low branch. It whacked him in the head, and the whole tree dumped all its accumulated rainwater on us both.

"What about it?" I finally said, a little irritated.

His eyes focused on me slowly. "How about what, Champ?"

"This gloomy spell you've took. I ain't never knowed checkers to put you in such a bad humor. Hell, I thought you liked checkers."

Rains nodded. "Yeah, I like checkers pretty well, I reckon."

"Then what's the problem?"

"There ain't nobody to play checkers with no more."

"Pert near everybody in the whole world knows how to play checkers, Rains. Hellfire."

"Well yeah, everybody knows how," he said, with just the faintest despondent echo in his voice. "But they're all too busy killin' each other to play checkers, seems like."

"I'll play checkers with ye if that's the only thing wrong," I said. "I'll play a game with ye this evenin'."

"You ain't no good at checkers, Champ. You ain't got the patience for it. Remember that one time, when you got mad and throwed the board off in the bushes? I never did find all the pieces. I had to get a whole new set."

"I remember, I remember." That had happened more than ten years before. It was like Rains to still be pouting about it.

"There always used to be somebody around to play checkers with," Rains said. Then he rode on in silence. I shook my head and trotted on up with the others, leaving Rains to bring up the rear. Talking to him when he was in such a state was even beginning to make me blue, and I couldn't afford to be blue.

Some things it's best not to dwell on.

~ ~ * ~ ~

When I got home I found Marthy out back splitting wood. She would raise the ax high over her head and bring it down with all her strength, grunting with the effort. Her eyes flicked up at me briefly as I came riding up, and I seen the quick shadow of relief in them that I had made it home alive one more day. Then she swung the ax again and *thunked* it into the log before her.

I slid out of the saddle and led my mare behind me as I approached Marthy.

"Set that ax down, honey," I told her. "Ain't no need for you to be doin' that kind of work." I turned and looked at the huge woodpile stacked up against the side of the house. "Hell, fact is, we done already got enough wood cut to last us half the winter."

"And if we don't cut no more," she said, not looking up from her task, "then halfway through the winter we'll run out. Then where will we be?"

The ax *thunked* again.

"Well," I said, "if it means that much to ye I'll cut some more. Just reach me that ax."

"I don't mind doin' it," she said.

Thunk.

I took my hat off and just stood there a few seconds, confused as hell. "Maybe you don't mind doin' it," I said finally, "but I wish you'd just let me. The neighbors will think I'm too lazy to chop my own damn firewood."

"The neighbors know better."

"They won't know better, if they see me standin' here watchin' my wife swing an ax."

"They will, too. Horace Carmichael has done stopped by once, while-ago, and tried to talk me into letting him cut this wood for me. I wouldn't let him."

Thunk.

"You know what he said, Champ?"

"No."

"He said it ain't right for the wife of a good Rebel hero like Champ Ferguson to be cuttin' her own wood."

"Rebel hero, huh. That's news."

"There's folks around here that would do every chore on this farm, just so you could be free to do what you do."

"That ain't right. It's my farm."

Marthy actually set the ax-head on the ground and leaned against the handle. "It is right, Champ. You need to be doin' – what it is you do. And when you ain't, you need to be restin' so ye can do it some more, or plannin' what you're fixin' to do next. Me and Ann will take care of things around here. Now you go inside and rest, Champ Ferguson, and plan."

Marthy hefted up the ax again. She brung it down even harder than before, like that log was the head of someone she hated with all her heart, like it was the devil and she was trying to beat him back into hell.

She ignored me after that, so I walked away. Seems like everybody around me was lost inside their own head anymore. I didn't want to set, or plan, or mull over anything. The more that folks around me done such things, the more uncomfortable I became. The more anxious I was to get back on the hunt.

Rains had it pegged, all right. I never was no good at checkers.

Chapter 17

I had told Bledsoe that my business wouldn't take long to finish. I figured I would ride up into Kentucky, go straight after the sons of bitches I wanted – one at a time or all at once, I wasn't particular – make a little small talk, maybe, and then send them on to hell where they belonged. Similar to what I had done with Reuben and Frogg. What I hadn't counted on was that them old boys had a strong sense of self-preservation. They was just like quail – once I shot one or two, the rest scattered. I reckon Reuben was too brave to scatter, and Frogg was too stupid, and that was their tough luck.

Me and Rains hid out in the woods down the road from my mama's house for two days, waiting for some sign of Jim. We made cold-camp on a timbered hill, where we could keep an eye on the road. We didn't even smoke in that time for fear of giving ourselves away; we had to be content with chewing. I doubt if a feller could have kept a cigarette lit anyways, it was raining so damn much. Two days with the rain soaking down into our bones, and nary a sign of my brother – nor anybody else, for that matter – coming down that road. They probably had sense enough to stay home in such weather.

"I reckon it's warm up yonder at your mama's house," Rains said on the second day.

"I reckon so," I mumbled. His statement irritated me. It put me in mind of all the days I had spent in that little house up the road, of warmer dryer winters and happier times.

"I'd say she's got coffee on to boil, this time of the day," Rains said. "Your mama always made good coffee."

"I'd say it's probably warm in hell, too," I told him, "but that don't mean I'm in any hurry to get there."

Rains crinkled his eyes up – he was confused again. "I never said nothin' about hell, Champ," he said. "I just said your mama makes good coffee."

"If we went to my mama's house lookin' for coffee or anything else, she'd have us both shot before we could reach the front door."

Rains was shocked. "She wouldn't shoot us, Champ. You're her son."

"Oh, yes she would."

"Well," Rains said. "I reckon you'd know better'n me, she is your mama."

"Gettin' shot might beat gettin' rained on, though." I said. "At least it would be somethin' different."

"I reckon I'd rather get rained on."

"You win, then. Slow death by rain it is."

"I swear, Champ. You've got to where you're gloomier than I am."

"Well, well now," I said, perking up a little. "I reckon I was wrong, we ain't the only fools in the world. Here comes somebody."

It was two somebodys, in fact. Two men came around the bend, their horses plodding slowly through the mud. One of the men I knowed right off. It was Tinker Dave, from down in Fentress County. I had to stare at his partner awhile before I could place him, though he looked familiar right off. After a moment I realized that it was Preston Huff, a brother to Alex Huff, who was one of the men I was laying for.

I waved my hand absently at Rains. I mounted up. He followed my example, and we picked our way down the hill to meet the travelers.

They wasn't expecting any company to come popping out of the woods. Tinker didn't seem too concerned about it, but Preston Huff sure as hell did.

"Howdy fellers," I said.

"Hello Champ," said Tinker.

Huff didn't say nothing.

"Ye reckon it's fixin' to rain?" I asked.

"It's as good a day for it as any," Tinker said.

"You're a long way from Jamestown, Tinker."

"Yep."

"It's a hell of a day to be travelin'."

"We had business that wouldn't wait. You're a long way from Sparta, your own self – I hear you've planted yourself down yonder now."

"Yep. The weather suits me."

"If ye cain't go to heaven," Tinker said, "ye might as well go to Tennessee. That's what I've always said."

I looked at Preston Huff. "What if a feller's goin' to hell?" I asked.

Tinker answered. "Then I reckon he'll get there, sooner or later."

"You're awful quiet today, Preston," I said.

"I ain't got much to say, is all," he said.

"You look kind of nervous, to me."

"I ain't nervous," Preston said, and the words came out fast enough to tell me that he sure enough was.

"I was hopin' I'd run into my brother Jim out here, I ain't seen him in awhile." I leaned over the saddle to spit a stream of tobacco juice into the mud. "A feller ought to keep up with his brothers, I reckon."

"There ain't much chance of ye runnin' into Jim around here," Preston said. "I hear he joined the regular cavalry a few months back – he won't be back this way for a spell, unless he's on leave."

"Why, I thought he was with the – what did he call that outfit, Rains?"

"Home Guards."

"Yeah, Home Guards. From out of Camp Dick Robinson. I thought him an' his Home Guard buddies was gonna stay right around here and set the woods on fire with their patriotic spirit."

"Most of the Home Guards has pulled out, too," Preston said. "They've attached theirselves to some of the regular regiments – it's time for the fightin' to start."

I grinned. "Your brother Alex is in the Home Guards there, ain't he Preston?"

"Yeah."

I leaned forward again. "I want you to do me a favor, Preston, next time you see that brother of yorn. Would you do that for me?"

"I reckon."

I spat again. "You tell him he is a damned worthless son of a bitch, and a coward. Tell him my horse shits out better specimens than him, and my horse don't even eat all that good nowadays. When I see that bastard I intend to cut him so bad his own dog won't know him, and all the Home Guard shit-asses in the state of Kentucky won't be able to save him."

Preston Huff's face colored up, his anger overtaking his fear. Tinker just looked kind of sad, same as Rains. Preston swallowed real loud and took a deep breath, I reckon trying to draw up some courage from his gut.

"I'm a Home Guard my own self, sir, here on leave."

"I reckon that's your problem, son, I don't really give a damn."

"Sounds to me like you're down on patriots," Preston said, straightening in the saddle.

"I'm down on sons of bitches. I ain't got no problem with you, Preston, so don't go makin' one."

"Sounds like you have some personal scores to settle, Champ," Tinker said.

"I never said that."

Tinker's face was still sad, and it was cold, and empty.

"Scott Bledsoe and some of his bunch came to my house the other day," he said. "Must've been about twenty of 'em, I reckon. Them boys have been keepin' pretty busy this past week. I reckon you know 'em."

"I know 'em," I said, "but I ain't seen none of 'em for over a month. I've been huntin'."

"While you was huntin'," Tinker said, "Bledsoe's company joined in an offensive with the Confederate regulars, as scouts – there was a sure-enough battle the first part of this week. It was at Mill's Creek, just down the road yonder by Logan's Crossroads."

"You don't say," I remarked. I tried not to show my disappointment that there had been a big fight and I had missed it.

"Reckon who won," Rains said.

"We won," Huff announced proudly. "Put them Rebs on the run, and even kilt their general, Zollicoffer. They've done buried him in Nashville. I was there – for the fight, I mean."

"My oldest boy Claude was there too," Tinker said, his mouth a thin line. "He was kilt." His face and voice betrayed no emotion, but his eyes shone wetly.

"That's hard luck, Tinker," I said. "I'm sorry."

"And my nephew, too," Tinker continued. "Odom Taylor. He lived here in Clinton County, you know. The poor boy held on for days, gutshot, but he finally died and I come here to bury him."

I didn't say nothing else, on account of there ain't much a feller can say. This was still early on, you see – after awhile speaking to folks who had just lost kin became so common there was never even any thought given to saying anything about it.

"My boy, he died quick. Me and my other son Dallas had hardly finished puttin' the dirt on him when Bledsoe rode onto my farm."

I felt the muscles in my back and arms tensing up at the same instant I seen Tinker Dave's eyes flash.

"Sons of bitches rode onto my property like they owned the place," Tinker said. "They told me and my son that we better by God be enlisted in the Confederate Army like loyal Southerners by the time they pass back through. While we stood there they ransacked my barn, and took all my saddles and my best tools."

Tinker's eyes narrowed and seemed to glow like a wolf's that is just beyond the campfire, and his fingers twitched just a little.

"When they left I took down my guns and rode so bareback, so hard that my horse like to have died, and cut them off. I opened up on them from cover, and sent two of the bastards straight to the devil."

Me and Tinker was setting stiff-backed in the saddle. Rains and Huff was both nervous and confused.

"We've always got along, Champ, and I ain't got a thing in the world agin ye. But there ain't gonna be no peace anymore, not for nobody."

We both moved at once. The same thoughts seemed to be running through our minds, the same drives, the same hates, like we had the same soul. Both our revolvers slid loose at once, lightning-quick, and we each looked down the muzzle of death wielded by the other.

Tinker's lips pressed together so hard it was like he had no mouth at all. Only eyes, eyes of flame. We stood that way for several seconds, both our partners afraid to move a muscle lest they accidentally start the rain of death to falling.

"Somebody has to die, Champ, you or me one."

I nodded, so slight that I knowed only Tinker could see it. Neither one wanted to pull the trigger. This was partly because, even though we had never been friends, we still shared a bond of respect and affection. But it was mostly because neither wanted to die, not before we could revenge ourselves on our real enemies. The personal ones, the ones who had dishonored our homes.

Again the same thought charged through the brains of two men. Tinker Dave and me, each throwing his self to the side, and holding close to the neck of his horse, while revolvers thundered. I missed him completely, and his ball cut through the sleeve of my coat. It burned the skin but didn't draw blood. Horses reined up, keeping us from drawing another bead. Preston Huff was already galloping away. Tinker got his mount under control and spurred its flanks, following his comrade – the whole thing took about five seconds. Rains fired a shot at Huff, which grazed his thigh, while Tinker tossed another shot over his shoulder at me.

"Come on!" I hollered at Rains, and we gave chase to the Union men. We pounded through the mud for less than a mile before we blundered into the trap.

Imagine my surprise. While me and Rains had been laying in wait for my brother, Reuben Wood's sons and their friends had been a mile away laying in wait for *us*. I don't know if Tinker even knowed they was there – it was blind bad luck that we ran into them.

I had pulled several yards ahead of Rains, so I took the brunt of the gunfire. I wasn't hit – I reckon the devil still had plans for me – but my favorite black mare took two bullets. She was still screaming when the load of buckshot hit her in the head. I was sent hurtling through the air – if the ground hadn't been so muddy I might've broke my neck. I come up out of that mud with two revolvers blazing at my enemies. I couldn't even see the bastards, they was behind cover, but I sure as hell shut 'em up for a few seconds.

Then Rains put a ball through the head of one old boy who had decided to get a better look at things - and he reached out for me, swinging me up behind him. Tinker had turned around and was coming toward us now. We broke into the brush and rode like hell in a headwind.

We managed to get away. Once again I had been chased out of my own home county, barely making it out alive. To top it off I had a new enemy, one who wasn't afraid of nothing except for the possibility of not killing enough Rebels to satisfy his appetite.

It was time to try something different.

Chapter 18

Me and my boys went on ahead and joined up with Bledsoe. We stayed plenty busy, too – we gave Hell to the Kentucky Home Guards every chance we got, and even had a couple of skirmishes with Federal cavalry squads.

Tinker Dave had gathered a bunch of Union-minded Tennesseans to his side in the meantime, and like as not every time we was up north hitting them they was down south hitting us. Every once in awhile we'd cross paths as each group was returning home, and shoot at each other. Edgar Whitley's red-headed cousin got shot through the lungs during one of them encounters; he died coughing blood into the snow, Edgar holding his hand.

Tinker was fast becoming a bigger threat than Rufus Dowdy or Elijah Kogier. From time to time word would get back to us that one of our boys had picked the wrong time to go home to his farm, and got caught by Tinker Dave. Whenever that happened, the lone Rebel wound up dead. Tinker stomped one man to death with his own horse. Of course, we was prowling the woods between Jamestown and Albany doing the same thing.

It was getting to where we was seeing more uniforms in our mountains, both blue and gray, and more organized regiments. Turns out that the battle which I had missed, the one the Federals won, had been a decisive one. It had given the Yankees access to the Cumberland Gap, and the upper hand in East Tennessee. Then 'Useless' Grant took Fort Donelson, which led to the fall of Nashville – and all the supplies and ammunition stashed there. The main Confederate forces had to fall back plumb to Mississippi after that. By March Union troops was having parades in downtown Nashville.

None of our group was a party to any of them actions, of course – those things happened a ways off from us. It wouldn't be long before we'd feel the effects of it, though, our territory being overrun by blue-bellied bastards.

It just meant we had to fight a little harder, and that was fine with us. Overton, Putnam, and White Counties was still pretty much solid Reb in their sympathies, and

Confederate cavalry regiments passed through often on their way to make raids in Kentucky.

It was in March of 'sixty-two that I met Colonel Basil Duke. Him and sixty of his troopers rode into our temporary camp outside Livingston. They was all dressed up in their snappy gray uniforms, sabers rattling as they bounced in the saddle, hats cocked on their heads like cavalry dandies have done forever.

The colonel was the biggest dandy of them all. Even his name was a dandy – Basil. I'd never heared such in my life, and I said as much to Scott Bledsoe.

"Sounds peculiar, sure enough," Scott said. "I've heard he's a good cavalry officer, though."

"I reckon a feller named Basil would have to learn from a young age either how to fight hard or how to ride like hell."

"He's Morgan's second-in-command, you know – and his brother-in-law."

I had never heared of old Basil, but I had heared of John Hunt Morgan – Colonel Morgan, at the time, they hadn't made him a general yet then.

Duke dismounted stiffly and marched over to where me and Scott stood, in front of the command tent – marched, not walked, like he was on a parade ground. He stared at us a moment, uncertain.

"I assume one of you gentlemen is Captain Bledsoe."

"I am," Scott said.

Duke glanced at me. "Then you must be Captain Ferguson." I nodded sharply.

Duke took a quick breath, like he had something unpleasant to get out of the way. "It's, um, it's customary to salute a superior officer, you know."

"I reckon that suits me fine enough," Scott said, "if'n you don't mind bein' identified that way it's your business. There's probably not any snipers around."

"Yes, well," Duke said, clearing his throat and glancing quickly at the trees around us. "I have heard quite a bit about you gentlemen. You have kept the enemy very distracted for us, and it is appreciated."

"Hellfire," I said, a touch of mockery in my voice. "It wadn't nothin'. Proud to serve."

Duke wasn't sure how to take my comments, so I reckon he decided to just ignore them. "It is our hope – Colonel Morgan's and mine – that your company can provide a more direct form of assistance to us."

"Anything we can do to help, just say the word," Bledsoe said. He must have sounded more sincere than me, because Duke immediately looked relieved. Not that I wasn't sincere, mind you – it had just angered me a tad, the way Colonel Duke seemed to think our actions so far in the war had been some sort of personal little favor to the "real" army. Of course, now that I look back on it, Duke may have took the wild stories about us too much to heart and may actually have been a little intimidated by us.

"By summer we intend to sortie north, make some raids deep in enemy territory," Colonel Duke said, "provide some distractions of our own. We plan to use this area as a base, and we hope we can rely on your men to assist us."

Bledsoe nodded. I smiled a little – I'd always wanted to take a trip up north, seemed like a good time for it.

"Right now we have more immediate needs, though," the colonel continued. "Perhaps you could assist me in provisioning my men for my return trip."

Scott and me looked at one another and grinned. "It just so happens, Colonel," I said, "that we know some upstandin' citizens over in Fentress County who would be happy to contribute to the war effort."

"Oh?" said Duke. "Loyal Southerners?"

"They will be when we're done with 'em, by God," I said.

"I see," said the colonel, and he even chuckled a little bit – though it seemed forced.

"We're fixin' to show you how we do it in the mountains," I said.

"I look forward to the education."

~ ~ * ~ ~

It was just after dawn when we rode onto the property of John Cobb. A black plume of smoke curled up form his chimney. Frost lay heavy on the ground, and our breath froze as it left our mouths – it being early March we would probably see no more snow for the year, but it was still sure-enough cold.

There was about a hundred of us. Duke and his cavalrymen made up the most part of that number. We trotted our horses easy toward the little farm house, there being no need to get in a hurry.

Me and Scott and Colonel Duke was in the lead. We reined in, the rest of our boys stopping a little piece behind us. I drawed out my revolver and fired a shot into the air.

A few seconds later John Cobb walked cautiously out the door, a shotgun cradled in his arm. His eyes widened when he seen how many visitors he had. He looked the group over, trying not to let the fear show in his features. The way things was in the Cumberland Mountains, most times a man had to study the faces in a group of armed strangers, in order to figure out which side they was on. Colonel Duke's boys provided enough gray uniforms for the truth to sink in on John Cobb damned quick.

"I reckon you're John Cobb," Scott said.

Cobb swallowed. "I am."

"What are ye up to this mornin', John?" I said in a friendly tone.

"I'm just – I was havin' a sup of coffee."

"John, John," I said. "You ain't got much ambition, for a farmer. Here it is, well past daylight, an' you still settin' around drinkin' coffee." I put a cigar in my mouth and struck a match. I smiled at Cobb through the smoke as I was lighting it.

"What do you boys want?" he asked.

"They way you go about farmin'," I continued, "this place is liable to just go to hell on ye. A feller that don't take no better care of his livestock than that – why, I don't know what to think."

"I reckon ye better put down that shotgun, Cobb," Scott said. "I'd be real easy about it, if I was you."

"What do they want, John?" a woman asked fearfully from inside the doorway. I seen it was Cobb's young wife. She had a baby in one arm, and another one swelling up her belly. Cobb lay his weapon gently onto the porch.

"Stay back, honey," he said, and she muffled a sob.

"This here is Colonel Duke," Scott said, and Duke tipped his hat politely. "The colonel is in need of some fresh horses – and some fresh meat. Reckon you could oblige him?"

"Do I have a choice?"

"You've always got a choice, John," I said.

"Go on and take what y'uns is after, then, and leave us alone."

Scott waved his arm, and several men rode toward the barn and the stable. In addition to four good horses, Cobb owned several beef-cows and some prime hogs. He stood on his front porch and watched as we took his animals away. Anger was starting to mix with fear in his expression. His hands clenched into fists at his sides.

"Now John," I told him. "It's a shame you've waited 'til now to be helpful to your country. Looks like you would've follered along with all the other good Tennesseans, and spoke out your support for the South."

Cobb didn't reply to me. Fear was getting the upper hand on him again.

"Your contribution is appreciated," Scott said. "But it ain't nearly enough. Reckon we're gonna have to visit some of your neighbors this mornin', too. And since we don't want you to run off and warn 'em – and spoil our surprise – I suppose you'd best get mounted up. Them boys has probably got your horse saddled up by now. We'll let you borry him for a spell."

Cobb looked very confused. "Wh-what?"

"We're takin' you into our custody, John," I said. "Now come along, we have a busy day ahead."

Cobb nodded absently. He left the porch and headed for the barn – he walked like a man in a funeral procession. Old John Homer, a wicked grin breaking apart his gray whiskers, led Cobb's horse to him and even offered the farmer a boost into the saddle. Cobb declined, swinging up on his own.

I nudged my horse's ribs and set off down the road. I noticed Colonel Duke sweeping his hat off to the Cobb girl and mumbling something to her. She stood on the front porch and watched us leave with her husband and his stock, her squalling as loud now as her baby's.

It went like that through the morning and into the afternoon, us stopping at the farms of one Unionist after another. Being as Fentress County was crawling with them, it wasn't a far piece between stops. At every farm we took the growed men prisoner.

We stayed on the alert for an attack by some of the Union bushwhacker groups. We was a big enough party it wasn't likely guerillas would attack us on the open road, but we was ready just in case.

We reached the Overton County line at about two o'clock. By then we had a sizable herd of stock, and fifteen prisoners.

We lined them up on the side of the road. Me and Scott and a few of our men walked down the line, stopping briefly to exchange words with each of them.

Jay Marlin was among the prisoners. I hadn't seen him since that camp meeting fight almost a year before, when I got in the fight with the Evans boys.

"We never did run them 'coons like we was goin' to, Jay," I told him.

"No, Champ. We never got the chance. Too much goin' on nowadays for such as that, I reckon."

I clapped him on the shoulder. "Maybe one of these days," I said, and moved on down the line.

The next one was a feller named George Woods. I had met him a time or two, but never really knowed him except to speak to.

Edgar Whitley knowed him. "This feller here was with Tinker Dave when they kilt my cousin," Edgar said. "I remember him plain as day. That'n beside him was, too."

Of the fifteen prisoners, three was identified as riding with Tinker and a fourth was on leave from a Federal regiment.

We herded all the Fentress County men into a barn. The farmer that owned the place was either off working, or close by with the good sense to stay hid.

We separated out the four who had been known to bear arms against us and took them outside. Several of Duke's cavalrymen remained in the barn, guarding our prisoners. Duke his self started to follow me and Scott out the door, but Scott turned around and shook his head.

"It might be better, sir, if'n you stay in here where you can't officially see nothin'."

Duke was a little pale around the gills. It looked for a moment like he was going to say something, probably something about chivalry and honor and what-have-you, but then he remembered whose territory he was in. The colonel simply nodded.

"I suppose you're right," he said.

These four prisoners had their hands tied behind them, ever since we'd found out the sort of men they was. We pulled them roughly behind the barn. Besides me and Scott, we had LeRoy Reese, Bob Timmons, John Homer, and four of Scott's boys. Rains was in the barn with the others. He was reliable in a fire-fight, but I knowed better than to include him in something like this.

We put ourselves between the four men and the barn wall, and drawed our pistols. It would've been better to line them up against that wall, I reckon, but there was folks on the other side of it. As it was, George Woods took off running. He never made it far. Nine men with six-guns can kill four Unionists pretty damn dead.

Scott went back to the door of the barn and called for the other prisoners to be brung out. Soon the eleven men – these without their hands tied – stood over the bloody bodies of their neighbors. Neither Duke nor any of his command came around the barn with them. Rains did, though, wearing the same sad look he always seemed to carry anymore.

"Do ye see what road these fellers has gone down?" Scott said loudly. No one answered.

"Do ye see?" he repeated, and several men nodded and mumbled numbly.

"Y'all can go down that road with 'em," Scott said, "or ye can support the Confederacy. Out in the open, in public – the good colonel in yonder, I'm sure, is even still takin' volunteers. Which had y'uns druther do?"

"I'd druther go on and volunteer," Jay Marlin said. The others agreed.

"Good," Scott said. "I'll take y'uns at your word. You're free to go on back home, or wherever you're of a mind to. But if we hear that any of y'all are fightin' for the Union – you see what's gonna happen."

"The same thing," John Cobb said, his voice shaky. "The same thing that's gonna happen if Tinker Dave hears we're for the Confederacy."

"That's the way it is, John," I told him. "That's just the way it is."

They set off walking slowly down the road toward Jamestown. All of them but Jay Marlin and his cousin Bobby – they asked to be allowed to volunteer for Colonel Duke's command, rather than go back home and go through the whole thing again at the hands of the other side. I vouched for them to Duke – I always liked old Jay, and was glad I didn't have to shoot him – and they was given back their horses. It made more sense for them to serve with the regulars than with us, in a way, because we still might not be able to trust them completely if they stayed close to home.

"You gentlemen seem to have things well in hand," Colonel Duke said. "We'll be on our way. When we return, the regiment will be with us."

"We'll see you then," Scott said. "Give our regards to Colonel Morgan."

"Oh, I intend to do that, I assure you. I think – I do think that with you men at our side, we shall give the Yankees something to remember."

Duke and his men – including the new recruits – rode away. We mounted up ourselves, and went back to camp. The four dead men we left where they lay.

Buzzards have to eat, too.

Chapter 19

Me and my boys reined in at Thurman Goodbody's farm outside Cookeville in the early morning, half an hour before sunup. There was about thirty of us, and I reckon we made sufficient noise to wake Goodbody up from his sleep pretty quick, because he showed up at his front door with a lantern after only a couple of minutes. He wore the same frightened, uncertain look John Cobb had worn two weeks earlier when we showed up at his house. Goodbody's disposition didn't seem to improve very much even when he realized it was only us, and that we was on the same side as him.

"Captain Ferguson, is that you?"

"Sure enough is," I told him.

"What are you doing here at this hour?" Goodbody was still quite anxious, and his jowly face quivered just a little bit. The notion struck me that maybe he was afraid someone had fingered him to us as a Unionist and we was after his blood. I considered letting him squirm for awhile. Goodbody was a wealthy man – one of the prominent loyal Confederates, and a lawyer. I never cared much for lawyers. His anxiety amused me.

"Settle down, Goodbody," I said. "No need for you to get your drawers wadded up. We're just passin' through, so to speak."

"At this time of day?"

"I got a message from Scott Bledsoe, said for me to meet him here. I've been away for a week, scoutin' for Colonel Duke and teachin' his boys the lay of the land. Captain Bledsoe has been down south in Alabama meetin' with some general or other. Seems like while we was gone some of them Union boys in Fentress County got all cocky and got to stealin' stock from good loyal Southerners. Hell, they even stoled some steers right out of my pasture in Sparta – snuck over in the middle of the night like they owned the damn place."

"I was not aware of any raids," Goodbody said. He was still a little too nervous to suit me, and I began to feel suspicion creeping up my neck. It must have darkened my face enough for Goodbody to tell, for he suddenly grew pale.

"They didn't come through Cookeville, evidently," I said.

"What is it that you and Captain Bledsoe plan to do?"

"I aim to get my damn cattle back, and everybody else's too. Maybe collect some interest."

"I see," Goodbody said, and nodded. "Well. I must go inside and get dressed. Would you men like some coffee?" He said it in a plaintive sort of way, not wanting to seem rude to a bunch like us, but at the same time hoping thirty rough men would not feel inclined to tromp through his house and deplete his supplies.

I could tell Rains was about to open his mouth and speak up. Rains was always eager to deal out hospitality, and just as eager to take it. I cut him off before a sound could escape him.

"That's all right, Mister Goodbody. You go on in the house and eat you some breakfast. We'll be content to just set out here a spell and wait on Captain Bledsoe – he should be along shortly."

Goodbody's face relaxed at the same instant that Rains's face fell. Goodbody nodded again sharply, and seemed on the verge of thanking us for declining him, and then he turned to go inside.

"Goodbody," I called after him, and he stopped in his tracks. He turned around slowly.

"Yes, Captain?"

I leaned forward in the saddle. "You feelin' all right, Mister Goodbody?" I said. "You seem ill."

"No, I'm – I'm in good health."

"Could it be you have somethin' you want to tell me, then?"

Goodbody took a deep breath. "Things have changed, in a way, while you were away. I'll wait for Captain Bledsoe, if you don't mind, and explain it to both of you at once."

"Explain it to us, you say."

"Yes. Yes, I'll explain – what has happened. It's a good thing, really." He swallowed hard. "It's a good thing, really, a very good thing. I'll be out directly." Goodbody rushed into his house.

I heared Bob Timmons chuckling beside me. "You know what, Champ?" he said. "That old boy is scared of ye."

"I get that feelin'," I agreed.

"Wadn't too scared to offer us a cup of coffee," Rains mumbled. "I surely could use me some coffee, this time of day."

"Most folks in this county is always happy to see us comin'," Timmons said, ignoring Rains. "They know we're a protection to 'em, from the Union bands, and they're grateful. Kind of makes a feller wonder, don't it."

"Makes me wonder, all right," I said. "Reckon I'll get to the bottom of it soon enough."

I swung down out of the saddle. No sooner had my feet hit the ground than young Peter Lucas appeared at my elbow.

"Want me to picket your horse for ye, Cap'n?"

I nodded. "Thank ye, son."

I handed Lucas the reins. His eyes shone with pride as he took them. It made me feel sort of peculiar, having a boy look up to me the way Lucas did.

I walked over to Goodbody's porch and set one boot up on his front stair, and rested my hand on my knee. After a couple of minutes I felt the urge, so I took out my tobacco pouch and rolled me a smoke. I stood there like that a spell, smoking and watching the gray dawn spread over the sky, and none of the men came near or bothered me.

In a little while, I heared the horses coming. It was Bledsoe, and he had sixty or seventy men with him. They reined in and dismounted, same as most of my boys had done, and Scott walked up to me and shook my hand.

"How'd things go down yonder in Alabama?" I asked him.

Scott nodded and smiled, then patted his breast pocket. "Real good. I got papers here – I'm now officially in command of a mustered company of cavalry. Got some for you, too, authorizing you to raise your own company." He pulled out a fat envelope and handed it to me. "You need to read this over real careful," he said. "It explains all about how to fill out your muster rolls and all."

I took the envelope and stuffed it into my coat pocket. "I'll give her a look afterwhile," I said.

"We ready to ride? I'm ready to teach them bastards from Jimtown and Albany a lesson. It don't matter if we're here or not, they'll learn not to come into our territory and fool with our people."

"Reckon ye better pay your regards to Mister Goodbody first. Seems like he has some news to tell us."

"What kind of news?"

"He wouldn't say, but he was skittish as hell about it."

"Let's find out, then," Scott said, and we stepped onto the porch and Scott pounded on the lawyer's door.

Goodbody appeared. He was dressed now, but he had not shaved.

"Hello, Captain," he said to Scott. "Please, won't you both come in for a minute? There's something we have to discuss."

"Long as you make it quick," Scott said. "We have things to do."

We followed Goodbody into his home, and he set us down at his kitchen table. His wife flitted briefly through the room, but he whisked her away and brought a coffeepot to us himself. He even poured for us.

I sat there and looked around. I reckon it was about the fanciest house I'd ever seen, with paintings on the wall and lacquered chairs around the heavy oak table. Dozens of books had lined shelves in the drawing room he had rushed us through on our way to the kitchen, thick books with leather covers and gold writing raised up on the spines. The kitchen floor was bare wood, all waxed and shiny, but the other rooms had soft carpets.

Goodbody pulled out a chair and settled down across the table from us.

"What's on your mind, Mister Goodbody?" Scott said.

"Yes," Goodbody said absently. "Where to begin."

We stared straight at him, and his face colored and seemed to shrivel, like a flower when a child directs sunlight on it through a spyglass.

"You gentlemen were gone, you see," he began, "and some of the town's citizens got together. It seemed wasteful to us, all this raiding back and forth, so we sent word to the Unionists in Fentress County that we wanted to meet with them, under a ceasefire as it were."

"What citizens would that be," I asked.

"Several businessmen, from here in Cookeville and from Livingston. The mayor. Judge Andrews."

"Go on," Scott told him. "You wanted to meet with some of their folks."

"Yes." He cleared his throat. "We set up a meeting, and we went to it, and we reached an agreement. No more of this raiding, is what we agreed to, by either side. Everyone is to just go home to their farms, and mind their own business, and let the soldiers conduct the war. Otherwise the whole Cumberland Plateau is going to be in ruins, just in ruins – it can't go on."

"Who was at this meeting from the other side?" Scott asked.

"Dave Beaty, and his son. Elijah Kogier. Rufus Dowdy. Some others."

Scott shook his head in disbelief. "So a bunch of politicians and store-owners go to a parley representing Confederate interests, and make a deal with the worst guerilla leaders in these mountains."

"There's been a lot of violence on both sides, and it has to stop."

I scowled. "But it didn't stop, did it. They've come over to our counties and stole our stock. Ours, and a bunch of simple farmers' – but nary bit of yours."

"That's – that's dreadful news," Goodbody said. "I can't believe they would violate the agreement like that."

"Are you callin' me a liar, son?" I said in an even tone.

"No, oh no, Captain. It's just – well, mistakes can be made, sometimes."

"Sounds like there's been some damned mistakes made, all right," I said loudly.

Scott leaned forward so his face was near to Goodbody's. "You are a damned fool, mister," he snarled. "All you've done is show the federals where our weak links are. Showed 'em who among us will roll over to them, and who they can view as a real threat."

I stood up, and the lacquered chair fell over onto the floor. "I got me some Confederate property to recover, by God," I said, "and some Yankee sumbitches to send to Hell. So if you'll excuse me."

"No, please no," Goodbody said piteously. "We mustn't violate our agreement! Maybe we can negotiate to get the stock back!"

"I never made no damned agreement," I said, "except my oath of loyalty to the Confederacy." I nodded then. "So that's why you've been so damn scared all mornin'. You wasn't scared of us. You was scared we'd carry out this raid, and the Unionists might take it out on you and your friends. And your property."

"It has to *stop*," Goodbody said.

"Kiss my ass, you little coward."

He clutched at Scott's sleeve. "Captain Bledsoe! Explain it to him, please!"

Scott jerked his sleeve away. "If I hear of any more 'upstanding citizens' dealing with the enemy," he said calmly, "I won't have no choice but to protect the interests of my country. Do you understand me?"

Goodbody looked like a lost child who has realized his mama is nowhere near.

I was already stalking out of the house. Behind me I heared Scott call back to our host, "Don't you forget, Goodbody."

The men all stiffened up when they seen how angry we both was. Some let their hands drop to their weapons.

"Mount up," I told my own men. "It's time to ride."

Scott climbed into his own saddle. "Anybody that raises arms against us," he said, "shoot them on sight."

We galloped away. Goodbody stared after us.

Chapter 20

We skirted around Dale Hollow Lake and struck north through Fentress County. We passed right by the same field where I had chased Elim Huddleston on that day of the camp meeting fight, right after I had stabbed Jim Read. I reined in my mare and sat there quietly, looking at the rocky field and pondering over the way life had gone for me since that day. My mind played over the possibilities, and I wished I had thought to carry a gun to that camp meeting. I could have killed several of them sons of bitches right then and there, and saved myself a lot of trouble on down the road. Or maybe if I had not gone that day at all, or if my brother had not stole that Evans horse without telling me about it – maybe then I wouldn't have started a snowball rolling downhill that would bring such misery and shame to my girls.

I tried to convince my heart that things could have been different – to make myself feel better, I reckon – but it didn't work, and I could not quite believe. I had the oddest feeling that nothing could have been changed, and that some dark force was pulling me along like an iron filing being pulled mindlessly to a magnet. We're all born to die, I reckon, but it struck me that I was born to kill. A sort of quiet sadness passed though me when I realized that, the same way the warmth of whiskey will pass through a feller's body and make him all peaceful and dull and forgetful.

I remembered then that I wasn't alone. I was on a sortie, riding with a hundred men, and there was no time for being thoughtful. Scott and Rains had both reined in beside me, as had about twenty other men. The others looked back at us, anxious, and Scott waved them on. They were all eager to recover their stolen horses and stock, maybe even recover more than they had lost.

"Been a lot happen the last year, ain't they?" Rains said.

"Yep."

Rains pointed across the field, to the white two-story farmhouse. "Is that where they cornered ye, that day?"

I nodded. "They was gonna burn the house down around my ears, but the old codger who lives there wouldn't let 'em."

"Reckon that's him, comin' yonder?" Rains said. Sure enough, a figure had just left the barn and started riding in our direction. Before long the man on the mule was close enough for me to see that it was, in fact, the same old farmer. I throwed my hand up to him in greeting.

"Howdy," I said.

The man didn't wave. He carried a shotgun across his saddle.

"What the hell do y'uns think you're doin', tramplin' across my field?"

"You ain't got nothin' planted in it," Rains said.

"That ain't the point."

"We're just passin' through," Scott told him.

"Well I reckon by God you'd better pass a mite quicker."

I laughed out loud. "Damn," I said. "You're a cocky one."

"You're liable to see how damn cocky I am, boy. I remember you. You're that'un that went runnin' through my front room that day."

"I never got to thank ye for your hospitality."

"My ass. Get the hell off my property and back where y'uns belong, you damn Rebs."

It was Scott's turn to chuckle. "He's got us pegged, all right," he said. The old man didn't take kindly to us laughing at him, and his grip on the shotgun tightened.

I drawed my Army Colt out of its slim-jim holster quick as a snake and leveled it right at the old man. I had seen in his eyes that he was seconds away from doing something foolish.

"You just take it easy, old man," I hissed at him, all laughter gone now. "We ain't doin' no harm to you."

His face colored up, but I noticed his grip on the shotgun relaxed a good bit.

"That's better," I said. "Now then – we're here after our stock."

"What stock," he mumbled, a lot more humbly than before.

"Mostly horses, but a good bit of cattle too. Includin' some steers of mine that was took from White County."

"I don't know nothin' about no steers."

I pulled the hammer of the Colt back with a loud click. "If you was to hear anything about 'em," I said, "I reckon you'd be sure to get word to me about it."

He swallowed, loud enough for us all to hear it, and nodded. "Anything I could do to help a man that's been robbed," he said.

I smiled. "Glad to hear it. Now you go on back to your house, friend, and don't come out again today. You understand me?"

He nodded again, jerkily. "I understand."

"Go on."

He turned the mule around and head toward the white house. I watched him all the way, in case he decided to spin around with that shotgun – I reckon he could feel the heat of my eyes boring into him. He never turned around.

"You got a way with people, Cap'n," one of the boys said.

"Hellfire," Scott said suddenly. "I plumb forgot."

"Forgot what?" I said.

He reached behind himself and dug through his saddlebags. "I brung you somethin'."

"You shouldn't have."

"It's a gift from General Bragg – he's heard stories about ye. Yeah, here it is."

Scott pulled out a knife, sheathed in a tooled leather scabbard. It rasped as he pulled it loose and into the naked sunlight – it was a Bowie knife, with a blade over a foot long. It caught the sun and glinted like silver.

"I'll be damned," I said, taking it carefully from him.

I hefted it, smiling. It had wonderful balance for such a big blade. The handle was carved from bone. "This is a damn fine knife."

The boys crowded close, each taking a good look and whistling or grunting their appreciation.

Scott grinned. "The general said the only thanks he needed was for you to gut a few Yankees with it."

"I can sure as hell do that." I shook my head, and repeated, "I'll be damned."

We left the farm behind then, and nudged our mounts into a canter to catch up with the other men. It was not long before we heard the gunshots from up ahead.

We arrived on the scene to find several of our boys chasing some uniformed Yankees into the woods, while several more was trying to run down a fourth Yankee who was on foot. We later learned they was local men home on leave from the Union army, and they had been trying to drum up some new recruits.

The man on foot ran like the devil was breathing fire on his ass, but he soon found there was no more room to run. They had herded him to the edge of a cliff. The man must have had some idea who was chasing him, and what sort of fate might wait for him if he was captured, because he never even slowed down. He jumped right off the edge of that cliff and sailed into the empty air. The boys jumped off their horses and fired rifles down at him, but they was wasting powder – he had busted open like a ripe watermelon tossed out of a hayloft.

I dug my spurs into my mare's ribs and raced toward the woods. The wind blowed my hat off and whipped through my hair. I angled off to the west, hoping to cut the pursued Yankees off. Several of our boys was right behind me.

The three men looked surprised to see me, and not too happy. One carried a shotgun –he raised it in my direction, but I sent a bullet into his chest before he could fire and he was sent tumbling out of the saddle. One of his comrades trampled over his body and almost got throwed off his own mount. While he tried to regain control, he was caught in a barrage from the men with me, and hit three times. He slid off his horse and laid on his side, next to the dead, trampled body of his partner.

The third man fired at me, twice. I felt the wind from one of the bullets as it whistled past my head. I was a mite calmer than he was. I took a deliberate aim and shot him in the mouth. Even as he was falling one of our boys sent a rifle bullet into his side.

I jumped out of the saddle and hit the ground running, launching myself at the second Yankee who sat wounded on the ground. I had unsheathed the new Bowie knife as I ran, and I plunged it into the man's chest with a powerful momentum behind the blow. It sunk in up to the hilt, and the already-bloody man rattled and gasped as he died. I jerked the blade out and walked over to the man I had shot in the mouth. He twitched and moaned on the ground, surely not long for this world, and so I ended his misery as well. The first man I had shot was already dead, but I stabbed him anyway – bloodlust was upon me, fogging my brain with a red mist, and I wanted only to hack and kill.

Our boys who had been pursuing the Yankees reined in beside us, disappointed that we had killed the prey they flushed. I crouched over the bodies like a hungry wolf, bloody knife in one hand and smoking pistol in the other.

We heard something crashing through the woods, off to our right. Soon we heard yells coming from that direction as well.

"Run boys!" the approaching figure said. "The woods are full of Rebs!"

It was a boy. He crashed right into the clearing where we stood over his dead partners, and his faced whitened when he saw us and realized his mistake. The boy – he looked to be about sixteen – was paralyzed with fear. He wore no uniform, only homespun clothes, but a musket was slung over his shoulder.

"Reckon you better unsling that gun, boy," Bob Timmons told him.

"Yes-yessir," the boy said, and he began to slowly lift the weapon over his head.

"You look familiar, boy," I said. "What's your name."

His eyes popped open wide and his bottom lip quivered. I knew I had seen him somewhere before, but in my frenzied state I could not place him.

"I asked you a question, by God!"

"Fount Evans," he stuttered.

The redness swirled even more madly around my eyes, blowing up like a tornado. Evans! One of the damned eleven Unionists who had humiliated my wife and daughter!

The boy was still in the act of unslinging the musket – he had frozen in mid-action when I spoke and he realized who I was. The Colt in my hand jerked upwards like it had a mind of its own, and it thundered out as the bullet left its muzzle and sought the boy's chest. I don't even remember pulling the trigger. A geyser of blood spurted out as the ball struck Fount Evans and knocked him off his feet.

I sprang on him, raising the knife high in the air. It hung suspended there for a fraction of a second which seemed to last forever, and in that time I looked into the boy's terrified eyes, and my own eyes were made of hellfire. The knife smashed into young Evans, and there was a crunching, cracking sound as his breastbone broke at the force of the blow. I prett'nigh pinned him to the ground, and I stared coldly into his face as he coughed up blood and soul and died there on the forest floor.

Scott Bledsoe was just arriving on the scene. "What is happening?" he said.

I looked up at him, panting. The boy's blood had splashed onto my face.

"You said to kill anyone who took up arms agin us. By God, that's just what I've done."

Scott stared at the boy and at me for the space of three heartbeats then he nodded curtly and turned away. The others followed him. A dark pall seemed to have settled over them all.

I pulled myself to my feet. I was strangely weak all of a sudden, like the life had bled out of me same as it did from Fount Evans. I left him laying in the leaves, all bloody and pale and broken. I realized then that not everyone had walked away – Rains still stood beside me.

"Lord have mercy, Champ," he mumbled. "Lord have mercy."

"The Lord ain't got no mercy, damn it to hell," I said from between clenched teeth.

"It was just a boy, Champ. Just a slip of a feller."

"He was old enough to buy the ticket, I reckon he was old enough to take the ride."

Rains looked near tears. He shook his head, his eyes glued to the body but unable to focus. "What's happenin' to us," he said softly.

I cleaned my knife on the boy's pants leg and returned it to its scabbard.

"I killed this'un, and I'll kill a sight more. There won't be a Evans left alive in these mountains when I'm done, and that's just the start of it."

I mounted my mare and trotted off after the others. I left Rains standing alone with the dead, to follow me when he took a notion or to go to hell. I didn't care which.

Chapter 21

We rounded up a good bit of stock. Maybe it was the animals that had been stole from us, maybe it wasn't, it don't matter. We took it and so it was ours to use as we seen fit. There was no more need for gunplay while we gathered the stock we wanted – when folks seen us coming they took off running.

Scott decided it was time to head home, thinking I suppose that we had done enough for one day.

"You go on," I said. "I reckon I'm gonna stay around a spell longer, if that suits you."

"Stay around? What the hell for?"

I shook my head. The fact was, my blood was up. It was racing hot through my veins, burning them like it was kerosene, and my heart was pounding eagerly like a hound's when he is on the scent.

"Ain't done," I said.

Scott took a deep breath. "Hellfire, Champ, 'fore long the whole county is gonna know we're here."

"I'll just take a few men, then. Or hell, I'll go by myself. It'll be harder for 'em to spot than if we all tromp around the county with a bunch of stock."

Scott grinned and shook his head with amused disbelief. "You cain't get enough, can ye?"

"I reckon when I've had enough I'll know it. I ain't had enough yet. I'm just gettin' started good."

"All right then. Take some of your boys. And be careful."

I nodded, and he turned his horse and rode back toward the southwest. "See y'uns directly," he called back.

"Who's goin' with me," I called to my own men. Everyone clamored to join me, but I just took twenty – the best twenty – and sent the other ones with Scott. Rains was beside me, of course, making no comment one way or another. He rode as easily as if he was a part of my body, and if I plunged into the mouth of hell there was never any question but that he would follow.

We pointed north. Deeper into Fentress County, deeper into Union country. We rode hard, hoping to outdistance the news of our presence in the county.

Our first stop was Elijah Kogier's house. I'd had about enough of him and his band. Luck was with us, because we caught the bastard by surprise. We rode full-speed into his front yard and began firing into the air. I put a couple of slugs into his house, up high so they wouldn't hit no children or nothing. I heared a woman screaming inside.

"Elijah Kogier!" I hollered. "Get your ass out here, or we'll burn this damn house down!"

The back door slammed and I seen Kogier hot-footing it across his back yard. His arms pumped and his legs pounded as he raced for his life, and launched himself at his back fence. He scrambled frantically, pushing his body upwards, trying to get over it.

"Fire," I yelled, and about two dozen bullets pumped into Elijah Kogier's body. He writhed and danced and twisted on that fence, screaming as the bullets tore his flesh apart. A woman and two children had come out the back door now, and their crying continued loud and long after Kogier's had stopped. He slumped and dropped off the fence like an apple falling from a tree.

John Homer had leaped out of the saddle and was walking toward Kogier's family. The daughter looked to be around thirteen, and beside her was a boy no more than nine. Their mother had collapsed in the dirt. Homer held his arm out and laughed.

"Here now," he said, "it ain't so bad, gals."

I turned in the saddle. "Homer!" I snapped. "What the hell are you doin'?"

Homer turned around, grinning like a kid on Christmas morning. "I reckon we need to give some comfort to these pore souls," he said.

"Get back on your horse."

"Cap'n," he implored. "These are some fine-lookin' women. I'll make it fast, I promise." This brought giggles from some of the other men, and he scowled at them.

"I gave you an order, Homer."

The old man was flustered, then his face brightened. "All right, Cap'n. Let's take one with us then, for later. This purty little gal here." He took a step toward them, and the girl shriveled up like a leaf in the fire.

I pulled my pistol and leveled it at John Homer. The sound of the hammer cocking was probably the loudest noise he had ever heared in his life.

"I won't tell you again, mister," I said. "If any man who rides with me tries to molest a woman, I will blow his damn brains out. No questions asked. Mount up, by God!"

Homer scurried back to his horse. Kogier's young son broke free from his sister's embrace and took a step in our direction. Tears and snot made his face shine, and his little fist was raised.

"When I grow up I'm gonna kill you!" he screamed, and his mother cried even louder out of fear for her young'un.

"You'd best start practicin', son," I told him, and I jabbed my mare in the ribs. "Come on, boys, we still got things to do!"

We raced away. Behind us Kogier's daughter had crawled to her daddy's bloody body and was holding it tight against her, rocking with it and crying in one long unbroken wail.

Our next stop was the Evans farm. We pounded up the steps and I knocked the door open. Old Woman Evans was there, her eyes still burning with hatred for me just like the last time I seen her. I didn't know if she had heared word about the death of her youngest son yet. There was a boy there, too, eighteen or nineteen, and he was scared so bad he looked like he might piss his britches. Through the house I seen the back door – it was still swinging. Beyond it the weeds in the field rustled. Someone had just cut through them.

"Rains," I said. "Keep an eye on this boy. The rest of you come with me."

I led the way into the high grass. I seen a man ahead, running every bit as fast as Kogier had run.

"Shoot him, dammit, shoot him!" I hollered. Guns boomed out all around me, and bullets cut through the grass. Still the man ran. Finally one of the bullets caught him and he stumbled. Another hit him then, and he fell roughly to the ground. Within seconds I stood over him. It was Floyd Evans.

He lifted his head and stared up at the cold muzzle of death I had shoved down into his face.

"Howdy, Floyd," I said. "How are ye doin'?"

"Please, Champ," he said.

I cocked the pistol. Floyd whimpered and squeezed his eyes shut tightly.

"Don't kill me, for God's sake," he said, and sobbed. "Sweet Jesus, please. I'll tell you where the others are, I swear! It was them done it, not me!"

"Say hello to your baby brother for me," I said. His eyes widened then, and he shrieked, and I shot him between the eyes.

I turned and marched briskly back to the house. Rains was still there, his gun trained on the youth. If he was smart he would have kept the gun on the old woman, she was probably a lot more dangerous.

I stopped in front of her. "Who's the boy," I said.

Tears rolled down her cheeks, but she choked back her sobs. "It's just our neighbor. Let him go, he ain't never done nothin' to you!"

I looked at the boy. "You ride with them Union renegades, boy?"

"No sir," he said, with great difficulty.

"But you come here to warn Floyd Evans. That's how he knowed to take off."

The boy gulped, his eyes trained on the gun in my hand.

I raised it and pointed it at him, and I heared the piss dropping onto Miss Evans's floor. "Get out of here, boy. I got nothin' agin you."

He ran out the front door, not caring about the stain on his britches.

"I reckon you aim to kill everybody I know," the old woman said.

"Just a few more. Tell them other sons of yorn that I'm comin' for *them*, though, for certain."

"I hope you burn in hell, Champ Ferguson."

"I expect I will, but I'll have company."

The other houses we went to was empty. Some of the boys was all for burning them down, especially Elim Huddleston's place and Tinker Dave's, but I wouldn't let them. If we burned them out they might rebuild somewhere different, and be harder to find next time.

It was after we cut back to the south and headed for home that we caught Alex Huff out on the road. He had four men with him. They throwed down their arms when they seen how many of us there was, all of them except Huff.

"Better put them guns on down, Alex," Rains told him. Alex looked at the shotgun Rains held on him and reluctantly did as he was told.

"I don't know any of you boys," I told Huff's comrades. "But I don't want y'uns on my backtrail, so I reckon you'd better ride with us for a spell."

"Like hell," Huff said. "You're fixin' to kill ever' one of us, and you know it."

I dismounted. I looked over the faces of all four of the Fentress County men with Huff. They was terrified, and his words was bringing them close on to panic.

"Y'all boys behave yourselves," I told them, "and you'll come to no harm." A couple of them slumped down in their saddles, obviously relieved. I walked closer to them.

"Don't believe him, boys," Huff said. "He's a killer."

I reached up and grabbed Huff by the shirt and pulled him down off his horse. Once I got him on the ground I gave him a hard back-hand across the mouth, then a couple more. I let him fall to the dust.

He looked up at me, and flashed me a bloody grin. "I told y'uns," he crowed.

"There's worse things than killin' men," I said. "I reckon you know about them things, you've done 'em."

Huff had climbed to his feet. "That wife of yorn, she sure enough has some plump titties."

I shot his kneecap. He collapsed, moaning, and I ordered him to get back up. He tried, and I shot the other knee. I emptied my revolver in his arms and legs. He lay on the ground, twisted and broken, and still managed to spit at me. I held out my hand, and LeRoy Reece gave me over his own revolver. I sent Alex Huff to hell a piece at a time, putting the final shot in his face.

We carried our prisoners with us into Overton County, through Putnam, and into White. They was as tame a bunch as you'll ever see. We finally turned them loose near the Calfkiller River in White County. They thanked us for their lives, like we was the best friends they had ever made.

I noticed for the first time the redbuds was blooming. They was all over the mountainside, flashing red and violet like fireworks. I had always loved to see them for the brief while they lit up the country, and looked forward to them every year. This year all I seen when I looked at them was big fountains of blood.

Rains still rode beside me. The sad look was gone from his face, had been gone in fact since before we killed Elijah Kogier. I took that to be a good sign.

"Go ahead, Rains," I told him.

"Go ahead and do what, Champ?"

"Shake your head, tell me what a sad thing this all is."

"Ain't no use in it."

"Don't tell me you've give up on bein' my conscience."

"I reckon I have. You ain't Champ Ferguson no more. You're just pure hate, walkin' on two legs."

"I reckon that pegs it pretty good."

"It's done too late," he continued. "After today we're all goin' to hell. No use fightin' it no more."

I set my mouth in a grim line.

"No use fightin' it no more," he repeated, and he rode on ahead of me.

The people of the town was waiting for us when we reached Sparta. They lined up on the sidewalks to shake our hands as we rode past, blessing us, and throwing praise at us like we was God's own angels. Men offered to buy us drinks, and women promised to cook us meals. Children begged my permission to join us when they was old enough, if it should turn out there was still Yankees to kill then.

The next day a couple of our boys – the Kirby brothers – was ambushed by Tinker Dave on their way home to Overton County. Tinker Dave cut their heads off and stuck them on tobacco sticks, and planted them on the side of the road leading to Jamesown as a warning to the rest of us.

Chapter 22

I stayed at my farm beside the Calfkiller as often as I could. I always growed restless there, though, and itched to get back on the trail – more now than ever. Home was just not the same place anymore. At night I would lie on the feather mattress beside Marthy and hear her breathing – knowing she was not asleep, and her knowing I was not – and yet still we would not speak, nor turn our faces to one another. I could feel her there beside me, feel the hate burning inside her for our enemies, a hate near as strong as mine. It saddened me. I wanted Marthy to dream sweet, peaceful dreams, and wake to the world she had known in the days before the War came. It was one thing for me to hate, but she should not have to. I reckon I began to understand a little of what Rains felt when he would look at me and shake his head in sorrow.

But my hate was different from hers, for Marthy's rage gnawed at her insides like a rat. Mine coursed through my veins, pressing against my heart, wanting violent release. It was like a separate living thing, breathing within my body, with a will of its own. Sometimes, when I was setting at the table eating supper or laying in bed in the darkness or feeding the stock, it was all I could do not to open my mouth and scream like a wounded bear. When I stubbed my toe, or cracked my skull on the doorframe, a shout would leap out of me – like my hate had been waiting there just under my skin, waiting for any excuse to explode. I had no life of my own anymore, and no joy. I was only a vessel to carry the hate.

In the hazy moments before sleep finally did claim me each night, images danced before my eyes. It was the faces of the men I had killed, and the men I was going to kill yet, and they was twisted in their pain and terror and I would fall asleep chuckling quietly to myself. Sometimes I wondered if I was insane, but I knowed I was not, and knowing that made it worse.

Ann would ignore the frenzy in my eyes and set beside me, hand me my coffee, and talk to me about horses. She got to where she talked more than she ever had talked in the other time. There was love in her eyes when she looked at me, and fear – not of me, but for me – and she would talk quietly. It was like her voice was a fishing line. She would cast it at me, hoping to hook my soul and reel it back out of the black waters, hoping to call me back to her. Maybe she hoped her voice would make the world normal again. Sometimes when I looked at her I seen Kogier's daughter, or Reuben Wood's, and I would smile and she thought I was smiling at her.

Her mother did not speak at all. She just went about her chores with her back stiff and her eyes distracted by visions like mine, and I could tell she was jealous of me. She was jealous that, even though we both hated, I got to act my anger out and kill like she hungered to do. I would almost rather have seen her face cold in death than see it hate that way, and I would rather be dead myself than to know that her condition now was on account of I had not been there to protect her.

So I would set, and taste the hatred red and black on my tongue, and know that – with honor gone and love grown waxy cold – it was all I had left to me in the world. And I would chew on it, swallow it back down like bile, listen to my daughter without hearing her words, and wait for the chance to go out and kill again. I had become a rabid wolf, and the den could not hold me for long.

It was better when I was on the trail with my boys. They was cold-hearted murderers all, and so was our enemies, and it felt natural it should be that way. Every breath of fresh air, every rustle of the breeze, was a reminder that I was outside in the open air of war and fighting could begin at the drop of a hat. My hatred was able to breathe out there, like a fire fed by the wind, and it made me feel alive. Even Rains was different now, all the tenderness and conscience starved out of his soul. He moved about the camp like a hollow ghost, and I knowed from looking in his eyes that he felt his Judgment was sealed so he might as well give in to it. I didn't even feel guilty, not for a second, at the fact that I was taking my truest friend into hell with me. I was glad for his company. Hell put no fear into me.

That's how I was feeling on that June day in 1862, setting in my camp in the woods around England's Cove, when the messenger arrived from Scott Bledsoe. That's the way I felt on the day I met Colonel John Hunt Morgan.

Chapter 23

On a bright morning around the first of June, Bledsoe's messenger arrived at my farm in White County. The air was already thick and muggy, foretelling a hot day ahead.

"What is it, Parker?" I asked him.

Parker was smiling like a puppy in a butcher shop. Fact is, he was not much more than a puppy – I'm sure he was a good bit shy of twenty years old. "Mornin', Cap'n," he said. "Captain Bledsoe sends word to ye that you ought to start gathering your company together."

I leaned against my porch-post and spat a stream of tobacco into the dust. "More trouble in Celina?"

Earlier in the week we had clashed with a local Union company in Jackson County, led by a feller named McCollough. We had killed about half of them, including their leader, then barely made an escape before a regiment of regular federals arrived on the scene. It was a Pennsylvania regiment – there was getting to be more and more pure-bred Northern Yankees prowling around anymore.

"Not hardly," Parker said. "I don't reckon we'll have much trouble from that quarter for a spell, after the lesson we learned 'em over there."

"What, then?"

"Remember that fancy lieutenant-colonel was through here back in the winter?"

"Duke."

"Yeah, him. He's back, this time riding with a full-bird colonel and a whole regiment. Colonel Morgan, his name is."

I nodded. I'd heard good things about the man.

"Anyways," Parker continued. "This Colonel Morgan is bivouacked just outside of town."

"Here in Sparta?"

"Yep. And he wants to meet with you and Captain Bledsoe, and some other independent captains. Sent word to us 'fore daylight. Captain Bledsoe has got men rounding up our company, told me to suggest you do the same.

Meanwhile, Colonel Morgan has invited y'all to his camp this evenin', for supper."

I nodded again. "Thank ye, Parker," I said. "I reckon you'd best get on back to your own outfit."

"All right, Captain," he said, and turned to go, then he froze. He was looking past me now, not moving. I turned around, curious. It was Ann. She was hauling a bucket of water into the house. She paused to smile at Parker, and he raised his hand in greeting. I could tell he wanted to say something as well, but the words seemed to get stuck somewhere and he just stared until she disappeared through the front door.

"Parker."

"Yes sir?"

"I said, I reckon you'd best get on back to your own outfit."

"Yes sir. Of course sir."

I did not miss the fact that he did not start calling me "sir" until after Ann showed up, and I was not just a guerilla captain but the young girl's father. He left then, with a good deal of reluctance. Ann was near marrying age – hell, I reckon she *was* marrying age – but the youthful shine in Parker's eyes brung the fact that she was becoming a young woman to my attention in a way it never had been before. I didn't like it, not one bit, but I knowed it was only a matter of time before I would not be able to do anything about it.

I still leaned against the porch-post. I took a deep breath of the good air and looked around my place. Mountains rolled in the distance – the closest ones pine-green and them further off colored a hazy blue. The tall bottomland grass waved gently, and my horses stood in it like that field was the whole world and they owned it. I couldn't see the Calfkiller from my house, but I knowed it flowed just a short distance away, gurgling in England's Cove.

It was a calm place. A beautiful place. It made my heart swell and ache at the same time, yearning to stand in the shade and watch them horses forever and yet still being pulled along by a deep-rooted rage that no green fields could ever truly calm.

Words came into my mind, words I had not called up. They was words my Ma used to sing in church on Sunday mornings, words about loving the Lord and walking through peaceful valleys and being saved from sin. The Lord had seemed real to me then, and close – as close as a thunderstorm or a starry sky. He was still real, but not close. Not anymore. My life now was about as far off from the Lord as a feller could ever expect to be.

Rains was right. We was riding a hard road to Hell, and there was no turning back anymore. It was not something I dwelled on much, but that morning – seeing my horses play in the sun, seeing my little girl growing into a woman practically before my eyes – I couldn't help it. It saddened me to know that peace was gone from me forever. I had traded it away and could never bring it back. I remembered the story the old preacher used to tell about Moses, how he had wandered forty years in the desert and was allowed only a far-off glimpse of the promised land.

I sighed. I was embarrassed by a wetness in the corner of my eye, and I blinked it back. I ducked through the front door, into the darkness and smoky shadows.

Marthy was washing the dishes from breakfast. She never even looked up. "Who was that," she said dully.

"Parker."

"Parker who?"

"Parker's his last name. Hell, I don't even remember his first name. He's from over in Putnam County – he rides with Scott Bledsoe."

"He seems nice," Ann said.

Her mother ignored her, but I smiled sadly.

"Yeah," I said. "I reckon he's all right."

"What did he want?"

"Brung me a message from Scott."

Marthy clattered the dishes. I remembered a time when she was easy with them, when she handled everything we owned with a soft hand like she wanted it to last forever.

"You spend too much time with Scott Bledsoe."

That one caught me by surprise, all right. I was at a loss for words for a second or two.

"What's that supposed to mean?" I finally asked her.

"Just what I said."

"Hellfire," I said. "It ain't like I'm off runnin' 'coons, or fishin'. We're fightin' a dern war."

"You go where he leads ye," she said.

"That's generally how it works."

"The more you ride with him, the more you're in his shadow. You ought to be the one runnin' things."

"I don't do ary a thing I don't want to do. You know that as well as anybody."

She grunted, a *hmf* noise which said nothing and everything. "Where are you all runnin' off to now, then?"

"I'm goin' in to town to meet with John Hunt Morgan."

"I've heard of him – he's been in the newspapers."

"Yeah, well. Sounds like Colonel Morgan has somethin' big in the works, somethin' he might want our help with."

"So long as you don't go off too far, to Virginia or somewheres."

I chuckled. "Why, would ye miss me?"

She almost smiled at that one. I smiled for her, the warmest truest smile I could muster. She shook her head.

"Yankees is Yankees," I said. "It don't matter where they are."

"There's Yankees enough right around here, more than enough to keep you busy for a spell."

I lit a smoke and puffed on it real slow. A part of me wanted to be touched at the idea Marthy might have such tender feelings, that she would miss me or worry if I ranged too far to fight Yankees. Another part wondered, though – wondered if maybe her concern was that if I went away I would no longer be fighting the Yankees she wanted killed. I was afraid to ask, and afraid to know.

"Reckon I better go get Rains," I said, "and have him start gathering all the boys. In case we have to be ready to ride soon."

She said nothing. She washed the same plate she had just dried. I walked up behind her, my boots heavy on the wooden floor, and wrapped my arms around her. Marthy's body had no give to it. I kissed her on the cheek and walked back out the door.

I caught my black mare and was saddling her when Ann came outside. I looked up at her and smiled, forcing a twinkle into my eye. She giggled – a short giggle. I had never noticed how sad it was to hear a giggle suddenly cut off by its owner.

"Reckon how long you'll be gone?" she said.

I shrugged. "No tellin', honey. Depends on how far I go, I reckon. You ain't got nothin' to worry about. We got lots of neighbors around here, and they're all good folks."

"I ain't worried."

"You ain't got to worry about me none, neither. You know that."

"I know, Daddy."

"All right then."

"It's just—" She cut herself off.

"It's just what?"

"It's just – it gets lonely here when you're gone."

"I know, honey. I know."

I hugged her, and she hugged me back, and I smelled the sweetness of her hair. Holding her was like holding sunlight and honey. I put my face down near hers, so that our foreheads touched, and looked into her brown eyes – I always had loved to do that. When all I could see of her was her eyes, she looked exactly like the baby I had rocked in my arms just a few years ago, and her expression was the same.

"I love you, Daddy."

"I love you too, darlin'," I said, and then I swung into the saddle and rode off. Out of the valley, and back to the war. I felt her eyes upon me. I felt her eyes long after I was gone, miles after.

Chapter 24

I rode alone into Morgan's camp, just outside of Sparta. Rains was busy spreading the word to all our boys, and I figured they would start showing up by dark – come morning my whole band should be present and ready to ride, and Scott's too.

A sentry stepped toward me as I neared the camp, a young feller near about as skinny as the musket he carried. He didn't exactly point the gun at me, and he didn't exactly point it away, neither. He wore his self a dandy uniform, all gray with no homespun mixed in, and his boots was shined up smartly.

"Halt, who goes there?" he said. I gave him a cold stare for a second or two, and I could tell he was struggling hard against his instinct to fidget under my gaze. I always thought it was peculiar how, when you dressed a man up in a fancy uniform, he took to saying things like *halt, who goes there* like he was born to it, when just the day before he would've said *who the hell are you*.

"Captain Ferguson," I said. "The colonel sent for me."

The sentry's eyes widened, and his spine stiffened up all at once like he was trying to add an inch or two to his height. He even saluted me, and I returned the gesture – it felt odd.

"Right this way, Captain Ferguson, sir," he said, and waved an arm toward the line of tents behind him. "The colonel is waitin' for you in the command tent – it's the one with the standard planted outside."

I nodded and rode past him. I heared excited whispers behind me – the sentry had called a couple of his comrades over to him. Before I reached the command tent, dozens of dismounted cavalrymen had closed in around me. It made me a mite nervous at first, being hemmed in that way, no matter what the color of their uniform. Then I seen the broad smiles they all wore and was put at ease.

"Captain Ferguson! Captain Ferguson!" many of them was calling out. I smiled and waved to them.

One young lieutenant shoved his open hand toward me. "Let me shake your hand, Captain," he said. I gave him a quick, firm handshake, and soon hands were pressing in on me from all sides.

"It's Champ Ferguson!" one trooper hollered to some of his comrades who had not yet joined the crowd. "Come get a look at him!"

The soldiers' earnest buzzing filled the camp.

"You're a hero, Captain! This is an honor!"

"Give 'em hell, Champ, give 'em hell!"

"Thank ye, boys, thank ye," I said.

"You scare them Yankees worse than hell scares a dying sinner, Cap'n!"

"You really fixin' to ride with us, Captain Ferguson?"

I had no sooner dismounted than three soldiers was scrambling to be the one to look after my horse. I was pounded on the back and greeted like a long-lost cousin, by men I had never seen before in my life. It was a heady feeling. I seen Scott Bledsoe and the Colonel standing at the entrance to the tent – Basil Duke was with them – and I couldn't help but notice the looks in all their eyes. It was part pride and part envy. This was a heady feeling too, but I was smart enough to know I'd have to step careful. Proud warriors ain't never been real partial to sharing the glory. I remembered Mama's stories about David from the Bible days, and how the more people loved him the more enemies he made among his own comrades. I was confident that Scott would be Jonathon to my David if need be – a true brother to the end – but this new colonel could wind up being a jealous King Saul. I seen the potential for it behind his smile.

John Hunt Morgan was a striking figure of a man. He was about my age, maybe a little younger, and his beard was full and flowing in the style of the day. His hair was long and curly – also the style amongst rakes and cavalrymen. His uniform was spotless and crisp, the trousers tucked into high shiny boots. A feather bobbed in his big hat. In all these respects he was similar to his subordinate Duke, but he was different in a way that is hard to put words to. Despite the uniform, he was no girlish dandy. He seemed tough as leather – the sort of man you would bet on in a horse race or a tavern brawl.

"Captain Ferguson," he said. "Welcome. My men have thrilled at the news of your exploits – as have I. Please, do come inside."

"Much obliged, sir," I said, and I followed as the three men ducked under the tent flap and stepped into the cool darkness. I could still hear the soldiers talking outside.

"A pleasure to see you again, Captain," Basil Duke said. His voice was admiring, to an extent, though not so much as his men's – but there was also a guarded tone to it, like he remembered the events of that last day I had seen him, and was just a little nervous to be in the company of killers like me.

"You too, Colonel," I told Duke. Scott greeted me with a friendly wink, which set me more at ease.

"Have a seat, gentlemen," Morgan said, and he pointed to a little table ringed with chairs. "They'll be bringing a bite of supper to us soon – roasted chicken, I believe, and biscuits, and other good things provided by the dear ladies of the town. I hope y'all are hungry. In the meantime, I happen to have some good brandy." He took out a bottle – Basil reached behind the table and produced tin cups. Morgan gave him the bottle, and Basil did the pouring.

Morgan lifted his own cup. "To brighter days for the Confederacy, gentlemen," he said.

"Here, here," Basil added, and we clinked our cups together. The brandy was good enough, I reckon, but I've always had more of a taste for whiskey.

Morgan drained his cup. "Fact of the matter is," he said, "brighter days have already begun. True, the Yankees drove us all the way back to Mississippi just a couple of months ago—"

"And now the bastards are taking their ease in Nashville," Duke said bitterly.

"Yes, the bastards are in Nashville. I've had no cause to forget that fact, Basil." Morgan's voice had become steel-hard, and Basil's face softened in regret.

"I know, John," he said. "But Mattie is fine. We'll get her someplace safe as soon as it is feasible." Duke looked over at us. "The colonel's fiancee lives in Murfreesboro, you see. In the middle of an occupying army."

"That has little to do with the matter at hand," Morgan said, but his very insistence proved to me it had a lot more to do things than the colonel was willing – or able – to admit.

"As I was saying. We were driven back, but even as we speak a counter-invasion is being planned which will put Middle Tennessee and Eastern Kentucky back into Southern hands. General Bragg is in Chattanooga and General Kirby-Smith is in Knoxville – both their commands in full force and ready to strike."

Scott nodded. "Good," he said. "This region could use some relief."

"They'll get it, Captain," Morgan replied. "We are going to see to it."

It was my turn to perk up. "What ye got up your sleeve, Colonel?"

"A raid. I plan to strike north into Kentucky – maybe even beyond – fast as lightning. My intention is to take the measure of the Union forces which Bragg and Kirby-Smith will be facing, and give them the intelligence they need to prepare for their strike. In addition to my own brigade, I have Colonel Hunt's Fifth Georgia Regiment. A regiment from Alabama, two squadrons of Texas rangers, and two independent Tennessee companies – one led by a fellow named McMillan, the other by Romulus Jones."

"I've heard of both of 'em," I said. "They think they're as mean as me and Scott."

Morgan chuckled. Basil Duke did not. He had seen firsthand who the mean ones was.

"Your help will be welcome as well," Morgan said, looking at each of us in turn.

"All you got to do is say the word, Colonel," Scott said, "and my boys will be ready to ride."

"Excellent. And you, Captain Ferguson?"

I was pleased to see that he was treating me on an individual level, as an independent captain and not as Scott's subordinate. A smile stole its way onto my lips – it was a wolfish smile, I could feel the coldness of it from the inside of my face. It made Duke go a little pale, but it made Morgan's eyes light up in answer with a coldness of his own.

"I think it's a hell of an idea," I said. "If'n you boys don't get movin' soon, by God, I'm liable to go without y'uns."

Everyone laughed – even Duke. "I'm going to like you, Champ Ferguson," Morgan said. "You and me are going to get along just fine."

~ ~ * ~ ~

The next day we set off. We headed due north. Crowds of folks gathered to see us off – old men and ladies, and little young'uns. There was even a band, and how they scrounged together a band in Sparta I have no idea. The band played *Dixie* and folks cheered as we rode past them. Marthy and Ann was right there, in the front of everybody, pressed by the crowd. Ann smiled and laughed and called out "Daddy!" I smiled real big myself, and tipped my slouch hat at her – she waved in delight.

Marthy held her head up high as a queen and stared at me. It was a look of steel, like she was drawing up strength and will from her huge reserves and sending some my way, just in case I needed it. *Be strong*, her eyes was saying. *Ride fast, kill hard, and then come home to us.*

I nodded to her. I didn't need her strength, but it was still good to have. Not as good as the softness she kept hidden deep in her soul – if it was still alive there.

I had ridden off to fight often in the past months, but never like this. There was a thousand men behind me, seemed like, and a thousand on either side. Spurs jangled and sabers gleamed and people cheered, like we was a machine fed by the coals of their admiration.

We got the same reception when we passed through Cookeville. Then came Gainesboro – there was quite a few folks out in the streets to greet us there, but not near as many as in the other towns. Gainesboro is so damn small that if three dogs get to itching at once, only two of them will get scratched.

Celina was pretty quiet. There was a strong Union element there, and I half-expected to run into a federal patrol. The Unionists was afraid to be seen, and the good Southerners was afraid to greet us for fear of what might happen to them once we was gone.

Then we crossed the Cumberland River, and soon after we crossed the border into Kentucky – near Tompkinsville. That's when we finally seen some Yankees. It was a regiment out of Pennsylvania. For some reason it really pissed me off to see a bunch of Pennsylvania farmers tromping around in my backyard with guns.

I reckon we all must have felt that way, because we tore into them Yankees like starving men at a church picnic. They was scared half-to-death, so it didn't hurt our feelings none to send them the rest of the way. The Yankees never really mounted a good resistance – they didn't take the time, they was too busy running into the woods by the hundreds. About half-a-dozen of them got cut off from the woods and hemmed in by the river. They throwed down their guns and throwed up their hands. Scott opened fire on them, and several of his boys joined in. I didn't, but only because the Yankees died too quick to give me a chance. Only one of them managed to make it into the woods, a major trailing blood from two wounds.

"Those men were trying to surrender!" Colonel Duke hollered. I hadn't realized he was so close behind us.

"Don't look like it worked too good," I said.

"We ain't got time to bother with prisoners," Scott said.

"We could have paroled them!"

"We did parole them," Scott answered. "Straight to hell." He pounded away then, his boys in his wake.

"Do you realize how this makes us look?" Duke said to me.

I nudged my mare closer to him. "You wait a spell, Colonel," I said. "Wait 'til a few of your friends get shot down tryin' to surrender, or get murdered in their sleep. Then come tell me how we ought to behave."

"We look like savages," he said dully.

"We are savages. That's the only way to win."

I rode away and left him, same as Scott had done, knowing Duke was going to raise a stink with Morgan on account of the incident. Nothing was ever said to me about it, though – Morgan knowed what we was when he asked us to come along. I felt sorry for Duke in a way, because he was living in a dream-world. I was later proved to be right. Grant and Sherman spent the last part of the war acting savage as hell, while General Lee and them was trying to figure out the politest way to get on with the fight. I reckon we all know who won.

The Pennsylvania boys scattered behind us like leaves in a hurricane. We kept riding. Three days later we hit some more in Lebanon, Kentucky, and five days after that we tore through a bunch in Cynthiana – just a few miles shy of Ohio. Our losses was slight. Morgan got his intelligence, and we gave the Yankees something to think about. We was wild-assed and woolly Southern boys, by God, and we was liable to show up anytime no matter how big a army they had. This was still my kind of fighting, the kind I was used to, except there was more men involved. The big battles would come later.

On our way home we swung to the west. We swooped into Gallatin in the middle of the night – that's right outside Nashville – and tore up some train tracks. We killed a few federals and then disappeared into the night before they could regroup and figure out what the hell was going on. That too was part of the message we sent to the Union command – but I suspect it was also a message to Morgan's sweetheart.

Chapter 25

"That Colonel Morgan, he's a good'un."

I nodded at Rains. "Yep," I said. "I reckon he is, at that."

"That other colonel, though, I don't think he likes us too much."

We had pitched our camp deep in the woods a few miles from my house, way back in the cove. It was raining. I pulled my slouch hat down lower over my face, so the rain wouldn't put out the match before I could light the cigarette in my mouth.

"Reckon maybe he don't."

I dragged on the smoke and shook out the match. The fact is, I didn't believe Colonel Duke disliked us at all – I just don't reckon he knowed what to think about us. He was damn glad to have us on his side instead of the other one, I'm pretty sure of that. I didn't feel like going over all them thoughts with Rains, though, setting back in the woods getting drizzled on. I could tell my friend was trying to strike up any kind of conversation he could. He was like that. Long as he knowed me, he still didn't understand there was times I found talk of any kind to be tiresome.

Morgan's brigade had moved on for the time being – I ain't even sure where to – until it was time for the big strike into Kentucky. Scott and his boys had scattered to their homes, and most of mine had done the same. There was only me and Rains and about a dozen others camped together. Them still with us was mostly men with no families to go back to.

We had been back from the raid for two days, and I still had not gone home – even though it was close enough that I suppose, if I looked hard enough, I could see the smoke from Marthy's cookfire. I don't know why I had not gone back yet. If my family knowed I was so close their feelings might be hurt about it. It seemed like the closer I got to home the tireder I was, like I was swimming through molasses. At the same time I was restless inside, restless to be back on the trail, restless to fight some more of the hate out of my system. I felt the same way a man feels when he has a high fever. He can't quite rest, and he can't quite do nothing. I don't know why.

"I wish't somebody had brung a guitar," Rains said. "Weather like this, seems like I want to hear gloomy guitar music. Seems like it makes me feel better, some way."

I tossed my cigarette butt into the wet leaves. I opened up my coat and fumbled around, trying to roll me a fresh one inside the coat without getting my tobacco wet.

"I got a harmonica," Rains said. "I never brung it, though."

I grunted. The last time Rains brung his harmonica along some of the boys threatened to shoot him – and I don't think they was altogether fooling. When I made no further sound, Rains filled the emptiness with a big sigh. Then he pulled himself up to his feet and slogged away, giving up on the prospect of getting any small talk from me today. He walked over a few yards, to where half-a-dozen boys was clustered together.

"Y'all want to play some cards?" I heared him ask.

"It's raining," one of them said.

"I got a deck," he replied. "They ain't marked, or nothin'."

"It's raining."

Rains went off by his self then, and sat on a wet log. He took out an old pocket-knife. I heared the soft *thunk* of him throwing it into the wet leaves over and over again. I reckon he didn't care if it got rusty.

It would be warm and dry at my house. This time of day Marthy would just be starting supper. The kitchen would be quiet except for the sounds of cooking. There would be no talking between Marthy and Ann. I knowed it well. Even though I remembered a time, dim in the past now, when there would have been talking, and laughing, and singing.

There was six men left alive out of the eleven who had come to my house in Clinton County that day and done my family wrong. *Six left.* I thought to myself, as the rain dripped off my hat brim, that some of them was probably warm and dry now too. Maybe they was in their homes, more likely they was in somebody else's – but dry or not, nary a one of them was comfortable. They was wondering, in the back of their minds, if this might be the day I catch up with them. Little did they know that the Confederate Army's upcoming push northward was actually keeping them safe from me; I was too busy to attend to them right now. That would change, though.

I wondered what I would do once they was all dead. I wondered what would be left.

Chapter 26

Boys, I seen my first full-scale combat in October of 'sixty-two, and let me tell you all, it was hell with the hair on. We was attached to General Braxton Bragg's force, doing scouting and reconnaissance – regular cavalry work. Bragg had spent the month of September making his way into Kentucky, his goal being to join up with General Kirby Smith – who had done took Frankfort. With the two outfits joined into one huge one, we'd have control of Kentucky for the South once and for all and could get down to the business of striking even farther north. Probably invade Ohio. The good people of Cincinnati, as I hear it, was scared shitless. They was shoring up their town and drumming up every militiaman who was out of diapers and had at least one arm and a couple of legs to defend against the coming invasion.

It didn't take no genius to figure out, though, that we wasn't fixing to invade anyplace except maybe hell unless we got ahold of some water. That summer had brung the biggest drought to Kentucky that anyone could remember, and water was harder to come by than virgins in a two-dollar whorehouse, if you'll pardon my way of putting it.

The ground was parched and blasted, and the grass was more dead brown than blue. Everything was dead or dying, seemed like, almost as if the Good Lord His Self had decided to make our surroundings fit the occasion. Maybe He was seeing fit to give us all a glimpse of where we was going to be sending one another before long. I halfway expected to see old Satan his self come ambling by, dragging his pitchfork on the dry ground, sucking on a rock to ease his thirst. That ground would be plenty wet enough soon, but we had no way of knowing that at the time.

Shoot, it got so bad that the whole army was on the move, right on the cavalry's tail, hoping to stumble across some water – not even caring that we had no idea where the Federals was, nor how many of them. Turns out the Yankees was doing the same thing, and it further turns out there was a hell of a lot more of them than we thought.

We all sort of bumped into each other, tired and thirsty and ornery, near a place called Perryville. And then it got hot, boys.

Now there's been many a time I have been shot at, as you well know if you've been listening so far. But never in my life had I knowed anything like this. Bullets was zipping through the air – *thip, thip, thip* – so thick it felt like a whole swarm of hornets was buzzing all around me. The wet splats of them smacking into bodies sounded like heavy raindrops in a pond.

And that's not to mention shells and the like screaming through the air, some of them plowing into the ground and sending men flying every which way in pieces. Others exploded over our heads and sent scraps of hot metal raining down on us like it was blown by a tornado. One shell whistled by and kept right on going – but it took Peter Lucas's head with it. Me and him had been riding side-by-side, and I had just happened to look over at him. His eyes wasn't all dreamy like they usually was, they was near about popping out of his head in terror. The boy had always wanted adventure, but I reckon this mess was not as romantic as he had figured it to he. Then all at once, as I was glancing at him, his head just disappeared. There was nothing there but a red bone sticking out of his neck. About a second later spurts of blood started spewing out of him. He swayed slowly then toppled out of the saddle.

Right about then I heared a wet smack real close by. I took a quick, frantic look over the front of my own body, for fear I had been shot and hadn't felt it yet. I seen that the source of the noise was a wound in my horse's neck – it was a hole about the size of a dime, from shrapnel I reckon. Seemed like it bothered me more than it did him. If we'd of been setting still I reckon it would've scared him into a breakneck gallop, but we was already in a damn breakneck gallop, so it didn't seem to matter much.

All around me, men was falling. Some of them was my own boys, or Scott's, most of them was regular cavalry. Them infantry boys was taking it even harder, bunched up together the way they was.

I didn't much care for it all, myself

And then we was on the top of a Yankee artillery placement. There was bluebellies clustered around the big guns, feeding them the shells they needed to spit death at us, and there was more bluebellies all around with muskets, who I reckon was supposed to protect the artillerymen from us. It didn't work, because we was mad as hell. We swarmed over them the way their bullets and shells had swarmed over us.

We trampled men down beneath our horses. We fired pistols point-blank into their faces and watched them explode and would have laughed, I reckon, if we'd had the time. Them regular cavalry boys, the ones who was wearing full-gray uniforms instead of just what they could cobble together like us irregulars was, they soon had them sabers of theirs swinging and flashing through the air like they was threshing wheat.

Me, I had to lean out of my saddle and swipe at Yankees with my Bowie knife, and I kind of envied them others their swords a bit. I resolved to come up with me one to carry on my saddle for occasions like this.

The Yankees tried to run away from us once they seen there was no turning us back. We rode among them, cutting them down at will, until we had prett'near killed them all.

Then it was time to charge up another hill, and do the whole thing all over again. It was rough work, like to wear a man out or kill him, one.

The day's fighting ended with Bragg sending out the order to retreat to the southeast. We run away, we never did get to unite with Smith for that surge into Ohio, and it turned out later that because of it Kentucky was lost for the South permanent. But the generals in the rear and the newspapers back home still insisted on calling it a victory. It's too bad wishing don't win wars, or we would have had the whole damn thing wrapped up pretty quick. The Union commander, D.C. Buell, was relieved of his command later in the month because he allowed us to escape when he should have had us at his mercy – at least in Abe Lincoln's opinion, I reckon.

We was outnumbered by more than two-to-one that day, and we still gave the Yankees four thousand casualties to our three thousand. Out of the hundred or so men I had brung into the fight, seven died and about a dozen was wounded, a couple of them bad enough that their fighting days was over for good. One feller we never found at all. He wasn't the sort to just run away, so I figured he must have caught one of them shells dead-on and exploded into a mist of blood, leaving nothing to mark his passage on this earth but some memories. And vague ones at that, because now I can't remember his damn name.

But they all fought hard, and they fought good. As I recollect back on some of the things I've done told you about my best friend Rains Philpot, it strikes me that maybe I've give you the notion he was a timid man Well, hell, I reckon he was, a good part of the time – but not when we was fighting Yankees. Rains drawed as much blood from the bastards that day as anybody did. With all his talk about going to hell, maybe that day convinced him it couldn't be no worse than where we was at right now, so he relaxed a mite.

Within a couple of weeks, Bragg's main force had made it back to Tennessee. Once there they positioned theirselves in Tullahoma, skirmishing here and yonder along the way. The cavalry kept making swipes at Kentucky, though. General Joe Wheeler captured the town of Loudon, and Colonel Morgan took Lexington. I was with him when he did. We whupped the hell out of 1500 Yankees and then rode into the town just as easy as you please, like we owned the damn place, rounding up every skulking Federal we found and taking them prisoner. Folks started attaching a nickname to the regiment, one that would stick when the colonel later had a full brigade. Morgan's Raiders, people called them, and I done my part to live up to the name. By the end of December Morgan had been made a general. Old Basil Duke took his brother-in-law's place as commander of the regiment, while Morgan was over them and several others to boot.

It still seemed like they had us on the run. We done all we could to disrupt the Union supply and communication lines. Morgan was playing hell with them all over Tennessee and Kentucky, and Nathan Bedford Forrest was doing the same.

Morgan thought it would be a good idea for me to break off and head back east, to my own territory, and do what I could to occupy the Yankees there. That plan of action suited me well enough. I gathered volunteers to me from every county I passed through along the way, and by the time I reached the Cumberland Plateau I had upwards of three hundred men with me. I right away set to harassing the Federals in Cumberland County – I put the fear of God into them sons of bitches. I had them running around in circles trying to catch me, like dogs trying to catch their own tails. We had us a hell of a time.

While I was at it I decided to take care of a little personal business. I had been out of the area long enough, maybe some of my dear old friends in Jimtown and across the border in Clinton County, Kentucky, had worked up the nerve to come out of their hiding places and into the broad daylight.

If they had, by God, I aimed to show them more than sunshine.

Chapter 27

I left LeRoy Reece in command of the main body of our company while I split off to look up old friends. I took about seventy-five men with me. I told Reece to keep moving, not to hit any Federal targets until I got back, but not to let no one hit him, neither. Then I turned north into Fentress County.

The first thing we done once we got there was to grab up an old boy we seen walking on the road. He never even looked up at first, when he heared our horses coming – I reckon he was used to Federal patrols and Union guerillas passing through all the time. The Federals was occupied a few miles to the south, though, looking for me, so we had little reason to worry about them.

When the farmer did finally look up at us, he got the surprise of his life. I reckon he hadn't expected to see that much gray coming his way again anytime soon. His eyes popped prett'near out of his head.

He was nobody I recognized – but I ain't from Fentress County, though I spent plenty of time there, so I didn't know everybody.

"Good mornin', neighbor," I said. I had reined my horse up beside him.

"Good – good mornin'."

"You know who I am, hoss?"

"I figure you're Captain Ferguson."

I smiled. "You figure right. And who might you be?"

"Robert Sorrell, Captain. Sir. Robert Sorrell."

"Well, Mister Sorrell, we got us a extry horse here just for you. He's fresh as new-cut hay. Why don't you just climb on up into the saddle and ride with us for a ways."

Sorrell gulped loudly. "I ain't got no troubles with you all, Captain. I'm just an honest farmer, I mind my own business."

"That's good to know. Come on now, let's go."

The honest farmer hesitated, his face turning paler by the second. I squinted at him.

"I have invited you to travel a ways with us, Mister Robert Sorrell. I have even been kind enough to offer you the use of one of our horses, so's ye don't have to foller along on foot. Are you refusin' our hospitality?"

Mister Sorrell hopped up on that damn horse so fast he almost plopped off on the other side.

"Where – where are y'uns takin' me, Captain?"

"Well, that part is sort of up to you." I nudged my own mount forward, and Sorrell did the same. He rode with me at the head of the column, looking like he was none too comfortable with the idea of having seventy-five Rebs staring at his back. On the other hand, he was probably also none too happy to have his neighbors see him riding along in the company of seventy-five Rebs whose leader was smiling like they was old friends.

"I aim to visit some people today," I told him. "Sort of to renew old acquaintances, you might say. Good, dear friends of mine."

He nodded nervously. I hoped he didn't shit his britches, it would make this an uncomfortable journey for us all.

"One friend I especially want to see is good old Tinker Dave," I said. "Me and him, we go way back. Do you know Tinker Dave, Mister Robert Sorrell?"

"I know of him," he replied weakly. "We ain't, you know, we ain't friends or nothin' .I just know him enough to throw my hand up to when I pass him."

"I know him real well," I said. "But what I need you to help me with, see, is there might be other friends of mine livin' between here and Tinker's farm that I might want to drop in on."

"Who?"

"I ain't rightly sure. That's where you come in."

"Me?"

"Yep. Anybody that is a good friend to Tinker Dave, why, that's just who I want to meet. People who have got the same political persuasion Dave does, if ye know what I mean. I always enjoy talking with people like that. Debatin' with 'em, and all. I reckon you'd know where Dave's friends are, and which of 'em might be home right now. On leave from their army regiments, or restin' up from where they've been out huntin' with Tinker Dave or Elim Huddleston. Stuff like that."

"I don't know any—"

I drawed my pistol out and pointed it at his face. I cocked it.

"Don't bullshit me, son. It is a very unwise thing to do. If you can't help me, see, I'll find me somebody that can. Once I take a notion to do that, why, I won't need you anymore. Ain't no telling what I might do then."

Robert Sorrel, he led me to several new friends that morning. I don't reckon he made any friends in the process, but that's the way it goes. By noon we had well over a dozen prisoners in tow. A couple of other fellers we knowed for a fact to be guerillas – them we just shot dead on sight.

Tinker Dave was nowhere to be found. His farm was abandoned – I reckon he had give up farming for good. I intended to burn it to the ground, but I seen the headstones out front and it gave me pause. It was the resting place of Dave's wife, dead many years now, and of the one son who had been killed fighting Rebels. It made me think of my own first wife, and my dead boy. I knowed this man, somehow, and I figured he knowed me, in ways that other folks wouldn't understand. We was the same. We was on different sides, but we was the same. Another man's house I would've gone on and destroyed. It would serve no useful purpose, though, for I knowed Dave wasn't coming back anyways until all the fighting was done – and there was something else that held me back. I would kill Tinker Dave Beaty if I found him, kill him quick and sure. But I wouldn't burn his house down.

"Come on, boys," I said. "Let's move on to Clinton County."

They followed without a murmur of complaint, not even the wild-eyed Timmons. He had learned long ago not to accuse me of being soft. Rains rode close at my side – he gave me a look of understanding, then turned his eyes back to the road ahead of us.

~ ~ * ~ ~

Looking at them quiet graves had made me feel a little blue, and the feeling lasted through the night. Rains stuck close to me after we made camp, silent and grim, like he was keeping watch to hold the blues away from me if he could.

The prisoners was a lot sadder than I was, though. They should have known that if I aimed to kill them I would have done it already. I was planning to carry them south with us to White County, and introduce them to the good folks representing the Fifth Infantry or the Eighth Cavalry, who would give them a choice between joining up on their side or going to a prison camp.

My own mood lightened considerably the next morning. We had reached Wash Tabor's farm, and damn if there wasn't smoke in the chimney. One of my boys was almost as happy as I was. Frank Burchett's brother had fallen into the hands of the Home Guards a few months before, and witnesses say it was old Wash who cut his throat. He had been little more than a boy.

Wash was walking out of his stable when we rode up. He froze stiff as a board when he seen all the rifles pointed at him. All the blood left his face, like it was preparing for the upcoming journey out of the old bastard's body.

"Dear God," he said as I rode closer to him. "Dear God in heaven."

Frank Burchett was beside me, and he laughed at Tabor's words. "You're off on that guess," he said. "You're way off."

Several of the boys went into the farmhouse, and they came out with two prisoners. I spared a glance at them – it was the Thrasher brothers, Will and George.

"What are you boys doin' here?" I said.

George took a step forward, then stopped when the man guarding him poked a gun barrel into his ribs.

"Howdy, Champ," George said. "We told Wash we would help him paint his house today. He's gettin' a little long in the tooth for that sort of work, and he give our Ma and Pa some vegetables while we was away, so we figured we owed him a favor. We was just havin' a cup of coffee 'fore we got started."

Will Thrasher made a shushing noise to his older brother, his eyes frantic. I almost laughed in spite of my anger at Wash.

"While y'uns was away," I repeated.

"Yeah," George said. "I won't lie to ye, Champ, me and Will is home on leave from the Eighteenth Kentucky Cavalry."

"Union cavalry," one of my boys said, and several of them grunted. Will grunted too, and it was plain to see he was furious at his brother.

"Hell, Will," George said, "they done know who we are and that we ain't with them, no sense draggin' it out and makin' it worse."

"Y'all just set tight," I told the Thrasher brothers. "I'll talk to y'uns in a minute. Right now I have business with Wash Tabor."

Tabor was whimpering. "Don't kill me, Champ, please. Please God don't kill me."

"Oh no," I said, my voice mocking. "You ain't never done nothin' to deserve dyin' for, have ye?"

"Blow his brains out," Frank hissed. "Blow his damned brains out."

"Jesus, oh sweet Jesus."

"Are you still a Christian, Wash?"

Tabor nodded. He was now sobbing too hard to speak.

"Seems to me like," I said slowly, "the last time you was at my house Wash – visiting with my family while I was away – they told me you said somethin' unkind about me. Somethin' about shovin' a cornstalk up my ass, as I recall."

Tabor's voice was a wordless, vibrating sob.

"That was plumb rude of you, Wash."

I blowed his brains out. They splattered all over the dusty ground. His body pitched back onto the mess and twitched a few times. Frank drawed his knife out and stabbed the old bastard several times while he was twitching.

"Somebody fetch me a cornstalk," I said. One was handed to me, and I set it into the nasty chest wound Frank Burchett had created. Wash was still now – the cornstalk raised out of his body like it had growed right through his chest.

I turned to the Thrasher brothers, and spoke to George. "I ain't never heared of you bushwhackin' nobody or stealin' no horses, Thrasher, so I ain't gonna kill ye. I have killed Wash Tabor, but he was a damned fine Christian, so I don't think he'd hold it agin me."

"You ain't gonna kill us?" Will said.

I walked up to him. "You reckon I should kill y'uns?" I said.

"No, no I don't."

"I don't know," I said to him. "Maybe the war would be over a whole lot sooner if we just killed everybody."

"It'd be a mighty hard thing, Champ," George said, "to just kill an unarmed man that ain't done ye no wrong."

I chuckled. "Sounds like it would be an awful damn easy thing, to me." I turned away and walked to my horse.

"Mount up," I told the Thrashers when I was in the saddle myself. "You ain't gonna die today, no more than any of these other prisoners we've got."

We was a few miles down the road when Elim Huddleston's guerillas hit us. They was about evenly-matched with us, and there was three or four shot on each side before they broke off and rode away again. In the confusion, though, all our prisoners got away. I hoped some of them would have the sense to leave this part of the country.

Huddleston was another thorn I reckoned I was going to have to pluck soon. He was on my list anyway, and my list was growing shorter. Huddleston, the two remaining Evans brothers, and John Crabtree.

And my brother Jim.

Chapter 28

It was well-past dark when we passed back down through Fentress County. It must have been about ten o'clock. I was hoping my enemies would figure I had done been there and gone once, and wouldn't be back for a spell, so's it would be safe for them to come out of hiding.

We stopped at Elim Huddleston's house, but there was no one there. We jerked one of his neighbors out of bed and used our gentle persuasion to convince the feller to tell us where Huddleston and his cronies might be. The neighbor wasn't in a mood to talk much, but his wife jumped right in when she seen that her husband's foolish loyalty – or fear of Elim – was fixing to get him killed.

"They're at the Piles place," she said, "several of 'em. I know, because just this afternoon Annie Piles was complainin' about havin' to feed 'em all."

"Piles," I repeated. "Where is this place at? I ain't never heared of it."

One of my boys stepped forward. It was Ephraim Crabtree. "I know where it is," he said. "Annie Piles used to be married to my first cousin, 'fore he died and she took up with that scrawny Piles feller. Her oldest boy John runs with Huddleston, always has."

He spat on the floor. "I'd hate to have to kill old John, him bein' kin to me and all, but Yankees is Yankees, Crabtree or not."

A smile crept over my face. "Crabtree," I said. "Of course. John Crabtree. Don't worry none, Ephraim, you won't have to kill him. I'll take care of that detail my own self"

It was close on to midnight when we reached the Piles farm. All was dark and quiet inside.

"Spread out, boys," I said, making no effort to keep my voice low. "Surround the house."

I reckon I had put the fear of the Lord into these Unionists after all, because they had posted a guard. A couple of rifle shots barked at us. One of my men, a lanky blond-headed boy named Young, took a bullet square in the Adam's apple. I pulled my pistol and returned the fire

– within seconds the others had joined in. There ain't no telling how many holes we put into that farmhouse.

The backdoor slammed open, and in the dim moonlight I seen two figures hightail it toward the brush. I shot at them, but it was too late – they had made it into the trees.

"Homer," I called out. "Take six men and flush them bastards out, whoever the hell they are."

The shooting from inside the house had stopped.

"The next'un runs out that door," I hollered, "is gonna be dead 'fore he takes his second step." I nudged my horse closer. "And the next'un fires a shot at us, I'm gonna burn this house to the ground, and ever'body in it."

"Don't do it!" a voice called out – it was an elderly man. "We got young'uns in here!"

"Somebody put on a light in there."

A woman's voice this time, from near the front door. "Who are you?"

"Never you mind who I am, just put that damn light on."

"I'm lightin' it now."

Another voice, a man's. A familiar voice. "If you light that lamp, woman, I swear I'll shoot ye myself!"

"I never asked all of y'uns into my house!" The woman hollered back at him. "Onliest one I asked was my son! And now you've brung Champ Ferguson down on us, and got us all killed, damn you! I'm lightin' the lamp!"

Behind me a little ways, Young was still thrashing a little bit. He had been gurgling ever since he was shot, choking on his own blood, and I could tell it had put all his comrades into a surly mood.

"Is Elim Huddleston in there?" I demanded.

The light came on, and the door swung open. Nobody stepped into it, though.

"No sir," the woman said. "Ain't no Elim Huddleston here."

"We'll see about that," I said. "I reckon you'd all better put down your guns and step out here, unless you want this house burned down around your ears."

"We're comin' out," the familiar man's voice said. "Don't go to shootin', for God's sake."

"Come out, then." I rested my hands on my saddle horn and waited.

They came out slowly, each one casting frightened looks at the Rebs all around them. There was an older woman, a young woman and three kids, a feeble-looking old feller, a sprite of a boy about sixteen years old, and three growed men. The young'uns all held on to the woman's skirts like I was a tornado come to blow them away into the night. A Negro girl walked out last – she was about the same age as the youth.

I touched the brim of my hat and smiled. "Howdy ma'am," I said to the older of the two white women "I reckon you'd be Annie Piles."

"I am," she said, her jaw jutting out. "This here is my step-daughter Vina and her young'uns."

I looked at Vina. "One of these men your husband?"

She shook her head, hers jaw clenched tightly.

The old man spoke. "Her husband died at Perryville. Kilt by Yankees."

The man whose voice had been so familiar to me was lingered near the back of the group, trying to keep his face toward the shadows. I turned to him. "Ye might as well give up on ary notion you got of runnin' away, John Crabtree," I said. "I know good and well who you are, and you'll be took care of in a minute." I glanced at his grown companions. "I don't know who the hell they are, though."

Crabtree's cousin Ephraim spoke up. "I know 'em. It's Jack Williams and David Delk. Ever'body knows they're in a Union infantry outfit – they must be home on leave."

Annie Piles spat at the ground near Ephraim's feet. "Shame on you, Ephraim Crabtree," she hissed. "Your daddy would be ashamed of you, runnin' with trash like this, pointin' fingers at your neighbors and your own kinfolks!"

Ephraim shrugged. "Hell, I don't know, Annie – if'n he was alive, he might be ridin' with us. You don't never know."

"Who's the squirt," I said, pointing at the boy.

"That's my other cousin," Ephraim said, "Donny Richardson. He ain't never run with no Unionists, or raised arms agin us."

I grunted, then nodded slowly at the youth. "See that you don't, son. You will by God come to a bad end if'n you do."

Annie gasped then, and choked back a sob. All the anger and fight left her face, like she had suddenly realized just who and what we was, and what it would mean for her own son. She fell to her knees.

"Don't kill my little boy," she said, "don't kill my John. You ain't that mean a man, to take a mama's only son away from her – you got a mama yourself, who would take care of her if'n you was gone?" Her voice was breaking. John looked touched and embarrassed and terrified, all at the same time.

"Your John is a worser man than I'll ever be," I told her. "I reckon you should've raised him better, but you've had your chance to and now it's gone." I motioned to my men, and several of them grabbed Crabtree, Delk, and Williams and bound up their hands. Annie Piles was near hysterics, refusing to take comfort from her trembling husband.

"Who was them two that got away," I said. "Somebody better talk fast."

The old man spoke. "It was the Evans boys," he said. "Mike and Will. Elim was here while-ago, but he left 'fore y'uns got here."

"I'll catch them some other day," I said. "And when I do I aim to unjoint their bodies and scatter the pieces so far the dogs won't be able to find 'em."

I singled out half-a-dozen of my men. "Y'all go in the house," I told them. "Turn it inside out, make sure there ain't no more hidin' in there. Take anything that we might need later."

"Anything?" one of them said.

"Anything."

"What about this little nigger gal?"

"She's property, ain't she? We can sell her – we need all the money we can raise."

"I've had that little gal since she was borned," Old Man Piles said. "She's the onliest worker I got around here."

"Life is tough."

The old man shook his head. "Y'uns Rebels is mighty hard," he said, "takin' a man's nigger away from him thataway."

"Take her!" Annie screamed. "Take anything, but don't take away my son!" Her husband held her back, which was quite a chore for his skinny frame. I paid her no heed – there was nothing else to be said.

John Crabtree looked back at her, the eyes fairly popping out of his head. "Mama!" he hollered. "Mama!"

I pondered on what him and his friends had done to my wife, and my own little girl, and the thought of it steeled my spirit.

We left another half-dozen men to stand guard over the Piles family. The rest of us marched our three prisoners over the hill, and down the road for a couple of miles. No need for the women and young'uns to hear what was happening, bad enough they had to watch all their belongings being carried off. Bad enough that old Piles should have to watch his nigger gal leave his possession.

I heared Annie's screams for a long time after we left, but I was immune to such sounds now, as much as I was immune to the sound of whizzing bullets or of whistling shells. The prisoners never said ary a word, knowing as they did their fate. They never even protested – they was Yankee soldiers holed up with Crabtree, the Evanses, and Huddleston, and there wasn't no denying what they was up to. Nothing good for me, that's for damn certain.

I stuck a cornstalk into what was left of John Crabtree later, same as I had done with Wash Tabor. They tell me his mama took it out with her own hands.

The next week I made the acquaintance of Jack Williams' father. Him and his slave Granville took onto my trail, wanting revenge for Jack's death – I didn't kill neither Williams nor Delk, by the way, my men did. I sure as hell did kill Crabtree and done a good deed when I did it. Anyways, they came up on me when I was alone and tried to get the drop on me.

Williams and the slave made two mistakes. Number one, they came looking for me. Number two, they found me.

May they rest in peace.

Chapter 29

I know what you're thinking. Just from looking into your face, I can see it. You are tired of hearing about all these bloody killings, they are all the same, they are starting to blend together in your mind until you can't even tell 'em apart no more. I understand. Hell, I'm tired of talking about 'em, for that matter. Just imagine what it was like doing 'em. After awhile it got to be where it was like a job of work – not much different from plowing a field. Row after row, one after another, all the same, without no end in sight, until a man feels like his skin is gonna melt in the sun and just soak plumb into the ground and his bones have to keep right on working – row after row. Row after row.

You're also thinking I am a heartless bastard. An evil man, maybe. You're right on that count, too. I can't deny it. I done things no human man should ever do. I done 'em regular, day after day, until I couldn't even feel myself doing 'em no more. I felt the sting, brother, believe me – setting in that courtroom and listening to them people accusing me, especially the women, I could feel it. It wasn't like when it happened. There was no heat of battle, no life-or-death situation. Setting in that hot courtroom here in Nashville and hearing folks tell and retell about what they seen me do – it brung it all home. The words and the place they was spoke at didn't seem to go together somehow, made it all seem different than I remembered it. I don't rightly know how to explain why that is. It made the things I done seem more real-like, and less real to me at the same time. I don't understand it.

Maybe it's because I don't have the rage and the hate no more. I finally let go of it, and it's like I'm drowning now, without it to buoy me up.

I set here and listen to 'em hammering on that damn scaffold. Hell, I know how this damn story is gonna end, same as you do. But there is still some telling to be done about how things came to this point – still some blood to wade through – and the story is worth the telling. Worth it because maybe you can learn from it, or someone else can, and save your own soul from what awaits me.

We both know how your story is gonna end too, after all. Everyone's story ends the same way – I just happen to know the exact date mine ends in advance. It's what happened on the way there – for all of us – that makes our story our own. And I reckon they're all worth telling, at least we hope so.

But don't hear me wrong, I still stick by what I said when I first set down here with you. Everybody I killed needed killing, and some of 'em needed it bad. And I never brung no harm to any women or children, or innocent folks who never done a thing to deserve it. I done what I had to do, and I ain't sorry I done it – I'm just sorry I was drove to it. I'm sorry we was all drove to it, and for what it has done to us. Everything I done, though – hell, ain't nary doubt but that I'd do it again.

They tell me I killed over a hundred people. Hell if I know. But as 1862 drawed to a close, there was only four men left I had to kill. The remaining Evans brothers, Elim Huddleston, and my brother Jim. Three of them I found on one bloody night just a couple of months after I got John Crabtree, but the fourth would elude me until near the end of the war. I'll get to that directly.

First, I'll tell you about something a little more pleasant. I'll tell you about General Morgan's sweetheart, who become his wife, and how it was that I met her.

Chapter 30

General Morgan married Miss Mattie Ready of Murfreesboro, Tennessee, on December 14. She had been whisked out from behind Union lines – everything was in confusion around Murfreesboro, as General Bragg and General Rosecrans was fixing to square off. Mattie swore she would not be separated from her true love no more than she had to be, not ever again.

Rosecrans, who I reckon didn't want to be disgraced like his predecessor Buell, he set to shoring up his defenses around Nashville. Bragg ordered us to strike north to Kentucky, in order to destroy the railroads linking Nashville and Louisville, and put a stop to Rosecrans' supplies.

On December 20 we arrived in the little town of Alexandria. That's in DeKalb County, which is right next to White County and my own home. Word of our coming had preceded us, and folks was gathered from all the little towns around to catch a glimpse of the famous general and his new bride.

Morgan, him and Mattie smiled and waved to the cheering crowds like they was a prince and princess moving amongst their royal subjects. The mayor informed Morgan that the local inn, which was called Browning's Tavern, had been set aside special for the charming couple. So far as I know, that was the closest thing to a honeymoon they had gotten so far.

Morgan told the mayor that his entire division – bivouacked in tents all over the DeKalb County countryside – would pass before him in review first thing the next morning, and the mayor and all the civilians was most welcome to come and observe.

Twilight was closing in, and the happy couple had disappeared to their hideaway, when a messenger appeared at my tent and stuck his head in.

"Beggin' the Captain's pardon," he said, "but you've got some visitors."

I waved for him to send them in. The flap opened further, and my little Ann scampered into the tent and into my arms – she hugged my neck so tight I thought I was apt to choke to death, and it seemed like the sweetest way of dying that God ever invented. I call her my little Ann, but even I could tell each month was bringing her closer to womanhood.

"Oh Daddy," she said into my beard, "oh Daddy, I've missed you so much!"

Marthy had walked in too. She sat down in my single rickety chair and smiled at me – her own smile, which most folks would not even recognize as one, but which was enough to set my heart on fire. I held out my arm to her – my free arm, for the other was wrapped around my daughter – and she took it and held it to her cheek.

"Hell, y'all," I said, with a grin. "I ain't been away that long. Just a couple of months."

"And you better not be gone that long no more, not ever again," Ann said.

Marthy got up and urged me to set in the chair in her place, and they both kneeled in the dust beside me. We talked for a long time – about everything, and about nothing, but nary a word about war. We talked about the crops and the stock, and about who-all was sick and who-all was courting, and about what meanness various of our neighbors had got into. We talked about Mattie Morgan – Ann saying how pretty she was, and me saying what a sweet gal she was, and Marthy saying what a flighty, pampered thing she seemed to be.

Then Ann kissed me goodnight and left – she was staying with some of our neighbors who had cousins in DeKalb County. This whole thing was like a big county fair.

Marthy stayed the night with me in my little tent, and I won't tell you no more about that because it's none of your damn business. But I will tell you that – while I was whispering words of love – she whispered back that, since I was going to Kentucky anyways, maybe I could catch some more of the men who had abused her and had in fact seen her even as I was seeing her now. I will tell you the whole world suddenly tasted sour to me, and the taste is still in my mouth.

She went on to say how much she wished Ann had been born as a boy, so that all she would ever have to fear was just getting killed. I reckon she said some more, too, but I wasn't listening. She was in her world, and I was in mine, and I couldn't weave them together anymore.

~ ~ * ~ ~

I reckon it was what you'd call an inspiring review. It was clear and fair, unseasonably warm and comfortable. General Morgan and his wife, as well as the mayor and several other prominent folks, stood on a hill and watched while the division passed by in the valley below them. Regular folks was all around, too, hollering and whistling. Flags waved. A band played.

We passed by the general one company after the other. I rode at the head of my company of irregular scouts, and I was tickled and warmed through to notice that the applause was loudest for us.

"Go get 'em, Champ!"

"Give 'em hell, Champ!"

And, from somewhere in the crowd, "We love you, Daddy!" I can't be sure if it was Ann or not, as lots of my men had families in the admiring crowd, but I like to think it was.

When we had all taken our positions the artillery was brung in, a battery of four guns. Then we all saluted General John Hunt Morgan, and the crowd cheered louder than ever.

If only that could be all there was to war.

Chapter 31

There is a certain spot on the Calfkiller River. It's about three-quarters of a mile from my house in White County, just before you come to the wild tangles of England's Cove, where me and my boys camped and hunted and hid so often. It ain't the same place where I used to go fishing with Ann – the water is more shallow. So shallow you can wade right across it most times, and the water there runs and gurgles over thousands of little stones. The stones is every color and shape you can imagine. It's a real quiet spot, never any sound but the running of the water over them stones.

I took to setting in that spot every once in awhile. Sometimes I would set there listening to the water, instead of riding on down the river to the house where Marthy and Ann was waiting. I would come just close enough to the farm that I could feel their presence – and maybe they could feel mine – but not close enough to see their faces or hear their voices. Sometimes I couldn't bear the thought of their eyes looking into my own, and trying to figure out what was on the other side of them, trying to catch a glimpse of the things I have seen. Sometimes I didn't want their voices talking to me, asking where I had been and what I had done – asking why I had done so much, or why I had done so little.

Sometimes I didn't want anybody talking to me except for the river.

It's a restful site, there where them rocks are. A feeling comes over me when I set there alone – a feeling of home, and of peace. There is a kind of quiet magic in the air. Maybe it's from the Indians. I know they camped at that spot. I don't know because somebody told me, I know because I can feel it. Once I found a stone stopper from a Indian jug there in the water. There's no telling how long it had laid there before I found it – a hundred years, maybe. Two hundred.

The water over the rocks sounds like voices talking. It sounds like the voices of all the people – Cherokees mostly, I reckon – that have lived beside that river and been happy there. Other times, when I close my eyes, it's like the voices of all the people I have killed calling out to me – not in anger nor hatred, just calling out that they are waiting for me to come and join them. Then a feeling of sadness creeps over me – but a peaceful sadness, just the same.

Not far from that spot there is a graveyard. It is a little graveyard, up on a hill, shaded by big oak trees. There's only a few people buried in it. My neighbor Horace Carmichael, he buried several of his cousins there in the middle of the war – all killed fighting Yankees.

When you stand on that hill you can look out across all the hills and valleys for a far piece in every direction. If you strain your eyes you can almost see my house from there – or you could, before the Yankees burnt it down. You can smell the sweet green grass, and the sap on the trees, and the smell of sunshine all warm in your nostrils – the smells of forever. And if you strain your ears you can almost hear the river, gurgling and calling your soul into it.

Sometimes when I go there to that little graveyard on the hill I just want to set in the grass – to set, and sink down, and sleep, and smell the earth and forget all the sadness of this world.

But I would always get back up. Get up, and climb into the saddle and head back toward the Cove. I would always check that the caps was set proper on my pistol, and that the edge was still keen on my knife. I didn't have time to rest yet.

Seems like there was always more killing to do.

Chapter 32

War don't stop for the holidays. Our raid into Kentucky came to be called "the Christmas Raid", and it lasted 'til into the new year of 1863. We was fighting and slashing the whole way.

It wasn't long before we was having trouble with the Union guerillas at the state line, harassing our rear. General Morgan kept Scott Bledsoe's company with him to act as scouts, and sent me and my boys south to occupy the guerillas on the opposing side. That suited me fine, as the Union bands in question was the ones headed by Elim Huddleston, Tinker Dave, and Rufus Dowdy. Sometimes them groups acted independent of one another, sometimes members traded back and forth from one band to another, but them three men was always at the head of the mischief.

Morgan sent Colonel Duke and some regulars along – I reckon that, technically, Basil Duke was in charge, but he knowed as well as I did he needed to stay out of my way and let me take care of business.

We caught Elim by surprise on New Year's Night – at his brother Moses Huddleston's house, with only a handful of men. In most ways it was an exact duplicate of the night we got John Crabtree – us surrounding the house and firing into it, and them shooting back.

What was different this time was that we had Basil Duke with us.

"Hold your fire!" Duke commanded. The air still popped with gunfire. I held up my hand, and the shooting stopped on our side.

"You in there!" Duke hollered at the house. "This is Colonel Basil Duke – I would speak with your commander!"

"Speak, then, damn it!" someone yelled from the house.

Duke cleared his throat. "You are surrounded. Surrender – come out with your hands up, and you will not be harmed! You will be paroled in the morning, and allowed to return to your homes – on the condition you give your words as gentlemen not to take up arms again!"

"Go to hell!" One of the Unionists snarled, and the shooting started back up. Most of it was directed at our position, as they was firing in the direction of Duke's voice. I knocked the colonel unceremoniously to the ground and fell beside him, or else we would surely both have been hit. As it was, a musket-ball tore through my overcoat so close to the skin it burned.

"Don't reckon they feel like bein' gentlemen today," I told him. "I reckon they also don't feel like throwin' down their weapons and marchin' out to be shot. Can't say as I blame 'em none."

"You will not be shot!" Duke screamed toward the house at the top of his lungs. "Surrender – you will not be harmed, I swear it!"

Until the Unionists made up their minds, me and the boys occupied ourselves by shooting at the windows. We heared a couple of pain-filled shouts which told us our fire was effective. I sent a couple of the other boys around to the back of the house to set fire to it. One of them was shot dead before he could make it back to safety, but the blaze was set. Before long it was burning real good.

The Union boys decided to convert over to being gentlemen.

"Don't shoot!" One of them hollered. "We're comin' out – don't shoot!"

Three of them straggled out, including Moses Huddleston. We stepped out to meet them.

"Where's your brother?" I demanded of Moses.

"Upstairs. He took a bullet in the chest and fell out of the rafters. He's dead by now. The bullet or the fall either one could finish him."

I grabbed him by the shirt. "Get your ass back into that house and drag him down here – I don't care if he's alive or dead! And any others that's in there, too!"

The Unionists reluctantly returned to the burning house and retrieved their comrades. Three bodies was dragged out into the yard. The first one was dead as could be, his brains leaking out a hole in his head. The second I recognized as the Huddlestons' brother-in-law, a man named Brax Simpson. Simpson had a serious chest wound, but it was not fresh – he was slowly dying from an injury received on one of their raids on Morgan's men.

The third man was Elim Huddleston. He was not moving.

I knelt beside him. I slapped Elim as hard as I could, over and over, until finally he opened his eyes. They stared at me weakly, and without focus.

"You still alive, Elim?" I asked him.

He groaned.

"Good," I said, and I shot him between the eyes.

Brax Simpson, injured as he was, whimpered because he figured he was next. I waved my gun at him, my gaze never leaving the corpse of Elim Huddleston.

"That one layin' yonder can live, die, or grow wings," I said, indicating Simpson. "I don't give a shit. But Elim, ain't no way he was goin' to hell before he looked in my face." I shot Elim again, just because it felt good.

Duke cleared his throat. "You men are our prisoners for the moment," he said. "In the morning, you shall be paroled."

I shook my head as I holstered my weapon. "Stupidest damn thing I ever heared of," I said. "You let these bastards go in the mornin', they'll be back shootin' at us again by nightfall."

"That may well be," Duke said. "But it is the manner in which gentlemen conduct warfare. We are not murdering savages."

"Well, maybe you ain't," I said. "The rest of us sure as hell are. If these fellers ever had the good fortune of capturin' you or me, our throats would be cut in a minute." I grinned at Moses. "Ain't that so?" He didn't answer. I reckon he had cut a Rebel throat or two in his time.

"These men shall not be killed, and that is all there is to it," Duke said, then he marched stiffly away – but not so far away he couldn't keep an eye on me. I reckon his conscience bothered him for turning the other way that one time while me and Scott had them Federals shot.

It puts me in mind, now I think back on it, of some words I am told William Quantrill used when arguing tactics with one of the refined Confederate officials – that war and barbarism are the same, and not two separate things at all. "For twenty years this cloud has been gathering," Quantrill said. "The cloud has burst. Do not condemn the thunderbolt."

I reckon he had the right idea. I could have got along fine with him, and with his boys too – the Youngers, and Frank James and his kid brother, and Bloody Bill Anderson. The Yankees herded Anderson's sister and some female cousins of the Youngers into a jailhouse and then undermined the foundation so it 'accidentally' collapsed and crushed the poor women to death. Their only crime was being related to loyal Southern men. Bloody Bill collected Yankee scalps, they say, had 'em streaming from his saddle. Wish't me and them boys could have rode together, we would surely have raised some Rebel hell. Bloody Bill and Quantrill is both dead now, though, and I doubt the Youngers and Jameses can ever amount to much without them. And we both know where I am.

I leaned in real close to Moses, lest he get to feeling too secure. "As long as you're with us," I said in a low voice, "I reckon you boys can make your selfs useful and lead us to where Rufus Dowdy is holed up."

Tinker Dave would've been better, but I knowed he was too smart to hole up in a house while there was a war on. He would be deep in the woods somewhere. His day would come later.

"Why would we do that?" Moses said.

I touched the knife at my belt. "I was told I ain't supposed to kill y'all, son. I was never told I had to turn y'uns loose with all your parts still attached."

"I know where he's at," one of the men piped up, and I nodded and smiled.

"I figured it might come to ye," I said.

Within an hour we was at the house Dowdy was last known to hide in. The dim glow of the fireplace through the front window was the only light.

LeRoy Reese creeped down and peeped in at the windows. He come back to report that there was two women and a couple of kids in the back of the house – Dowdy's family, most likely – and four men sleeping in the front room.

Duke straightened up. "Then it shall be a simple matter to inform them that they are outnumbered and surrounded."

Reese ignored the colonel, and stepped closer to speak softly in my ear. "One of them horses down yonder I know for a fact belongs to Will Evans."

I immediately drawed out my Bowie knife and set off for the little house on foot. I sensed that Reese and Rains was right behind me, and probably Timmons as well. I heared Duke sputter angrily, but he had the sense not to make too much noise, and to keep an eye on the prisoners to make sure they didn't holler out a warning.

I never slowed down – I strode purposefully in the moonlight, the twelve-inch blade of my knife flashing with each step. The red misty rage was clouding up in my eyes, turning the moonlight to the color of blood.

I kicked open the door. I took a quick glimpse around in the dim firelight as I entered the front room. The four men inside all jerked their heads up from their pillers.

Two of them was sleeping in a bed, the other two on the floor. One of them last two was scrawny as a stray dog, and the second man went to the other extreme – neither one was an Evans, nor anybody else I recognized. The fat one tried to get to his feet. I kicked him hard in the face and sent him sprawling. I stepped right over the mangy one, headed toward the bed.

Both remaining Evans brothers lay there, trying to untangle their selfs from the covers. Will Evans had pulled a revolver from under his piller and was in the act of cocking it.

I leaped through the air like a panther, my knife raised high, right into the bed with them. Will's eyes bulged near out of his skull as his fingers tightened on the trigger.

The knife-arm came down, knocking his gun aside just as he fired - the bullet went into the wall. I grabbed Will's wrist with my free hand, trying to twist the weapon out of it. Mike Evans grabbed me from behind. He had one arm around my throat and the other going for my knife.

Mangy had got up and run out the door – straight into Reese and them, who shot him full of holes. Stout-boy stayed hunkered on the floor, hands over his head, whimpering. Timmons and Reese grabbed him by the feet and pulled him out the door. He screamed all the way.

The women appeared in the doorway from the other room. It was Dowdy's wife and oldest daughter. "Don't be shootin' in my house!" the wife screamed. "I got young'uns in the next room - don't y'uns be shootin' in this house! Rufus ain't here!"

I was only dimly aware of all of this, as I was tangled up in the bed with the two Evanses – all of us struggling and kicking, and Will biting my arm trying to make me turn loose of his gun-hand. He angled his wrist to get a good shot at my head and pulled the trigger a second time - the shot was loud as thunder in the little house, and I heared the ball whistle past my ear and into the wall like his first one had done. Mrs. Dowdy screamed again. If she'd of had a shotgun, I don't doubt that she would've emptied it into all three of us in order to end the danger to her young'uns.

I rammed my head backwards into Mike's face. I heared his nose crunch. This made the second time I had broke it, the first time being with a rock on the day of the camp meeting fight in Fentress County, which seemed like a different lifetime to me now.

Naturally, he let go of my knife-arm when I busted his nose. The second he did, my blade plunged down – with all the strength I could muster into it, all the strength of my hate and frustration – into his brother's chest, where it sank to the hilt. Will Evans gasped and gurgled and dropped his gun. While he was still dying, I jerked the long blade out and swung it around in a powerful roundhouse, driving it into Mike's side.

I squatted atop Mike Evans, my hand at his throat crushing it as I plunged the knife into his gut over and over again. Blood splattered on the walls until they was like the walls of a slaughterhouse. I kept stabbing long after the bastard was dead, and long after the women stopped screaming.

Two years ago I was just a good old boy – just a rough-necked farmer that gambled a little and drank a little, got into a scrap now and then, maybe took a horse or two that I shouldn't have. I was no different than most of my neighbors.

Now my life was in tatters. I was hunted like a dog by my enemies, even as I hunted them – my own brother among them. My other brothers and sisters and my mother I had not seen in ages, and they would no doubt spit in my face if I seen them now. I was sleeping in the woods, come rain or snow. I was a danger to my family when I come near them – and on the rare occasions I risked it, I no longer felt at home. My wife and daughter had been shamed in my absence. Marthy had been driven deeper into the cold shell I had spent years coaxing her out of, the soul smothered out of her, and she was trying to drag our tender daughter into that hell with her.

And it all started with these Evanses, and their brothers, and their damned horse. I was lost in a world of screams and blood, and I could never go home again, not really. I knowed it was also due in large part to the damned Yankees up North who wouldn't just go away and leave us alone – and Lord how I hated them – but for me it had all started at a picnic, with these Evanses.

And so I stabbed them until I didn't have the strength to stab them anymore. I stabbed them until tears rose into my eyes, and sobs choked my throat, until I growled and wailed like a lost, mad wolf

All was silent now, except for my own ragged breathing. The women and children had been rushed away from the grisly scene. The fat man, whose name I learned later was Greenville Murphy, was outside the house with the other prisoners we had taken.

Rains Philpot stood near me. He stood like he was prepared to protect me from anything that might give me threat, even if it was the Devil his self.

Colonel Basil Duke stood in the doorway. He watched, terror stamped on his face, as I stepped off the bed and stood in the flickering fire-shadows. I held the knife loosely at my side. Red gore dripped off it and spattered the floor. Blood covered my face – it matted my hair.

"Dear God," Colonel Duke managed to gasp. "Dear God in Heaven."

"Hell," I answered, my voice a hoarse croak. "God is in Heaven. We're in Hell."

I brushed past him on my way out the door, leaving a bloody smudge on his gray sleeve.

"We're all in Hell."
Rains quietly walked out behind me.

Chapter 33

General Morgan and the rest returned from their raid a few days into the new year. They set up camp at Lake Sligo, a few miles from DeKalb County's seat at Smithville. I brung my boys along with Colonel Duke and his few troops – although I reckon officially it was them that was bringing me – and met up with the main body.

Old Basil, he give me a snooty look and pulled off from us soon as we got there. He hopped off his horse, leaving a sergeant to tend to it, and marched away. He walked so fast his saber beat agin his leg like a flutterwheel blowing in the wind. I'd be surprised if he didn't get a bruise from it. I knowed right where he was going, and I smiled grimly to myself

He was gone looking for his brother-in-law the general, to chaw on his ear about what a savage bastard I am, and how I'm liable to give killing folks a bad name.

I didn't give a shit.

I told the boys to take their ease, because I figured they deserved it. Me and Rains walked off, and it wasn't long before we found Scott. We shook hands and clapped one t'other on the shoulder and laughed a goodly bit.

"How did y'uns do?" I asked him. "Did ye give 'em Rebel hell?"

Scott let out a breath that was half-laugh and half-sigh. I noticed for the first time how tired and gaunt he seemed. There was bags under his eyes, and he looked a mite thinner than he had when I seen him last.

"We done good," he said. "I'd be sorry as hell if we hadn't of done good, wore out as I am. We rode about five hundred miles, all told. Most of it with sleet in our beards."

"What did y'uns get done?"

"Tore up about twenty miles track. Burnt four bridges. Ain't no tellin' how much Yankee supplies we destroyed."

I nodded, and grunted lowly. It was a grunt that told, in one sound, of my approval – and that I understood bow rough it had been, and that I regretted I had not endured it with him.

"I hear you fellers have been busy your own selves," Scott said. "I hear Elim Huddleston is in Hell, if the devil ain't too particular to have him."

I spat, which was all the comment I had concerning the life and death of Elim Huddleston.

"I hear you give him plenty of company, too," Scott continued.

Rains smiled. "You shore do hear a lot, Cap'n, to of been up in Kentucky for two weeks."

Scott chuckled. "Good news travels fast, like they say."

"I ain't for certain it was good news to old Basil," I said. "I reckon that, far as he's concerned, the whole Rebel and Yankee armies ought to take turns bein' one t'other's prisoners ever' other day. Maybe have a picnic together or somethin' on Saturdays. That would most likely be the civilized way of doin' things."

Scott laughed. Rains didn't laugh, both because he's a little on the slow side when it comes to catchin' a joke, and because he had been there and seen the blood drainin' out of Basil's face in anger; he knowed that it was no laughing matter.

A regular captain walked stiffly up to us. He looked like he had put enough starch in his uniform to do a whole division. I recognized him as Morgan's adjutant.

"Gentlemen," he said, "the general wishes to see you in his tent."

"All right," I said. "Captain Bledsoe, do you know the location of the general's tent?"

Scott grinned. "Captain Ferguson, I know it well. Shall we?"

"I reckon we should." I glanced at Rains. "Come along, Sergeant," I told him. Rains looked over his shoulder, to see if someone else had walked up behind him. Seeing that no one had, he figured out I was talking to him, and he trotted into step behind us as we walked toward what I reckoned was the right direction.

The captain cleared his throat nervously. "I beg your pardon," he said, "but General Morgan only told me to fetch Captain Ferguson and Captain Bledsoe."

"You mean Captain Bledsoe and Captain Ferguson, I believe," Scott said with a stern voice which the other man couldn't quite peg as serious or joshing.

"That's what I said, Captain Bledsoe and Captain Ferguson." It was my turn to stare him down. He sort of wilted a little.

"Sergeant Philpot here," I told him, "is my adjutant." I could hear Rains's gulp of surprise. "Not to mention my personal secretary. He goes ever'where I go – for record-keepin' purposes."

"Ah, I see," the man said. "Very, um, very well."

"Good day, Captain," Scott told him, and we resumed our walk.

"Champ," Rains whispered. Then, when I didn't say anything in reply, he hissed at me and said again, a little louder, "Champ!"

"What's on your mind, Rains?" I said, not looking back.

"Well, hellfire, Champ. You know good and well I cain't write my own name, never mind keep no dern records and sich."

"I know."

"Then how come ye to make me a adju – a adjective?"

"Didn't see where it could hurt none," I said. "I had to tell him somethin' as to why you was taggin' along. I couldn't very well tell him you was my conscience; after all, he just wouldn't understand. Besides which, you've been doin' a piss-pore job at it lately."

"Oh," he said, and studied on it a few seconds. I could tell it hurt his feelings a little bit for me to say he had failed me at something, even when I said it as a joke, and even when he didn't know what the hell I was talking about anyways.

"Well," said Rains, "why do ye have me comin' with ye?"

"Because you're my adjutant," I said, as if it should be obvious. "If'n me and Scott aim to get these folks like Basil Duke to take us serious, we've got to come up with a adjutant or two apiece."

We walked a little further, and then Rains spoke again. "Hey Champ."

"What is it now?"

"I never knowed I was ary sergeant."

"Well, I reckon ye are. A sergeant, or a loo-tenant. Or a corporal. Or somethin'. Ye have to be, else I wouldn't never of made ye ary adjutant."

"Oh," he said yet again, but this time he said it like he finally understood. That almost made me laugh out loud, as there wasn't anything for him to understand – I was just making things up as I talked.

"How do ye have him wrote down in your muster roll?" Scott asked, greatly amused his own self

That question made me pause. Muster roll. I was supposed to have drawed one of them up a long time ago, but I had never give no more thought to it. It occurred to me I might need me a adjutant or a secretary for real. With Rains in the position that might pose a problem or two, as he couldn't write his own name. Knowing his nature as I did, I realized that - except for the reading and writing part – he would probably do a good job at it. Rains was good at taking care of little details, once you nudged him in the right direction. He would've been right good at butlerin', now that I study on it, maybe in some of these fancy Nashville houses. Onliest thing that might hold him back is that he don't wash often enough. That, and the fact that most of your colored house servants acts and looks more dignified than he does, which would make it stiff competition for him to get a butlering job.

"I done forgot how he's wrote down," I said in response to Scott's question about the muster roll. Then I put it out of my mind, and didn't give no further thought to muster rolls until them federal lawyers brung it up at my trial.

Morgan sat waiting in his tent, at one of them folding card-tables – a nice one, too, I reckon it must have been donated by one of the locals, as I doubt he would tote something like that around with him. But you don't never know, with generals.

A mug of steaming coffee sat at his elbow. He had a thin cigar in his mouth, and was wearing a wry smile. Colonel Duke sat nearby – his face was all soured up. He looked like somebody had pissed in his oatmeal, and then hadn't even bothered to stir it up.

"Come in, gentlemen," Morgan said, and Duke winced at the idea of the word being applied to such as us.

"Good mornin', General," I said. "I hear y'uns done right well up yonder."

"Damn right we did," he said, and the amused smile grew into the big grin of a proud child. "And next time we'll do even better. I hope you'll be able to join us then."

"Me too, sir," I said. My voice was grim, because it had occurred to me that my brother Jim would likely stay away from our old stomping grounds, knowing I had done caught everyone but him. I was going to have to range further if I hoped to find him.

"Part of the reason for our success, though," Morgan continued, the grin melting, "was that you were down here protecting our rear and keeping the Yankee irregulars occupied." Now his face was every bit as grim as mine. "As I understand it, you gave them plenty to think about." He moved his head to include Duke in the statement.

"We done our best to," I said.

Morgan nodded. "You keep it up. You too, Captain Bledsoe. Your service to the South is invaluable."

Duke bristled, but did not seem surprised. His spine stiffened a bit.

"Thank you, General," I said, and Scott echoed my words soon as I started speaking them. Rains was silent – he was most likely trying to figure out what an 'adjective's' role was in proceedings like this.

Duke cleared his throat. It was a habit he had whenever speaking in my presence. I'm liable to of give the poor old boy consumption, or something.

"General," he said, maintaining his protocol even when talking to his brother-in-law. "General, I must protest. The behavior of these men, particularly Captain Ferguson, has been nothing short of reprehensible."

Morgan nodded slowly, like he had expected this to be coming. "Captain Ferguson's behavior is such," he said, "that loyal Southerners love him and traitors have nightmares about waking up to find him standing at the foot of their bed. When we speak of reprehensible, let's not forget to mention the good citizens murdered in their fields by Elim Huddleston and Rufus Dowdy. Let's not forget the Confederate troopers shot dead whilst trying to surrender."

That had happened to one of Morgan's lieutenants not long before. The general had turned his head when the man's comrades refused to take any prisoners at the next engagement.

"So long as Captain Ferguson or Captain Bledsoe do not take it into their minds to burn Jamestown, Colonel, it is not for me to question their methods."

"We'll be sure to clear it with you first, sir," Bledsoe joked.

Now, you might think that last exchange was a reference to what Quantrill done at Lawrence, Kansas. I know you've heared plenty about it – how he burned the town to the ground, and killed every adult male. This was because Lawrence was the home base of the Union guerillas that fought agin him.

It wasn't a reference to that. The sack of Lawrence wouldn't be for two or three months yet. Hell, even I wouldn't do such as that. There was still a few loyal men in Jimtown, after all, and in every other town in Eastern Tennessee and Kentucky.

"Perhaps so," Duke said. His voice reflected the knowledge that he was beat, he just didn't want to let up yet. "But there is something else which you have to consider."

Morgan lifted an eyebrow. "Yes?"

"The people love you. The enemy respects you. General Bragg is perhaps a tad jealous of you." His eyes flickered over the rest of us, uncomfortable, knowing he shouldn't be talking like this in front of subordinates.

"Go on."

Duke cleared his throat again.

"You've opened this can of worms," Morgan continued. "You might just as well pour them all out."

It was Duke's turn to nod. "Very well. We know that Wheeler's division is going to be split into two wings. Everyone assumes you'll be in command of one, perhaps even promoted to Major-General. The decision is Bragg's. If our scouts were to precipitate some action which created a scandal, you would be held responsible. Your rivals would make sure of it."

Morgan's face went slack. He apparently hadn't thought that far ahead. His expression reminded me of a young boy that had been playing hooky, thinking about nothing except how good the fishing was, who suddenly realized he had been seen by a neighbor who might or might not tell his pa.

"The shooting of prisoners, for example," Duke continued, for he knowed that he was on to something and he planned to push it as far as he could. "Or of enemy soldiers attempting to surrender."

Just when it looked like the general was about to be swayed, Scott spoke up.

"Soldiers," he said. "To me, that means regular troops."

Duke wrinkled his nose. "I should think it goes without saying that we don't want to go around shooting private citizens in the streets. Or in their homes."

"Beggin' the general's pardon," I said, "and the colonel's too – but I ain't stupid. I know the difference between regular Union troops and local guerillas. There is a difference."

"Granted," said Morgan, clearly hoping I was going to give him a way out. "But why don't you explain it to us."

"I ain't got nothin' personal agin your average Yankee soldier," I said. "Me and him is on opposite sides, and it's my sworn duty to kill him if we're in combat.

"But your guerilla, now, he's a different animal. He is from these mountains, and in these mountains he knows who of his neighbors is loyal. And where they live. If'n we turn him loose today, he's gonna be waitin' on us when we go home on leave. He's gonna bushwhack us – individual-like – ary chance't he gets. There's certain ones of 'em that I know have done such. There's certain ones that have publicly swore to get at me any way they can."

I made myself stop for a minute and take a deep breath. My voice had been rising the longer I spoke. I didn't figure it was in my best interests to holler at General Morgan, or at Colonel Duke either one.

"There's even a danger of 'em comin' into our homes while our duty takes us away," I said, more softly than before. "Sich things has been known to happen. I've heared of cases."

I paused again. Some of the color had drained out of Duke's face, and he stared at his own feet. I noticed that none of the other'ns was looking me in the face, neither, not even Rains. They all knowed what had happened in my house. It shamed me that they did.

Nobody spoke. I figured I might as well go ahead on and cap it off.

"If I was to capture any regular federals, or if anybody under my command did, they'd be secure in my hands. They'll live to go home safe and sound to New Jersey, or wherever the hell it is Yankees come from. Even the ones that've joined up here in Tennessee or Kentucky.

"But these other bastards, now, I've been known to kill them for the public good. Ones in blue uniforms included. If they're here on leave and runnin' with bushwhackers, then they're here for the purpose of bein' bushwhackers their own selves. I figure they ought to be treated the same as they treat us."

I stared direct at Basil Duke. "I have also been known to preserve people prisoner, and even to let 'em go. It all depends on what I know about 'em. Their politics don't matter too much to me. I act honorably towards honorable men. Wild dogs and sons-of-bitches I shoot. I reckon that's all I got to say."

Scott stepped a little closer to me so that we was even, side-by-side. "Everything that Captain Ferguson said, I stand by it my own self"

Morgan nodded, and sighed. "All right, men. Then I'll tell you where I stand." He glanced at his brother-in-law. "All of you. If anyone attached to command from here out, whether trooper or scout, should kill any federal soldier in uniform – met in combat – after he has offered an honorable surrender, the consequences will be the most severe imaginable. On the other hand, what you irregulars do to one another is your own business – or at least, none of mine. It's out of my purview. So I will trust you to continue acting on your own discretion in such matters. It has worked well so far."

He was sure enough figuring out how to work this "general" business. He was telling us to keep on doing like we've been doing, which made the public – the loyal ones – happy. But if the public or the higher officers started getting unhappy, or if me or Scott was to go too far, it would be our ass in the bear-trap and not his. That suited me fine.

Duke acted like he was about to protest again. I reckon being married to your commander's sister gives a feller a extry ration of nerve. He never got the chance to say nothing, though, because Morgan's adjutant appeared at the tent-flap with a dispatch in his hand. Morgan waved the man in, and looked at the paper.

Rains watched the adjutant leave, trying to press into his mind how the feller carried his self, just in case I was serious about expecting it of him.

"Damn," Morgan said under his breath, His face was twisted with shock, turning quickly into rage. "Damn, damn! Damn!"

"What is it?" Basil demanded.

"It's from General Bragg. While he had us and Wheeler tearing up railroad tracks, Rosecrans moved on him at Stone's River. He's boasting about how many Yankees he killed on his retreat." Morgan looked up, his jaw quivering with pain and anger.

"We've lost Murfreesboro."

All was silent. We was all thinking the same thing – a few railroads tore up is a useful thing, but it might have been a hell of a lot more useful if'n all of us and General Wheeler's bunch had been at Stone's River.

"I had just sent Mattie home to her folks when we left," the general said in a dull voice. "Because I thought it was safe. Now she's stuck there again."

Duke put his arm on the table, and stopped just short of touching Morgan. "What else does it say, John?"

"Tells us to set up camp for winter. At McMinnville – that's just forty miles or so from Murfreesboro."

"Shall I have the men get ready to move?" Duke asked. His face was much gentler than it had been when his only thought was how to stop me from being an embarrassment to civilized folks. Now his features showed only his worry – worry over his commander, and worry over what this news would mean for his country.

Morgan nodded. "Yes. Take care of it, please."

Duke was on his feet at once, and brushing past us. Morgan waved a hand in our direction, but spared us no glance.

"You men can go too," he said. "But stay close – I may need you soon."

"Yes sir," Scott said. We all three turned to leave. I cast a glance over my shoulder – the general sat slumped over his table, hand clenched into a fist, like he was praying for someone to strike out at.

I knowed the feeling.

Chapter 34

"Captain, are you willing to take on a private mission?"

I looked at Morgan, a little taken aback. He had invited me and Scott back to his tent the day after we had got the news about Murfreesboro.

"Hell, General," I said, trying not to laugh at the question. "You know me – I'm willin' to take on damn near anything."

"Yes," he replied, and a twinkle briefly lit in his eye. "But this is something – outside of official channels."

"I can't think of many things I've ever done that was inside official channels, sir."

"What about you, Captain Bledsoe?"

"You can count on me, sir," Scott said. "Whatever it is."

"You haven't even heard the nature of the mission."

"Don't have to, sir. Me and Champ, we can handle it."

Morgan nodded, pleased. He had expected no less. Everybody that rode with John Hunt Morgan was like that, you see – ary one of us would have follered him straight into the gates of hell without a backward glance, and we wouldn't even have considered the possibility that the Devil might come out on top. We all knowed Morgan could never be wrong, and that his Raiders could never be beat.

There was a day coming, not too far off, when a good many of them boys – and Morgan his own self – would pay dearly for that kind of thinking. If you was to have told them that ahead of time, though, I doubt a single one would have done things any different. Especially the general.

Hell, I reckon the same thing could be said for the whole South – we was cocky, and we was proud, and by God the notion of defeat never entered into our minds. Not even now – with the War over – we don't quite believe it. I reckon you've heared that song that's started going around here lately, *I Am A Good Old Rebel*. That's us, brother. *I won't apologize for what I was, and what I am; I won't be Reconstructed, I do not give a damn.* Fifty years from now there'll be old Rebels still singing that tune, and they'll mean every word. Every damned word.

Morgan drummed his fingers on his little card-table-turned-desk. It was just the three of us in there. "I have three other men picked out and ready for this mission – volunteers like yourselves. I believe a small squad has a greater chance of success. Further, this is a – personal matter. I won't risk my entire command for my own selfish purposes. So there will be six of us – the six I have deemed the best."

Scott's eyebrow went up. "You're goin', sir? On such a dangerous mission, with so little protection?"

Morgan smiled. "The six best," he repeated.

"Damn," I said. "What are we fixin' to do, sneak into the White House and twist Abe Lincoln's pecker?"

Morgan laughed himself breathless. "Lord," he finally managed to say. "I wonder how they'd describe that in the newspapers?" He had another fit of chuckles. Fact is, I'm sorry I won't be around to see how you put it.

"No, Champ," he said, "I plan nothing that dramatic. I merely intend to slip across enemy lines into Murfreesboro, and liberate my wife."

Scott whistled. "Rosecrans has his whole army quartered there."

"That's the beauty of it," Morgan said. "It's the last thing anyone would expect – even from us."

"What does Colonel Duke think of this plan?" I said.

"Colonel Duke knows nothing about it," the general said. "Nor shall he, until we are well on our way. I intend to leave sealed orders to be opened later, with instructions on what to do in the event we don't return."

He had another chuckle. "Basil would definitely not approve."

"No sir, I reckon he wouldn't," Scott said.

I privately felt that Basil would not approve of corn shucks in a outhouse, but I managed to hold my tongue.

Morgan's other three men joined up with us just before dawn. We mounted up and rode west. We wore Union overcoats over our Confederate colors – I say colors instead of uniforms, because me and Scott and all our boys never had ary uniforms as such. Just whatever gray we could cobble together, mixed with every other color under the sun. Morgan had traded his usual ostrich-plumed headgear for a simple black slouch hat, the kind I always wore.

The blue overcoats meant that, if caught, we would be executed as spies. This was business-as-usual for me and Scott, but it was an unheared of risk for the general.

We was barely outside of camp when a rider approached from our rear. Morgaan reined up his horse in annoyed disgust.

Our uninvited guest soon scooped off his hat and hollered out to us. We all recognized him right off.

"Basil!" Morgan cried. "What the hell do you think you're doing?"

Duke reined up beside us. "I might ask you the same question, John," he said. "But I think we all know exactly what we're doing."

He was wearing the same sort of blue coat the rest of us had. He saw us staring at it, and shrugged.

"When I determined from the quartermaster that several of these captured coats were missing," he said, "I thought perhaps I might need one, as well."

"Then you aren't here to try talking me out of my foolishness?" Morgan said.

"No, I intend to join you in it. It would have been easier had I been in on the plan from the beginning, you know."

Morgan paused, biting his lip, obviously searching for words. Duke held up a hand, palm outward, as if to stifle the general's thought before it could be expressed.

"I know what you're thinking," Duke said. "You have obviously picked your squad well – only the best. You fear I will be a liability."

Morgan just looked at him sadly. He couldn't bring himself to wound his friend's pride, even by muttering a simple "yes" to his question.

"I will pull my weight," the colonel said stiffly. "You are my commander, and my friend. Mattie is my sister-in-law, even though once removed. By God, you will not go without me. Sir."

Morgan sighed. "It saddens me that you would open your orders early, colonel, despite my command not to."

"Those orders rest on your desk," Duke replied, "still sealed. I don't need orders to tell me what you're up to, John. I know you."

"We've wasted enough time," the general said. "Let's ride."

We left DeKalb County behind us, on a direct course for Murfreesboro.

~ ~ * ~ ~

For awhile there, I thought we was going to get away with it clean. For one thing, it was a sorry-ass day to be taking a ride – rain drizzled down on us the whole time, dripping off our hats and down our beards. It wasn't a driving rain, but was just hard enough to cause misery instead of refreshment – not quite frozen, but cold as hell. You know the kind of rain I mean. When you feel that kind of rain you head into the house, most likely, and leave the outside world 'til a more agreeable day.

That's what most folks in Middle Tennessee was doing that day, too. At least, them was who had good sense and no pressing duty. Fact is, a good part of them who had pressing duties must have let good sense get the upper hand, and they went on inside too. We never seen ary a soul, all day long.

We did see a few deer, and all of us would surely have loved to bring one or two down and make us a better dinner than what we carried in our sacks. Maybe you like cold cornbread – try it sometime when it's damp with cold rain and horse sweat, old hoss, and tell me what you think about it then.

But we was traveling fast and light. We couldn't take no time to dress out ary deer, nor could we carry any meat with us – and we didn't dare attract any attention with gunfire. Not to mention it would be next to impossible to get up enough of a fire to cook the blamed venison with if we had it, the weather being like it was.

All we could do was watch them deer amble down the field and lick our lips, and dream. I personally was hoping maybe we could kill a few Yankees that had brung boxed lunches with them.

One thing you don't hear folks talk much about, when they're telling old war stories, is the hunger. Sometimes they was plenty of food to be had, you just didn't have time to eat none of it on account of you was too busy trying not to be shot or gutted to death. Other times you didn't have nary a bite, and you had all the time in the world to set and think about it.

This was especially true later on in the war, when the whole South had been tore all to hell. Men was too busy fighting to plant crops. Them that did, they had them took away by first one side and then the other, 'til there wasn't anything left. Folks from up in Io-way and Michigan and New England, they had their people back home growing food for them and carrying on life as usual. It made me want to kill a couple of extry Yankees every day just out of pure spite, so they wouldn't be able to go home and eat good. Bastards.

Some fellers got to where they would chaw on their belts, or suck on rocks. Me, I'd set and dream about biscuits all broke open and steaming, and runny eggs, sawmill gravy and pork chops and grits with honey. The memory of them tastes settled down into my gut, and was enough to quiet my belly for a spell.

Them was the kind of thoughts running through my mind as we rode through Cannon County. Not was I going to get shot today, but was I going to eat good tomorrow or the day after that.

It was well past dark when we entered Rutherford County and approached Murfreesboro. The cold and wet got worse, funny enough, when we swum our horses across the river. We started seeing folks then, all right – and most of them was dressed in uniforms. It was too dark to see many details. They wasn't Confederate uniforms, though, and somehow I don't think they was Mexicans or wandering Frenchmen. We was passing right through enemy lines.

Nobody seemed to pay us too much mind, and that suited me fine. I like to fight Yankees, and it did sure enough aggravate me that this was ground we had held a month ago – but that didn't mean I was raring to take on a thousand of them at a time. They might well have qualified as Philistines, but I ain't no Samson on my best day. My wife has kindly hinted around now and then that I might have the jawbone of an ass, but I think she means something else by it

The thought struck me that this kind of warring felt different to me than what I had been doing the past couple of years. If I had been in charge of this little company on my home grounds, and I happened to run across a few dozen federal troops or Home Guards, I have no doubt I would've ordered a quick charge in amongst them. We would have killed a few – having the element of surprise – and then high-tailed it into the brush, daring them to follow. If they had, we would've picked them off one by one. If my brother Jim or some of my personal enemies was amongst them, I would've jumped right into the middle of the bunch all by my lonesome and to hell with what happened next.

Nowadays I was engaging in actions agin enemies I didn't know personal. The fighting was planned, and it was all based on military necessity and politics. I had never been one to fight over politics before, but I was kind of getting used to it. It was as much luck as anything else that had put me on the side I was on, but in time I had come to believe we was right – and there's such a thing as a cause that's worth fighting and even dying for, a notion I would have took to be foolish before all of this started. But because I didn't take it personal, like I had most of my earlier fights, I was able to approach it with a more level head.

In other words, I was hoping like hell that nobody figured out who we was.

We rode right into town, and up the muddy streets 'til we reached the house where Mattie was staying with her sister. Morgan hopped out of the saddle, giving the reins over to one of his men, and bounded up the steps and onto the front porch. He knocked on the door, taking care not to be loud enough to rouse the neighbors.

A young lady came to the door. She wore a look that would curdle fresh milk – then the visitor swooped off his hat and flashed one of his boyish grins, and she almost cried out in joy at the sight of her beloved brother-in-law. He made a quick stifling gesture, whispered briefly, and she rushed him inside.

The rest of us stayed put. We all glanced around from time to time, fidgety, watching for patrols. One plump citizen, umbrella protecting his fine clothes and fancy hat from the rain, strolled up to us. He looked into my face, his own features smug.

"Gentlemen," he said, "I just want you to know something. I came out into the elements just so I could speak with you."

I reckon he wanted me to say something, but I just stared at him. He cleared his throat.

"This town is full of traitors," he said, "as you well know. But I wanted you to be aware also that there are plenty of loyal Americans, who are happy to see the Stars and Stripes flying above our streets, and who appreciate all your sacrifices. God bless the Republic, sir!"

Basil was clearly insulted the man had spoke to me instead of to him – that, without rank or insignia to go by, anyone would assume I was a leader instead of him. He shifted in his saddle and huffed softly.

My head wasn't swelled up by it none. Fact is, the notion had flashed across my mind that I'd be doing the whole world a favor if I cut this dumb bastard's throat. Scott must have caught my look, because he broke in real quick-like. I was a little irritated by his lack of faith in me. Hell, I wasn't fixing to actually do it, I don't think.

"We're much obliged to you sir," he said, doing his best to hide his accent.

"Please," the man answered, "come into my home and have some coffee – to warm your bones on this chilly night."

"We dare not, kind sir," Basil said. "We are keeping an eye out for rebels and spies." The colonel winked. "Perhaps if we're lucky we'll catch John Morgan himself."

"I doubt that, the coward," the man said.

"Please, sir," Basil said with a smile. "Return to your home before you catch your death."

I spat a stream of tobacco – not right toward the man, but I had judged the wind right and the juice spattered all over his shiny shoes.

"Yeah," I said. "Thank ye."

Old Mister Stars-and-Stripes looks down, his cheeks flushing. He cleared his throat again. I reckon folks like him and Basil, who are prone to speechifying, needs to keep their windpipes good and open.

"Good night, gentlemen," he said, "and God bless you."

He rushed down the street towards his own house – the rain was picking up – and missed the rare treat of seeing the cowardly General Morgan skipping down the front steps with his eager bride.

Mattie had been supplied with a Yankee greatcoat and a slouch hat all of her own, and her husband helped lift her into the saddle of a spare horse. I believe the gal was wearing britches, which shows just how serious she was about leaving town.

"Any trouble?" Morgan said.

"No," said Duke. "But we know of a neighbor Mattie's family should keep an eye on."

Curiosity showed in Morgan's features.

"Don't worry," I told him. "By now he's probably sat his fat ass in front of the fireplace and started singing the Battle-Hymn of the Republic to his dog. Poor animal."

"Let's ride," Morgan said, and we rode.

Morgan wasn't of a mind to swim our horses across Stone's River, like we had done on our way in. I reckon he didn't want Miss Mattie to get no wetter then necessary. Besides, the horses was beginning to get a little skittish – the rain was now accompanied by thunder and an occasional flash of lightning.

He decided we would use the ferry, instead. We rode right up to the pilot, and Morgan told him we had to use his ferry for pressing government business. The pore feller had probably long since learned better than to ask anybody in uniform for fare money - he just sighed and cowered down in his slicker, and set off into the elements.

We had no sooner disembarked on the other side than a squad of Union cavalrymen approached us. There was about twenty of them, led by a lieutenant.

"You men must be lost," the lieutenant said. "We're patrolling this sector."

"Patrols are doubled tonight," Morgan answered. "Weather like this is perfect for saboteurs to prowl around in."

"I wasn't informed."

"Since when do generals let regular folks know what's going on?" Morgan said. "They usually don't know themselves from one minute to the next."

The lieutenant laughed in agreement, and it looked like he was going to let us pass. Then several things went wrong all at the same time. I reckon God must have been having another slow day, and needed a diversion.

A big gust of wind come up and made Basil's overcoat flap completely open, at the very moment that the biggest lightning flash of the storm lit up the sky.

That lieutenant stared, wide-eyed, for a couple of seconds at the gray uniform and colonel's insignia which showed from under Basil's coat. Then the lieutenant clawed for the revolver at his hip. Morgan was faster, and fired a ball into the man's chest. We spurred our horses and charged through the Yankees. They was slow, but they wasn't dead, so pretty soon the air was hot with gunfire.

No commands was needed. We all knowed our reason for being there. We closed ranks behind the Morgans to take the brunt of the fire, and to keep Mattie as safe as possible. One of our boys, a sergeant named Phelps, took a bullet through the arm. He grunted and dropped his sidearm, but he never slowed down.

Basil Duke had his horse shot from under him. He was throwed hard into the mud, and sat there dazed for a few seconds. There was three of the Yankees who, instead of setting in the saddle firing their rifles at us or even dismounting and shooting over their horses' backs like some of their comrades, had done took to chasing after us. I could see that they would be on top of old Basil in seconds.

I didn't have time for any committee meetings. I wheeled my black mare around and laid the spurs to her. I drawed out my revolver and shot the lead Yankee smack in the forehead. I was fixing to do the same for his partners – and their intentions towards me was none too friendly neither, as I felt a bullet tug at my nice warm Yankee overcoat.

All my gun did was snap. Rainy weather is hell on black powder, I don't know if you educated folks are aware of that or not. Half our enemies was having the same trouble, which explains why we didn't take much worse casualties than we did. I was lucky to have got one shot out of the thing, and that was because the chamber was in the firing position and wasn't exposed.

Basil had come to himself. He come running straight at me and tossed his saber up in the air. I grabbed it, galloped past him, and lit into the two Yankees. Off in the distance I seen the other'ns was mounting up to give chase to us as well.

One Yankee shot his pistol at me, and the ball whistled past my ear. I rode right betwixt them and swung that sword with all my might – damn if I didn't take that old boy's head clean off. The other feller lunged his saber at me like he was aiming to stick me with it. I swung down, backhanded, to deflect his blade – then I ran my own up into his guts.

Them other Yanks was drawing close. I spun around and rode like hell. I paused long enough to lift Basil up behind me. He held on for dear life – I don't reckon he had ever been so happy to see a damn barbarian in his whole life.

Scoff and a couple of the other boys had fell back, and they unleashed a rifle volley at our pursuers which made them stop and have a quick thought about all the beautiful things in life. We got away.

Old Basil, he was a changed man when we got back to Smithville – at least where I was concerned. I was now the greatest tool for glory ever produced by the Confederacy. I have to admit, he was raised up a notch in my estimation, too – he might not be the best fighter in the world, but he had the guts and the loyalty to be in the thick of things anyway. I figured I could put up with his tight-assed ways. He made that saber a gift to me, which was fine, because them things comes in damn handy. Especially when it's raining.

Morgan moved his camp to McMinnville, as he had been directed, and set his wife up there with a local family. He took the rest of the winter off from campaigning.

"He sure does love that little gal," I told Scott one day, not long after our little adventure. For some reason seeing the two of them put me in mind, not of me and Marthy, but of me and my first wife – who had been so full of life and passion. It made me feel sort of warm and achey, both at the same time.

"He does that," Scott replied, his voice sober.

"What's wrong with you, hoss?" I asked him. "Don't you approve of true love, and sich?"

"He loves her too much," Scott said, his voice soft so no one else would hear. "Too much for wartime, anyways. She's gonna get him killed one of these days, or else a lot of good men who follow him. That, or he'll spend so much time lookin' after her he forgets to fight, and it'll cost him his command."

A lot of folks had been whispering stuff like that lately, but I hadn't expected it of Scott Bledsoe.

"You need to get you a woman, Scott," I told him. "You're too serious all the time."

"I need to win this damn war, that's what I need," he said. "So it'll be safe for me to have a woman, one of these days."

"All right, then," I told him. "In that case, just have some whiskey. And one of these ceegars we liberated last week – they're damn good."

I shoved the bottle at him, and he pulled from it. We sat together under a big pine tree. The smoke and the whiskey vapors mixed together with the smell of the pine needles in the cold air, and blended into the smell of brotherhood and friendship. I realized then that was all some men could ever expect out of this life - and that was all right, because in some ways it was more real than anything else a man ever knows.

Chapter 35

"How come ye don't go home and see your family, Champ?"

I was lighting a cigarette. I looked up from the flame and stared at Rains through the smoke.

"I will," I said.

"Oh," Rains replied, and nodded.

It was just the two of us, in the woods at England's Cove – not too far from the Calfkiller. Damn cold, I huddled close to the campfire. It was mid-morning, and I could done tell I wasn't likely to get no warmer today, unless I set fire to my clothes. I had sent all my boys home for a week or so, with directions to meet back at the Cove come the first day of February.

"Why don't you go home, Rains?"

"What – to my house, ye mean?"

"Well, yeah, that's what folks generally mean when they say 'go home'."

"That old shack has probably fell to pieces and growed over with brambles by now, I reckon. I ain't got no folks there to keep it up fer me. Just my Uncle Rafer, and he's been drunk for thirty years. I ain't got no folks nowheres, really, not since my ma got took with the consumption and my brother got kicked in the head by that hoss. You know that, Champ."

"I know."

I puffed at the cigarette, trying to make it last – the cold made my fingers too numb to roll another one for awhile. I wished I had some more of them cigars, or that I carried a pipe with me.

I did have a bottle of whiskey I took a nip from now and again, to warm my gullet, but I couldn't afford to go overboard with it. If I got drunk, my enemies might come up on me. Besides that, if I passed out I didn't trust Rains not to just sit there and watch me freeze to death, or roll over into the fire. That's the problem with consciences, I reckon, whether they're the kind that's in your head or the kind that rides around with you. They talk a lot, but you can't count on them to actually do much.

"You 'member that hoss, Champ. He was spotted all over, but his hind-end was all black. Kicked like hell."

"I remember."

He stared into the fire. "I reckon my home is wherever you're at, Champ."

"Yeah," I said softly. "I reckon so."

"You wantin' to get shed of me?"

I smiled. "No, Rains."

"Sometimes I think you're tryin' to get shed of ever'body."

"Sometimes it crosses my mind," I said. "But I reckon you talkin' is like the trees rustlin'. The world wouldn't seem natural without it."

Rains smiled, pleased at that thought. Then he said, "You don't seem as mad as ye was, Champ."

"I wasn't mad. I was just tryin' to light my damn smoke."

"I don't mean just now. I mean all the time. You seem sort of blue here lately."

I grunted, but didn't answer him. I hadn't give it much thought. Maybe there was something to what he said.

There was a certain number of men I had set out to kill, and I had killed them all but one – my own brother. I wanted to catch him, and then again I didn't. Once I killed him it seemed like there wouldn't be anything left. Hate had been blazing in me for so long that maybe nothing was left but ashy coals.

"Know what I think?" said Rains.

"No, but you're fixin' to tell me."

"I think you don't want to go home, because Marthy might not like it that you ain't so mad anymore. On account of she's always gonna be mad."

"You think too much."

"Ann don't care about that none, though," he continued, as if I had not spoken at all. "She misses ye. She'd be happy to have ye there, no matter what ye feel like."

I tossed the cigarette butt into the fire.

"I just want it to be over, Rains. I just want it to be over."

He nodded. I knowed he did too – no matter what the end would be.

I stood up and stretched. "Let's go home, Rains. I'm hungry."

He jumped to his feet. "Me too, Champ. I'm starvin'."

~ ~ * ~ ~

Marthy smiled with her eyes, but her mouth was forced down into a scowl. A stranger to her would never have known, nor even suspicioned, that the scowl was not real.

"Well, well," she said, hands on her hips and her form filling the doorway, forcing me and Rains to stand on the porch and wait to be let inside. "Look what's come draggin' into White County," she continued, "lookin' like two cats left out in a storm."

I stood, arms folded across my chest, staring at her. I felt the twinkle growing in my own eye.

"Ain't y'uns got nothin' to say for yourselves?" she asked.

"Howdy, Miz Ferguson," Rains said, trying his best to muster a polite smile even though his mouth was about froze shut. After a pause, he added, "Sure enough is cold this time of year, ain't it."

"Depends on where a body is at," Marthy replied. "I find it downright cozy, here in the house."

I moved forward. "Step aside, woman," I told her. "The man of the house is home."

"Man of the house, my foot," she said, but she stepped aside.

The warm air hit me, and it felt like the loving breath of God Almighty. Leastways, from what I hear. A much hotter and less comfortable air than that is bound to be hitting me here before long, I reckon.

Ann looked up from her sewing. Her face was lit up brighter and warmer than the fireplace she sat beside. She stood up, not even setting aside her needlework, and I scooped her into my arms. I swung her around, me laughing and her giggling, and she kept squealing out, "Daddy! Daddy!"

"Lord bless," Marthy said. "Y'uns is gonna break somethin' in here in a minute."

I let go of my little girl and grabbed holt of Marthy instead. I squeezed her, and she squeezed back. "Ain't no tellin' what I'm liable to break, woman," I said.

I looked at Ann. "I reckon daddies is supposed to prang their young'uns presents when they come home," I said. "But all I prung was Rains. He's pretty handy when ye need somethin' toted, though, and he makes a right fair adjutant."

It wasn't like I thought it would be. I felt home. It was almost like all the bad things of the past two years had never even happened. Marthy didn't mention none of it, neither – not right off. Oh, she did that night and the next day, and started pushing at me – and I started itching to leave again. There was still a right smart of fighting to do, and things was heating up closer to Sparta.

Still, that winter wasn't as cold as some have been. I've seen colder. And that one day, and that one moment; was like something magic – something that flashes away in an instant, and lasts forever, something that fills up your soul and leaves it empty, something that tingles from its beauty and hurts from its briefness.

That one moment was my life, and my life was that one moment. If I wind up burning in Hell for a million years, I'll still have that moment to draw up. The joy of it will dull Hell's pain, and at the same time it'll hurt worse than the fires will – but so long as I have it, I'll be all right. I'll be all right.

You'll have to forgive me. I'm talking foolish. Men tend to ramble that way, when they're fixing to die. All you can do is set and listen to the words, because you're too busy living to get the sense of them.

You'll understand one day.

Chapter 36

For the next few months, things just kept going downhill for the South. General Bragg and General Rosecrans kept dancing around each other in Tennessee, skirmishing here and yonder, especially around Murfreesboro and Tullahoma – but nothing ever seemed to come of it. We wasn't nowheres close to taking back Nashville, like many of us had hoped – the Union military governor was still setting in the capitol, every breath he took an insult to loyal Southerners. Maybe you've heared of him, Andrew Johnson. Now he's setting in the White House, as much a bastard as ever.

Bragg's officers complained about him hot and heavy – Forrest among the loudest. According to some of them, Bragg's decision to retreat from Murfreesboro during the Battle of Stone's River come at a time when the Confederate forces was in control of the field. We quit and run off right when we was winning, in other words – or leastways, we was a fer piece from losing.

In June Rosecrans advanced on Bragg, with heavy fighting around Tullahoma. This kept Bragg from heading down to Mississippi to relieve Vicksburg from a siege that had went on for weeks, under the direction of Useless S. Grant. Vicksburg finally fell, and because of it we lost the whole West.

Back in the East, our boys did win at Chancellorsville. Of course, that didn't much matter considering that Stonewall Jackson was killed. One of his own men shot him by accident. At about the same time Grant was taking Vicksburg, Robert E. Lee's invasion of the North ended hard in Gettysburg. Some say that was the turning point.

General Morgan had a couple of minor skirmishes through the winter. He made up for it in the springtime. My company and Scott's, and a couple of other irregular outfits, coordinated ourselves with Morgan. All of us took to hitting the Federals every chance we got and then scampering away. We was hoping to take some of the pressure off of Bragg's main force. We did distract them a right smart – for a while there, us and Morgan's regulars was tying up Union forces that outnumbered us ten-to-one. They never knowed where we was going to pop up next. But we was like bees swarming around a grizzly bear. We annoyed, we distracted, we slowed them down – but we would never be able to stop them on our own.

Morgan come up with a plan to take the Federals' attention off of Bragg – and at the same time draw the whole country's attention right square onto John Hunt Morgan. It was an unexpected plan, and it was a bold plan – but it was not exactly what I would call a smart plan.

With his 2500 cavalry troopers, General Morgan invaded the North. It was understood that us scouts and irregulars was more valuable staying in Tennessee and harassing Yankees here. Morgan and his own boys, though, they crossed the Ohio River and attacked Indiana, figuring to sweep through that state and into Ohio.

Some have said John Morgan was trying to hush up his critics, who claimed his devotion to his new wife had made him soft. Others have went so far as to say maybe the whole scheme was his way of impressing Mattie. Me, I think he done things the way he did because he was John Hunt Morgan, and everybody should've figured on just such a move from him.

The Raiders done fine at first – riding through Indiana with hardly any resistance, and scaring the hell out of the whole Union. It was kind of like a scrawny little feller in a bar fight. At first he has the upper hand, because everybody else is so surprised that he would even think about hitting them. After a few minutes, though, everybody sort of wakes up and realizes it's only a scrawny little feller, after all, and they gang up and beat the shit out of him.

That's what happened to Morgan's Raiders. One skirmish after another – one long running fight – ate away at his forces. A couple of weeks later they was covered over by Yankees in Ohio. Morgan escaped into Pennsylvania with only three hundred men left, the Yankees hot on his trail.

Morgan had hoped there'd be a huge uprising of Copperheads – Northerners that sympathized with the South – in his defense, but it never happened. He was finally brung to bay and captured back in Ohio, and him and his officers was put in the Ohio State Penitentiary in Columbus.

Four months later, Morgan and some of his men – including old Basil Duke – busted out of that prison and made their way back home. There was a big party for them in Richmond, and everybody heaped Morgan with praise for his daring and his courage – but nobody much took him serious after that. They figured him as too reckless. He was never able to find his way back into the spotlight again, which must have been far worse for him than setting in an Ohio jail had been. It's a damn shame. A few more men like Morgan, willing to light out and actually do something instead of just setting around thinking about it, and things might have turned out different.

About a year later the Yankees caught him in a trap in Greeneville, Tennessee. Him and a hundred of his men was shot dead. The Confederacy lost a great hero that day – even though they had long since stopped telling him so – and I figure I lost a good friend.

I ain't said much about what I was doing through them first several months of 1863. There was plenty of fighting, make no mistake about that – but it was pretty much the same as always. Nothing really stood out.

That was about to change. Rosecrans broke the stalemate. Not content to hold Bragg in place, the Union general left Tullahoma and moved east, his goal being to whip Bragg and take Chattanooga.

Sparta was no longer a safe haven. Up to now, there had only been scattered units of Yankees around – never before had there been a whole army. Hell was about to break loose in Middle Tennessee, and this time in my own back yard.

Chapter 37

On July 29, 1863, George Dibrell come back to Sparta. Yeah, I know – I ain't even mentioned the man's name up to now, who he is or where he had went, and now here I say he came back. You must think I'm getting ahead of myself, or that I've got forgetful in my "old age." I did mention him once, early on, but I reckon you've forgot.

Well, the fact is, I didn't know who George Dibrell was my own damn self at this point in the tale. I reckon I might've heared the name, but I didn't store it away or nothing.

Dibrell was from Sparta – he owned a big farm a few miles north of town, even owned several slaves. Wasn't but a handful of people in Sparta – or any of the other towns close by – that owned slaves, and them that did usually never had but one or two. They just didn't have the money. So a man with several slaves, why, right off you know he's kind of well-to-do. Dibrell, he was a county commissioner, or a court clerk, or something of the kind. I never could keep them public officials straight, and they sure as hell never could keep me straight.

Anyways, this here Dibrell mustered his self up a regiment at the beginning of the war. It was made up of men from White County, with a good many from surrounding counties topping it off. The Eighth Tennessee Cavalry it was, with Dibrell commissioned all good and proper as a colonel - they rode off in 'sixty-one to fight in the big battles, leaving the little stuff back home to scruffers like me and Scott Bledsoe.

Oh, I never mentioned whether they was North or South. Why hell, son, they was South. A total of ten companies was raised up in White County during the late war, and nine of them was Confederate. I'll tell more about the single Union company later.

So that's how come me not to know anything about him. Them boys rode off before I ever moved down from Clinton County, Kentucky. After that, they was attached to Nathan Bedford Forrest, and I was doing what little official riding I done under Morgan.

Reason they came back was, Rosecrans was getting damn close. There was a whole Yankee corps camped at McMinnville now. Forrest sent the Eighth Tennessee up to Sparta from North Georgia to keep an eye on Rosecrans.

First thing Dibrell did was set up headquarters at his own farm, in his own house. His men camped out in his fields. Second thing he done was set up patrols on the road to Spencer, which lays pretty much in-between Sparta and McMinnville.

Third thing he done was send for me. He sent an orderly out to my farm to fetch me, same as Morgan had done – except this time, instead of reporting to a colonel in a muddy tent, I was reporting to a colonel in a fancy house. I sent word to my men to assemble there, too, in case the colonel had anything he wanted done quick-like.

By the way – just like with Morgan – Dibrell was a colonel when I met him, and got promoted to brigadier general not long after. I reckon I'm just good luck that way. Hell, come to think of it, my old admirer Basil Duke wound up being a general before it was all over, too.

Me, I started out as a captain of irregulars, and now six months after the war I'm fixing to be a hanged captain of irregulars. Life is hell for poor boys.

The colonel welcomed me all warm and polite-like, even shook my hand. He had steel-gray hair and a well-trimmed beard, and was a little on the short side. He sort of put me in mind of an older Basil Duke, but he wasn't hardly as tight-assed.

Mrs. Dibrell was bustling around the house, directing women-slaves here and yonder. She was a round little woman, and seemed to be tickled to death to have her husband home. They had them a growed son, but he was serving in a different outfit entirely, so she didn't get to have them both home at once. Dibrell's son was already a general, in fact – that would have to feel peculiar. It would sort of make a man feel proud and embarrassed, at the same time. I thought briefly of my own little boy, dead for so long now, and wondered what would have become of him in this war.

"Captain Ferguson," Dibrell said as he gripped my hand. "It is a pleasure to meet you in the flesh, after hearing so much about your exploits."

"Thank ye, sir," I said. I would've said something along the same lines back to him, but hell, I hadn't never heared of him until just a couple of days earlier. I reckoned he probably hadn't heared all of my exploits, nor them of the boys that rode with me, or else he wouldn't never have shook my hand. Hell, if he got word of some of the exploits of Bob Timmons and John Homer, he might be tempted to arrest me.

Colonel Dibrell introduced me around to his officers – there was about a half-dozen of them there – and they all treated me with the same politeness the colonel had. They each shook my hand like they meant it. One stout captain name of Leftwich - I recognized the name, for I knowed that the Leftwiches was wealthy big-wheels around Sparta - he looked all apologetic as he let go of my hand.

"I wish I could stay and talk to you further," Leftwich said, "but I'm leading a patrol toward Spencer. Have to keep an eye on those Yankees, I reckon!"

"It pays to."

"I did want to say, though, I've heard a lot about you. My sister and my wife have mentioned you often in their letters – it's a lot easier to be off campaigning when I know you're here to protect my family and my property. The people of Sparta have made you one of their own – everyone I've spoke to loves you."

I chuckled. "Well, thank ye, Captain," I said. "I really do suspect, though, there's plenty that don't love me none, even around here – they just ain't exactly in your circle of friends, so I don't reckon ye hear from them much."

Leftwich smiled. "I'd say you're right. A pleasure to meet you." I nodded, so as to say I felt likewise, and he walked off – pausing only to whisper briefly with Colonel Dibrell before passing through the front door.

Mrs. Dibrell came up to me, still all a-flutter. "Oh, Captain Ferguson," she said. "You should've brought your wife – how lovely that would've been!"

"Well, ma'am, I thought this was purely a army business kind of thing, else I might've done it."

The colonel appeared at my elbow. "No apologies necessary, Captain," he said. "You are correct – this is official military business. Later we will certainly have a social event for all our officers, and the Fergusons will of course attend – when we can afford the time for it."

The colonel's wife floated off - at least it looked like she was floating, with that big poofy dress she was wearing. She reminded me of some strange bug skittering around on a pond. She was mumbling under her breath about how long it had been since they had a party at their house.

My eyes lit up just a little at the colonel's words, but thankfully nobody noticed. I personally don't give a damn about big houses and fancy parties and polite people – but Marthy would love it, and I'd set through near about anything to see her smile again. Maybe mixing it up with the bigwigs in our new hometown would make life taste a little sweeter to her. I figured it could only help, and hoped the colonel wasn't offering his house up to roughnecks like us only to be civil, without meaning to actually have us. I figured him as sincere. Being an officer, I begun to see, has its advantages – shoot, I sometimes forgot I was one.

Three of Colonel Dibrell's niggers come into the front room. They was wearing red jackets, and smiling to beat the band. Partly I reckon that was on account of they're supposed to smile and be polite, but I think even they was happy to have something going on in the house for a change.

The niggers took our coats and led us all to the dining room, and seated us at a big eating-table. They brung out all sort of vittles, and ladled stuff into our plates for us. I had never had ary nigger to wait on me thataway before – I didn't hardly know how to act. I wasn't sure whether I ought to say "thank ye" or not. It didn't seem right not to, but nobody else was, so I didn't. Still, it was kind of nice – I could see where a feller might get used to it.Damn if they didn't have two or three forks laid out next to my dish, and a couple of different spoons. Them other officers, being well-brung-up men, switched back and forth from one utensil to another. It give me kind of a pause for a spell – I surely did hate to make a fool out of myself in such high company - but I finally shrugged and figured to hell with it. I picked out what seemed to be the stoutest fork out of my bunch, and went to work with it. If'n anybody didn't like it, I reckoned they should just be glad

I didn't take out my Bowie knife and eat with it instead. I ate like I meant it, smacking my lips and grunting my approval, as I was brung up to believe that was the polite thing to do. Mrs. Dibrell's eyes widened. She almost said something, but caught herself. The colonel's eyes twinkled, and he chuckled into his napkin – more at his wife than at me.

We talked as we ate – about the course of the war so far, and about what still needed doing. They told me a little about their battles riding with General Forrest, and I told about my experiences with General Morgan.

We discussed how – though most folks in the area was loyal – there was a few well-to-do Unionists who was lending support to the enemy. One of the biggest of these was an old man named John Rodgers, who lived at Rock Island - another little town in-between Sparta and McMinnville. This John Rodgers had went to Texas with Tennessee's former governor Sam Houston all them years ago, and become a major-general in Houston's Texican Army. He was at his commander's side when Houston accepted the surrender of Santy Anny.

Just like his old friend Houston – by then a senator from the state of Texas – Rodgers declared his self a Union man when war broke out. There was some talk that he was even a personal friend of Abe Lincoln. Besides his big house at Rock Island, the old codger was also running a health resort on Bon Air Mountain, just east of Sparta on the road to Knoxville. Union spies come and went from his house like fleas from a doghouse, and for all anybody knowed they was even venturing as far as that mountain resort, using it as a base to spy on us.

It was strongly hinted at – though never spoke out loud there at the table – that General John Rodgers, retired, might well need a visit from Captain Champ Ferguson, active, Confederate States Cavalry. I stored that nugget away in my mind, adding it to my list of things to do.

That night the colonel invited me to sleep in his house, like his regular officers. I wasn't sure what to do at first – Rains and the others was camping outside in the fields with the troopers, and I hated to be in comforts not offered to them. At the same time, I appreciated that Dibrell was treating me the same as if I was regular-army. I stayed.

A nigger led me upstairs to a soft feather bed. I reckon it was about the most comfortablest bed I had ever stretched out on - it felt like sinking down into a cloud.

Maybe it was because the bed was so soft that I had such dreams. Soft dreams.

I was a boy again, playing with my brothers in the river – splashing water on little Jim, both of us laughing. Then I was growed, setting in the dewy woods under an oak tree, kissing my Ann Eliza – falling into the warmth of her soft mouth, floating, feeling her moist fire burning against me. I opened my eyes, in the dream, to see Jim staring at us. His eyes was both sorrowful and hateful, at the same time.

Nothing like that had ever happened in real life, or if it had, I never noticed it. I was too lost in my Ann Eliza, just like I've been lost all these years without her and never noticed that.

Then I was back in that jail in Jimtown, hearing Marthy's words to me after the camp meeting fight when I stabbed Jim Read.

"I just wish't you'd forget things," she said, *"or let 'em go, ever' once in awhile."*

And as she said it she was setting naked in the dust, Jim behind her whipping her back and shoulders with a quirt. She never winced. Her face was twisted with hate, and her eyes cold as death.

"Kill him, Champ," she said, her voice different from before. *"Kill him – hunt him, never stop. Look what he's done to us."*

I was froze, not knowing what to do. Marthy switched back and forth, one voice to the other and back again.

"Forget things, or let 'em go."

"Kill him."

And now Ann Eliza was under me, squirming, moaning, her legs wrapped around mine. Marthy's eyes looked on me, filled with hurt and hatred, just like Jim's was. My mama was there, hoeing at the weeds on the ground, chopping, slashing. The air all around me was filled with their voices.

"Kill him, Champ, look what he's done to us."

"You're not my son anymore."

"Forget about things. Let 'em go."

"Champ – don't stop, honey, don't stop."

"You're a damn traitor, brother, you don't deserve the name you carry."

"Look what they've done to us."

"You've betrayed me before."

"Don't stop honey. If you stop I'll die, if you stop I'll die."

"Kill him, Champ, hunt him down."

"Kill him, Champ."

"You're not my son."

"Kill him."

"I'll die."

"Kill him."

I awoke, drenched with sweat, to the sound of gunfire. I shook my head in the darkness, and realized the dream was over. There was not ghosts outside, but men.

Fighting and war and death had come for me, was waiting beyond the door for me, and I was grateful to them.

Chapter 38

I pulled on my boots and grabbed my weapons. The whole house was in an uproar. The shooting had been a good distance away, but there was a lot of it. I ran down the stairs, tucking my extra revolver into my waistband as I ran, and passed through the front door. I heared other officers coming behind me, but I was the first one onto the porch.

"Reese!" I hollered at the top of my lungs. "Reese!"

Within seconds LeRoy Reese appeared, flanked by Rains and Crazy Bob Timmons.

"Get the boys saddled and mounted!" I said. "Does anybody know what the hell's goin' on?"

"Heavy fightin' a mile or two down the road, is all I can make out," Reese said.

I heared steps behind me. It was Dibrell – from the comer of my eye I seen that he was just now pulling on his braces.

"The patrol," Dibrell said. "Captain Leftwich's patrol."

Someone cried out that a rider was coming. Soon we seen him galloping up the road – a single trooper in gray, one of Leftwich's men, pushing that horse like he was trying to outrun the devil. The man fairly leaped out of the saddle once he had drawed his horse up.

"What is it!" Dibrell snapped at him.

"They hit us about twelve miles down the road, sir – when we was hallway home." The man, a private, was pale. He paused to take a ragged gasp of air. "It's a whole damn brigade, colonel!"

Dibrell chewed hard on his lip. "What is your company's status, soldier?"

"We've been givin' 'em a runnin' fight, colonel – I reckon they'll all show up here in the next few minutes."

Dibrell nodded curtly. "Get a fresh horse, son." Without turning, he said, "Major Lewis!"

"Yes sir," the major replied at once. He was a tall, skinny man with muttonchop whiskers that stood out, bristly, from his cheeks and made him look like a porcupine.

"We're going to fall back to Wild Cat Creek, and cross the bridge."

I nodded to myself - that was a damn good idea. Wild Cat Creek wasn't very big, but its banks was steeper than the walls of Hell - the only way for horsemen to cross it was at the bridge, unless a feller wanted to skirt it for several miles. If we took cover and laid fire onto the bridge, it would buy us a passel of time – which we would need, if the scout wasn't exaggerating the size of the enemy force.

"Captain Ferguson!" Dibrell said, and I turned and gave him my complete attention.

"Yes sir," I said.

"Can your company hit the enemy hard enough – and fast enough – to check them until the rest of us have made the creek?"

"Hell yeah," I said. "Um, I mean, hell yes, sir. I'm on my way."

"Excellent. Delay them as much as you can, Captain, and then you and Leftwich both ride like hell for the bridge. Make sure you arrive well in advance of the enemy, or you won't have time to cross."

I bounded down the porch-steps. Rains was waiting for me, mounted, holding the reins of my horse. I fair leaped into the saddle. It was my favorite horse, a black gelding with a silver blaze I had named Jimbo.

I took a quick glance around. LeRoy Reese had already got all the boys mounted and ready to ride. About seventy of them had showed up at the colonel's house the night before – less than half of what you would expect on a good day. The actual number of men who rode with me was always changing, depending on the weather, the time of year, and God knows what else. I figured about another hundred would straggle in during the next week, once word got around. Dibrell had about two hundred and fifty men, plus the thirty or so that the Yankees was presently shooting at.

Seventy was what I had to work with on that particular morning, though, so seventy was going to have to do. I wasn't too awful concerned about it, no how – I didn't figure there was much that could slow down seventy wild-eyed Tennessee sons of bitches. Shows how much I knowed.

I waved my boys forward, kicked Jimbo in the ribs, and hollered, "Move out!" I let out a long Rebel yell. Everybody joined in, all whooping together as we pounded down the road, headed south toward the sound of gunfire – much, much closer than it had been while-ago.

We almost run right over the top of poor Captain Leftwich and his scared troopers. Their eyes lit up with hope when they seen us – then fell to despair when they seen it was only us.

"Fall back to Wild Cat Creek," I yelled to Leftwich, barely slowing down. "We'll take it from here!"

Leftwich's men kept riding for safety, but the captain his self stayed still and watched us pass him by. He looked like he wasn't sure whether we was brave or stupid. I admit, I was puffed up a little on the inside when I seen that. Yeah, step aside, I almost felt like saying – let us show you what real men can do.

Then, a few minutes later, I rounded the bend and seen about fifteen hundred Yankees barreling down on me.

"Shit!" I yelled. "Shitfire!"

I glanced at my lieutenants. They was a group of very unhappy Southern men. Even Bob Timmons looked less crazy than I had ever seen him.

"Holy damn shit," I said, because I was still searching for just the right words to describe our situation.

"I reckon I should've brung some more powder," Rains said.

"Foller me, boys," I hollered – and I turned and rode back the way we had come. Bullets was whizzing through the air all around me. Seeing our hind-ends made the Yankees take heart. They rode faster, and now it was their turn to whoop and holler.

Once I got back around that bend, though, I didn't stick to the road. I headed straight up the wooded incline on the right side instead. I waved for LeRoy to go up the opposite bank. Both sides was just steep enough to give us an advantage on the Yankees, but not steep enough to keep our horses from climbing them. I could sense a shift in my men's spirits once they figured out what I had in mind. Our whole company divided in two and went up into the trees, flowing smoothly like we was the waters of the

Red Sea – parting just long enough to lure the old pharoah in so we could close back and crush him.

Some of them Yankees was still smiling when they rounded the bend and we shot them out of the saddle. The next bunch had a chance for their smiles to fade, and to say some words along the lines of what I had been saying a few minutes earlier, before we shot a few of them. Most of them didn't get shot, but they did have about fourteen hundred of their Yankee brothers run right up their ass. They had one hell of a disorganized mess on their hands there for a spell.

It didn't take very long, though, for the Yankees in the rear to pull the same trick we had. They clambered up into the tree-covered hills and come at us through the woods, taking away our brief advantage.

Old John Homer took a bullet smack in the face. He fell off his horse and flopped a time or two, and that was all she wrote for him. It was kind of a tough loss – John Homer was a blackhearted son of a bitch, but so long as we kept him at war at least he was a blackhearted son of a bitch toward Yankees. Still, I couldn't think of nobody that would shed any tears over him. He was the sort of man who'd be robbing and killing, raping too, no doubt, whether there was a war on or not. Maybe we was better off shed of him, after all.

Now of course, I wasn't thinking all these things at that very moment – that came later. Right then all I knowed was we needed to get the hell out of there before they swarmed over us

We raced off to the north again, finding our way back to the road. We left Homer and two other old boys dead in the woods.

We turned behind us and shot as we rode. Times like that is when it comes in handy to have several guns, hoss, because we sure as hell wasn't able to do any reloading. The enemy slowed down and fell back a little, to stay out of the range of our guns. I was hoping that between them slowing down and the several minutes we had stopped them in their tracks, we had bought Colonel Dibrell enough time. Hell, even if the Eighth did manage to get into position and get ready for them, we was still going to be outnumbered by almost five-to-one.

I was happy as a fox in a two-story henhouse when we got to Wild Cat Creek and I seen all them gray uniforms lined up on the far side of the bridge. We pounded across that thing like our feet was on fire and our asses was catching.

There is an open clearing about three hundred yards wide that has to be crossed before you ever reach the bridge. At about the time we was crossing over to the other side of the creek, the advance of the Yankee brigade was pouring into the clearing. Dibrell's men opened fire on them. Now, I told you I was happy to see gray uniforms - but the men in them uniforms wasn't standing right out in the open, they was in the woods with plenty of cover. We rode hell-for-leather into the trees with them, and then we dismounted and grabbed our rifles and joined in the fun.

Son, we shot the fire out of them Yankees – but they kept coming. Pretty soon that whole big clearing was full of them. If it hadn't been for the steep banks of the creek, they would have swarmed into the woods and right over us. As it was, though, they got bunched up at that bridge and we laid into them. Before long they figured out that it wasn't really a healthy place to be, and they retreated.

After a little while they tried it again, throwing a fresh regiment at us - I heared later it was the Fourth Regulars – with the same result. We poured volley after volley into them. Well, they pulled back and then tried it a third time. One thing about them Yankees, they can be god-awful stubborn. Maybe they figured we was bound to run out of bullets eventually, or get tired, or come down with bad colds, or something. We kept right on a-shooting.

Turns out they was actually just keeping us busy. While we was occupied shooting holes in their front ranks, they sent another bunch around to flank us – not being familiar with the area, though, they had no idea how long it would take. By the time they had backtracked and crossed the Calfkiller River, thereby swooping plumb around the Wild Cat, and hit our rear – it was well past midmorning, and we'd had the time to strengthen and prepare our rear. Colonel Dibrell had figured them to try just such a move. Instead of catching us by surprise, we caught them – and pushed them away.

We still knowed it was only a matter of time, badly as we was outnumbered. The colonel decided we should fall back about a mile to the mouth of Blue Springs Creek, which was an even better position.

We moved out. We kept expecting to see some sort of pursuit, but there was none – in fact, there was no more sign of any Yankees at all. Dibrell ordered me to send out some scouts to see what was going on at the Yankee position. I sent LeRoy Reese and a couple of other boys.

They was back in no time. Reese's boys was grinning. He looked like he was close to cracking one his own self, a rare thing for him.

"What did you find?" the colonel asked.

"Nothin'," said Reese. "Nothin' to find. They retreated. They're headed back south towards McMinnville."

A cheer erupted from the regiment. Colonel Dibrell turned to face his men, and waved them down into silence with his arms.

"By God!" he cried out to them. "So long as they're running, we may as well chase them!"

There was another cheer, much louder than the first – it prett'near rattled the leaves out of the trees. Then there was the sound of spurs jingling and sabers rattling, as the men climbed into their saddles.

It was a bold move, I reckon, riding out of our protective shelter and giving chase to an enemy several times our own size. It was bold, and reckless, and damn if I didn't thrill to do it. I was starting to really like this old colonel. He had the gumption of Morgan and the good sense of Basil Duke, rolled into one.

We rode hard for eighteen miles, all the way to the Caney Fork River, but we never could catch up with the enemy. They had got too big a head start on us, and besides, they was in a pretty big hurry their own selves.

By the time we got back to our camp at the colonel's house, we was starved about half to death. We had missed breakfast and dinner both, and here it was nearly suppertime.

We had no need to worry about getting fed. Not only had Dibrell's slave women been hard at work cooking all day, but so had every woman for miles around. There was more people at the colonel's house than you'd expect to see at the county fair – and more food, too.

Somebody had got word to Marthy. Her and Ann had cooked up a mess of food and brung it to the Dibrell place in our little wagon – it was only a few miles' ride. Half the men in the regiment, in fact, had their families show up to eat with them. We had us one hell of a picnic, right out there in the Dibrell fields.

I didn't appreciate the way some of them young soldiers was looking at my daughter, but every one of them had sense enough to watch his step. That's where raising a gal gets to be harder on a man than raising a boy would be, I reckon.

Colonel Dibrell walked over and laid a hand on my shoulder while I was eating.

"Your men did well," he said, after he had nodded politely and half-bowed to Marthy. "We would have been hard-pressed without you."

"We give them Yankees somethin' to study on, I reckon," I said with a grin.

Dibrell's smile was not as broad – it was half-sad, tainted by worry. "They gave us something to study on as well," he said. "If they'd had better guides, things might have gone differently. We shall have to be more cautious in the future."

"Maybe so," I said, "but so will they."

"Indeed. That's what worries me. Perhaps they will."

He patted my shoulder again, and wandered off. I put his gloom aside. We had won a tough victory, and a complete one – we deserved to celebrate it.

In the back of my mind, though, Dibrell's words gnawed at me. We had been lucky – we might just as easily have been at our own funerals as at a picnic.

Chapter 39

Soon after the skirmish at Wild Cat Creek, Colonel Dibrell had that "special function" he had promised his wife. I was invited to attend, just like the regular officers of the Eighth Cavalry. I reckon Scott would have been included if he'd been around – he had his company here and yonder, attacking Unionists around Jackson County one week and tearing up railroad tracks between McMinnville and Murfreesboro the next. I wondered what he was up to often, but none of the regulars ever mentioned him. His name wasn't associated with Sparta and White County the way mine was, even though a couple of his main lieutenants was from the area.

Marthy was in a tizzy over going up to that big house to eat supper, with them bigshots and their wives. It's a funny thing, but whenever a regiment of locals gets raised up they don't never put any braid on the pore boys. Marthy went on and on for days about how she didn't have no decent dress to wear to such a fancy place, and didn't have the time or the wherewithal to make one.

I was kind of figuring on riding up to Jimtown or somewheres, finding a suitably rich Unionist with a suitably built wife, and appropriating one. I never had to, though. When some of the women in town found out about it, they give her several pretty ones, and do-dads to match. Any other time Marthy would have refused them, being too proud to accept charity - but she dearly wanted to look her best at that fancy eating-table I had told her about.

What Marthy hadn't figured out yet, but I had, was that there wasn't ary such thing as charity where the Ferguson family was concerned. The people in Sparta would of give me anything I asked for, out of pure love. The people in some of the other towns would have done the same, except out of fear.

When we walked out of our house and to the wagon, fixing to head up the road towards the Dibrell house, Marthy spread her arms wide and twirled one time, letting the dress billow in the wind around her. She laughed like a little girl. Me, I grinned so wide the top of my head nigh fell off.

I helped her onto the seat, then climbed up beside her and took the reins.

"Champion Ferguson," she said, "you better be on your best behavior tonight."

"I'm always on my best behavior, Ma," I said. "Ask anybody. Get up there, hoss."

There was no need for her to worry about me attracting attention to myself by my coarse and ungentleman-like behavior. I was ever' bit as coarse and ungentleman-like as ever, but the guest of honor was Colonel Dibrell's commander – General Nathan Bedford Forrest – so nobody paid much attention to me.

General Forrest sat at the head of the table. Watching him made me feel a whole lot better. He acted like he didn't much care whether he used that left-hand fork to eat his meat, to eat his vegetables, or to comb his beard with.

"Miz Dibrell," he said – it was the first time he had spoke since we sat down and started eating – "these here is some damn fine biscuits."

A couple of the younger officers seemed to be a little shocked at such language, right there in front of the womenfolk, but nobody was stupid enough to say nothing. Except for me, of course.

"Shore as hell is," I grunted in agreement, and went on eating. Marthy kicked at me under the table. I ignored her. General Forrest looked up at me, a grin spreading across his face, and then he chuckled softly. Taking their cue from him, all of his junior officers laughed out loud.

Forrest nodded sharply. "Reckon you're Captain Ferguson," he said, and I nodded back at him. "Been hearin' a lot about you, Captain," he added. "Most of it good." He winked. "We could get a lot done if'n we had a few more like you."

"I've heared a lot about you too, General," I said. "Proud to have ye in Sparta."

That was two year ago, mind. Forrest hadn't even got started good yet – hell, I reckon that by now there ain't a living soul in this country that ain't heared about Nathan Bedford Forrest. Some figures what they hear to be good, and some figures it to be plumb awful – about the same as folks look at me, I reckon.

I figured everything I heared about the general back then to be good, and I still do. Me and him is a lot alike, even beyond the fact that we're big, tall, rough cobs with hot tempers.

Word was Forrest's own men was more scared of him than they was of the enemy. That's how come them to fight so hard and win so often. They would a heap rather ride straight into a Yankee cannon as to turn around and ride into General Forrest, who might have them shot or even beat the shit out of them with his own hands. He had little patience with retreats or surrenders. More than once he had been known to ignore direct orders to do so.

He had also got in a gunfight with one of his own junior officers, and killed the man. I heared of another time when the general was pacing in circles, hands behind his back, trying to figure him up a strategy – and one of his junior officers kept interrupting him, trying to get his attention for one reason or another. The general finally got irritated enough to take notice of the man. Without even breaking stride, General Forrest punched the officer so hard in the face that it knocked the old boy plumb out. The general kept walking in circles – ever' time he come to where the man was laid out senseless on the ground, he just stepped over him and went right on pacing.

One way Forrest scared the enemy was by telling them they better surrender right now, because once the fighting started he would be accepting no surrenders. They knowed he meant it. He had backed the threat up too many times.

That miserable son of a bitch Sherman knowed how serious a threat Nathan Bedford Forrest could be. Later in the war, Sherman said Forrest was a devil that needed to be hunted down and killed, if it cost ten thousand lives and bankrupted the treasury to do it.

We went on eating for a good spell, the ladies making small talk and the menfolks focusing on their food. After awhile, though, I happened to catch General Forrest's attention. I looked him square in the eye, man to man, and spoke.

"General," I said, "what d'ye think about our position here?"

Forrest scowled. "I think General Bragg is a damned idiot, is what I think," he said. "Pardon my language. I reckon I'd better not take on that subject 'til afterwhile, when there ain't no ladies present.

We all chuckled excepting the general his self – he looked dead serious. He attacked the steak set before him, sawing at it like it was Abe Lincoln's liver.

"I'll tell y'all one thing, though," he added after he had chewed a mouthful. "Winnin' means fightin', and fightin' means killin'. That's why I like what I hear about Captain Ferguson yonder. To hell with Braxton Bragg and his notions about holdin' back reserves. If'n it was up to me I'd turn around and hit Rosecrans with ever'thing I've got. You just cain't beat a good charge, boys. The women in Memphis run out in the street in their nightclothes just to get a look at us when we rode through, and I reckon before it's over they'll be doin' the same thing on the streets of Nashville. That is, if Bragg don't retreat us plumb over to Europe by then. I swear, if that man retreats any faster he's liable to trip and fall up his own ass. Pardon my language."

Forrest's eyes was blazing so hot that for a minute there I almost thought he was going to jump up and shoot one of us, just to make his self feel better. Mrs. Dibrell chuckled nervously, and her husband tapped his glass.

"Gentlemen," Colonel Dibrell said, "one thing I know about women is they like to gossip uninterrupted. I suggest we move our man-talk into the drawin' room and leave the ladies to their idle chatter. There is French brandy and Cuban cigars waiting for us."

Now I fretted over Marthy. When she heared them words about ladies and their idle chatter, I half-expected her to jump up and slap the good colonel upside the head with a slab of his own ham. I felt her body tense up next to me, but it relaxed after a couple of seconds. I reckon she figured out what Colonel Dibrell was up to – namely, avoiding any more embarrassing outbursts. Son, he don't know how close he come to getting his self one from quarters he hadn't bargained on.

We went and stood in the drawing room, and got to talking about farming and hunting and raising horses. Forrest knowed a lot about all of them subjects, and he softened up while talking about them, to the relief of Colonel Dibrell. I reckon it was pretty well understood by the whole crowd it was in everybody's best interests to keep the guest of honor off the subject of his superior, General Bragg.

Me, I was enjoying my little taste of the good life. There is just something about being in the company of men on a warm summer evening, good food still settling in your belly, with good liquor and good 'bakker, one just as smooth as the next. It made a feller feel like he was getting a taste of what heaven might be like if the Devil was in charge of it, and had got rid of the damn wings and harps.

Forrest seemed to be at ease with it all. He had been borned a pore Tennessee farm boy, but he had done made and lost a couple of fortunes. I reckon his life before the war was about like his military career, in a way – he's about the onliest feller I ever heared of that started as a private in 'sixty-one and wound up a general.

There was one thing nobody brung up, though, and that was the slaving business. It was one of them things that polite folks calls a "undelicate matter". Ever'body knows that before the war Nathan Bedford Forrest was the richest slave trader in the state of Tennessee.

It didn't make much sense to me. Not slavery – I reckon I understand that well enough – but the way them rich slave-owners acted about it. Like Colonel Dibrell, for example, and Captain Leftwich, and one or two other officers of the Eighth. They made their living off the work of slaves – which I ain't arguing against, mind you, the preachers say it's God's will and all – and yet they act embarrassed at the evidence of it. You take a feller like Forrest, that buys and trades in human flesh, and them bigshots act like he's the lowest kind of criminal. He's cruel and inhuman, so far as they're concerned – a monster. But they sure as hell let him do their dirty work for them.

I reckon that makes it sting a mite for folks like that, when such a man ends up being richer than they are. It's even more uncomfortable, I would think, when he becomes your commanding officer. It was like eating supper with the man that runs your bank, and that has a huge knobby wart on his nose. There was a embarrassment that nobody would admit to – they would bow and scrape and cow-tow, and look everywhere but at him.

There's a big farmhouse in White County, a few miles from town, that's got a big stone auction block in front of it. That's the place where slaves always got sold in the Sparta area. I only passed by there a couple of times. Once me and Rains had rode out yonder because they was auctioning off that nigger gal we had took off the Evans place and I wanted to make sure I seen for myself how much she fetched – for all I knowed, that auctioneer was liable to gyp me.

The gal didn't seem to mind it much, as I reckon she figured one master was about the same as another. There was a few more sold that day, though, that seemed to mind the whole thing a right smart. It was a buck and a woman, and a couple of young'uns. They belonged to a old widow-woman who was having to pay off her dead husband's debts, and this particular nigger family was being sold off piecemeal. Lord how they squalled – even the man. They had to beat him over the head to shut him up when his young' uns was being took away from him.

It didn't bother me too much – I had seen a lot worse in my time. Shit, I've caused a whole lot worse. Life is hell for ever'body, I reckon ye have to take what is dished out to ye and go on, wh'er you're black, white, or green.

Rains was upset about it, though. He's always been real tender-hearted about such things. For a minute I was afraid he was going to start blubbering, just like them niggers was doing – I was all set to whop him on the head if'n he did, before anybody seen what was happening. Our whole company would be a laughingstock if'n we started crying over niggers, hellfire.

Still, there for a second, the whole thing made me think about the day – so many years ago – that my little boy died, and how I had wailed and cried and pounded my fists in the mud, and begged the Lord and cussed Him and begged Him some more. I reminded myself that I was a white man, and not cursed by the Almighty, and that such a fact made a world of difference. I put it out of my head and tried not to think about it no more. I never went back to that auction block again, though. From then on I trusted the auctioneer to do me right when I sent them Unionists' niggers to sell.

Thinking back on it, I reckon I can understand how them bigshots was a little embarrassed to have General Forrest setting in their house, after all.

After awhile, the ladies called us back in and led us to a big room right in the middle of the house. The Dibrells had hired theirselves somebody to play their big piano – Lord, that thing was fancy-looking – and everybody commenced to dancing. I grabbed holt of the crook of Marthy's arm and swung her right out onto the dance floor, though she flushed and told me to let her go. I hadn't never done none of that box-step dancing they was all doing, but I had always set socials and square dances on fire, so I figured I could handle it.

I pressed her close to me, and laughed in her ear, and swung back and forth with her. I closed my eyes and lolled my head back. I swam in the music, and carried her with me, letting my feet do whatever the hell they wanted to. I felt everybody's eyes on us. I didn't give a damn wh'er I was making the proper moves or not, I just danced. Soon I felt Marthy relax in my arms and swing with me. I wanted to swing her around the room, around the world, away from everything ugly that ever was or ever would be. For awhile – just for a little while – I reckon I did.

Chapter 40

I'm glad I got to meet General Forrest that evening. A couple of months later there was a change in command. Forrest got so fed up with Bragg that he requested – and they give him – a transfer to the East, and a promotion to go with it. It was a damn big loss for our little section of the war. Dibrell was moved to Joe Wheeler's command. Wheeler was a fine general too – I wish't we could of kept both him and Forrest, and shipped Braxton Bragg off somewheres else.

Forrest leaving wasn't the worst of it, though, not by a long shot. The worst part – so far as us Tennesseans was concerned – was what Bragg had done that made Forrest so damn mad, mad enough that he even talked about killing the damn fool the next time he laid eyes on him.

What happened was we lost Chattanooga. The whole damn Confederate Army was forced to skedaddle, the Yankees on their tail. Colonel Dibrell and the Eighth Tennessee Cavalry was forced to leave their homes to the Yankees and follow Bragg to Georgia. The Yanks, meanwhile, left several regiments to hold the area.

Men like me and Scott Bledsoe, and George Carter down in Spencer, we was all that stood between our people and an occupying army.

It wasn't long before I got my first look at how things was fixing to be from now on. My lesson was learnt the hard way. I had took a small patrol – about a dozen men, all of them old boys who had been with me a long time – and rode over to my old stomping grounds, up above Jimtown and in Clinton County. I hadn't been up there in a spell, with so much scouting to be done for Colonel Dibrell. I sure didn't want the dear companions of my youth to forget about me, after all. I was hoping we might even get lucky and run into Tinker Dave or Rufus Dowdy and catch them unawares.

Heading up into Union country thataway always had been sort of a risky notion. Riding the main roads could mean running into a mess of Home Guards, which might outnumber you – and running through the woods had its own dangers. You never knowed what thicket or mess of trees might have one of Tinker Dave's scouts or snipers setting in it. Still, it was nothing we hadn't faced before.

This time was different. The roads, and even the woods, was crawling with Yankee soldiers. We would no sooner duck into a blind or a draw and let one bunch pass, than here come another'n. They was ever' one riding from the north towards the south.

"It's gettin' mighty damn hot in these woods," Will Simmons whispered.

"They's a nice breeze a-blowin'," Rains said, "when you're out in the open. 'Course, we ain't been out in the open much."

"Shit, Rains," Simmons said. "I ain't talkin' about the weather. I'm talkin' about all these damn Yankees."

Rains frowned. "They's a lot of Yankees out today, Will."

Bob Timmons snickered. I hoped he didn't poke no fun at Rains, this wasn't hardly the time for it. Besides, I hadn't been too sure my own self that Simmons wasn't complaining about the actual weather. The son of a bitch was always whining about something.

"Ye reckon we ort to turn back, Cap'n?" he whined to me. "This is makin' me kindly jumpy."

Harry Cropper leaned over the side of his horse and spat 'backer juice. Some of that breeze Rains had mentioned broke through the trees – it grabbed a gob of the juice and blowed it back on Cropper, splattering against his big belly. He ignored it.

"I reckon it'd take more'n a few million Yankees to make me jumpy, by God," he growled. "I'll take 'em all on."

"Ye might get a chance to, the way things are lookin'," Jory Williams said. Sweat was running out from under his stringy blond hair and into his eyes, and he wiped a sleeve across his face. I sort of regretted bringing Jory along on this trip – he was loyal, but he wasn't no natural-born scrapper like the other'ns.

"What do ye say, Champ," LeRoy Reese asked softly.

"I say we've done come all this way. We ort to at least scout around and see what-all's goin' on. Hell, many bluebellies as we've seen ride by, there might be more behind us now than in front of us."

Reese nodded his agreement. "Must be a whole division in this county."

"I don't much like it," Simmons said. "But you know what you're doin', Cap'n."

I sure as hell hoped so. "Let's move," I said.

It wasn't twenty minutes later that our luck give out, and we run smack into a squad of Yankees. We didn't stop to shoot at them, we just turned tail and lit a shuck out of there. Not being so pressed for time as we was, I reckon, they sent several bullets after us.

Our luck had run out on us at first, now it decided to piss on us for good measure. While hightailing it from the first squad we blundered into a second one.

We wheeled to the right, hoping to push through their flank and get away. We exchanged fire point-blank – we was so close together I felt the heat from the burning powder.

Cropper was right beside me. A Yankee bullet hit square in the center of the 'backer stain on his belly. I heared the air whuffing out of him. He weaved in the saddle and they shot him again, this time blowing his brains all over my shirt. There was more of them than I would of figured. I wondered if he was jumpy yet.

Jory hollered out a grunt of pain. I didn't have time to spare him a glance – I was leaned forward into the wind, knees squeezing old Jimbo tight, and slapping his rump for all I was worth.

The bullet twisted me around and prett'near knocked me off my horse. My side was on fire, and was flowing wet, both at once't. I held on and kept riding.

"Lordy!" I heared Rains cry out, pain wringing the word as it flew into the air among the smoke and bullets. I throwed a quick look back over my shoulder this time. I seen that he was still alive, and still riding even though he clutched at his left shoulder, so I didn't slow down.

Somehow or 'nother we made it out of that hornet's nest. We had lost Cropper, and I learnt that Simmons had been shot dead as well. Me, Rains, and Jory had been wounded, but none of us serious. Jory had took a ball in the upper leg that broke the bone, though, so he would be going home for a spell. At least that way I wouldn't have to worry about him none. I'll never forget him trying to warn me about the Evans brothers at the camp meeting that day, and how much the world had changed – at least the loyalty of friends like Jory and Rains hadn't changed none.

My wound was not much – just a graze in my side. It was fine once't I got the bleeding stopped. I still have a groove in my flesh there.

But there would be no more riding into Jamestown in broad daylight, or on the main road, bold as brass. From now on we was going to have to stick in the woods, and come and go like thieves. We soon learnt it wasn't just Jamestown – it was every town around, even Sparta.

I reckon that now would be the time to talk about the one single Union company to be raised up in White County. About a year or so before our fight at Wild Cat Creek, Governor Andrew Johnson had commissioned a feller named Will Stokes to raise up a regiment of Union cavalry using Tennesseans. This was the Fifth Tennessee Union Cavalry. Stokes, a lawyer, got his hand shot off by a cannonball in one of their first engagements, and had it replaced by a heavy brass ball. They say that when he give orders he would pound at his desk with that brass ball, and would sometimes splinter the wood. I reckon he was happier with that than he had been with his real hand, on account of he dearly loved to crush things. And people.

Stokes's Fifth was one of the regiments sent to the Upper Cumberland to stamp out the Reb guerillas. First thing he done when he got to Sparta was to put out a call for volunteers.

There wasn't many Unionists in White County, but there was a few. They had mostly laid low and kept quiet for the last couple of years – but now the wind was blowing in their direction, so they started to poke their heads out. I reckon some of them was like that rich feller I had met in Murfreesboro on the night we snatched away General Morgan's bride – they'd pretended they hadn't ever heared of an American flag, 'til they seen one flying over their courthouse. Then all of a sudden they was all claiming to he Ben Franklin's bastard grandsons.

Stokes wound up with enough volunteers to fill out another company for his regiment. They chose as their commander an old boy named Joe Blackburn – somehow or 'nother Blackburn wound up with the rank of captain, and was Stokes's second-in-command. He commanded his company of White County men and several others to boot, and commenced to roving around the area trying to make trouble for me and Scott, and other good Southerners. Blackburn had been treated porely by many of his neighbors in the early days of the war, on account of he had spoke out openly about his Union sympathies, and now he was taking his chance to get even.

One of the first things Blackburn done after the main Confederate forces pulled out was to ride over to Gumspring Mountain, to the house of an old man named Miles. This here Miles had a nephew that rode with me, a right handy feller with a pistol name of Odell Miles. The old man had also spit in Blackburn's face once't when they passed each other on the square and Blackburn had something to the effect that all Rebels needed to be hung.

The tables was turned. Captain Blackburn called on Miles with about three dozen home-growed bluebellies at his back, and called the old man out.

Blackburn asked him where his nephew was hiding. Miles cussed and spat at him again. Them Yankees grabbed the old man and tied a rope around his neck, and throwed the other end around a tree – then started to pulling on it. Miles was dragged up into the air and left to dangle for a long spell, choking and swinging. Then they dropped him to the ground in a heap. Blackburn lifted him up by the hair of the bead. I know what-all went on even though I wasn't there, on account of the neighbors seen the whole thing.

"Where's them Rebels at," Blackburn said.

"Go to hell," Miles answered with a croak.

They strung him up again, for longer this time. Then a third time, and a fourth, until finally the old man broke and told them the name of the feller whose house his nephew had been known to stay at from time to time. They left Old Man Miles laying there, the rope still around his neck. He lived, but his throat was all crushed and he could never talk after that at no more than a whisper.

Blackburn's Yankees tore out, headed for the house Miles had named. His nephew Odell was sure enough staying there, along with two other of my men. One was named Bussell – like Odell Miles, he didn't have no family, and so was happy to be put up by good folks who would have him and feed him suppers and all.

The third man was there because he was wounded, and couldn't go to his own home – it was in Fentress County, and Tinker Dave would know to keep an eye out for him there.

It was Jory Williams.

The bluebellies drug all three of them out of the house. They tied their hands, and shoved them up agin the wall, and shot them like dogs. There wasn't no speeches made by the good captain – there wasn't no chance for my boys to say ary last words – the Yanks never took the trouble to spit on their dead bodies. Jory, Odell Miles, and Bussell was left laying where they fell.

Once them good, loyal boys had twitched their last, Blackburn finally spoke. Witnesses say it was the only thing that him or any of his men said the whole time.

"Burn it down."

Blue-coated troops, some of them natives of that very area, scurried to carry out Blackburn's order. In just a few minutes, the house of the family that had put up the dead Rebels was ablaze. At least they was allowed to pull the bodies out away from the burning house, so's they could be buried proper.

I know what you're probably thinking. Here I am, going on about what them Union bastards done, getting mad just talking about it after almost two years. And yet, I've sat here and told you about things I've done that amounted to about the same thing. I've shot down Union guerillas that was dumb enough to try and surrender to me. I've ordered Union supporters' houses burnt down. But there is a big difference. That was me, doing it to them. This here, though, was them doing it to my friends – my people – and by God, it made my blood boil.

Once I heared about this mess that had happened, I swore to myself there would be an accounting. I put Joe Blackburn on my list, right up yonder with Tinker Dave and Rufus Dowdy, and my brother Jim. I meant to kill him one day. Some of them other fellers had been on my list a long time and yet they was still alive, true – but on the other hand, that list used to be a whole hell of a lot longer. And as you probably know, because they brung it out at my trial, it's a lot shorter right now than it was then.

It's kind of funny in a way, now that I think about it. I never kept a tally of the men that rode with me, but I doubt if I ever lost track of one single man was agin me.

The next week after Jory and them was killed, me and my boys rode down to Rock Island. We paid a visit on the home of retired General John Rodgers. If they aimed to punish the people that helped us, I aimed to punish the people that helped them. Rodgers and his family had been entertaining and helping to feed the Yankees ever since Rosecrans first made it this far east, but it was going to stop.

We burnt the Rodgers house to the ground. I reckon I would've killed the old man if'n he had been there, but he had died of a heart attack a few weeks before – his sons had continued on making life comfortable for Yankees in the meantime. The old woman, she bellered and bawled – but hell, they're a rich bunch, and I reckon if worst come to worst they could move out to that health resort they owned on Bon Air Mountain.

Since I wasn't able to tell General Rodgers what I thought of him in person – and what I thought of people like him, that would welcome invaders with open arms – I pissed on his damn grave. Later on, General Rosecrans sent some men out to the site and had them put up a sign. The sign told how John Rodgers had been a war hero and a personal friend of Abraham Lincoln, and anybody caught defacing his grave would face the wrath of the Union army.

Next time I happened to be out there by that grave, I shit on it. A man's got to shit someplace ever' once in awhile, and that was the best spot I could think of to do it. I hope by God they found it and mailed it to Mister Lincoln.

Chapter 41

Life kept on getting rougher for us. We had to stay on the move. We would hit them in Putnam County, and then ride like hell to Jackson County and hit them there. Sometimes we split off into smaller groups, and other times we would join together with Bledsoe or Carter into one big group.

We lived in the woods. When it rained, we lived in the mud. When it was cloudy, we lived in the dark. We never went home no more, unlessing it was late at night or early in the morning. We rarely had a campfire, or a fresh-cooked meal, but at least we never stayed hungry for long – sometimes we stole supplies from the Yankees, or took them off traitors. More often than not, food was give to us by the people. They left sacks of biscuits on the roadside, or hung hams off of tree limbs deep in the woods, or just wandered among the trees and rivers 'til they found one of us to give it to.

It was a hard life. Boys, I ain't been fishing in near about three year, and I used to fish most ever' day.

There wasn't never no rest to be had, and there ain't been since. Ever' day there was somebody hunting us, ever' day there was somebody to fight. Sometimes they kilt some of us, sometimes we kilt some of them.

A couple of times, in the thick of some skirmish or 'nother, I had a quick glimpse of Tinker Dave Beaty. Our eyes would meet for a second, and then the fighting would carry us away from each other like dead leaves in swirling water. I didn't see ary bit of hatred in his eyes, and I didn't see ary bit of fear. I seen in him what he seen in me. Cold and tired, and hungry, and sad, and stubborn, and mad at the world for turning the way it does. I seen pride and respect, and understanding. We was caught in the same trap. If I kilt him, or if he kilt me, it was just two creatures doing what they was born to do, nothing else but that.

If I had seen Blackburn or Rufus Dowdy, it would have been different, I know. I would have seen hate and fear in two equal parts, with no room for anything else. I would have fought agin the tide of battle, swum agin it like a man caught in whitewater, trying to reach them and cut their hearts out. But not Dave. I wouldn't turn away from killing him if he was in my sights, but I wouldn't go out of my way to, neither.

If I was to see my brother Jim, I don't know what I'd do nor how I'd go about it. For all I knowed, Jim was already laying dead on some battlefield back east, at the hands of a stranger. I surely hoped so.

Ever' once in awhile I would pass by citizens, alone or in groups. Maybe it would be me and Rains running into a couple of wrinkled old hunters, or maybe it would be my whole company riding past some farms on our way to or from a fight or some act of sabotage.

When they seen me they would holler out my name, and the tiredness and the fear would leave their eyes, replaced by a sparkle. Sometimes they would salute, or pump their fist in the air.

"Give 'em hell, Champ!" they would say "Give 'em hell for us!"

Boys would join us from time to time, finally turned old enough to leave the farm and fight Yankees like their daddies did, and their brothers, and their uncles. Bob Timmons liked to tell us some of the tales he had picked up from them boys – tales about what heroes we was, how brave and true, like we was something out of the Bible. Which we was, but we was usually more Canaanite and Philistine than children of Israel. Reese would shake his head sadly at them tales, and Timmons laughed at them like they was the biggest joke in the history of the world.

Sometimes I wondered if it even mattered who I was, or what I had ever done. So long as there was one man that stayed and killed Yankees after ever'body else had give up on the notion and retreated, that one man would be a saint in the people's eyes, even if he was the lowest man this side of Sodom and Gomorrah. If such a man never come along, maybe they'd make him up. I don't know. I never did know exactly what to think about it all.

But it felt good. It felt good to find bushels of food set out in the woods, that I knowed the owners couldn't spare. It felt good when them bushels had notes on them that said, *God Bless Champ Ferguson*. Women holding their babies up to see me pass by – old men straightening up from the weight of age to look me in the eye – them things was never a joke to me. I might not understand it, but it wasn't no joke.

There was folks crowded outside that courthouse during my trial, and outside these prison gates right now, hollering my name. Most of them are Unionist sons of bitches, chattering away like a bunch of damn monkeys, wanting to see me swing. Some of them come to Nashville all the way from Jamestown and Albany, just to watch this party. I reckon I'm getting ahead of myself a little, but you done know they're fixing to hang me, so I ain't giving nothing away.

Some of them, though, is good loyal Southerners who ain't afraid to speak their mind even in front of the guns of an occupying army. They call out encouragement to me. A couple of times I even heared them say "God Bless Champ Ferguson!" I tell ye again, that ain't no joke to me, son. It means something.

It never meant nothing to Marthy. She didn't understand it, and she didn't really care. Whenever I would talk to her about pride, she would talk about sense, and then the next day it would be the other way around. Woman's idea of sense and man's idea of sense is two different things, and the same way with pride, even a knothead like me knows that much.

One time I had gone to the house late at night, when I was pretty sure it was safe. It got to where that only happened once't a month or so, even though I was within twenty miles of the house most ever' single night. It was just too big a risk, with so many folks knowing where I lived and all.

This particular night was right after New Year's, in 'sixty-four. Ann was sleeping. Marthy wanted to wake her up, but I wouldn't let her. I just stood over her bed and watched her in the candlelight, touching her hair soft as a feather – she moved, and smiled, and I knowed I was in her dream with her. I used to watch her sleep thataway when she was a baby. I was afraid back then that if I looked away a fever would come and take her, and when I looked back she would be gone. Her face as a baby and my little boy's face as a baby mix together in my memory, 'til I can't tell them apart. My boy's name was John. I know I ain't mentioned it before – I don't aim to again.

"You need to clear out of here, Champ," Marthy said. Her voice was low and dull, and flat, like somebody speaking at a funeral.

I shook my head. "I reckon I'm all right 'til daylight."

"I don't mean get out of this house, for the night," she said. "I mean get out of this country, for good. Or at least 'til the war's over."

I turned to look at her. The firelight made shadows dance on her face. "What the hell are you goin' on about, woman?"

She settled herself into a straight chair. "You cain't go on like this. The Yankees has got Tennessee, it's time you face up to it."

"I don't reckon I'm scairt of a few damn Yankees," I said, and immediately them words brung the image of Harry Cropper into my mind – blood spreading onto the 'backer stain on his gut.

"No, I don't reckon ye are," she said. "You ain't got sense enough to be. But there's Yankees in other places, and you can fight them – with the rest of the Confederate Army behind ye, instead of by yourself."

I turned to the fire. The heat from it warmed my face.

"I cain't do that, honey. These people here depend on me. I have to protect 'em."

"You cain't protect 'em, Champ. All you're gonna do is make it worse for 'em."

"Like hell," I said, maybe too quick.

"They're punishin' them that helps ye," she continued, her voice still flat. "Spikin' wells, burnin' barns – when crops come up they'll burn them. And it ain't no secret what Sherman told 'em – make the people suffer if'n they harbor guerillas. Pretty soon they'll quit askin' who it is in particular, and just burn out ever'body. On account of you."

"It ain't like that, and you know it," I said. "They'd be doin' worser'n all that if I wadn't here to make 'em hold back, from fear of what I'll do back to 'em."

I felt her hand on my arm, felt her presence behind me. "There's other battles," she said.

I stared into the fire for a long time. I bit my lip. Finally I couldn't hold it back no more, and it come busting out.

"These people has been good to us. I have a duty to 'em, and you act like you don't care. Sometimes I think—"

"Sometimes you think what?"

"When the war started you didn't want me rangin' off, you wanted me close by so's I could hunt for Jim. Now he's left the country, and you want me to do the same, so's I'll find him."

"You said you wanted to find him." The hand left my arm.

"I do. But this war comes first right now. Defendin' these people. I can always find Jim when that's been done."

I heard her feet on the floorboards, heard the creak of her body settling back into the chair. I turned now, finally, to look at her.

"The Lord didn't make you to be no defender, Champ Ferguson. You ain't no damn good at it. When was the last time you defended somebody and they stayed defended?"

I didn't answer. I felt my cheeks burn, no longer from the fire.

"The Lord made you to be an avenger," she continued. "He made you to hunt things down and kill 'em. You need to stick with what you're good at."

"I can do both."

"You ain't got no focus, that's always been your problem. Jim gets out of sight and ye forget about him. Maybe you don't want to find him at all."

"I'll kill him."

"You've killed ever'body but him, so far."

"I'll kill him, dammit!"

My hands balled up into fists. I wanted to hit something. I would have shoved my hands into the fire if that would have made her quit talking. Her voice was a knife all of a sudden, slipping under my skin and twisting.

"I never expected you to defend me, Champ."

"I should have been there that day."

"Is that what you think? I never expected you to defend me. Men always say they're gonna defend somebody, and they never do. I never expected you to. I just wanted you to make him pay."

I shook my head. Tears blurred my eyes. "Knowing what they done – made me feel weak, and helpless. It made me feel as helpless as when Ann Eliza and our little boy died."

"It ain't the same."

"It is."

"Do you think I don't know what it is to have a baby die?" she asked.

"You don't."

"I had a baby die before I even met you, Champ. Two years before I met you."

My mouth opened on its own. "What?"

I had met Marthy when she was sixteen – she was living with her daddy and her little brothers and sisters.

"It was borned dead," she said. The tone of her voice was no different on this subject than it had been on any other. "It was borned dead, and I was glad."

"What are you sayin', Marthy?"

"Men say they're gonna protect you. My daddy called what he done protecting me." She looked into my eyes, and hers was cold. "I never expected no man to protect me, not even you."

Then she looked away, into the fire. "I just want you to make him pay."

"What did your daddy do, Marthy?"

"My daddy is dead, it don't matter no more."

"What did he do?"

She rocked gently in her chair. "I just want you to make him pay."

"I will, Marthy."

"Swear it."

"I swear it."

She never looked away from the fire, and didn't speak no more. I got up and went into the other room. I sat beside Ann's bed, and watched over her through the night.

Chapter 42

We met up in Cumberland County, near the banks of the Obed River. A light snow was coming down – soft powder dancing in the air around us, whispering as it hit the trees and the ground. Despite the fact that hundreds of men was gathered together, there was very little noise – the snow was blanketing us all, smothering our sound. I love snow falling in the woods. If'n you listen, you can almost hear God breathing.

The snow wasn't the only reason for our silence, though. Our hearts was heavy. The Yankees had our homes, and we couldn't get them back – the best we could hope to do was make sure the Yankees wasn't comfortable in them.

My company had joined with Scott Bledsoe's, and George Carter's. We also had about thirty Tennessee-born Texas Rangers who had come home to fight Yankees. Come the morning, we aimed to head southwest into White County and hit whatever enemy we found, hard. Then, as always, we would run away – melt into the trees, hide our tracks as best we could by riding through the icy rivers. We was a pack of wolves, lean and rangy and starving – near-crazy with the quiet need to tear apart our prey.

We built a few fires. The dark clouds and the snow would hide our smoke. We ate what little rations we had, and settled in to wait for the next day's ride. The three of us – me, Scott, and Carter – huddled around the same fire with our lieutenants. I had Reese and Rains with me. Scott had three old boys, including Hank Kirby. Hank is the one I've mentioned before as being from White County – he had joined Scott's outfit at the very beginning, and stuck with him even after many of the others from around Sparta had come over to me. They hadn't done that out of disloyalty to Scott, but on account of my company was the one defending their homes. Most of them that rode with Scott was from Putnam, Jackson, or Overton Counties. Kirby, though, he stuck as close to Scott as a short shadow.

"Damn Stokes, that damn son of a bitch," Kirby said. That was how a lot of our conversations was starting off nowadays.

"Damn son of a bitch," George Carter echoed, nodding. Then he stuck a corncob pipe in his mouth and commenced to lighting it.

Carter was a beefy man, even though our rations was scarce. His face was always red too, no matter what the weather or the time of year. There was nothing soft about him, though – he was stout as an ox, and twice as stubborn. He came from down Spencer way. It was a little town, not big as a speck, named after Tom "Big Foot" Spencer – one of the long hunters from the early days, and a friend of my Grandpa Champion Ferguson. They had hunted bears and fit Cherokees together back in the old days, when Tennessee was all wilderness.

Carter was about ten years younger' n me. We looked as different as day and night – me all lanky and rawboned and four inches over six foot, and him eight inches shorter and a good deal rounder, his face smooth and red. On the inside, though, me and him was about the same. He didn't believe in taking no shit off of nobody, and he would as soon spit in Saint Peter's eye as not. And he hated Yankees with a passion. He had about eighty boys riding with him, mostly from around Spencer, Pikeville, and McMinnville. There wasn't as many of them as there was of us, or of Scott's bunch, but they still made the Yankees set up and take notice. We was always right proud to have them with us.

Kirby was still grumbling about Colonel Stokes. Ever' once in awhile he would kick at the ground.

"What the hell are you so dang tore up about?" Carter's man Lenny said. Lenny was as tall as me, and twice't as big – built like a bear. He even looked like a bear. The only part of his face not covered with hair was his eyes.

"Stokes has been stirrin' up trouble for months," Lenny added. "Are you just now figurin' that out?"

"That's easy for you to say," Kirby said. "You ain't got nary wife and young'uns – and even if ye did, they'd be in Van Buren County. Ain't no Yankees goes to Van Buren County, it ain't worth the trouble."

"So?"

"So, that son of a bitch Stokes is eatin' me out of house and home while I'm huddled out here in the woods like a scared varmint."

Stokes had moved his headquarters from Alexandria to Sparta, the better to keep an eye on troublemakers, I reckon. He had shut down several businesses in town and used the buildings either to house his troops or store his supplies. Meanwhile he was stripping every farm bare for miles around to feed them troops. Kirby's farm over by Bear Cove had been picked clean, and mine had too – I bet they enjoyed ever' bite they took out of my stores.

As cold and miserable as we was, it made us feel even worse to know our women and children was just as hungry. The men from other areas could rest no easier, because they knowed it was just a matter of time until White County was bled dry and it would be their turn.

"Whinin' about it ain't gonna do ye ary bit of good, Hank'" Scott told his lieutenant. "We all hate Yankees. Yankees is bastards. Let's talk about somethin' else."

I lit my pipe, sucking the smoke in deep. Cigars was hard to come by and it was too damn cold to roll cigarettes. After I had puffed a few times and got it going good, I took the pipe out of my mouth and pointed it at Rains.

"Rains, we need another topic to talk about. You're the best feller I ever heared of for wanderin' completely off the subject – why don't you put your talent to good use and start us off?"

Rains's most common expression stole onto his face. It was the expression of a man who was not sure wh'er he had just been complimented or insulted. He nearly always settled on complimented, no matter if it had been one or not, just to make his self feel better.

He cleared his throat, to announce that he was liable to say something important.

"A feller was tellin' me here while-ago that Jesus wadn't no person a'tall – he was a rabbit."

Everybody sat real still and stared at him. I let my pipe go out. I shook my head and finally broke the silence.

"Well, Rains, that sure as hell is a different subject all right."

"I know, y'uns think I'm joshin' ye. But I seen it with my own eyes. This feller pulled out the Bible and showed me right where it says that."

I stared at him blankly again. "Rains, son, you cain't read."

He looked hurt. "Well shoot, Champ, I know that. This other feller could read, though. He spelt the word out for me and ever'thing. Sure enough, Jesus was a rabbit."

"lf,n ye cain't read," Lenny said, "how do ye even know it was a Bible he was readin' out of?"

"Well, it looked like a Bible. It had a real serious look to it."

"You crazier'n hell," Carter said.

"Jesus was the Lamb of God," Reese said. "I reckon it stands to reason he was the Rabbit of God, too."

Rains shot his comrade a grateful look, and then a smug smile spread across his face. "The Rabbit of God," Rains repeated.

"Rabbi," Scott said.

"What?" said Rains, and several others echoed him.

"Rabbi," Scott said again. "Jesus was a rabbi."

"What's that?" Lenny asked

"A rabbi is a Jewish preacher."

Carter laughed. "Now what are ye sayin', that Jesus was a Jew? Hell, that's crazier'n sayin' he was a rabbit."

Scott chuckled. "Maybe I'm wrong," he said. "Maybe Jesus was a rabbit."

"The Rabbit of God," Rains corrected him.

Carter reached behind his back, into the saddlebag he had been resting on. He pulled out a bottle of whiskey.

"All right, boys," he said. He was grinning like a wicked schoolboy, and his voice was low – he looked around his self real sneaky-like, to make sure none of the men at the other fires could see what he was doing.

"Now that it's dark," he explained softly, "we can pass this bottle around a few times. Them other'ns won't know any different." He uncapped the bottle and took a long pull from it, then wiped his mouth with his sleeve. "It saves their feelin's from bein' hurt, us bein' quiet this way. It's a noble thing."

He reached the bottle over to me. The weight of it in my hand felt good. So did the whiskey sloshing around inside as I turned up the bottle. I sucked smooth liquid fire deep into my belly. I felt tingly and alive. Hell, I needed a good drink if Rains was aiming to discuss religion. I passed the bottle on to Reese, but I surely didn't want to.

"A feller told me the other day," Rains said, "that they found the door to Hell, and it's over in Chiney some'eres."

Reese pressed the bottle into Rains's hand. "Hush and drink," he said. "If ye drink enough maybe you'll start makin' sense."

I closed my eyes and puffed on my pipe. I listened to their voices, and floated away on the sound of them.

The strange feeling come back over me that I'd had the last night I was with Marthy. She wouldn't talk no more about her daddy, nor explain what she had meant – but she didn't need to explain. I'm a growed man, and I know the world is a evil place. I didn't want to think about it.

So I thought of something else instead. I thought of Ann Eliza – of our first year together. I felt her in my arms, warm and wild – I heared her voice in my ear, whispering things no one had ever said to me before and never would again. I had a hell of a lot of fun at the time, but I didn't realize I was living the best days of my life. I wished I could go back and live just one of them again, knowing how special it was.

I shook my head. Maybe the other fellers thought the motion was a silent comment on Rains's foolishness, but it wasn't. I was trying to shake the images out of my mind – the good ones and the bad ones alike. I had never been one to dwell on the past, or the future neither. That's how come I was able to enjoy them days with Ann Eliza as much as I did. I lived in them completely.

Who knows, I remember thinking. Maybe one day I'll look back on this as one of the good times. Not the cold and the hunger, or the fighting, but just setting around the fire with my brother soldiers – warmed by smoke in my mouth and whiskey in my veins, the soft snow sighing to me as it fell.

I looked across the fire and seen Scott staring toward me, understanding in his eyes. Somehow, he always seemed to know what I was thinking, without me having to say it. We both grinned.

Life is hell, boys. Take your pleasure where you can find it. Write that down if ye have to.

~ ~ * ~ ~

We went into White County looking for Yankees, and it turns out – as usual – they was looking just as hard for us. Several companies of Stokes's command had took the Old Kentucky Road north up to Cookeville, then doubled back and rode south through Dry Valley, right at the head of the Calfkiller. They knowed that was my territory. They aimed to beat the bushes along the Calfkiller, and try to scare me up. Stokes had put Blackburn in command. Tinker Dave's bunch rode with them as scouts. Stokes his self was in Sparta, preparing a nice victory speech about how I had been made an example of.

I didn't know all this the night before, of course, but I found out pretty quick the next morning. My neighbor Horace Carmichael had got wind of it in town, and – knowing about where we was – sent one of his boys north to bring me the news. Blackburn and Tinker Dave was going to find some Rebs, all right – a hell of a lot more than they had counted on. We beat a trail to Dry Valley, so we could be waiting for them.

We set ourselves up along both sides of Dug Hill Road, then sent LeRoy Reese and Bob Timmons on ahead to invite Blackburn to our party. We was in the high ground along the road – the river was a short ways off.

Reese and Timmons seen the Yankees coming. They shot at them, and then turned tail and run like hell. Blackburn give the order to his men to give chase. Tinker Dave tried his best to talk him out of it, but Blackburn wouldn't listen. He smelled Reb blood.

They came pouring down that road, into the valley. We waited 'til they was all there, and then we closed in on them and opened fire. It was a slaughter.

The guns echoed in the valley like thunder tearing apart the sky. Men screamed, and died. It was like shooting fish in a barrel – they was packed together so close they barely had room to fall when we shot them.

They broke ranks and scattered in every direction like quail. We spurred our mounts forward and converged down into the valley. Yankees charged right up the hill at us, hoping to break through – they had no place else to go.

Their eyes was bugged out and their mouths twisted in fear. We shot at them and they shot back. Hank Kirby grunted as a bullet smashed into the right side of his chest, just under the collarbone.

I had emptied all three of my revolvers by then. I had a few pre-loaded, capped cylinders in my coat pocket, but there was no time to change them. I pulled out my saber and spurred old Jimbo. If you thought that first Yankee's eyes was popping before, you should've seen him when I come barreling down on him swinging that sword. Jimbo rammed into his horse – while the Yankee was struggling to stay in the saddle, I run a foot of steel through him.

A few yards away I seen another bunch breaking for it. Most of them didn't make it. One who did was Tinker Dave. A man riding next to him yelled as two shots took him in the torso. Tinker Dave grabbed the man's reins and the two escaped together. The man looked familiar. I realized after a second, while I was pulling my sword loose from my dying enemy, that the shot man was Dallas Beaty – Tinker Dave's last living son. I found out he died the next day from his wounds.

A big group of Yankees had panicked and run the wrong way – into the river. I reckon it's safe to say they wasn't from Blackburn's company of White County natives. We follered them into the water and massacred them. The Yankees found there was as many Rebs on the far side of the river as was chasing them, and they was still trapped. I was keeping my eye out for Blackburn, but he had escaped already.

I reined Jimbo up and leisurely reloaded my guns. I kept a cold eye on the proceedings all the while. George Carter was wading around bashing wounded Yankees' brains out with a rock, mindful of saving powder and shot. A couple of Blackburn's boys managed to make it back out of the water near me. I calmly shot them down.

All told, we had killed more than half of the Fifth Tennessee Union troopers that had come into the valley. The Calfkiller was turning red. Blue-clad bodies floated slowly in the water. It was prett'near the beautifulest damn thing I had ever seen.

Chapter 43

Of course, Colonel Stokes had to cancel his little speech. They tell me he was practicing it when the first survivors of the battle come tearing into town. He had planned to do his talking at the town square – instead, by nightfall, the square was filled with the dead bodies his men had gone to Dry Valley and pulled out of the river and the wooded hills. They was laid out side-by-side, about fifty of them. A few of them was local boys, so there was a little bit of wailing and carrying on - but there wasn't a hell of a lot. Most of the townfolk filed past the dead Tennessee Yankees and smiled.

Stokes sent a dispatch to his superiors, asking for more help in catching me. Within a few days, Governor Andrew Johnson was asking for more federal troops to fight the deadly menace of Champ Ferguson. That's the way it always seemed to go – no matter how many independent companies I was fighting alongside, folks on both sides called us "Champ Ferguson's bunch". Scott didn't seem to mind who got the credit, so long as the cause was served, but I could tell that it ate away at Carter.

Tinker Dave was in Sparta, fretting over his injured son that he knowed would most likely not recover. Joe Blackburn, he was fretting over his injured reputation, which also might not recover.

Hank Kirby was hurt bad, but it looked like he would pull through. Where the Yankee bullet hadn't killed him, though, it seemed to be like his own stubbornness was liable to. He insisted on being carried to his own home in White County to recover – about the stupidest notion I had ever heared of, and everybody else agreed with me. Scott tried to talk his friend out of making his self a helpless target thataway, but Kirby wasn't having none of it. He had been kept away from his family long enough, and here was a chance to be with them for a spell. Maybe he was so tired of fighting he didn't give a damn wh'er he died or not, so long as he had a few hours of peace first. We carried him home.

Days went by, and the Yankees never bothered him none. They had to of known he was there. Stokes – reinforced by troops from Indiana – was combing through the woods looking for Rebs to kill, and never give ary bit of attention to a wounded one right under his nose. I was expecting to hear that Tinker Dave or Rufus Dowdy had come to Kirby's house and cut his throat, but three weeks passed by and they didn't. Tinker Dave had went home to Jamestown and buried his son, and then disappeared for a spell. Knowing Rufus Dowdy, I figured he was hiding under a rock somewheres in fear we was after him next. Which we would have been, had we knowed where he was.

It looked like Kirby had been give time to heal up enough to be moved again. It looked, too, like the Yankees had forgot about him in their craving to catch me – but that situation couldn't last forever. I reckon Scott finally decided his lieutenant had done got enough of a furlough, and it was time to take him someplace safer. He snuck down to Kirby's house in Bear Cove, driving an old buckboard. It took him about an hour of arguing, but he finally convinced Kirby to get in his wagon and leave with him.

What Scott didn't know – but all of us should have figured on – was that Blackburn had a couple of scouts posted in the woods near Kirby's house, waiting for just such an occasion. One scout kept watch on the place while Scott argued with Kirby, and the other one took off down the road to fetch Blackburn. If Kirby and Scott hadn't both been so stubborn – if Scott had left after five minutes, with or without his friend – all that faced him would've been two scouts, and maybe he could've got away. Instead, when Scott walked out the door to clear a spot in the wagon for Kirby's mattress, he found his self staring down the rifles of twenty Yankee soldiers.

"Reckon we got you now, you Rebel scum," Blackburn said.

Kirby's wife come out behind Scott, and screamed. A couple of soldiers grabbed her and pulled her off to the side. She told folks later that Scott Bledsoe looked around frantically in every direction. When he seen there was no escape, a calm look come over his face and he sighed. He run his hands once't through his thick, wavy, chestnut-colored hair. He straightened up and looked Blackburn square in the eye.

"Do what you've got to do, you sons of bitches. I'll show ye how a brave Southern man dies."

"Fire," Blackburn commanded, and eighteen rifle balls crashed into Captain Scott Bledsoe, the bravest man in Tennessee, and the best friend an old boy like me could ever have. He collapsed in the dust, and never let out another sound. Blackburn walked into the house, took out his pistol, and blowed Hank Kirby's brains out in his own bed, his young'uns huddled in the next room.

Blackburn come back outside and walked over to the sobbing widow. "You tell 'em, woman. Tell 'em this is what's comin' to all of 'em."

She gathered herself together enough to spit on him, but he paid it no mind. I reckon he was used to it.

~ ~ * ~ ~

Edgar Whitley came rushing into camp at about dinner-time with the story, no more than two hours after it happened. The news had spread like wildfire.

I felt my knees buckling under me. I stumbled over to a log and collapsed onto it. It felt like somebody had took a sledgehammer to my gut. Everybody moved away from me. Everybody, as usual, except Rains – and even he kept a little distance and stayed quiet.

Scott was the only man on this earth who knowed what my life was like, and understood it. Onliest other one who come close was Tinker Dave, and he was a Yankee. All of a sudden, I felt all alone in the world in a way I had never done before. I felt cold and empty on the inside, in a way that the snow and the hunger had never made me.

I kept seeing Scott's face before me. I kept feeling his presence beside of me, and hearing his laugh off in the woods. Then – slowly at first, then more quickly – the cold melted away. It turned warmer and warmer until it was white-hot. I felt comfortable – almost good – with the familiar rage. It was something I could bear. It was something I could act on.

First Jory, and now Scott – in almost the same way. It had to stop. There would be no more – there would be no more. I stood and paced in a small, tight circle, my hands clenched into shaking fists. I let all the frustrated anger still pent up from the situation with Marthy and Ann and Jim flow into me as well. I felt like a wall with a fire hiding inside it – smoking, smoldering, ready to explode. I screamed like a wounded bear.

"I swear, by God, I will kill that bastard," I hollered. Nobody asked which one – they knowed I meant Joe Blackburn. "Jesus Christ His Self cain't stop me. By God, I swear."

~ ~ * ~ ~

Like ever' church in Tennessee or Kentucky I had ever knowed of, Cherry Creek Baptist had services on Wednesday evenings same as on Sundays. Them righteous folks didn't like to go for a full week without praising the Lord and seeing their neighbors, and having their neighbors see them praise the Lord. Quite a few of Blackburn's home-growed Yankees attended this particular church, and sometimes Blackburn his self did.

This Wednesday they was fixing to have some company. My boys was a bunch of hell-raising sons of bitches, and I figured it was about time they found Jesus. If'n we found Joe Blackburn too, well, so much the better. A righteous man should want to die in church, in my opinion.

We could hear them in yonder singing. They was bringing in the sheaves. I never did figure out what the hell that was all about.

"Remember, boys," I said. "Shoot high, 'less'n I tell y'uns different."

I drawed out my pistol and shot into the church house. The boys all done the same. Bullets splintered wood all over the top of the building. I reckon Rains thought I didn't notice he was purposely shooting so high that he missed the church completely.

Women and young'uns was screaming. Men was hollering for us to stop. The preacher run to the door waving his arm, begging us not to shoot.

I raised up my hand, and the firing stopped.

"This is the house of God!" the preacher said, half-sobbing. "Y'uns have done shot Ann Gooch in the arm!"

"That was a accident," I called back to him. "But that's what happens when ye let traitors come in and pray with ye."

"God loves all of us, son."

"Good. Then He'll be glad to see a few Yankees comin' to join Him." The preacher's eyes widened. "You send Joe Blackburn on out here, now."

"He's not here."

I nudged Jimbo forward. "I reckon we'll see." I went up the steps and through the front door – still on horseback. I rode straight up the center aisle.

Folks was hunched over, hiding in their pews. One woman, who I figured had to be Miss Ann Gooch, sat bawling and staring at her bloody arm. Here and yonder I seen patches of blue uniform.

My eyes settled on one. He melted under my gaze like ice in the sun. "Step up here, boy."

He didn't move. I cocked my pistol. "I said step up here." He stood – it didn't look to be easy – and walked out into the aisle. "I take it you're Fifth Cavalry, boy."

"Company – Company D, sir," he said, his voice shaking. I leveled the gun at him.

"Where's Blackburn."

"He ain't here," the boy whined.

"You tell him," I said. "Tell him he ain't safe nowhere. I'm fixin' to hunt him down and kill him. Once't I'm done with that, I might take a notion to go to the governor's mansion and shoot Andrew Johnson – only thing I hate worser'n Yankees is Tennessee Republicans, which is all Johnson is wh'er he wants to admit it or not. You got all that, boy?"

"Yes – yes sir."

"The next time I see this church full of Yankees, by God, I aim to burn it down. This is Rebel country, and nobody better forget it."

With that I turned Jimbo around – knocking over the preacher's podium – and rode back out the door and down the steps. I hoped somebody would make a move toward me, but none of 'em did.

We rode off. I didn't hear no more singing. I doubt if there was any.

Chapter 44

It was two days later that we caught them. Blackburn was at the head of about twenty men again – it might well have been the same twenty who had killed Scott. It was the early morning hours, just after dawn. I don't know what would possess the man to travel with such a light detail when he knowed I was dead-set after him – maybe he figured I wouldn't be up and around at that time of day. I reckon he found out different.

Me and about fifty of my men had set up a cold camp in the rocky crags around Wild Cat Falls. This was just off the road to Crossville, about a mile east of the relay station of the Nashville-to-Knoxville stage line. A lot of famous folks had laid over at that station, I reckon, from Andrew Jackson to Davy Crockett. It was in-between Sparta and Bon Air, where the Rodgers family had that health spa the Yankee officers was so fond of visiting. I figured it would just be a matter of time before Blackburn passed by, but I wouldn't have guessed it would be so soon. Maybe the Lord was smiling on me – or maybe He just didn't want me shooting up no more of His churches.

They was caught by surprise in the open road – it wasn't much of a battle. It was a lot like the fight at Dug Hill Road, but on a smaller scale. Instead of being caught beside the river, this time Blackburn was caught with steep hills and cliffsides on his right and a dropoff on his left, with no place to go but to Hell. Old Joe Blackburn was a pure terror when the odds was twenty-to-one in his favor – but put him at a disadvantage, and he fell apart. He could have used Tinker Dave and his boys that morning, maybe he would have had a fighting chance that way. He didn't have Tinker Dave, though. There'd be no escaping for him this time.

Gunsmoke clouded the road like a morning fog. Men and horses screamed, a piercing noise that cut through even the gunfire. I caught a glimpse of Blackburn, blood streaming down from a wound in his upper arm, his face white as the ghost he was about to become.

I dug the spurs into Jimbo's sides and raced toward him. I was so intent on Blackburn I didn't pay no attention to his men. One of them drawed a bead on me, and shot. I seen the muzzle blast out of the corner of my eye at the same instant I felt something like an ax handle slam into my side. I was knocked out of the saddle, and sent tumbling to the ground – practically right at Blackburn's feet. The whole world was spinning around me, but I could see the glint of triumph and joy in Blackburn's eye. He raised his saber and wheeled his mount around.

My boys seen what was happening. A volley of shots rang out over my fallen body – punching holes in the soldier who had shot me, Blackburn's horse, and Blackburn his self. He fell to the ground a few feet away from me, and his horse fell on top of him. The dead animal pinned Blackburn to the ground. I got a good look at the body of the Yankee who shot me. It was the boy from the church. That's what I get for leaving a Yankee unshot, I reckon.

I pulled myself to my feet, wobbling unsteadily. I was bleeding like a stuck pig, and I wasn't for sure wh'er I'd been kilt or not. It hurt like hell. Blackburn was worse off than me – he was shot through the guts now besides the arm, not to mention he was wearing a dead horse. His weapons had went flying.

Blood frothed and bubbled from his mouth as he glared at me. He was wheezing. "You go to hell, Ferguson," he snarled, his voice hoarse and cracked.

"See ye there," I answered, my own voice none too steady.

I bent over him. When I did, pain shot through me so intense I like to have fell plumb over. I was determined, though, that Captain Joe Blackburn feel Rebel spit on his face one more time before he died. I hawked and spat. Then I drawed out my Bowie knife. I grabbed him by the hair of the head, trying to ignore the pain about to make me pass out, and cut his throat. I sank to my haunches and sat in the road, watching his eyes bulge as he choked on his own blood and died.

It wasn't good enough. I wanted to kill him again. I wanted to cut him into pieces with his own sword. Nothing would ever be enough to repay him – or his Yankee friends – for all the pain and misery they had caused me.

The fighting was over. All of Blackburn's men was dead, along with a few of mine. LeRoy leaned over me and examined my wound.

"It ain't too bad, Champ," he said. His hands was busy wrapping a bandage around me.

I tried to grin. "Like hell," I said.

"Bullet hit a rib and bounced off. 'Course, the rib's broke – I don't think it's pokin' into nothin' vital, though."

"Help me up."

"You better lay still for a spell, Champ. We'll prang a wagon for ye."

"Ain't got no time for ary wagon, there's liable to be more Yankees comin'. I'll ride."

LeRoy's eyes narrowed. "You go bouncin' around in a saddle, Cap'n, that broke rib is liable to puncture a lung or somethin'."

"By God, I said I'll ride!" I looked around. "Rains! Come here and help me up."

"I'm comin', Champ," Rains said.

LeRoy shook his head. "You're about the most pig-headed man I ever met."

Rains pulled me to my feet, and I winced. Edgar Whitley brung Jimbo around. I leaned against the horse's side and caught my breath. Then I put a foot in the stirrup.

"Give me a hand, boys." Rains and Edgar boosted me into the saddle. I bit my lip to keep from hollering.

"They's some folks back in the woods about a mile or so from here that'll give us some beds to use," LeRoy said. "For you and Graham, and Lowery. We'll all make camp behind their house and guard y'uns while I send somebody after a wagon to move y'uns someplace safer. Plus we got six boys needs to be took to their families for buryin'."

"We got us some new horses, extry guns, and plenty of ammunition now, though," Bob Timmons said with a grin. He was pulling on a pair of boots he had took off a dead Yankee. The Yankee looked familiar, even though I didn't know him – I found out later he was a cousin to one of our own boys that got kilt that day.

We moved out. I rode off from the other'ns. "I'll be right with y'uns," I said.

"Champ," LeRoy said, exasperated.

"Y'uns go on," I said. "Just for a minute."

I rode around a bend in the road, to where there was a cliff on one side. The rock was a good sixty or seventy foot high. The top was flat, and covered with trees and brush. A few small trees growed out the side of it. It was perched near the edge of a dropoff. When you stand at the base of the rock and look to the north, you can see for miles and miles. At night you can see the fires from towns below – Sparta, Cookeville, Smithville, McMinnville, not to mention the little villages here and yonder. If there hasn't been too much of a dry spell lately, and Wild Cat Creek ain't down, you can hear the waterfall.

All them towns, all them counties – and Yankees in control of it all. It made my heart sick to think of it. It's damned odd. At the start of the war, I didn't care much one way or the other – but now it made all the difference in the world. In my heart it cast a shadow even over my own feuds and private hates, something I never thought would happen. I couldn't rightly put my finger on exactly when it had happened, or how, but I was changed.

I thought of Scott Bledsoe's lonely grave. I hoped he could rest a little easier knowing that the men who killed him was laying dead theirselves – but I knowed he wouldn't. He would never rest easy, not even in death, knowing his home was controlled by Yankees. I'm sure that, if Scott had been give the choice, he'd druther have seen Joe Blackburn and his men go alive and free, if such a trade would of meant driving the Yankees away.

I hadn't changed quite that much. I aimed to go on doing what I done best, until they kilt me too. Not just for me and Marthy, and the memory of Scott and Jory and all my other friends who had fallen, but for my people, and my home. For the South.

I realized I wasn't alone. I looked over my shoulder, and was not the least bit surprised that the clopping I heared was from Rains Philpot's approaching horse.

"Ye need to come on, now, Champ," he said. "Ye need to lay down and rest. We have to get that rib set, and get that hole sewed up."

"Yeah," I said. "I reckon."

Rains looked at me with sad eyes, like a hunting dog whose master had left him behind. He started to speak, then hesitated – and then got the words out.

"You still got me, Champ."

I smiled a faint, sad smile in spite of the pain, and nodded slowly. "I know it, Rains. I always got you – sure as the sun comes up in the mornin'." Rains looked happy, and grateful, and relieved.

"Come on, now, Champ," he repeated.

We rode off slowly. The buzzards was already circling. It seemed like they follered me ever' where I went anymore. I wasn't sure if it was because they knowed I keep them in business, or because they knowed it was only a matter of time 'til they got me too.

It didn't matter.

Chapter 45

Many's the time over the next few weeks that I would cuss my stupidity in letting myself get wounded. To be shot by somebody I'd had under my gun, and let go, was nothing short of embarrassing. It just goes to show I'd been right all along in how I done things. If'n you kill somebody you know aims to kill you first chance they get, it's self-defense in advance. And it's just plain smart. Plus, I had let my guard down. In my rush to get my hands on Blackburn, I had blundered right into a bullet. A feller cain't afford too many mistakes like that when he's in the fighting business.

I had plenty of time to think about it. My busted rib might not have made me ary cripple, but I wasn't able to charge around on horseback for awhile, neither. I surely couldn't go home to my farm – I didn't want to end up like Hank Kirby, and I surely would have.

There is an old abandoned cabin deep in the woods around England's Cove. It was so far back in the tangled brush only a handful of people knowed about it, that I was aware of. Back several years before the war, me and Rains had come down to White County on a hunting trip with a couple of old boys who was from there. One of them, Charlie Parmer, got throwed off his horse about a year later and broke his neck. The other'n, his cousin Will, had joined up with Dibrell's cavalry and rode off to Georgia with the rest of them.

The four of us had got kindly turned around one day when we was running a fox – we was all drunker'n hell, it's a wonder we didn't shoot ourselves – and wound up wandering them woods for hours. That's when we stumbled on the cabin, so growed over with vines that Rains walked smack into it so hard he liked to have knocked his self out cold. In all the time we'd been hiding around them woods during the war, we had never went back to the cabin – it would've done us no good if 'n we had a passel of men with us, and the times it was just me and Rains we was always having to stay on the move.

Now it was time to go to that cabin and stay put for a spell. Rains went with me. I almost wished he hadn't of –

he fussed over me like a mother hen. Like to have drove me crazy. Still, having him there felt good in a way.

We snuck through the woods in the middle of the night sometimes, to my house. There I would steal an hour or two with my family, and be gone well before daylight.

LeRoy kept the boys together during that time. They hit the Yankees now and then, here and yonder – just enough to let them know we was still around. Folks just assumed I was with them. They made their hits fast, and nobody bothered to stand out in the open and get a good look at them. We kept my injury a secret best we could – so the Yankees was looking for dozens or hundreds of men on horseback, not for one wounded roughneck.

There was an old boy that had rode with us just a couple of times, name of Terry Webb. He didn't stand out as being especially handy nor especially worthless, and in fact I would've forgot all about him if he hadn't started making a name for his self in other ways. He was a lot like John Homer – not a wild redneck like me and George Carter, but more along the lines of being lowdown and wicked.

Once't Webb seen that riding with me included getting shot at as often as doing the shooting, he dropped out. Him and his brothers got together a gang of cutthroats and commenced to doing all kinds of meanness in the region. Robbery, kidnapping, rape, murder – wasn't nothing too low for them skunks. They called theirselves Rebels, but they preyed on the people of both sides. They was real active while I was stove up in that cabin, and LeRoy and the boys was leading the Yankees on a chase all through the Cumberland Mountains. With Yankees and us both occupied, the Webb gang had them a field day.

The worst part is – just like everything else that got done in the Upper Cumberland – somehow or 'nother a lot of it got blamed on me. There wasn't none of it brung up agin me at my trial, and that's good, but there's still tales circulating in Putnam and Jackson Counties and around of vile things that them rulicky sons of bitches done, only the tales say I done 'em. The Yankees finally caught them and wiped them out – and if I'd of caught them I would've did the same – but the damage was done. I wanted to make sure you're set straight on that matter. I've done some mean things, sure enough, but I ain't never harmed no women and children, and I ain't never robbed nobody purely for the sake of my own gain. And I never harmed ary loyal Southerner. I got actions enough all my own to hang for, without taking the blame for a bunch of sorry-ass cowards.

~ ~ * ~ ~

One day toward the end of April I got bold enough to venture out alone, pretty much in the open, and in the broad daylight. I rode through the woods to my favorite spot on the Calfkiller, just a stone's throw from my house. I hitched old Jimbo to a tree – he was all I had left. I had give the rest of my string for the general use of my company 'til I could get back to them.

Then I went and sat at that shallow point where the water bubbles over the rocks, and sounds like distant voices. The sun shone bright and yellow on the river. I closed my eyes.

When I opened them up again, I seen Ann walking toward me on the opposite bank. She didn't seem at all surprised to find me there.

"Hellfire, gal, what are you doin' out here?" I said, but my voice was warm and bright as the April sunshine.

"Come to see you, Daddy." She waded across and set down beside of me.

"I never told nobody I was comin' here," I said.

"I come out here most ever' day," Ann answered. "I figured I was bound to run into ye before long."

Jimbo nickered at her, anxious to be petted, even though he had only seen her a few times since I'd had him. She reached out and stroked his flank.

"What made ye think I'd come here?" I asked. I had never told anybody about the place, nor about how it made me feel.

"I've seen your track along the bank before," she said. "I recognized it. Besides, this place just feels like you."

I chuckled. "Like hell. This place is peaceful and quiet. And beautiful."

"I know."

She leaned her head on my shoulder, and I put my arm around her. When she looked up I grinned, and placed my forehead on hers. So close to being a woman now, and yet her eyes was still the same as when she was a baby.

The voices in the river whispered to me as always – accusing, consoling, damning, inviting – but this time I didn't listen. They no longer seemed as real, at least for the moment.

We sat there for a long time. We never talked none. We just sat.

Chapter 46

It felt good to be back in the saddle and back on the warpath. For a little bit, it even seemed like things was looking up some. Colonel Stokes and his Fifth Tennessee had lost most of their bite – after several battles and skirmishes, and a lot of desertions due to low morale – by summer Stokes didn't have but two hundred men. He packed up and left Sparta. The Fifth set up its new headquarters in McMinnville, where they could be closer to reinforcements. The other regiments sent to help him had all been called away somewheres else.

We didn't want to rest on our laurels. We decided to range out a little bit, and give the rest of the Yankees some attention too, so's they wouldn't be jealous. There was still the Fourth Tennessee Union Infantry, quartered at Kingston – about halfway between Sparta and Knoxville. I heared they had them a whole herd of horses crying out to be rescued from Union hands. I never could say no to a horse.

I took a few dozen men over to Kingston, a distance of about fifty miles. George Carter come along too, with half-a-dozen hands. He didn't want to be left out of the fun, or lose any credit. I went ahead with a couple of scouts to check it all out – I like to see such things for myself, rather than trust somebody else's judgment.

I whistled softly. I just had to shake my head at the Yankees' foolishness. There must have been five hundred prime horses in that valley down yonder – as valuable as a gold mine by that part of the war – and had just five men posted to guard them. The rest of their company was quartered about two miles down the road. The moon was high in a cloudless sky when we rode down into the valley. We went up to the sergeant in charge. He kept on puffing on his corncob pipe 'til I rode close enough for him to see that my clothes wasn't blue. Then the pipe dropped out of his mouth and his eyes went wide.

"Evenin', Sarge," I said. "Captain Champ Ferguson, Independent Tennessee Confederate Cavalry, at your service. We come here to take these horses off'n your hands. We can go on ahead and kill you fellers too, while we're at it – if that's what you reckon it'll take."

"Um – nossir. I don't reckon it'll take that."

"Good."

I waved, and my men rounded up all the guards and disarmed them.

"Y'uns set down," I told the Yankees, as the boys rounded up the horses. The sergeant was the first to hit the ground.

"Who's your commander, Sarge – Major Reeves?"

"Yes sir."

"Well, you give the major my regards. Tell him to come see me sometime, if he wants to. I'm always ready for company."

We took Major Reeves's horses and headed south with them. I learned later that Reeves took the rest of his company and started a pursuit as soon as the disarmed guards sent him word.

The poor boy must've been right confused on what to do – set out after me with a single company, or ride a few miles east and gather his whole regiment, giving me time to get plumb away. He settled on the first choice. He couldn't have won out, either way. He figured that out, eventually – realizing he didn't have enough men to accomplish much even if he did catch me, the major turned around and went back to Kingston. He was mad as a hornet, I figured – but as it turned out, I'd had no idea just how mad he was.

~ ~ * ~ ~

Reeves showed up at White County three days later, at the head of his whole regiment.

First off, naturally, they headed for England Cove – everybody knowed that was my territory.

Maybe the good major figured we would have a camp set up close by the old river road, with a sign posted that read "Champ Ferguson Headquarters," and five hundred horses tethered in a corral. I reckon he was disappointed.

That herd had been cut into a hundred pieces. Each man on the raid had took a horse or two for his own use, and the rest had been divided up and distributed to loyal neighbors in White County, folks we could trust to hold a few horses for us until we needed them. As usual, we had done something similar with the *men* in our company – we divided up and scattered.

This time, Reeves didn't turn around and go home. Instead, he led his troopers to every house in the area. If he seen stock that looked like it might have once belonged to the U.S. Government, he took it and called it "reclaimed." If it didn't look suspicious, he took it anyway and called it "captured." He took the people's valuables, he took their money, and what was too big to carry off he burned.

They hit my house, too. I don't reckon they knowed it *was* my house, otherwise they would probably have burned the whole place to the ground. They hit every home from there to town, in fact, a distance of fifteen miles. Reeves later bragged that "the most unparalleled plunder was committed."

The Yankees arrived in Sparta in the middle of the afternoon, towing along nine of my men they had managed to catch unawares in their own homes. Reeves declared martial law. Every man in Sparta was arrested and herded into the town square, where they was kept all through the night. Women and children cried in the streets, expecting their menfolks to be shot dead and the town burnt down around them.

While armed guards kept watch over the citizens, the rest of the regiment ransacked the town. Reeves set up a command post in the courthouse. Just like at the outlying farms, everything of value was either stolen or destroyed.

The next morning Reeves addressed the people of the town. He told them there would be no more mercy for them who gave aid to guerrillas, or who resisted the Union Army in any way.

He turned everybody loose, except for the nine men of my company, but told them he was coming back with reinforcements. They would then stay until they had captured all guerrillas – and live off the citizens' crops in the meantime. He would burn the town if that's what it took, and it would be no great loss anyways since it was little more than a nest of Rebels.Then they rode off.

My men that they captured went to prison.

I didn't learn about none of this until the next day, as me and a few of the boys had been giving some Union sympathizers hell over near Livingston. I come home to find a pile of rubbish in front of my house – broke dishes, ashes, charred farm tools. Marthy told me everything that had happened.

I felt the familiar rage rising up in me, burning my face. "I'll get all the boys together," I said. "We'll ride over to Kingston and hit their command post in the middle of the night, burn it down. We'll take back everything they stole, and then some."

"You won't," Marthy said.

"What?"

"If you do that, they'll be right back here the next day. This time they'll hit every little community in the county – Bon Air, Cassville, Cherry Creek, everywhere. They'll burn houses, and they'll kill people."

"What the hell am I supposed to do, woman? Stand still for this?"

"This happened because of you, Champ. You know it's true."

I felt like the breath had been knocked out of me. People had lost everything – and the harder I tried to defend them, the more they would lose.

"You need to gather your boys together, all right," Marthy said. "Then you need to clear out of here, like I've been sayin' all along. If ye don't, there won't be nothin' left in this county but burnt chimneys and bones."

I took a deep breath. She was right. I nodded. "I'll be back," I said.

"I know ye will, Champ. You always come back."

I kissed her, and I kissed Ann, and I rode away to start gathering the company together, them that wanted to come. Most did. By the next day we was riding south, toward Georgia, to offer our services to General Joe Wheeler.

It was a couple of weeks later that Rufus Dowdy's Union guerrillas came in the middle of the night and burnt my house down. Marthy and Ann barely managed to get away with their lives. I reckon Dowdy and them had heared I was going to be away for a long spell, so they felt safe. The neighbors got together and built Marthy a new house, near the ruins of our old one.

It was fall of the year before I even learned it had happened. There was nothing I could do about it, no how. There was nothing I could do.

Chapter 47

We had been with Wheeler's cavalry little more than a month when he sent us – as part of a detachment which included several other companies –up to Virginia for a spell, to report to General John Breckenridge. A big force of Federal cavalry, commanded by General George Stoneman, was pushing east into Virginia, tearing up railroads, and trying to cut off the Confederacy's salt supply. There was a huge salt works just a few miles northeast of Bristol, at a place that had come to be called Saltville.

We met the Yankees in a large meadow, within sight of the salt works. The battle was as vicious and bloody as any I had been a part of – two cavalry forces crashing together, pistols flaming and sabers flashing, the fighting so close that when you killed a man you would be spattered with his blood. The air was thick with smoke, and with screaming men and horses, and the whistle and thud of bullets. The grunts of men killing mixed with the groans of men dying.

Faces and bodies would appear before me in the fog – from out of nowhere, seemed like – and disappear just as quick, trampled under my horse's hooves.

Edgar Whitley had been riding close beside me. A Yankee rode near and begun to grapple with him. I was fixing to help Edgar out, but another Yankee charged at me and I had no choice but to focus, for the time being, on saving my own skin. My Yankee made to slash at me with his sword, but I caught his wrist with my left hand. With my right, I jammed my Colt's into his ribs and pulled the trigger. He blowed away like chaff in the wind.

I returned my attention to Edgar just in time to see him run through by his opponent's saber. A foot of bloody steel come busting out of my friend's back, and he screamed. The Yank quickly pulled the weapon out and shoved Edgar away in the same motion – Edgar fell heavily from the saddle and his horse ran off, leaving me face-to-face with his killer.

It was my brother Jim.

For a moment – quick as a breath, long as a lifetime – we was both too shocked to move. The battle swirled around us, and we just stared at each other. Then he was raising his sword, and I was raising my gun. He jerked to the side as I fired, and the bullet caught him under the right collarbone. He dropped the saber, and grabbed hold of his horse's neck to keep from falling.

I spurred my horse forward – and at that moment another Yankee come crashing into me.

I was mad as hell. I didn't have time for such distractions. I pulled my trigger on the man, but all I got for my trouble was a dry snap. The gun was empty. I brained the man with the barrel, backhanded, with all my strength. No sooner had he fell than another damn idiot come flying through the air at me, tackling me and knocking me out of the saddle. We rolled together on the ground. I managed to get my Bowie knife from my belt, and rammed it into his chest up to the hilt.

I stood up, breath coming in ragged gasps, and looked around. Jim was nowhere to be seen.

There was still plenty of other bluebellies in sight, though, and I figured a good many of them would be tickled to shed my blood. I needed to keep moving. I took the time to check on Edgar – he was dead. He had been a good old boy, and a loyal friend.

I took fresh weapons off a couple of corpses, quickly caught myself a riderless horse, and was back in the thick of things. All the while, even as I defended my life, I kept an eye peeled for Jim – but I seen him no more for the rest of the battle.

~ ~ * ~ ~

We won the battle, and the Union force skedaddled back to Kentucky. They left their wounded on the field to be captured. I dismounted and walked among the dead bodies, looking closely at the ones built like my brother. Part of me hoped to find him alive, and part of me hoped to find him dead.

One Yankee I kicked over groaned loudly—he was still alive. I bent over for a closer look. It was not Jim. Angry at the man for wasting my time, I blowed his brains out. I done the same for the next one I came across who was still breathing. If the fight had gone the other way, and it was me who lay bleeding on that field, I don't doubt for a minute that some Yankee would've cut my throat for me.

A few yards away some of the boys had rounded up some nigger soldiers and forced them to their knees. Some of the niggers was crying and begging, some was snarling in hate, and some just stared off into space with dull eyes. They knowed what was coming, sure enough – there was no secret made about the fate of niggers who took up arms against the Confederacy.

Some looked on it as revenge, and others just looked on it as destroying enemy property. Me, I didn't give a shit. I hated ever'body in a blue uniform, and would sooner kill them as eat.

Rifles boomed out, and niggers commenced to falling dead. One of them had jumped to his feet, though, and run toward me. I put a bullet in his chest and stepped over his twitching body. I did not pause at the pile of dead niggers – I would not find Jim there, so it was not worth bothering with.

"Howdy, Cap'n," someone said a few minutes later.

I turned to look. It was my lieutenants—LeRoy, Timmons, and Rains. It had tickled Rains half to death when I'd decided one day to start calling him a lieutenant.

"Reckon we put the fear of Jesus into them bastards, didn't we," Timmons said with a grin.

"I seen my brother Jim," I said, and a hush fell over them.

"You sure?" LeRoy said after a few seconds.

"I'm sure. I wounded him, but he got away from me. Y'uns help me find him."

LeRoy nodded. "We'll be proud to, Champ."

I nodded back. "Rains, you come with me. Y'all two go on and check at the hospital, in case he's done been took there."

"We'll find him, Cap'n," Timmons said, and they set off. The saltworks was just a stone's throw from Emory and Henry College—the main building of the college had done been seized and set up as a hospital.

Me and Rains come upon a pile of bodies, close by to a brushpile, and commenced to poking at them.

"Damn you, Rebel scum," a voice rasped at us. It was a stocky Union sergeant, bleeding from a chest wound. He may have had more to say, I don't know. My bullet cut the conversation short.

"Help me, Jesus, help me," whispered another voice. It was a scrawny nigger kid, his arm lifted up to the sky. The other arm was a twisted mess.

"I'll help you straight to hell," I said, cocking my pistol. Rains laid his hand on my arm.

"Let him go, Champ," he said.

"What?"

"It ain't but a boy. He cain't hurt nobody."

"Not now he cain't, but he might later." I was still sore about the boy I'd had in my sights at Cherry Creek Church and let go, the one that shot me not long after.

"Let this'un go, Champ. Do it as a favor to me. So much killin' – let's leave one to go home to his mama, just one time."

I grunted, and uncocked the gun. "He'll prob'ly bleed to death anyways."

"That's up to the Lord, I reckon," Rains said.

We moved on down the line.

~ ~ * ~ ~

It wasn't too much longer 'til LeRoy and Timmons came back.

"We fount him, Cap'n," Timmons said.

"Where?"

"He's in the hospital all right," LeRoy answered. "On the third floor."

"You sure it's him?"

"We ain't neither one been around him much," LeRoy said, "but we seen him a few times before the war, in Jamestown mostly. I went up to his bed and got a good look – it's him. He was out cold, never knowed we was there."

"Them other fellers in the room with him," Timmons said, "they claim him as bein' a Lieutenant Smith, of the Thirteenth Kentucky. He might be a lieutenant, but he ain't no Smith."

"Show me."

We went to the hospital. It was a fancy brick building, built for rich boys to frolic in while some professor learned them how to lord it over common folks. The third and fourth floors had been set aside for seriously wounded

Federal prisoners – there was a couple hundred of them. There was two stairways, one at either end of the building, and a guard was posted at the foot of each one – just in case one of the injured Yankees felt cocky enough to try hobbling out.

The four of us entered the building and walked toward the staircase. The guard stiffened and brung his rifle up to his chest, like he thought he was in a parade or something.

"No one is allowed upstairs without the proper clearance," he said. He had a thick Irish brogue.

"Step aside," I told him.

"I can't do that, sir, not without the—"

I rapped him over the skull with the barrel of my revolver. He crumpled to the floor, and we was properly cleared. We went upstairs.

They pointed out the room, and the bed – it was in the far corner. I went over to it, past a whole passel of injured and terrified Yankee prisoners. A couple of them had the strength to set up, and a couple more had the strength to hide under their covers. Them that couldn't move, and was conscious, just give me a bug-eyed stare not too different from the one William Frogg had give me just before I shot him.

I stood beside the bed and looked down. The open windows give off plenty of light. The man laying there opened his eyes and gave me a grim smile. There was no doubt – it was my brother.

"Howdy, Lieutenant Smith," I said.

"Howdy, Champ."

"Reckon you know what I'm here for."

"Reckon I do."

I pulled the revolver out and leveled it at his face. I cocked it. One of the prisoners gasped, and another'n whimpered. Jim's expression did not change.

A million things run through my mind. All the memories I had of me and Jim – running and playing together as boys, drinking and brawling together as men, setting in Mama's kitchen on cold winter days. Then I remembered holding Marthy in my arms as she shook with sobs, listening to her story of what Jim done to her. I remembered the empty look in my daughter's eyes.

All my life had led me to this moment. All my mama taught me about family, and about the Lord – all I had taught myself about pride, and revenge, and manhood. If I pulled that trigger, it seemed to me like, my own life would be over too. I would be poured out, empty, like a liquor bottle tossed into the weeds once the shindig was over. Empty.

I wanted never to have found him. I wanted to kill him and be done with it. I wanted to be a million miles away. I wanted to step into one of them memories of the good times in my life, and have someone explain to me why it is such times only last a short while and are gone forever, like redbuds on the hillside.

Jim sighed. "I don't mind dyin' much," he said. "I'm wore out. Besides, it means I can be with Ann Eliza. It means I can be with my son."

"You ain't got no son."

"Yes, I do. Little John. Now I can tell him who his daddy really is."

"You've poisoned my life enough without tellin' lies on your deathbed."

"Look in my eyes and tell me I'm lyin', Champ." The smile growed wider. "There ain't nothin' you thought was yours that I ain't had, sooner or later."

The redness took over. I pulled the trigger. The bullet took him right between the eyes.

His head bounced once, and came to rest back on his pillow. His legs jerked a couple of times.

"What's going on here!" said an angry voice. I figured it was the doctor, but I didn't turn around. I was watching the smoke as it curled out of my barrel and melted away, and the brains as they oozed onto Jim's pillow.

The doctor pushed past Rains and grabbed ahold of me. My reaction was pure instinct. I backhanded him, hard, and grabbed his collar. I pulled him closer as I shoved the revolver into his face and pulled back the hammer.

Rains was there at once. "Let him go, Champ. Come on, now. It's just the doctor."

I couldn't speak. My eyes clouded with unshed tears, and there was a wild animal howl stuck in my throat, wanting to claw its way out. I let go of the doctor, and Rains pulled him away.

I walked numbly out the door and down the stairs, gun still in my hand. No one moved to stop me. No one followed neither, at least not right off. The Irishman at the foot of the stairs was awake now – he stepped out of my way.

I walked back to the meadow, among the dead bodies and the stench of war. Burial details was moving around now—they had a long job ahead of them.

After awhile I came upon a dead horse. It was my own Jimbo. I sat down roughly beside him. It had never seemed funny to me until that very moment – the first horse I had assigned a name to since I was a young'un, I named Jimbo. Of all things. *It's just as well that he's dead*, I thought, without being really certain of just who I was talking about.

I was still setting there when the gray-uniformed soldiers came to arrest me. I didn't resist.

Chapter 48

It wasn't what you would call a real serious arrest. They didn't tie me up, or nothing. All's they done was ask for my weapons, and assign a guard to ride along with me until we got back to headquarters. I'm glad they didn't assign that Irish sergeant I'd whacked as my guard, it might of got uncomfortable.

General Wheeler seemed inclined to forget the whole business – to sweep it under the carpet and pretend it never happened. That suited me well enough. I felt drained most of the time, like I was sleepwalking. I didn't want to think about Saltville no more – even though the image of Jim laying dead in that hospital bed was branded into my brain and refused to fade.

"I suppose you know you've done it now," General Wheeler said when I seen him next, and shook his head sadly. "A damn shame, too. You're the best scout I've got, and we need you. I'll do my best to keep you out of jail, but if you fall into enemy hands you'll be dead for sure."

I shrugged. "I would've been anyway."

"Yes, I'd say you're right," he answered with a grunt, then laid a hand on my shoulder. "Champ, I'm fond of you. The general feeling is, these men you've killed have done something to richly deserve it – most of them, anyway."

He stared at me, wanting some answer, but I gave him none.

"Be that as it may," he said finally. "I'll do my damnedest to keep you in my service, and to get these charges dropped. But for Christ's sake, try to behave in the meantime."

"I'll try, sir."

It was the general's turn to shrug – I don't think he believed me. He ordered me to my post, and we got back to the business of giving hell to Sherman.

The incident wouldn't die, though – thanks mainly to that damned doctor I had almost killed. He raised such a fuss to so many people, and so loudly, the Confederate command couldn't ignore it no more. They sent word for me to be fetched from Georgia and sent back to Virginia to be court-martialed. I was slapped into a jail cell in February, to wait while they gathered enough evidence to try me. General Wheeler protested the best he could, considering he had a war to occupy him. As usual, Reese was left in command of my company in my absence.

I sat in that damn jail for two months. The longer I sat, the more I got over the grief and shock of what I had done and what Jim had said before he died. My son *was* my son, I knowed that much—Ann Eliza would never have betrayed me thataway, especially not with Jim. She never liked him much anyways.

That meant Jim's dying breath had been spent trying to poison my life. Trying to destroy the purity of one more thing I had which he never would. He was so ate up with jealousy it rotted him inside. After awhile I figured he was most likely better off dead, though I still wished it hadn't of had to be me that done it.

They finally turned me loose, on account of they claimed there just wasn't enough evidence. I reckon there was so much damn evidence that a blind man would trip over it, but Wheeler had brung the authorities around to his way of thinking – that I was a hell of a lot more useful on a battlefield than in a jail. I reckon that doctor, who'd been in such a rush to testify agin me, shit a brick when he found out nobody wanted to listen.

I got back to my company at the first of April – they was in North Carolina by then, and things was looking bad for ever'body. The whole army was half-starved, outnumbered, and just plumb wore out.

Timmons came stumbling into camp one evening – his eyes was red and he sniffled his nose. If I didn't know him better I'd of thought he had been crying.

"What the hell's the matter with you?" I said. "The price of whiskey go up again?"

"General Lee surrendered," he replied numbly, and the whole company began to buzz.

"What?" I said.

"Lee surrendered his troops," Timmons said. "Colonel Ward of the Eighteenth Georgia got a dispatch, read it to his men. Ever'body's talkin' about it."

"That cain't be!" somebody said, in a fearful tone which told me they knew well that it could.

"Well, it is," Timmons said, and he dropped heavily to the ground. "It is."

"Just because Lee surrendered, that don't mean nothin'," LeRoy said. "We ain't in no Army of Northern Virginia. Bobby Lee don't speak for us. By God, we can still keep fightin'."

I sat down heavily on a stump. I clasped my hands together in front of me and squinted at them. Things had been rough on us Southern boys for a good spell, and kept getting worser by the day, but I had never really let myself think about the possibility that the fighting might be over soon. Without any revenge to take, or any war to fight, I didn't have any idea what my life was going to be.

Killing had become my life, peculiar as that sounds. The same blue feeling crept over my soul that had come upon me when I'd held a gun at my brother's face, seconds away from pulling the trigger. It was like standing on one of them swinging bridges, and having it fall – a sick, empty feeling in the pit of your stomach, knowing you're fixing to plunge down into forever with nothing to hold onto.

Rains set down beside of me. He leaned sort of close and spoke in a low voice.

"Dern, Champ. Ye reckon we might can go home 'fore long?"

"We'll see," I told him. "I ain't sure if we can or not. We'll see."

What I told him was true. War or no war, fighting or no fighting, I wasn't for sure if any of us on the losing side could go home at all, not really. I wasn't sure if we'd ever know what home *was* again.

~ ~ * ~ ~

It didn't take long – within a few days, word started trickling in about one general after another surrendering his command. The Union Army offered a general amnesty – anybody that had took up arms against the government was free to take them up on the offer. All you had to do was make an official surrender, and you could go on home to your farm like nothing had happened. Of course, Federal troops was going to be occupying every state – nothing was going to be the way it had been. We was a conquered people – hell, not even a people, really, just a bunch of ragged upstarts. We had no identity. We was just rebels.

I told my men to do whatever suited them, as I hadn't made up my own mind yet. LeRoy Reese was keen on the notion of going south to Mexico, as many was doing, and hiring out as mercenaries in the civil war they was having down there. Reese bought into the idea that Southern boys could raise enough money thataway to finance a new Confederate Army, and give the whole rebellion thing one more shot. It was a foolish dream, and I told him so – but it would be a way to stay busy, and stay men, instead of going home and bowing down to a bunch of damn Yankees.

Little by little – first one-by-one, and then by two's and three's – my men began to drift away. Some drifted home, other'ns just drifted. Whenever I'd actually see one in the act of leaving, a sudden change would come over his features. The quiet joy of freedom from suffering and danger would quickly melt into a grieved, shameful expression when they seen me, and they wouldn't meet my eyes.

"Let's light a shuck for old Mexico, Champ," LeRoy said, for what must've been the tenth time.

"Hell with that," said Timmons. "Bad enough gettin' shot at on account of your own politics – I don't see ary reason to get shot over a bunch of damn greasers. Remember-the-by-God Alamo, that's what I got to say about Old Mexico."

LeRoy gave him a surprised glance. "Shitfire, Timmons, I figured you'd be the first to strap on his gun and go with me, if'n I went. I thought you liked a good fight."

"I like a good breath, too."

"Ain't much point breathin'," LeRoy said, "not with the Yankees tellin' ye which way to spit and how far."

Timmons shrugged, and grinned. "I say we head west," he said. "The West is wide open, hoss – especially for old boys with our unique talents. We could make us a easy fortune."

"You sayin' we should become the new Webb gang?" I asked him, and I'm sure he could tell I wasn't real pleased at the notion.

He shrugged again.

I looked around at the men lounging by the campfire. There wasn't but twenty of us left. I sighed, and stood up.

"We might not all agree on where to go from here," I said, "but seems to me like we all agree on one thing."

"Yankees can go straight to hell," LeRoy volunteered.

"All right," I said, "we agree on *two* things. The other'n is this – we don't know where to go, but we know we cain't stay here. It's over. The war is finished."

There was groans. A couple of them was deep, wounded-animal sounds.

"Best we can do if we keep goin' is to get slaughtered," I said.

"Sounds like you're givin' up, Champ," LeRoy said. There was hurt in his voice.

"I reckon I need to be gettin' back home," I said softly, "now that I can. I don't know what I'll do after that – I reckon I'll just wait and see. If'n I was a single man, LeRoy, I'd go to Mexico with ye in a heartbeat. But I ain't. I got me a family needs lookin' after – and somebody needs to be there to make sure they ain't made to suffer for the things we done."

Rains was nodding. "Ayep," he said. "We need to be gettin' on home." I knowed that if I'd said we all needed to swim to France, he'd of already kicked off his shoes and got ready to wade in after me. Home to Rains was wherever I might be.

LeRoy stood and took a step closer to me. He held out his hand – when I took it, he squeezed tight as a vise. There was warmth in his hand. It flowed up my arm and inside of me. His jaw was set tight, and his eyes shined.

"It's been a pleasure servin' under ye, Captain Champ Ferguson. It's somethin' I'll brag to my young'uns about one day, once't I have me some – but I cain't go back with ye."

I nodded my understanding, and shook back even harder.

He let go, and turned slowly to face the other fellers. "How 'bout y'uns? Anybody want to come with me, shoot some Mexes in the name of ole Davy Crockett?"

"Might as well," Frank Burchett said, and stood up. A couple of others joined him. They went about the business of saddling their horses and gathering gear while the rest of us sat and drank coffee in silence, not wanting to watch them.

We sat around the fire long into the night after LeRoy and his partners left, silent except for the sound of our guts growling. One by one, the other'ns turned in, but I stayed – staring into the flames, watching the faces in them.

Rains sat beside me, of course. He had a blanket wrapped around his shoulders like a shawl. He wanted me to speak, craved for me to – I felt it, as close and warm as the heat from the fire – but I never said ary a word, and he didn't neither. Along about midnight, he slumped over agin me, dead asleep. I lowered him down and spread the blanket over him, then got up and took a fresh spot on the other side of the fire.

The night went from black to blue to gray. Birds started singing, and roosters crowed, but I still never moved except to poke at the fire ever' once in awhile when it threatened to die.

The other boys began to stir finally, and climbed stiffly to their feet. I stood myself, and stretched.

"Reckon I best be on my way," I said, and I started tending to my horse. Everybody else done the same.

Bob Timmons headed southwest, where the rest of us went due west. Four other'ns went with him – two of them was the remnants of the Tennessee-born Texas Ranger unit that had been with us since our days with General Morgan. I didn't say nothing – didn't seem like there was nothing to say – but Rains spoke up nervously.

"See y'uns fellers," he called out after them. "I reckon."

Timmons throwed up his hand, but never turned around.

"Hope them boys comes out all right," Rains said.

"Best they can hope for is a bullet 'stead of a rope," said Ephraim Crabtree. "Reckon they'll be trouble enough for somebody in the meanwhile."

I said nothing. I just loped on ahead. I felt the other twelve behind me, but no one hurried to catch up—not even Rains.

~ ~ * ~ ~

It was in Cumberland County, Tennessee – not far west of Crab Orchard – we run into some familiar faces. There was two old boys coming down the road from the opposite direction. They was skittish as soon as they seen such a large group of men – they got even more skittish when they seen the patches of gray amongst our homespun clothes – and they got flat-out scairt as hell when they seen me, and we recognized each other. I reckon we ought to of knowed one t'other, we'd growed up together.

"If'n it ain't the Duvall boys," I said. "Howdy Van, howdy Bug."

Van Duvall swallered so loud that if we'd of been near the water it would probably have scairt the fish.

"Howdy, boys," Rains said, in his usual friendly tone.

"I ain't seen you boys in years," I said. "Not since the War started, and y'uns stole our horses. And tried to talk old Reuben into shootin' us dead."

Van had turned pale as a ghost – maybe for practice, since he no doubt figured he was about to become one.

"Don't kill us, Champ," he said. "Sweet Jesus."

I stared at him. The familiar burning was gone from my belly – I was cold as ice inside. I hadn't made up my mind wh'er that was good news for Van Duvall or not.

"How ye doin', Bug?" I said.

"I reckon I'm gettin' along good enough, Champ. Got kicked in the ribs by a horse awhile back, still hurts me a right smart."

"You spoke up for me and Rains that day, Bug. I'm glad you made it through the war. Champ Ferguson don't forget who is friends is – I owe ye."

"Aw hell, Champ, they wadn't even payin' no damn attention to me no way," Bug said.

"Don't matter."

Van whimpered. He was adding up what this might mean for him.

I didn't even bother to glance at him.

"I'm lookin' out for ye too, Champ," Van said. "I can help ye."

A couple of the boys laughed. "Looks like he's doin' all right by his own self," Ephraim Crabtree said.

Van shook his head. "Everybody knows you ain't made no surrender yet, Champ."

"How the hell would anybody know that?" I said, irritated he'd said something I felt obliged to question. He chuckled nervously.

"Oh, if you was to make an official surrender, Champ," he said, "ever'body would know."

"What's your point?"

"Point is, they're layin' for ye. They know you're bound to come home sooner or later, and if you ain't surrendered they can shoot ye on sight – no questions asked."

"Who's 'they'?"

"Tinker Dave and Rufus Dowdy. They're both patrollin' the roads into White County, waitin' for ye."

I nodded. Seemed like I still had some unfinished business to tend to, sure enough. I hadn't forgot about Rufus Dowdy burning down my house – and I reckon Tinker Dave hadn't forgot about his boy Dallas spurting his life's blood out on Sparta soil.

"Seein' as how we ain't surrendered," Ephraim said, "I reckon we can still have us a military engagement or two."

"Reckon so," I said. Van grinned.

"I'd say we ought to kill that grinnin' sumbitch, though," Ephraim added. Van stopped grinning.

Bug, who'd been quiet for a spell, spoke up. "Come on now, Champ. We don't mean ye no harm. The war's over, leastways so far as we're concerned."

"Leave him be," I commanded Ephraim. "He ain't worth the trouble."

"Wouldn't be much trouble," Ephraim replied hopefully.

"Leave him. Let's go find Tinker Dave and them."

I turned my horse away from the Duvall brothers, and put them out of my mind. I seen a quick movement from the corner of my eye, and heared a loud shot. My head jerked around.

Rains still had his revolver leveled at the brothers, smoke pouring from the barrel. A hide-out gun fell from Van's fingers, and then he dropped off his horse – a red hole in his chest. Bug's face was white with shock.

Rains kept his gun pointed at them. "Soon as ye back was turned," he explained, "Van pulled out that gun. He meant to shoot ye in the back."

"Damn you, Van," Bug said, his voice breaking into a sob. "Damn you, you stupid—"

Rains looked at me, questioning.

Bug glanced up, and realized what the look was about. "Go on!" he hollered. "I done told y'uns, I ain't fightin' no more. Go on!"

We left him there, holding his dead brother.

Chapter 49

"Heared you been lookin' for me, Tinker."

It had took a few days – and some slow, careful going – but we had worked our way around the Unionists without being seen. For a day-and-a-half we had sat in the brush and watched them, while they sat in the brush and watched the road for us. Tinker Dave had about twenty men with him – there was no sign of Rufus Dowdy. Finally Tinker had stepped out of sight of his followers, deeper into the brush – to squat down and have a mess. It was the moment we had been waiting for. I waited 'til he had finished his business and straightened back up. A feller like Tinker Dave deserves better things than to be blowed back into a pile of his own shit. Me, Rains, and two others was standing in front of him when he turned around – he stared down the muzzles of our guns. He jumped at the sight of me. I held a finger to my lips and spoke to him in a low voice.

"Not a sound," I whispered.

I could practically hear the gears clicking behind his narrowed eyes. He was weighing his chances, and his options – and like Scott Bledsoe at Bear Cove, he realized he didn't have any. Then, I could tell, he considered hollering out to his men – he would die at once, but they would probably get most or all of us. I shook my head at him.

"Don't have to be no fight, Tinker. Just come with us."

He nodded. He had a good notion we was fixing to lead him off somewheres and kill him, out of earshot of his men – but he also knowed he might could buy his self a few more minutes by going along. I reckon he was counting on thinking up a way out of the mess by then. I know I would've been, in his place, and we was a lot alike.

He nodded again, and walked off with us. We all four still had our guns on him. My other men fell in behind us. There was no sound except our feet on the forest floor. Once we got him to where we'd tied our horses, I spoke.

"It's been a long ride, Dave."

"Ride's over, Champ. War's over."

"Don't reckon folks hide in the bushes waitin' to ambush somebody once wars is over."

"You're still in rebellion. You need to just give it up, and folks wouldn't feel like they *had* to lay for ye."

"I'm sure little details like that would make a world of difference to folks who wants to kill me."

He shrugged. "It would make a difference to me."

I stared at him sadly. "Yeah, Dave, I reckon it would – but you're about the only one. And I ain't made up my mind yet. Quittin' fightin' and surrenderin' is two different things, and the word *surrender* kindly sticks in my craw. I sure don't aim to get shot whilst I'm figurin' it out."

Tinker Dave raised his chin, and stared level into my eyes, his gaze like steel. "Go on and get it over with, then, if'n ye aim to kill me. My men will miss me any minute."

I chuckled. "If'n my boys was to come lookin' for me ever' time I took a long shit, I'd kick their asses. Even if it was Rains – and I'm surprised it ain't been."

"Hellfire, Champ," Rains said, embarrassed.

"I hear Rufus is lookin' for me, too."

"He was," Dave said. "Once't he finds out your close't enough to git found, I reckon he'll stop lookin' damn quick."

I heaved a sigh. "You was a good man, Dave," I said, and my Bowie knife rasped as I drawed it out of my belt. "I don't mean nothin' personal."

Quick as a streak of lightning, Tinker Dave's elbow jabbed into the gut of the man closest to him, Elmer Matthews. He grabbed Elmer around the neck and throwed him forwards into me – then he ran for the brush.

"Hold your fire," I told the boys. "I've got him."

I cocked my Colt as I pulled it loose and pointed it at the retreating guerrilla. Dave moved through the woods like a rabbit, headed for his own camp. Soon he would disappear completely. I took careful aim, drawed a deep breath and let it go – and squeezed the trigger in the instant between breaths.

The bullet clipped Dave's right shoulder, I seen the blood spurt. He lurched to one side for a moment, then kept running – out of sight. I don't think I missed on purpose – missed killing him, that is – leastways, not so far as I know. Hell, maybe I did.

Either way, Tinker Dave had escaped. We didn't have time to run after him, his own boys would be alerted by the gunshot and was likely already on their way.

"Damn," Elmer Matthews said, rubbing his sore neck. "What do we do now, Cap'n?"

I put my gun away. "Y'uns do what ye want," I said. "I'm goin' home."

~ ~ * ~ ~

My new house had been built next to the ashes of my old one. I seen it for the first time in the gray light of dawn. My boots thumped on the boards of the front porch—a tired, hollow sound. I let myself fall forward, so I was leaning my shoulder on the doorpost, and I lifted my arm to knock—the arm was heavy, like it was weighted with lead. All the energy and life seemed to have drained out of me and soaked into the ground like the spring rains which was falling gently around me. The arm fell heavy against the door once, and then a second time, but after that I couldn't manage to lift it no more.

The door opened, and Marthy stood before me – her eyes misty, but her features hard as stone.

"I'm home," I said. "It's over."

"Is it all over?"

I nodded. "It's all over."

She put her arm around me, and guided me through the door. Ann was there in an instant, her face as bright and joyful as if it was Christmas Day. She covered me with kisses and tears, and whispered, "Daddy, oh my Daddy!"

I sank into a chair, and breathed in the smells of this new place – so familiar, so different. I looked around.

"It ain't as good as Abe Lincoln's got it in the White House, but I reckon it'll do."

"Abe Lincoln?" Marthy said. "What are you talkin' about – ain't you heared any news?"

"I been on the trail a spell, ridin' slow."

"Abe Lincoln's been dead for two weeks, Daddy," Ann said. "Somebody shot him dead."

I grunted. "About time. A shame they waited 'til it was too late."

"Why was you ridin' slow?" Marthy said.

"So's not to run into any Yankees."

"The war's over. They done give amnesty to surrenderin' Rebels."

"A surrenderin' Rebel ain't no rebel a-tall, is he," I said. "I reckon I need to, but I ain't got around to it yet – and all the Yankees around here knows it."

"I swear," Marthy said, plainly irritated. "Of all the stubborn fools, you and Rains Philpot takes the cake."

"Rains?"

I had completely forgotten about Rains. He had held the reins of my horse while I slid to the ground and walked up to the house. I looked out the window. Rains was still out there—still in the saddle, still holding the reins, still getting rained on. Still looking pitiful, like a loyal dog forgotten by his master.

Marthy followed my gaze and sighed. She throwed open the door. "Don't just set out yonder in the rain, you lunkhead, come in the house!"

He hesitated. I hollered out the door at him.

"Stable the horses first, Rains."

"All right, Champ," he said.

~ ~ * ~ ~

The spring shower got heavier and heavier, and by evening had worked itself up into a storm. The wind howled around the house like a banshee – the shutters banged against the walls so hard it sounded like cannon, and the heavy rain like bullets.

"Come on," Marthy said, pulling at me.

"Come on where?"

"Down to the cellar – this is liable to turn into a tornado!"

I nodded. "You get Ann down, I'll be right there."

She took Ann – and Rains too, who needed to be led like a child in everything except killing.

I ran outside and stood in the storm, my face lifted up to it. The sky was roiling and black, lit by bolts of lightning. The wind whipped my coat around me like a flag. The rain stung at my face like bees.

I lifted my fists and hollered – hollered as loud as I could, to be heard above the wind. I screamed, and I cussed – not in words, but in an animal-wail. Like a wolf. I didn't know who I was cussing, or why – I only knowed that I hated the storm, with all the hatred my heart could muster.

The wind blowed harder, and howled so loud I couldn't hear my own voice screaming. I lost my footing, and it blowed me down – it sent me rolling like I was a scrap of newspaper. I struggled until I had raised myself up onto my knees, and hollered some more. I was soaked to the bone now. The rain washed away the tears which suddenly pouring down my cheeks.

"Damn you!" I screamed at the storm. "Damn you!"

I felt arms around my waist. Ann had run out into the storm, and grabbed aholt of me.

"Come inside, Daddy!"

"No! No, no, no!"

She held tight – if I stayed, she would stay too. Lightning blasted a tree not far away, and it exploded like hell cracking open. I grabbed Ann, and together we ran back into the house.

Marthy was waiting for us. "Champ, have you gone plumb crazy?"

I wouldn't answer her.

The next day I sent Rains into town, to tell them I was surrendering.

Chapter 50

"They're coming, Champ," Rains said. "They'll be along in a few minutes."

We stood in the stable. It was early afternoon.

"Did you surrender?"

"Yup," Rains said. "It wadn't that hard. I just said 'I surrender', and they said 'good'. Then they took my pistol, and turned me loose. They never took my rifle or my knife, just my pistol."

I nodded. "That don't sound so hard."

There was a moment of silence, then Rains spoke again. "You want me to stay close by, Champ?"

"No. No, if it's all the same to you, this is somethin' I'd druther do all alone."

"Yeah," he said sadly. "I'll come around tomorrow, to see if'n ye need help. You know, with farmin' or anything."

"That'll be fine."

"Reckon I'll just go on back to town, then." His face suddenly brightened a little. "Say, there might be a checker-game goin' on down at the store, or in front of the courthouse. I ain't played me no checkers in a long time."

I smiled, in spite of myself. "You can play checkers anytime ye want to now, Rains. You go on."

He put a hand briefly on my shoulder, then walked away. I meant to go outside my own self, to set on the porch and watch for the soldiers come to accept my surrender, but I couldn't bring myself to move. I sat in the stable, drawing what comfort and power I could from the presence of my horses.

~ ~ * ~ ~

"Champ Ferguson."

I turned my head slowly. Colonel Joe Stokes stood in the doorway of the stable, the brass ball he used for a hand resting on his hip.

"That's me," I said.

"Come out into the open, Ferguson."

I stood up and walked stiffly through the door. As soon as I passed through, I was struck in the back of the head by a pistol barrel – a Yankee soldier had been crouching at the door. Several men fell on me, punching and kicking.

My arms was jerked up behind my back, and I heared the shackles clicking shut on my wrists.

"What the hell are you doin'!" I said.

Marthy and Ann had run out of the house – soldiers grabbed them and kept them from reaching me. Stokes was laughing.

"So – I've finally captured the great Champ Ferguson."

"You didn't capture me, I'm surrenderin', you dumbass!"

"I don't accept your surrender."

"You have to accept it!" Marthy said. "There's amnesty!"

He ignored her and squatted down beside me.

"If you wanted to surrender, Ferguson, you should've done it while Lincoln was alive."

"What does that have to do with anything?"

"In addition to all your other crimes, you threatened to kill Andrew Johnson when he was governor – and now he's president. Bad luck for you."

"Amnesty!" Marthy repeated, screaming it this time.

"Amnesty is offered to all surrenderng Rebels," Stokes said, "with the exceptions of Jefferson Davis and Champ Ferguson—by order of the President of the United States." He leaned closer to me. "You're an important man, Ferguson. It must feel nice."

I was jerked to my feet and led to a horse. Ann strained against her captors, stretching her arms out toward me.

"Daddy! Where are you taking him!"

Where they was taking me, of course, was right here – to this Nashville prison cell. But I reckon you already knowed that.

~ ~ * ~ ~

My lawyer has done the best he was able to, but the deck was stacked against him from the first. The Federals claim that, since I never filled out no muster rolls for my company, I was never a member of the Confederate Army – and therefore every man they can prove I've killed has been an act of murder, not of war. They say this, yet they give me a military trial – my fate in the hands of a military commission instead of a jury of my peers. They say this, yet their own records show me to be a Confederate cavalry captain, and General Joe Wheeler his self got on the stand and testified that I was under his command.

And of course, there was the witnesses. Lots of them. From Union soldiers who had seen me killing wounded Yankees at the Battle of Saltville, to the men in the hospital room who'd seen me kill "Lieutenant Smith". There was the Confederate doctor I had almost killed that same day. There was widows and orphans by the wagonload, to describe how I had gunned down helpless citizens – and every time my lawyer tried to introduce evidence that Union guerrillas had done the same to us, it was throwed out as irrelevant.

It was more of a circus than a trial, from the very beginning. Crowds thronged around the courthouse – part of them chanting for my death, part of them for my release. Reporters swarmed all over the place, trying to set up interviews with everybody except the "murder victims" theirselves – and I reckon that was only because they couldn't find a spirit medium talented enough to drudge the old boys up out of hell.

One afternoon I traded hats with one of the Yankee soldiers guarding me—a scrawny kid, a good foot shorter than I was—and we convinced a couple of out-of-town reporters that he was Champ Ferguson and I was the guard.

"Don't step too close, son," I said. "He's ferocious as hell."

They shuddered, and jotted merrily away in their little notebooks.

The highlight of the whole shebang, in my opinion, was when they put Tinker Dave on the stand as a witness for the prosecution. Dave looked over at me and nodded politely – he looked sort of embarrassed. He was introduced as "the celebrated Union scout, David Beatty."

Tinker Dave proceeded to tell the court how me and him had tried to kill one another for years – how our bands had shot at each other from ambush, and how we had each killed members of the other's company as they tried to surrender. He pointed out it was never anything personal, it was all on account of the war. The prosecutor's was happier to see him get off the stand than the defense was. He nodded at me again as he got down.

The newspapers went on for pages about how many low-down Rebels the celebrated Tinker Dave had shot dead, and there's even talk of running him for the state legislature. Whether you're a hero or a criminal don't depend on what you do, I reckon, it depends on whether or not your side wins.

The reporters I spoke to later was surprised at what I had to say on the subject of Tinker Dave.

"Well, there are meaner men than Tinker Dave," I said. "He fought brave, and give me some good licks, and I give him some back. He's dealt kindly with me other than that. There are meaner men than Dave." Then I chuckled. "He's the only thing I ever aimed at and missed – write that down. I wish to God I'd had a clean shot at Rufus Dowdy, though. That would've made the world a better place, sure enough."

No one was surprised when they sentenced me to hang.

Chapter 51

They let Rains in to see me for a few minutes, yesterday. It was depressing as hell. He just sat there, on the other side of the bars, looking all lost and helpless.

"I should've stayed by ye, Champ," he said, his voice cracking. "I should've stayed by ye."

"Aw, hellfire, Rains," I said, trying to make my tone cheerful. "You've always stuck by me – you're the truest friend ever was. You only left that day 'cause I made ye – it wouldn't have made ary bit of difference, nohow."

"I shouldn't of listened. I should of been there – I could've at least kilt one or two of 'em."

"And they would've kilt you."

"Better that—than live to see this." His eyes was shining wetly.

"You'd best go, Rains, 'fore they drag ye off. They ain't exactly what I'd call considerate."

He shook his head slowly. The tears had welled up in his eyes and was rolling freely down his cheeks. "I don't know *where* to go," he said. "I don't know what to do."

He got up and shuffled slowly away. He paused at the outer door, and turned. "Goodbye, Champ."

"Goodbye, Rains."

"I'll see ye on the other side—wherever you wind up, I reckon that's where I'll be too."

"I'll be waitin' for ye."

He turned away, trying to choke back a sob – he was only partway successful. A low keening sound escaped his throat, and echoed in the hallway after he was gone.

"Goodbye, Rains," I said to the empty air.

~ ~ * ~ ~

They *was* considerate enough to let my family stay with me last night—*my* last night—and even remove my chains. The guards let them in at about six o'clock. Them guards, I reckon I ought to add, was a couple of good old boys. So was the two that watched over me in the daytime. They made things as comfortable for me as they could, under the circumstances. They brung me tobacco, and we played cards through the bars. They brung me all the cakes and pies and such the local ladies baked up for me, and checked them real close – in case they contained weapons from my supporters, or evidence of poison from any of my enemies who couldn't be content with just seeing me die without having a personal hand in it. The food they brung me was good, too – beefsteaks and biscuits, and nary a navy bean in sight, only warm-brown pinto ones. I'll eat white beans if'n I have to, but I'd druther not. They brung a barber in to shave me before them newspaper boys took my picture, and I joshed and kidded with them the whole time.

There wasn't much talking done last night. I just swept my womenfolks up in my arms, and then set them on the cot beside of me. They pressed their faces into my shoulders, one on each side, and cried softly – until my arms went numb from the tightness of their grip, until my shirt was soaked through with their tears. I just held them, and made gentle, reassuring noises, and kissed their hair from time to time – and floated in their presence, breathing it in. Have you ever noticed that tears have a smell? It's a salty, bitter smell, but it's soft and sweet, too.

My eyes misted up a good deal, but I never cried none. I smiled. All the voices that hollered out at me in my dreams was quiet now – all I could hear was the sleepy breath of my family, and it filled the whole world. What was going to happen tomorrow didn't matter none, not to me. This was the moment of heaven I'd dreamed of during all them cold nights sleeping in the wet leaves – a lot of my partners had died before they could taste it again, so I didn't figure I had much to complain about. If it was all of heaven I would ever see – it was enough.

I didn't sleep at all. I was still awake, still holding them, when the roosters crowed. I'll have plenty of time to sleep directly. If'n I can just be laid to rest on that little hill by the river, over yonder in White County by my farm, I know my dreams will be easy ones.

I fought hard, boys, and I done all I could. We all did. But the fighting is over now.

Ann clung to me tight when they opened the door up this morning to take them away. I had to pry her fingers off of me. Her sobbing and wailing was pitiful to hear, and it broke my heart clean in two. I reached out and held her face in my hands.

"Sweet little gal," I said. "Sweet beautiful, Ann. Don't you fret none about your old daddy, now. I'll be with ye forever, watchin' over ye. You'll feel me there, honey. You'll feel me." I put my forehead against hers one last time, and seen them loving, tearful eyes look into my own. I could fall into them and let my spirit float forever, seemed like. With all the evil I've done in this old world, I know that I brung something beautiful into it, too.

"I love you, Daddy," she said through her tears. "You're the best Daddy ever was." Then she broke down again, and they led her away.

I kissed Marthy soft on the mouth. She was hard – she was making herself be, like she always has. Her jaw quivered in her effort to be strong for her and me both, and for Ann, and for the whole faithless, lost world. I found myself wishing she could be soft for me this one time – but she is what she is, and she is the very human model of love, in her own way. I reckon the things her daddy done, that she only spoke of once, made her so hard on the outside. I had just about softened her up, and brung out the loving little girl who hid inside her, when my brother Jim come along and undid it all.

"You die like a man, Champion Ferguson," she said. "You show them. You be *strong*."

"I've lived strong, and I'll die strong, Marthy honey. You put me on that hill I told ye about – with me in the soil, won't nothin' grow there but hardwood."

Nobody had to lead her away. She walked off on her own power, her back straight as a ramrod – even though her shoulders shook just the least bit.

Mama never came to see me, of course, nor any of my other kin from Clinton County. I'd been dead to them for years, after all – this hanging just made it official. I kilt my own brother for revenge, and some would say that's a horrible sin, but to kill your kinfolks – for real, or only in your own mind – for *politics* is a sorry damn thing.

I reckon they'll be coming for me soon. Let them come. I'm wore out.

Chapter 52

At ten o'clock on Friday morning, October 20, 1865, Champ Ferguson was led from his cell to the prison courtyard. For his final meal he had requested, and received, a pint of brandy, but he showed no effects from it. He was dressed in a black broadcloth suit tailor-made for him by the local chapter of "Ladies of the South," with no hat. Escorted by his guards, he carefully walked to the scaffold, pausing only briefly to regard the cherry-wood coffin which rested near the structure, and climbed the steps.

The scaffold was surrounded by soldiers. Three hundred special passes had also been issued, to privileged observers, including not only prominent loyal Unionists, but reporters from around the country. An artist from *Harper's Weekly* was present. Thousands of other people thronged around the prison gate, but were not allowed entrance. A detachment from the Fifteenth United States Colored Infantry guarded the entrance, and this rankled many of Ferguson's supporters. Ferguson's supporters may well have rankled the colored soldiers, as well, but they did not show it.

Ferguson's wife and daughter waited in a nearby brick building, until such time as they could claim his body. A wagon waited near the prison gate to transport the coffin.

The provost-marshal approached the prisoner to bind his hands.

"Is that really necessary?" Champ said. "I don't reckon I'm goin' noplace."

"I'm sorry," the marshal said, "it's the rules." Champ placed his hands behind his back and allowed them to be tied. "Is that uncomfortable?" the marshal asked.

"No, it's fine."

Colonel Shafter, the prison commandant, ascended the scaffold. He was accompanied by a preacher. The colonel took out a sheaf of papers and began to detail the charges of which the prisoner was convicted. The reading took twenty minutes. Champ nodded at some of the charges, and shook his head vigorously at others.

At one point, while Colonel Shafter was describing the death of Elim Huddleston, Champ laughed and spoke.

"Hell, Colonel, I could tell it a lot better than that."

Shafter cleared his throat and continued.

Once all the charges had been read, including the primary charge of guerrilla activity, and fifty-three counts of murder, Shafter paused.

"Champion Ferguson," he then said, "for these crimes you are sentenced to be hanged by the neck until dead. In accordance with this sentence, it is my duty to carry out the execution." His eyes flickered toward the crowd, and the many reporters present. "The accused may make a brief final statement."

Champ blinked sweat from his eyes. "Ary chance't somebody could take the handkerchief out of my back pocket for me?"

The colonel nodded, and reached behind the prisoner for the handkerchief. He quickly wiped Champ's brow with it. When his face was close to the condemned man's, he whispered.

"Make it brief, Ferguson," he said, not unkindly. "The longer this takes, the harder it'll be – on all of us."

Champ nodded his understanding.

"I hope there's no hard feelings," the colonel added. "There's nothing personal in this for me. I'm only doing my duty."

Champ smiled sadly at his words.

"I got nothin' agin ye, Colonel. Thank ye, for your kindness."

Shafter sighed, and stepped back. "Do you have anything to say?" he asked, in a voice louder than he had been using before.

"I got plenty to say, if I just knowed how to say it." Champ looked over the crowd – he nodded and smiled at a couple of friendly, familiar faces. He took a slow, deep breath.

"I surrendered on good faith. I didn't think they'd treat me like they've done – else they never would've got their hands on me."

Reporters scribbled furiously.

"I'm the same man now that I was before the war. I'm a Southern man – I was a Rebel, and I'll die a Rebel. I don't believe I done nothin' wrong. I've kilt a good many men, to be sure, but I never kilt nobody that wasn't lookin' to kill me. All that I done, I done in defense of my life and my cause.

"It's a lie that I took no prisoners. I took plenty, and they're alive today. Ask the Yankees how many of my men, or Scott Bledsoe's, they ever took prisoner – most ever' one they caught, they kilt. I knowed that, and so I fought back all the harder.

"I'll say it agin, I'll die a Rebel." He looked then at the courtyard around his scaffold, and the blue-clad soldiers there, and a look of disgust flitted briefly across his face. "My only request is that my body be removed to White County, Tennessee, and buried in good Rebel soil. I'll not rest in a place like this."

Champ closed his mouth, and set his jaw.

"Do you have anything else to say?" the colonel asked.

Champ shook his head. "I reckon not. I'm ready to die."

The colonel gestured to the executioner – he took his place beside the condemned man. The preacher stood before Champ, closed his eyes, and began to pray.

"Dear Lord, take pity on this errant sinner, and have mercy on his soul. We pray in Jesus' name, amen."

"Lord have mercy on all our souls," Champ said.

The hangman fitted the noose around his neck, tightened it, and dropped the burlap sack over his face. He returned then to his station beside the rope which released the trapdoor.

"Now," Shafter said, and the trapdoor opened.

Champ Ferguson felt the world fall from beneath him for one final, brief moment.

Epilogue

Champ Ferguson was laid to rest in the France cemetery, not far from the Calfkiller River and his own farm, only a few miles outside of Sparta, as he had requested. Mourners crowded around the little hill, so numerous many were forced to stand in the road. Songs were sung over the grave, some of them church songs, but *Dixie* and *Good Old Rebel* were sung as well. The mourners gradually dispersed and returned to their homes where they would tell their children and grandchildren tales about their hero, and curse the Yankees who had despoiled their county.

Champ's family left, too – eventually Ann married, and the young couple took her mother along with them to the Indian Territory, to make a new start.

When night fell, everyone had left – except Rains Philpot. He sat beside the fresh grave, rocking back and forth to keep warm in the chill autumn air. He would leave too – once he figured out where to go – but not yet. Not yet.

Afterword

Almost a century-and-a-half after his death, Champ Ferguson remains perhaps the most beloved figure in the lore of Sparta, Tennessee. Flowers and Rebel flags are placed regularly on his grave, and historical re-enactors commemorate his exploits. A marker has been placed at the cemetery by the Sons of Confederate Veterans, stating that Captain Champ Ferguson and his companions were the area's sole line of defense against Union guerrillas. Other counties, it should be noted, could say with just as much honesty that Union guerrillas were their only defense against Champ Ferguson and his companions. In 1942 a biography – *Champ Ferguson, Confederate Guerrilla* – was published, and has remained in print for most of the intervening years. Written by Thurman Sensing, it sought to extol Ferguson's virtues and minimize his failings.

In some neighboring counties, where many citizens have ancestors who were slain by Ferguson, he is remembered as a brutal thug. The historical marker placed near his birthplace in Albany, Kentucky, calls him a terrorist. Such interpretations are seldom welcomed in Sparta.

The truth is the quiet grave at the northern end of White County contains the bones, not of a monster or a saint – but of a very human man. Close your eyes if you go there, breathe deeply the smell of soil and green grass and Tennessee river water. You can almost feel his presence. If you do, you will know that he has found peace at last.

The End

Recommended Reading

For many years, Champ Ferguson was ignored or minimized by Civil War historians. In the decade since this novel was first published, in 2002, that has changed; there are now several historical works touching on Champ and guerrilla warfare in the Upper Cumberland. I have listed below several nonfiction books which you may want to consult for more information about the subject.

My highest recommendation goes to the work by Brian McKnight.

Confederate Outlaw: Champ Ferguson and the Civil War in Appalachia ~ Brian D. McKnight
Cumberland Blood: Champ Ferguson's Civil War ~ Thomas D. Mays
A Savage Conflict: the Decisive Role of Guerrillas in the American Civil War ~ Daniel E. Sutherland
Let Us Die Like Brave Men: Behind the Dying Words of Confederate Warriors ~ Daniel W. Barefoot
True Crime in the Civil War ~ Tobin T. Buhk
Champ Ferguson: Confederate Guerrilla ~ Thurman Sensing (1942)

You can also read my cover article about Champ Ferguson in the journal *Civil War Times* at this website: http://www.historynet.com/champ-ferguson-an-american-civil-war-rebel-guerrilla.htm

And available in May, 2015 from the University of Tennessee Press: *People of the Upper Cumberland*, edited by Calvin Dickinson and Michael E. Birdwell, which features my chapter "Legacy of Blood: The Legend of Champ Ferguson."

About the Author

Troy D. Smith was born in the Upper Cumberland region of Tennessee in 1968. He has waxed floors, moved furniture, been a lay preacher, and taught high school and college. He writes in a variety of genres, achieving his earliest successes with westerns -his first published short story appeared in 1995 in Louis L'Amour Western Magazine, and he won the Spur Award in 2001 for the novel Bound for the Promise-Land (being a finalist on two other occasions.) He is currently teaching American history at Tennessee Tech, and serving as president of Western Fictioneers -the first national writing organization devoted exclusively to fiction about the Old West.

Also by Troy D. Smith